PRAISE FOR J

"*The Girl from the Papers* is a paints an alluring portrait o: public enemy era. Wright does a stellar job penning complex characters fighting for self-worth and identity in all the wrong places. This haunting tale is a poignant reminder that no matter how dark the path one chooses, redemption is possible if one simply turns around. Readers will be captivated from beginning to bittersweet end."

AMANDA COX, Christy Award–winning author of *The Edge of Belonging* and *The Secret Keepers of Old Depot Grocery*

"Readers of suspenseful historical fiction rejoice! Jennifer L. Wright has written a fast-paced, sit-on-the-edge-of-your-seat story that will keep you up past your bedtime to find out what happens next. Even better, though, is the thread of inspiration Wright wove into *The Girl from the Papers*. Throughout Beatrice's story we're reminded that no matter what chaos enters our life, nothing can separate us from the love of God. Be sure to grab yourself a copy!"

SUSIE FINKBEINER, author of *The All-American*

"*The Girl from the Papers* is flat-out brilliant. If you're looking for a gripping historical novel with nuanced and complicated characters, this is it. Jennifer L. Wright pulls no punches, nor does she take the easy road through a gritty story. For fans of unflinching fiction such as *The Nature of Fragile Things* by Susan Meissner."

KATIE POWNER, author of *Where the Blue Sky Begins*

"Jennifer Wright ignites stories about women and girls with a passion, heart, and heat that can't be extinguished. In *The Girl from the Papers*, Jenn plunges readers straight into a Bonnie and Clyde–inspired story to explore the dreams and drive of a young girl struggling to break free from life's abuse and doldrums and become a high-flying star. But what will young Beatrice Carraway discover in the glare of the newspapers' spotlight? This story won't let go until its final pages surrender her life-changing truths with bold lessons for us all."

PATRICIA RAYBON, award-winning author of *All That Is Secret* and *I Told the Mountain to Move*

"Brimming with grit and beauty, *The Girl from the Papers* is a poignant study in human frailty and unending mercy. Set in the bleak days of the Depression, a young woman searches for a love that will heal her wounded heart in a story that is as hopeful as it is heartbreaking. *The Girl from the Papers* will remain in your thoughts long after the last tearstained page is turned."

STEPHANIE LANDSEM, author of *Code Name Edelweiss*

"Jennifer L. Wright brilliantly takes her readers on a journey of crime and passion, faith and surrender in her latest novel, *The Girl from the Papers*. From the first words of the brief yet intriguing prologue to the final heart-wrenching pages of this Great Depression era tale, Wright's extraordinary storytelling offers an intense, page-turning experience I will not soon forget. Bravo!"

MICHELLE SHOCKLEE, award-winning author of *Count the Nights by Stars* and *Under the Tulip Tree*

"Once again, Jennifer L. Wright sets the gold standard for vivid imagery and poignant descriptions. Inspired by the infamous exploits of Bonnie and Clyde, *The Girl from the Papers* is an edge-of-your-seat kind of read, both heartbreaking and hopeful. This book delivers the perfect balance of high-speed suspense and moments of profound introspection."

NAOMI STEPHENS, Carol Award–winning author of *Shadow among Sheaves*

"Sometimes what we want isn't what's best. It's a truth Jennifer Wright explores in this story of a waitress–turned–infamous bank robber. Despite being West Texas dirt, Beatrice Carraway has always wanted to see her name in lights. Unfortunately notoriety as the Salacious Sheba drags her into the dark underworld of criminals willing to do anything for the next big score. A nod to Bonnie and Clyde, *The Girl from the Papers* is an insightful escapade about the importance of being known and loved anyway."

JANYRE TROMP, author of *Shadows in the Mind's Eye*

"This is historical fiction as it is meant to be told: a glimpse (based on true events) through the eyes of people caught up in the maelstrom of world events beyond their control."

LIBRARY JOURNAL on *Come Down Somewhere*

"Intelligent and arresting. . . . In the moving historical novel *Come Down Somewhere*, a nuclear test has explosive consequences for a burgeoning friendship."

FOREWORD REVIEWS

"[A] lovely debut. . . . Wright's adept depiction of the times capture the grit of the Dust Bowl. Fans of Tracie Peterson should check this out."

PUBLISHERS WEEKLY on *If It Rains*

"The treatment of historical events is gritty and unflinching, similar to other Dust Bowl fiction, like Susie Finkbeiner's *Cup of Dust* and Kristin Hannah's *Four Winds*. Character growth is the highlight of this novel."

LIBRARY JOURNAL on *If It Rains*

THE GIRL FROM THE PAPERS

THE GIRL FROM THE PAPERS

JENNIFER L. WRIGHT

Tyndale House Publishers
Carol Stream, Illinois

Visit Tyndale online at tyndale.com.

Visit Jennifer L. Wright's website at jennwrightwrites.com.

Tyndale and Tyndale's quill logo are registered trademarks of Tyndale House Ministries.

The Girl from the Papers

Copyright © 2023 by Jennifer L. Wright. All rights reserved.

Cover photographs are the property of their respective copyright holders, and all rights are reserved. Woman © Mark Owen/Trevillion Images; man © philipimage/iStockphoto; sky by Raychel Sanner on Unsplash.com; landscape by Mick Haupt on Unsplash.com; car © Biswarup Ganguly/Wikimedia Commons; art deco border © Tartila/Adobe Stock; fabric texture by Rawpixel.com.

Author photo taken by Jonathan Wright, copyright © 2022. All rights reserved.

Designed by Libby Dykstra

Edited by Sarah Mason Rische

Published in association with the literary agency of Martin Literary & Media Management, 914 164th Street SE, Suite B12, #307, Mill Creek, WA 98012.

Proverbs 13:20 and John 4:14 are taken from The ESV® Bible (The Holy Bible, English Standard Version®), copyright © 2001 by Crossway, a publishing ministry of Good News Publishers. Used by permission. All rights reserved.

John 8:11, Matthew 26:52, and Lamentations 3:19-24 are taken from the Holy Bible, *New International Version,*® *NIV.*® Copyright © 1973, 1978, 1984, 2011 by Biblica, Inc.® Used by permission. All rights reserved worldwide.

The Girl from the Papers is a work of fiction. Where real people, events, establishments, organizations, or locales appear, they are used fictitiously. All other elements of the novel are drawn from the author's imagination.

For information about special discounts for bulk purchases, please contact Tyndale House Publishers at csresponse@tyndale.com, or call 1-855-277-9400.

Library of Congress Cataloging-in-Publication Data

A catalog record for this book is available from the Library of Congress.

ISBN 978-1-4964-7756-9 (HC)
ISBN 978-1-4964-7757-6 (SC)

Printed in the United States of America

29	28	27	26	25	24	23
7	6	5	4	3	2	1

For Erin:

In a world where friendships come and go,

sisters are forever.

Ecclesiastes 4:9-10

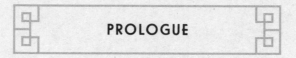

PROLOGUE

NOW

My mama always told me I would live and die as a nobody.

Here at the end . . . I couldn't help but wish she'd been right.

CHAPTER ONE

My earliest memories are of sequins. Sequins and bruises. But the sequins came first.

Growing up in the small West Texas town of Wingate, color was a rarity. Shades of brown and yellow stretched for miles around our gray town, the lone reprieve the soft green of grass or pale purple of wildflowers that sometimes sprouted in the spring—but only if the rains came. And the rains rarely came.

So I had to rely on my sequins.

My mother said it was my father's idea to start me on the pageant scene. He put my name down for my first beautiful baby contest in 1911 because, in his words, "there weren't nothing or no one more beautiful than our Bea." And he must have been right—I won my first trophy at only five months old. And then I just kept on winning them.

In fact, it's hard to remember a time I *wasn't* onstage. I have hazy memories of pageants and shows when I was little: my mother's tight smile behind the scenes and my father's watery eyes in the audience, before his death in 1914 (an unfortunate alignment of my father, a frayed rope, and a pallet of bricks on a construction site in Pumphrey—a gruesome blessing, according to Mama, that perhaps saved him from an even worse fate in the fields of France a few short years later). But it's after his death that my recollection really comes into its own—and what it recollects is the limelight.

"And now, here's Little Miss Beatrice Carraway of Wingate, Texas, performing 'Alabama Jubilee'!"

"Look at her go, folks! I've never seen a four-year-old who could tap that way!"

"Truly, the face of an angel. Miss Beatrice Carraway, Little Miss Firecracker of 1916."

With my little sister, Eleanor, in tow, it was a constant flurry of dresses and dances, performances and preening, rouge and road trips. We traveled all over Runnels County, and when that got too small, we traveled even farther. To Sweetwater and Abilene, San Angelo and Odessa. Even to Dallas, the mother of all cities (at least in my childish mind), where we stayed with my nana and grandpop, who had a house across the Trinity River. From their upstairs window, I could see the downtown skyscrapers glinting in the sunlight, a sparkle in the world matched only by my sequins and trophies. It couldn't have been a coincidence.

For nine straight years, the universe revolved around me—my shows, my schedule, even my money, without which my widowed mother would not have been able to keep my sister and me fed and clothed. I was a blossom in a garden of weeds, a star whose light kept the darkness of my father's death away, a savior to my family and a gift to the world.

Until one day when I just . . . *wasn't* anymore.

"Mama!" I scowled at my reflection in the mirror as I scrutinized my cheeks. They were too pale; the cheap rouge my mother had purchased just wasn't cutting it the way the good stuff used to. "I need the Mary Garden face powder! This Mennen stuff makes my eyes look like dirty bathwater. They are *supposed* to look like the sky." I batted my lashes at myself for emphasis as I waited for her response.

Nothing.

"Mama!" I yelled again.

But the house only popped and creaked with the late-fall winds.

Blowing an irritated snort out of my nose, I smoothed my blonde waves before making my way from my bedroom and into the hall. The putrid scent of something burning assaulted me. My toes curled over the threadbare rug, which barely insulated them from the cold hardwood beneath, as I followed the smell to the small kitchen at the rear of the house.

My five-year-old sister stared at me from the far side of the table, her bare feet swinging over the yellowed linoleum, an uneasy smile on her face.

"Eleanor," I said slowly. "Where's Mama?"

She shrugged.

"El, what—?" My question broke off as I saw smoke billowing from a pot on the stove, blacker than the iron range itself. I let out a yelp and ran toward it, barely remembering to grab a towel to protect my hand before yanking the crock off the flame. Coughing, I threw the smoldering pan into the sink, pulling open the back door with one hand while shooing out the smoke with the other. My eyes and nostrils burned with the stench.

Eleanor sat at the table, mouth still twisted in a nervous smile. Her dark eyes—she'd gotten our father's instead of our mother's, like me—gazed at the small puffs of smoke wafting from the pot.

I scraped my tongue with my teeth, trying to remove the taste of char from my mouth. "El, were you trying to cook?"

She shook her head.

I looked into the pan, the blackened remains of *something* stuck to the sides and bottom in one unrecognizable clump. "What is this?"

Eleanor pointed to the counter, where a box of oats stood open. "Oatmeal? Is this oatmeal?"

She nodded.

"Was Mama cooking you oatmeal?"

A nod.

"Then where is she now?"

At that moment, the door to the side bedroom flew open, and my mother burst forth from its depths. Well, a version of my mother, at least.

It was the smell that got to me first. More overpowering than Eleanor's neglected breakfast. Not lye and dirt and yesterday's dinner, but flowers and a hint of musk. The woman before me had bright-blonde hair pulled back at the sides and deep-blue eyes set against long black lashes. But where my mother was normally plain and—dare I say—frumpy, this woman's complexion was smooth, her lips glossy, her figure not hidden beneath a shapeless, well-worn dress. No, this woman's dress was blue muslin and formfitting, calves lengthened and accentuated above new leather heels. To top it all off, her cheeks were pink and rosy—a rosiness that could only be achieved with the Mary Garden face powder I was told we could no longer afford.

I narrowed my eyes, but my mother brushed past me like I

wasn't even there and grabbed the smoking pan with a shout. "Eleanor! Eleanor, honey, I'm so sorry! I completely forgot this was still on the stove."

My sister gave a small shrug, averting her eyes. I, on the other hand, cleared my throat.

"I'll make you something else. Let me see what we have . . ." She began rummaging through our meager pantry, completely oblivious to my tapping foot. "No . . . no, there's no time for . . . but maybe I could—"

I cleared my throat again.

"—break into our summer preserves. I believe I still have some strawberry rhubarb from Mrs. Moore's garden. I was saving it for—"

I cleared my throat *again*, this time with as much sass as I could muster. Which was a lot.

My mother finally sighed, a deep and aggravated exhale from which anyone else would have shrunk back. "What is it, Beatrice?"

"You almost burned down the house."

"Oh, stop it."

"You did. *And* you're wearing *my* rouge. I thought you said we couldn't afford it anymore."

"We can't."

"Then how come you have it? *I'm* the one who's going onstage, not you. If anyone in this family is going to wear it, it needs to be me." I glanced at the clock above the doorframe. "And I need it now because we're going to be late. It's an hour and a half to Big Spring. You know I have a preshow ritual, and I hate to be rushed."

My mother turned her back and continued to rummage inside the pantry. "We're not going to Big Spring."

"What?"

"I said we're not going to Big Spring."

I glanced at Eleanor, but my sister was busy poking the burnt remains of her breakfast.

"What do you mean we're not going? It's the Harvest Pageant, and I—"

"And you came in fifth last year. And third the year before that."

I stuck out my chin, pretending her words didn't land like a punch. "It . . . it was a fluke," I stammered. "But I have a new routine. I—"

"Bea—"

"I've learned all the words to 'Poor Butterfly' and some real swell taps to—"

"Beatrice."

"—go along with it. You've only seen me in practice, but boy, once I get that dress on—the one with the red sequins, remember? From the Fourth of July pag—"

"Enough, Beatrice!" The shrillness of my mother's voice was a knife through my plea, and when she spun around to look at me, there was a redness in her cheeks that had nothing to do with the coveted rouge. "We won't be reusing your Fourth of July dress because you didn't win that pageant either. Or the one before that. Or the one before that. You haven't placed first in over a year or in the top five in six months. You've grown out of your cuteness, and your childish talents aren't enough to take you to the next level of the circuitry."

I recoiled as if physically struck. But Mama wasn't finished yet.

"Your father may have thought the sun rose and set on you, but he's gone. Dead. And we cannot afford to keep traveling around for a losing routine. If you haven't noticed, we are barely keeping things together as it is now. We are not going to Big Spring, and we will not be going to another pageant or show from here on out. So enough, Beatrice. We are *done*."

The silence that punctuated the end of her tirade was thick, obscene even. Pride wrestled both anger and sadness within my nine-year-old chest. No, I hadn't been winning lately; I would give her that. But that didn't mean I *couldn't*. I just needed another chance. A *good* chance, with the right dress and the right song and the right face powder. I was Beatrice Carraway, after all.

The star. The showgirl.

And what was a showgirl without her show?

"Mama—"

"Beatrice." My mother closed her eyes. Her hands reached up to rub them, then stopped as if she'd remembered her makeup. "I've said my piece. It's done. Decided."

Heat flushed up my neck. My lips twisted into a ferocious pout. "What about me?" I snapped. "Don't I get a say in it?"

With another dramatic sigh, she lifted Eleanor from her spot at the table. "Once you start making money rather than draining it, then you can have a say. Now go get dressed. Both of you. Something nice. Maybe they'll have something for you two to eat at church."

"Church?" We'd never gone to church a day in our lives. "I ain't going to no church."

"You will if you want to avoid a tanned backside."

I clenched my jaw. I wanted to scream at her. To stomp and kick and break things until she saw how stupid she was being. I wanted to force her into that car by sheer stubborn willpower and make her drive me to Big Spring so I could prove her wrong. My entire body twitched with a building tantrum.

My mother held my gaze, her steely eyes steadfast and

unflinching. Daring me. On her hip, my sister dipped her chin to her chest, refusing to look at either of us.

Eleanor. The sight of my sister's dark-brown locks hanging over her face—hiding her when she could not be hidden—deflated my rage as only she could.

I took a deep breath. I would not shriek. I would not rave. Not now. But not for my mother's sake. No. Because the only thing I cared about more than pageants was my sister.

I shot daggers in my mother's direction before retreating down the hallway.

"Scowl all you want," she called after me. And then, quieter: "You're not enough to save this family anymore. Now it's my turn."

I held my head high, pretending not to hear. Pretending it didn't hurt. No matter what my mother said, I could still put on a show.

CHAPTER TWO

The Wingate Baptist Church was bigger than it looked from the outside.

We'd had to pass it every time we made a break for bigger, better places beyond the town limits. Even though it was one of the nicer structures (redbrick with a fresh white steeple—not like the weathered clapboard that made up the rest of the town's buildings), I still found it unimpressive. The churches I saw in Dallas and Abilene were massive, towering stone structures with colorful glass windows and ornate wooden doors. Compared to them, this building looked like a shanty.

So imagine my surprise when we walked inside—my mother adjusting her too-tight dress, gripping my sister's hand with knuckles so white, you couldn't even tell she wasn't wearing gloves like all the other church ladies—to discover an atmosphere charming and quaint. The carpet was a cheerful shade of maroon, the rows of pews carved out of shiny wood with cushions to match the floors. The smell was different but pleasant—a mix of perfumes and candles, a marked difference from the manure outside.

And the *people*. I saw some familiar faces, like our neighbors, the McGraws, along with their redheaded pest of a son, Bert, who was always spitting his tobacco over the fence between our yards, and my schoolteacher, Mrs. Guinn. But most of the people were new. And not just new but *fancy*. Never in my life had I seen so many different types and colors of fabric—in Wingate!—or wide-brimmed hats not made out of straw. These were not the same people we saw down at the Five 'n' Dime or Corner Drugs. Were they?

Maybe it was like the difference between me in my sequins and me out of them, the difference between plain ol' Bea Carraway and *Miss Beatrice Carraway*, singer, actress, and pageant queen extraordinaire. Makeup and nice clothes made all the difference.

Too bad right now I was wearing a plain cotton dress covered in small lilac flowers—faded lilac flowers at that—with ugly copper buttons running all up the front and a frayed lace collar. The dress wasn't *terrible*—it was an "everyday dress"—but it only served to remind me what I was supposed to be wearing and wasn't. Where I was supposed to be and wasn't. And that was enough to sour any positivity I might have begun feeling about this stupid, ugly church.

I melted into the nearest pew, sulking.

"Get up," my mother hissed. "We're not sitting here."

I crossed my arms and ignored her. One pew was the same as another. I wasn't moving.

Sharp nails dug into my upper arm, causing me to yelp. "Get *up*." It was the loudest whisper I'd ever heard. "Now."

Sighing, I allowed myself to be led to a different pew, one closer to the pulpit. We squeezed in, my mother first, Eleanor second, me last. At least being closest to the aisle, I could make a quick exit when this nonsense was over.

"Well, good morning, ma'am. I don't believe I've had the pleasure."

A smooth baritone wafted over the din of the congregation. My mother had seated herself next to a tall man with dark hair, and he was now standing, making a small bow toward her in an absurdly formal way.

From my seat, I couldn't see my mother's face. But I heard her giggle. At least I think it was her. I'd never heard that sound come out of my mother's mouth in my entire life.

"I'm Emma Mae Carraway," she drawled, her voice as sweet and thick as honey.

"Well, Mrs.—"

"Miss."

A beat. The smile on the man's face grew wider. "Well, *Miss* Emma Mae Carraway. Your name sounds just like a song."

That giggle again. I tried to catch Eleanor's gaze, but she was preoccupied with a thread on the cushion.

"I'm Charles Thomas, and I am delighted to share a pew with you this fine morning." He gave my mother's hand a dainty shake, his fingers lingering on hers for much, much too long before letting go suddenly and picking a small ball of lint from her arm. It was an intimate gesture, bold and unexpected, but he never batted an eye. He was handsome for an older man, I decided, not a hint of baldness or stubble on his defined jaw. His eyes were a deep chocolate brown, and his smile reached all the way to their depths.

And yet something about him set my teeth on edge.

"Thomas, Thomas . . . ," my mother was saying, flipping her

hand one way and then the other. "I do believe I've heard that last name before. Are you related to Clyde Thomas of Drasco?"

Drasco? We didn't know anyone in Drasco.

"No, ma'am. I'm not. At least not that I'm aware of. It's a fairly common name, mind you, but my Thomas is tied to the oil refinery outside of town."

"Thomas Oil Refinery? You're *that* Thomas? Well, I never would have imagined. A polite gentleman such as yourself in such a hard, messy business."

"I take that as a compliment, Miss Carraway. I must clean up quite alright then."

Charles laughed. My mother laughed. I sneered.

Charles Thomas. Of course she knew the name. Everyone in Wingate—heck, everyone in Runnels County, maybe even the whole state of Texas—knew that name. One of those men who went off to war but didn't return injured or depressed or broken like the rest of them. No, Mr. Charles Thomas somehow came back richer and bigger and more important in ways I didn't understand. What I did understand was Mama didn't have that dress or that laugh before she met Mr. Charles Thomas today, and it wasn't a coincidence. I let out a little cough of displeasure.

My mother turned her head sharply, her face a battle between surprise and annoyance. "Oh, Mr. Thomas—"

"Charles. Please."

"Charles." A titter. "Forgive my manners. Allow me to introduce my daughters. This here is Eleanor Jean, my youngest, and my other daughter, Beatrice."

Eleanor did not look up from her thread. I bit the inside of my cheek and did my best to give Mr. Charles Thomas a smile I hoped passed for friendly—but dubious.

"What lovely young ladies," Charles said, extending his hand.

I offered mine hesitantly, and he shook it with the same delicacy he had my mother's.

He gave a quick raise of his eyebrows, another flash of that perfect smile. "Beatrice, it's an honor to meet you. You are quite the little looker. The apple didn't fall far from the tree, that's for sure." He shot a sideways glance at my mother, who blushed. "And it's very nice to meet you as well, Eleanor."

My sister still didn't look up.

"She's . . . shy," my mother said tightly.

We were saved from any further conversation by the swelling of organ music and the rustling of bodies as hands reached for hymnals. I grabbed one but didn't even bother to open it. What was the point of wasting my voice on songs so old-fashioned and dreary? I was supposed to be singing songs by Nora Bayes and Belle Baker—modern, upbeat songs where I was the star, not drowned out by the weak, wobbly voices of the masses. And not only that, no one was even looking at me. No, everyone's eyes were forward, staring at the rugged wooden cross hanging behind the pulpit. The only person's eyes who were not on the cross belonged to Mr. Charles Thomas, whose gaze flitted between the organ and sideways glances at my mother.

When the music ended, I settled back into the pew with my arms folded across my chest. A sweaty man with thinning hair and wire-rimmed glasses stepped onto the stage and began droning on and on about someone named Job and all these bad things that happened to him thousands of years ago. It was even more depressing than the off-key songs. Beside me, Eleanor's attention had moved from the thread on the cushion to the thin pages of a Bible, flipping them back and forth with curiosity. On the other side of her, my mother sat ramrod straight, her chest thrust forward, her eyes glued rapturously to the preacher, as if his words were the most fascinating and important thing she'd ever heard. As if she couldn't feel Charles's constant glances at her bosom.

I slumped back further in my seat, frowning. How long was this man going to talk? My dress was itchy, my rear end was sore, and I wanted to get my mother home where no one would stare at her like that again. It made me uncomfortable in a way I couldn't fully wrap my mind around. It wasn't that I wanted Charles to look at me—never, ever, ever—but still. *I* was the star of this family, the beauty, the one people looked at and talked about and fawned over. What was she thinking parading around like that?

My mind flashed to the words she'd spoken that morning: *"You're not enough to save this family anymore. Now it's my turn."*

Not enough. What could she possibly have been talking about? I tilted my head and sought out my reflection in the silver vase of flowers sitting near the front. Sure, my front two adult teeth had recently come in. They were bigger and slightly more crooked than the baby ones that had been there before, but they were still cute. And yes, my hair was a bit brassier than the platinum blonde it had been when I was five or six, but it still had a natural wave the other girls would kill for. And the right makeup would cover up the new blemishes that had started appearing over the past few months—if my mother would open the purse strings and splurge a little like she used to.

I was still pretty enough. I was still talented enough. My name was still famous enough, at least in West Texas. I was still *enough*, no matter what Mama said. And after this ridiculous church service was over, I'd make her realize it.

After what felt like hours of preaching and *amen*ing and singing, the service finally ended with a long-winded prayer and a blessing for the week to come. I grabbed Eleanor's hand and made to move into the aisle, only to be stopped cold by my sister's flat-out refusal to leave our mother's side. And Mama, unfortu-nately, wasn't budging.

On the other side of her, one of Charles Thomas's large hands was once again cupping her palm. "Now, Miss Emma Mae, you must promise me you'll be back next Sunday."

"Oh, Charles, I'll try." She dipped her chin and shook her head shyly. "It's been years since we've been. I've found it so hard since . . . since my dear Ernest passed away."

I squeezed my sister's hand. We'd *never* been to church, not before or after my father's death.

"I'm so sorry to hear. How long has it been?"

"Almost six years," Mama sniffed.

Charles produced a hankie from his front pocket, which she accepted with exaggerated gratitude. "Grief is a mountain, Miss Emma Mae. But I'm glad to see you've finally begun your descent down the other side. The good Lord was cheered by your presence in His house today . . . as was I."

"You're very kind, Charles."

I groaned internally even as my skin began to prickle. I didn't like where this was going. Not one little bit.

"In fact, I was so cheered by your presence that I'm not quite ready to leave it. Would you do me the honor of accompanying me to lunch? You and your daughters, that is. The café on the corner has the best chicken-fried steak this side of the Mississippi." His lips twitched with an excited smile. "My treat."

I chewed the inside of my cheek, watching the two of them. The invitation was for all three of us, but Charles Thomas's eyes were squarely on my mother. They reminded me of a coyote's on a chicken coop. A challenge. A hunger. Only not the kind a chicken-fried steak would fix.

My mother took his arm lightly as he led her from the

sanctuary. Eleanor and I followed behind. As we made our way into the bright sunshine, I turned to look at Eleanor, only to find her already staring at me.

"Bea."

One word, but it was enough. She glanced ahead, at our mother side by side with a stranger, and then back to me. Her fingers squeezed mine with a grip that wasn't just a consolation; it was a plea.

I managed a weak smile as I pulled her hand to my chest. So it wasn't just in my head. My five-year-old sister was a girl of very few words, but she always got her point across: something had just shifted in our world. And I wasn't sure it was for the better.

CHAPTER THREE

"Penny Fulton thinks she's such a dish." I kicked at a rock, sending it flying. "Old man Barron's jalopy has better pipes than her!"

Eleanor winced as I swung my foot at another rock but missed. The toe of my black boot turned gray with dust. It only made me angrier.

"I was perfect for that part. Just perfect. The only reason she got it was because her daddy is the mayor. Or maybe because her chest has already come in. Or so she pretends. I know a wad of stockings when I see it."

My sister's cheeks turned red. She pulled her schoolbooks toward her stomach, the strap binding them dragging in the dirt beside her. I grabbed it and shoved it in her hands so she wouldn't trip but didn't skip a beat in my tirade.

19

"It was a stupid play anyway. I only auditioned because I knew the sole way a boring old story like *The Magic Rose* would have any hope of succeeding was if it had a real catch as its lead. But if dumb old Penny Fulton is the direction Mrs. Galloway wants to go, then so be it. She wouldn't know talent if it bit her in the rear. Let the stupid thing fail. I don't even care."

Eleanor gave me a sideways glance and a quick nod before turning her attention back to her feet. I always appreciated her silence but even more so now. She'd been there; she'd sat in my room as I'd rehearsed hour after hour, quietly and in the dead of night, after Charles—I still refused to call him Father—went to bed for the night. She knew how much I wanted this part—no, *needed* this part, if I was being completely honest. Without pageants, school plays were all I had left.

Well, school plays and church. I wasn't crazy about either one of them, but at least the plays allowed me a little individuality, a chance to shine brighter than the Baptist church children's choir ever did, where I was shoved between a dozen no-talent kids all dressed in the same drab robes, voices merging into one toneless, tedious clump. The plays were also my way of sticking it to my stepfather—a small, private victory that sustained my pluck even in his worst moods.

Miss Emma Mae Carraway had become Mrs. Emma Mae Thomas in the summer of 1920. We'd moved out of the Sears and Roebuck home my father had built and into Charles's blue-and-white two-story house on the east side of town, away from our crunchy yellow yard and that tobacco-spitting nuisance Bert McGraw. This new house was surrounded by acres of waving grass, our nearest neighbor over a half mile away. Charles's house had a library and a proper sitting room. The deep walnut floors were polished and buffed to a shine brighter than pomade. Eleanor and

I each had our own room; not only were they bigger than the living area in our old house, they were both covered in thick woolen rugs that warmed our feet and provided the perfect sound barrier for my secret dance rehearsals.

Because that was the trouble. The house was grand, money flowed freely, and we never went to bed hungry, but that didn't mean things were better. Charles had a very specific way he liked his things, and we were now his things. The house needed to be kept in a certain order, the food prepared a specific way, and his wife and children were to look, act, and speak in a manner befitting their new last name. That included modest clothes (though it killed me not to remind him that my mother's flashy outfit was what attracted him to her in the first place); quiet, submissive voices, especially when addressing him; and most importantly, absolutely no singing, dancing, or performing, unless the singing was in church and the songs were subdued hymns to the Lord.

And if any of those standards were breached, well . . . let's just say Mr. Charles Thomas took his God-given role as head of the household and steward of our souls seriously. Very seriously. He was "hitting us to save us," he always said. And if our bruises were any indication, we were as saved as one could possibly get.

At first, I refused to yield. I gave up on the idea of pageants because I had neither the money nor the transportation to get me there, but when the school announced its rendition of *Cinderella*, I was the first to put my name on the audition sheet. I would have gotten the part, too, if Charles hadn't heard me rehearsing and beaten me so severely my welts wouldn't have healed in time for the grand performance—and Cinderella couldn't have welts, could she?

It should have been enough to make me quit. But no one ever complimented me on my *brains*. I took to practicing in secret, with

Eleanor my best and only confidante. I tried out for a role in every play—seven since that first one—no matter how small (though I very rarely chose the smallest roles). I was *made* to be a star, and it was frustrating that no one else could see it. Not my mother, not Charles, not even dowdy old Mrs. Galloway, who had yet to cast me in a featured role. I *was* good enough. No, not just good enough. I was the best, bruises and all.

But I didn't have a chest like Penny Fulton.

I sighed as our house came into view. "Thanks for letting me get it all out, El. It's easier to pretend nothing's wrong when all that rage isn't sitting in my gut." I gave her arm a quick squeeze. "How was your day? Any more trouble with that Mulligan boy? Need me to whup him again?"

She shook her head, her smile warm enough to melt the last of my bitterness. Almost.

We wiped our feet on the mat, then removed our shoes before stepping into the hallway—another one of Charles's rules. Eleanor put her books neatly on the hall bench while I dropped mine irritably on the floor. I'd get them later before he came home from work. Right now I needed something in my stomach to quell the ache in my heart.

"Girls? Is that you?"

My mother's voice rang out from behind the kitchen door. I knew she was preparing dinner—chicken, by the smell of it—because Charles wanted to eat as soon as he walked in the door at five fifteen. She always got started around four, which meant she already had a snack ready for us by the time we got home at a quarter after. One of the very few benefits to such a well-oiled schedule.

I pushed open the door and found her at the counter, hair pulled back in a tight bun and stuffed under a handkerchief, frilly pink apron swinging in time with the strokes of a wooden spoon.

Her face was weary but beautiful, red lipstick beneath a small cut, the faint green of an old bruise still visible beneath her otherwise-flawless powder. "How was school?"

I bit down on my tongue. I wished I could tell her all about stupid old Penny Fulton and that brainless Mrs. Galloway. But my mother—for all her injuries—was loyal to her husband above all else. "Fine."

Eleanor grabbed a cookie. "Fine," she echoed quietly.

"Well, why don't you girls go tidy up? Bea, I see a rip in your skirt. You know how your father will hate that. Leave it with the laundry, and I'll mend it tomorrow. In the meantime, put on the brown one. The one with the stripes. He loves that one on you."

I shoved the rest of my own cookie in my mouth and glanced down. Sure enough, there was a small hole near one of the black pleats. I stuck a finger through it, trying to remember how it got there. Probably when I'd given it a violent pinch trying to keep myself from screaming when the cast list was passed out.

"The back porch needs swept and the chickens fed, too. Make sure your rooms are tidied up as well."

Eleanor gave me a shrug, a few crumbs still hanging from her lips; then we trudged up the stairs to change and get started on our chores. I needed to forget about Penny Fulton, about *The Magic Rose*, about the whole unfair mess. There'd be another play, and I'd stuff some socks in my own shirt next time. But for now . . . for now there was just chicken poop and ragweed that needed cleaning up.

Charles's truck rumbled up the drive precisely at five fifteen, just as Eleanor and I were washing up for dinner. I was wearing the brown skirt, I'd wiped any trace of dirt from my face, and I'd carefully pinned my hair back from my eyes. My hair was now past my shoulders—Charles thought short hair was a mark of either pretend masculinity or overt sexuality—but a few wisps around my face still refused to grow. He insisted they be pinned back, which I did, but only when he was around. I secretly loved my short strands; it was as if my hair was waging a covert war of its own. We took our places in the dining room as he walked in the door.

"Emma Mae? Girls? Are you here? I'm home!" The same words every evening, as if we'd ever be anywhere else.

I held my breath as he rounded the corner, my eyes searching his face for any telltale signs of his mood. If he was smiling, I could relax a little. A good day at work usually meant a good day at home, with little chance for an angry tirade or backhanded slap over a minor offense. But today his brow was furrowed, his forehead creased. The corners of his mouth pulled down slightly at the corners.

It was a bad day.

My mother rushed forward, pausing for a moment to remove the apron she'd almost forgotten. She took my stepfather's lunch pail and moved to take his coat, but he grabbed her instead, wrapping an arm around her waist and kissing her in a way no child should ever have to witness their mother being kissed.

I stifled a gag.

"Welcome home, honey," my mother said breathlessly. "Fried chicken with country gravy and collard greens."

"Smells delicious." He gave her another kiss before disappearing into the kitchen to wash up.

The three of us waited behind our chairs. We were to stand until he returned. We could only sit after he sat. Another one of his ridiculous rules. And even then, we still weren't allowed to eat. Charles liked to pray first.

And pray. And pray.

"Heavenly Father, thank You for the blessing of our daily bread, for the nourishment and strength this food provides to our bodies. We thank You for the rain, the sunshine, the soil that allowed these collard greens to grow, for the chicken who sacrificed its life, and for the hands that prepared this meal for our benefit." He paused and I knew without looking he was throwing a wink at my mother, who would blush as if he didn't say the same stupid thing every night.

"Lord, we continue to ask for Your mighty hand to work in our lives, particularly those of Eleanor and Beatrice. Our enemy the devil walks about like a roaring lion, looking for someone to devour, and he has his sights set on these girls. I pray specifically for Beatrice, Lord, that You would change her heart, convict her of the sin of vanity, sift that part of her that continues to offer the devil a foothold in her life. Save her from the fires of hell that surely await her should she not repent of her wicked ways: her insolence, her vain conceit, her lack of respect not only for You, but for those You have put in authority over her. Father, open the eyes of her heart . . ."

Beneath the table, I dug my fingernails into my palms, keeping my head bowed and eyes firmly shut. I knew he was looking at me; he was trying to get me to take the bait, have an outburst, so he could feel justified in his judgment.

"Lord, the depravity of this generation is unfathomable, and my daughters are teetering on the precipice. Let them not . . ."

I stopped listening. Instead, I focused on the pain in my flesh as my nails dug further into the soft skin. I pushed until tears sprang to my eyes, until I was sure there was blood, until the pounding of my heart inside my ears drowned out the sound of Charles's voice. He was probably railing against Eleanor now, about how the devil had tied her tongue and would soon bind the rest of her if she didn't open her mouth and speak the saving words of Christ. This was almost more painful than the horrible things he said about me. Eleanor wasn't wicked; she was just quiet. And there wasn't a doggone thing wrong with it. She spoke when she had something worth saying and someone worth talking to. And in the two years he'd been in our lives, that person had never been our stepfather.

I think he prayed for me because he hated me. I think he prayed for Eleanor because she hurt his pride.

His prayers continued until the steam from my collard greens evaporated and the chicken in front of me turned gray and rubbery. When he finally said *amen* and picked up his fork, the last thing I felt was hungry, but I ate anyway, quickly and without comment, wanting to be done and away from the table as soon as possible.

Charles, on the other hand, was in no such rush. "How was school?" he asked, his fork and knife hovering over his plate.

I looked him in the eye as was required. "It was fine, thank you."

His mouth twisted into one of his famous smiles. It still gave me the willies, even after all this time. Especially now that I truly knew the man behind it.

"Good to hear. No issues with the teacher? The schoolwork? Other kids?"

Just Penny Fulton. You think I'm *vain?* "No, sir."

He stared at me as he twirled his fork around on his plate, the scrape of metal abrasive and unpleasant. I could see the words forming on his lips, the next challenge, the next test.

My mother, however, intervened first. "How was your day, honey? You seemed so tired when you got home. What can I do to help?"

It did the trick. Charles's stare abated, his posture slackening.

He reached a hand out to my mother's and gave it a squeeze. "Ah, Emma Mae. You're so good to me. It was a doozy, let me tell you. I had twenty men at my office door when I got in this morning, all scrambling for a chance to be on the next detail—it's an extra three dollars a week, you know—but I only had six spots to give out. So then there was sob story after sob story about . . ."

Gosh, he loved to talk about himself. But at least it gave me a chance to inhale the rest of my food in relative peace. Across the table, Eleanor was picking at her vegetables, her long dark hair covering her face like a curtain. Hiding.

I clenched my teeth, feeling the lackluster chicken rise in my throat. She wasn't as good as I was at blocking out our stepfather's words. No matter how many times he said them, her shoulders always shrank, her chest concaved. She would never protest, but I knew she felt every single word like a bee sting.

"May I be excused? Please?" I spat the last word with barely contained fury.

My mother and stepfather looked at me, surprised. I'd been so consumed with my own resentment, I'd unknowingly intruded on their conversation. The silence left behind was earsplitting.

"Beatrice," my mother said with a nervous giggle. "You interrupted."

"Sorry," I mumbled.

"I beg your pardon?" Charles's voice was sharp, just this side of menacing.

I swallowed, giving my blood a chance to cool. *It's not worth it, Bea. Not worth it at all.* "I'm sorry, *sir*," I repeated, using my years of pageant training to inject a cheerfulness I did not feel into my tone. "How rude of me. I simply wanted to get started on the dishes so we could have more time for our Bible reading tonight."

"Well, that's lovely. Isn't that lovely, Charles?" My mother rubbed my stepfather's thumb with her own, trying very hard to pull his gaze away from mine.

After what seemed an eternity, it finally did, the battle of wills not over but reduced to a stalemate until the next conflict. He gave me a curt nod, and I retreated to the kitchen, where a mound of pots and pans awaited my sponge and elbow grease. I didn't mind. There was something comforting in scrubbing, in the rhythmic scraping of the scour pad and harsh, burning smell of lye. Not to mention, it freed me from the presence of Charles, his oppressiveness penned on the other side of the kitchen door for as long as it took me to finish.

So naturally I took my time.

Tonight, however, I had only just begun the plates—mere moments after Eleanor had brought them in from the dining room with a grim smile—when Charles's booming voice shocked the wire scrubber from my hand, sending it flying.

"Beatrice! Get in here! Now!"

Eleanor just managed to catch the dish she was holding before it hit the floor. Her other hand trembled beneath the drying towel, which was as white as her face.

"I said *now*."

I wiped my hands on my skirt, creating a damp spot for which I'd surely get scolded. But that was the least of my worries. I grabbed Eleanor by the shoulders, trying to force her eyes to me. "It's fine," I hissed. "It's fine. You keep washing. I'll be right back."

She nodded shakily. She didn't believe me. I didn't believe me either. But I stepped into the hall anyway, head held high with a courage I wished we both felt.

Charles stood next to the bench, a piece of paper in his hand. "What is this?"

I cocked my head to the side. My eyes darted over Eleanor's books, stacked neatly on the far side, and came to rest on mine, still in a heap on the floor. My *books*. I'd meant to pick them up. Why hadn't I put them next to Eleanor's when I came in, like a sensible girl?

You were too distracted by that no-talent Penny Fulton, that's why.

"I'm sorry, sir. It was my mistake. I won't let it happen—"

"What is this?" he repeated. The paper in his hand made a terrific crumpling noise as he squeezed it.

My stomach rolled, the lump of barely digested chicken and vegetables twisting dangerously. The cast list. Why, oh, why hadn't I thrown away the cast list?

"It's a . . . a cast list. For the school play."

Charles's face hardened further. If that was possible. "And why do you have it?"

"They gave it out to everyone. So we could see who was going to be in the play."

"You're lying."

Sweat broke out under my armpits. "No, I'm not. They gave it to everyone."

"I told you no more shows. No more plays. No more recitals."

"I'm not." My voice was high-pitched and desperate. *Easy, Bea. Tone it down. This is just another performance. Sell it—don't steamroll it.* I tried to take a deep breath inside my constricted chest. "See for yourself. I'm not on there."

He hesitated before moving his glare from me to the sheet, which he scanned quickly and wordlessly.

I took a step back while he was distracted. "See? I'm not on there. No Beatrice Carraway, er, I mean, Thomas." He insisted we go by his last name, which I did, everywhere but inside my own head. "I'm not in the play."

The floor creaked beneath my weight. I paused midstep as his focus returned to me. "You're hiding something."

"No, I'm not."

He clicked his tongue over his teeth. "You are. I can tell when you're lying."

A few hairs came loose from their pins as I shook my head vigorously. "I swear I'm not."

"You tried out for this play, didn't you? That's why you have the cast list. Against my express wishes, you tried out for a play. Again."

"No, I—"

"And by God's mercy, you didn't get the part. Once again He's kept you from falling headfirst into sin, though you are bound and determined to go to hell with stage lights burning, aren't you? *Aren't you?*"

I opened my mouth to speak but thought better of it, choosing instead to take a step toward the door. Charles, however, was ready. He rushed toward me, rumpled cast list in one hand, the other grabbing a fistful of my hair. I screamed out in pain.

His pupils were black. "I've been patient, Beatrice. So very patient. But this ends tonight."

The toes of my shoes scraped against the wooden floor as my feet struggled to gain traction. I swung my arms wildly, trying to knock his grip from my hair, knowing full well I was no match for his height or his strength. That didn't mean I'd stop trying, though.

"Charles? Charles, what are you doing?" My mother's face appeared from the dining room. Confusion morphed into shock as her eyes took in the scene before her. "Charles!"

She took a step forward, though whether she was reaching for me or for him, I couldn't be sure. He pushed her backward with one powerful shrug, sending her reeling. "Stay out of this, Emma Mae."

He dragged me through the mercifully empty kitchen. I hoped Eleanor was good and hidden, and not just because I did not want her to see whatever was about to happen next. She was perfect and good and blameless, but Charles was rarely satisfied with punishing only me.

He pulled me from the house. My sweat chilled instantly in the cool evening air. The sweet smell of hay and freshly tilled earth created an aroma I'd always associated with freedom, an eerie distinction impossible to reconcile with Charles's fingers still wound tightly through my hair. He dragged me off the back porch and toward the barn. Tufts of grass ripped from their roots, releasing small clouds of dust from beneath my feet as I tried to dig my heels into the ground. We passed the chicken coop, the vegetable garden, the weathered fence around the horse corral. All the while I kicked and huffed and swung my arms, trying desperately to get in one punch—just one—that would stun Charles long enough to loosen his grip.

The corral sat empty; our two horses were already in the barn. The gate let out a shrill creak as Charles yanked it open, pulling me inside. The earth within the circular pen had disintegrated into a fine powder from years of stomping hooves. My stepfather's breath came through his nostrils in angry bursts as he hauled me over to a large metal trough and jerked my body into a standing position. He finally released my hair but wrapped both arms around my torso, pinning my limbs to my sides to keep them from flailing. The strength of his grip pressed on my rib cage, stealing my breath.

"Beatrice Thomas." The stench of tobacco and sweat choked my already-restricted lungs. "Do you repent of the sin of vanity?"

I clenched my teeth, trying to breathe and not to breathe at the same time.

His arms tightened, crushing me. A whimper escaped my lips.

"I said, do you repent of your wickedness?"

A tear broke free from my eyes despite my best efforts. I tasted blood as I willed them to stop, willed *him* to stop, willed myself to keep breathing.

I felt Charles's chest rise and fall against my back. In the distance, the slam of a door, a rustling of grass as footsteps approached. I hoped it was Mama and not Eleanor. Maybe this would be the time she would intervene. The time she would finally stand up and choose me first.

"Charles." Her voice, though I couldn't see. She remained behind us—from the sound of it, just barely inside the corral. "Charles, please stop."

He didn't answer her. Instead, his feet swept mine, causing me to lose my balance. I tumbled toward the ground, but Charles's arms remained firmly around my upper body, preventing my fall. My face now hovered at the edge of the trough. The smell of animals and algae collecting on the filmy surface of the water caused me to gag.

"She needs to be taught a lesson. She needs to be cleansed."

My terrified reflection stared back at me. Gnats and horseflies buzzed around, curious at the intrusion, as a wad of what looked to be regurgitated oats floated past, breaking up my image. When the water stilled again, it wasn't me I saw but Charles, behind me, eyes narrowed, mouth pressed into a thin white line.

"Do you repent of the sins of lying, vanity, and pride?"

I don't know why I did it. For all his power over me, all my terror, a bigger emotion was rising. An emotion planted years ago, with that first slap, that first unkind word, maybe even with that first lustful stare in my mother's direction: rage. Rage not only at my stepfather, but at this God he proclaimed to worship, a God who gave him authority to belittle and beat his women, to cover his house in a cloud of never-ending dread, to decide who was bad and who was good. A God who allowed this man—this evil, hateful man—to presume to be his own lord. No, I would never repent to a God like that.

Or to my stepfather.

I stared at Charles's reflection in the water before me. And then I spat on it.

His reaction was swifter than I anticipated. With one swoop, he lifted me from the ground and threw me in the trough, his hand pressing down on my head until my nose touched the slimy bottom. Putrid water filled my mouth and nose. My arms flailed wildly but still he held, until my muscles felt too full of water to move. Just when I felt as if my lungs would burst, he released me, and I bobbed to the surface, spitting and gasping against too much and too little air.

I could just make out the sound of my mother's screams—briefly—before being forced beneath the brown water again.

This time under the surface felt longer. Or perhaps it was only my imagination. My body was filling up with water. My brain and my heart and my lungs were floating away, bumping against the confines of a body now too tired to fight. And then suddenly there was air again. And light. And my mother's screaming. And Charles's question.

"Do you repent?"

I tried to open my mouth but my mind was no longer communicating with my muscles. Everything was numb. Dead. Worthless. And submerged once again.

I don't know how many times I went under. My mind stopped

recognizing numbers or shapes or words. The blackness of the water was no longer outside my body but inside, bearing down on my brain until all I could see was darkness. It no longer even hurt; the burning had long since extinguished. It was a gentle nothingness, the pull and push of water reduced to a dull sensation on a shell of a body I barely inhabited.

And then a coldness on my skin that broke through the numbness, a voice from the shadows calling my name. "Beatrice! Beatrice!" The smell of lavender and Crisco, soft hands on my cheeks. My mother. It was my mother. I tried to open my eyes, but they were weighted down with too much water. "Beatrice, please wake up."

A rough grip on my neck, searing pain awakening the parts I'd long since left for dead. "She's got to say it, Emma Mae. She's got to say it or else she's doomed to the fires of hell for all eternity. I can see it in her eyes—she's been touched by the devil and this is the only way to cleanse her."

I tried to free myself from his grasp, to run from the water that was going to cover me again and again and again. But my strength was suffocated, trapped beneath the dirty liquid coursing through my veins. Only my eyes functioned; they burned as they rolled around, searching . . . and landing on him.

His face was calm. Not a single strand of hair out of place. He could have just as easily been sitting in a Sunday morning pew as kneeling by a water trough in a horse corral after trying to drown his stepdaughter. "Say it, Beatrice. Say it and be saved." His brow lowered, creating a shadow over his already-dark eyes. "Do you repent?"

I searched for any sign of concern in his face, any twitch of the lip, any crinkling of the forehead that might convey regret or genuine distress for me. Instead, I saw nothing but contempt. He wasn't trying to save me; he was trying to break me, to bring me under his authority—what he saw as his God-given authority—and complete the trophy case he thought he was getting when he married my mother.

This wasn't about my soul. It was about his ego.

I said the words he wanted to hear. I said them, but I lied. And when I was lifted out of the water that last time, it was as if by a stranger, gently and with reverence. He hugged me and lifted his hands to heaven, thankful I had finally seen the light.

My entire body ached as I lay in bed that night. I felt changed, but not in the way Charles intended. Because I did not feel cleansed. I did not feel saved. When I had come up out of that trough, I had not seen God. I had seen only Charles Thomas.

And I vowed that this night in his wretched home would be my last.

CHAPTER FOUR

I did not go to school the next day. I didn't let Eleanor go either. When I returned to the house the night before, limp and soaking, her eyes had met mine through the crack in her bedroom door. I didn't know how much of my "cleansing" she had seen, but I did know she saw me then . . . and she knew. Without words, she knew what had happened. And she knew what had to be done.

Charles was all sunshine and kisses over breakfast. Rubbing Mama's back as she poured his coffee. Snorting over the morning paper's funnies and mooning over Harding's election. Giving Eleanor his bacon—her favorite—and me an extra slice of honeyed toast—my favorite. Even his morning Scripture reading and prayer were upbeat, a passage from Psalms about the greatness of God and a petition for His blessing over "my beautiful wife and two lovely daughters, the greatest earthly treasure You have bestowed upon me, Your humble servant." After breakfast, Eleanor and I grabbed our things and headed out the door, turning left at the end of the long drive, like it was any other morning.

We continued along the road until we reached a place where the fountain grass concealed our movements should anyone happen to be watching from the house. Then we ducked into the field and circled back to the barn. His horses, creatures I once saw as majestic and gentle, seemed to glare at us from their stalls as we climbed the rickety ladder up into the hayloft. They were a part of *him* now, guilty because it was their corral, their trough, their master. I knew it wasn't fair, but it didn't stop me from hating them—and from being sure they hated me too.

Eleanor's eyes spoke her anxiety, wincing at every popping floorboard, every disgruntled snort from the animals below our feet. She picked at a hangnail on her thumb as her gaze darted from me to the house. I should have been nervous too; if he suddenly decided to check on the horses, remembered a chore he'd forgotten the night before, or simply decided he didn't feel like going to work today—not likely but still a possibility—we would be caught and punished. Punished beyond what had happened the night before because my disobedience would prove the disingenuity of my confession. And even worse, this time it would include my sister.

All of those things should have terrified me. Should have had me weighing the risk, deciding it was too heavy, and heading off to school like I was supposed to. But the memory of last night burned in my lungs. Or perhaps it was still the dirty trough water. Either way, it drained my strength but toughened my resolve.

The sun had crested the top of the magnolia tree before we finally heard our stepfather's truck grumble to life. The stench of ragwort drifted in from the fields as he bumped down the drive, the yellow flowers we called "stinking willies" attaching to my mind an odor I would always and forever associate with this moment and the backside of a man I hoped to never see again.

We waited fifteen minutes before climbing down from our hiding place just in case Charles forgot something or got the wild notion to return. Eleanor's fingers trembled in mine as we crossed the pasture to the house. Her breath was short and rapid, coming out in slightly congested whistles, the lone sound across a yard that was somehow silent, not even the grasshoppers daring to make a chirrup. I pushed open the back door with a creak that seemed to echo for miles.

Mama was at the kitchen sink, back turned, but spun around at the sound. Her body tensed as she took in the sight of us. Suds dripped from the half-washed breakfast plate in her hands, leaving dark spots on her Clarks. "Beatrice! Eleanor! What are you doing here? What's wrong? Did something—?"

"Nothing's wrong," I said calmly. "We're fine. Well, as fine as we can be after last night."

At my words, her shoulders deflated, and she gripped the plate with both hands as if to keep it from slipping. "Beatrice." Her voice was tinged with a weariness I wanted to believe was an apology, even though my heart knew it was too late for that now.

"He almost killed me last night, Mama. You saw it." *And did nothing,* I wanted to add. But I had to keep my cool. I only had a little time, and not one of those seconds could be wasted on sorrow or anger. I had to focus on the facts. "He can call it whatever he wants—saving my soul, cleansing my sin—but the fact remains he held my head in that trough until I passed out. Until water filled my body and came out of my nose because it had nowhere else to go. He tried to *kill* me."

"Beatrice." My name again but softer. Weaker.

I swallowed the hard lump in my throat. I would not allow myself the luxury of stopping. "It may have been the first time he went that far. But it was not the first time he hurt me. Or Eleanor." I squeezed my sister's small, cold hand. Her hair covered her face. "Or you."

Instinctively my mother put wet fingers to the yellowed remainder of a bruise beneath her eye.

"I'm not going to sit around and wait until it happens again. Because it *will* happen again. You might never admit it, but you know it's true." I paused, giving her a chance. A chance to tell me I was right and she was sorry. For her to even say my name in supplication again would have been enough. But her lips remained closed, her eyes on the floor, the sporadic drip of water from her fingertips onto the linoleum the only sound.

The child in me crumpled, wanting to cry. Despite everything, she was still my mama; I wanted desperately for her to act like it. With an urge as instinctual as a newborn's, I longed for her to see me, to love me, to *choose* me.

But that was not who she was. It was not who she'd ever been, really. And I couldn't expect her to be different now just because I was. That expectation was childish, and I was no longer a child. So my disappointment was fleeting; even before I let myself truly feel it, I stuffed it deep down inside me, beneath the last parts of youth Charles had suffocated the night before.

"We're leaving. Eleanor and me. Today. We're going to Dallas to stay with Nana and Grandpop. You can come but—"

"Don't do this, Bea. Please." Tears collected in the corners of her eyes as she finally raised her head and met my gaze. "He's a good man. He made a mistake last night, but he's a good man. We have so much more than we ever dreamed of with him. Food fit for kings, a beautiful home, plenty of money for clothes and books and—"

"Makeup?" I interrupted, an edge to my tone. "To cover the cuts and the bruises he gives out just as generously?"

"Not more than we deserve," she said shakily. "He's saving us, Beatrice. We just don't understand it because we spent so long in sin."

I squeezed Eleanor's hand so hard my fingers began to throb. "That's a load of manure, and you know it. There wasn't a dog-gone thing wrong with us until Charles walked in the picture. We were happy."

"Happy?" The intensity of my mother's question caused me to jump. Beside me, Eleanor whimpered. "You think we were happy? Open your eyes, Beatrice! We barely had any food. We were behind on rent payments for the house. The only pair of shoes Eleanor owned had a hole right through the sole!"

I glanced over at my sister's feet. She tucked one foot behind the other, embarrassed, even though her holey shoes had long since been replaced with the brown-and-white lace-ups she wore now.

"Your father left me nothing but you girls and a mound of debt. I poured every penny I had into your pageants and shows, and for a while, it earned us some income and allowed us to get by. But the older you got, the less you won, and it just wasn't enough anymore. Without Charles, we would have been homeless in less than two months. No matter what you think about him, he *did* save us, Beatrice, and I am not going to walk away from that because of a few hiccups and your own hardheadedness."

Blood pounded in my ears. A few hiccups? My own hard-headedness? I'd thought my mother was weak, but now I could see she was a fool. And all my resolve to keep my emotions in check evaporated with my patience. I opened my mouth to object only to close it again at the soft squeeze of my sister's hand. She'd pushed her hair out of her face, emerging from her safe space to stare at me, her dark eyes pleading for the deliverance I was in danger of disrupting.

I took a deep breath, willing my fury back down my throat. She was right. Without speaking a word, she was right. As always.

"You can stay, then. But I'm leaving. And Eleanor is coming with me."

I moved to go past her and up the stairs, where I'd already packed a small suitcase for each of us.

"And just how do you think you're going to get there?"

"The bus," I said without turning around. "Eleanor and I have some change we saved from turning in cans we found along the side of the road." Truth was, I didn't know if it would be enough. I didn't even know if the rusty old bus that serviced Wingate would go to Dallas. But I wasn't going to let that be the thing that stopped us.

"You don't even know how to find Nana and Grandpop's."

"I know their address. I'll ask someone for directions when we get there." I stomped up the stairs, pulling Eleanor along with me.

My mother followed. "And what are you going to do when you get there? Nana and Grandpop don't have enough money to feed and clothe you forever."

"I'll get back in the pageant scene. Or find a role in a play. There are way more opportunities there than here. *Paying* opportunities."

"And when you don't get the roles?"

When. Not *if,* but *when.* Her words were deliberate and cutting, but I absorbed them like one of Charles's slaps. I pulled Eleanor's suitcase from under her bed and shoved it in her hands. "Then I'll find another job until I do. Maybe I'll quit school. Or maybe I'll be like the kids we saw last time we visited—school in the morning, work in the afternoon. Ain't no different from chores." I pushed past her and into my own room.

"And what about Charles? What will you do when he comes to bring you home? Because you know he will."

I pulled my suitcase out from under my bed, smoothing down the *Little Miss Runnels County 1915* sash I'd glued to the front. "Let him try. After I tell Grandpop what's been going on, I'd love to see him try to step foot inside that house. In fact, I'd welcome it."

I turned to face my mother. I'd hit a growth spurt over the summer and now came up to her nose. I tilted my chin so I could look her in the eye, challenging her. But though her lips twitched with more feeble objections, they remained unspoken, and after a moment, she looked away. I turned and met Eleanor back in the hallway. Descending the stairs, side by side with my sister, I walked out the front door.

We'd only just reached the magnolia when my mother found her voice again. "Wait! Beatrice, please. Wait!"

I felt Eleanor stiffen beside me. I paused but did not turn around. From behind us came the swift sound of gravel crunching as my mother ran toward us.

"Please don't do this to me, Beatrice. Don't go. Please . . ." A hitch of breath, a waver in her tone. "Please don't leave me alone."

I turned. Doggone it all, I turned around. I wish I hadn't. Because the woman who stood before me looked nothing like my mother. Her apron was askew, damp spots darkened the fabric under her arms, and mascara flowed down her cheeks in black rivulets. But it was her eyes that wounded me the most—the beautiful blue ocean within them was lifeless. Defeated.

The young child inside me roared forth once more. I felt a stab in my heart that caused my chest to deflate. Numb hands dropped my suitcase. Beside me, a tear dripped from Eleanor's eye. I licked dry lips, clenching and unclenching my fists, willing the lump in my throat to subside enough for me to speak.

"You have to choose," I said finally. "You have to choose us or him. We don't want to go . . . but we can't stay. So you have to choose."

My mother's shoulders heaved as sobs racked her body. Her gaze flitted between us and the house, between me and my sister, between the ground and the sky. The emptiness in her eyes had cleared at my words, replaced with surprise, then grief, and what I later realized was resentment. Because when we finally left forty-five minutes later in my mother's old car rather than the Wingate Blue Line, she was in the seat next to me, a cigarette hanging from her lips, dried mascara crusting her cheeks.

My mother might have chosen me that day. But she never forgave me.

CHAPTER FIVE

"If you'll just give me another chance—"

"I'm sorry, Miss Carraway, but my decision is final."

"I had a cold that day, see, and my voice came out all nasally. If you listen now—" I gave a loud, exaggerated inhale through my nostrils—"it's all cleared up. Night-and-day difference. Let me do one song. One song is all I—"

"Miss Carraway." Albert Hamilton was a short, round man with hooded eyes and a mustache like a half-decomposed caterpillar on his upper lip. It quivered when he frowned. And he was frowning now. "As I've said before, my decision is final. I encourage you to try out for my next production in the spring. That is, if you're not plagued once again by congestion."

He pulled his hat off a rack in the corner and made to reach for the door behind me. He was late for a luncheon, a fact he'd made very clear when I'd barged in fifteen minutes ago. The conversation was over, had been over before it had even started. No amount of begging, pleading, stomping, or explaining was going to put me on the stage for Dallas Community Theater's production of *Treasure Girl*. Not as Kitty, not as Mary, not as Ann, the role for which I'd auditioned. Not even as a chorus girl, a part for which, at nineteen years old, I was way too old and way too qualified after all the smaller roles I'd notched in over the past few years to build up my name. Which was how I knew Mr. Albert Hamilton must be prejudiced against me in some way.

I should cut and run. Hike up my stockings and concentrate on the next audition, the next theater, the next director who perhaps wouldn't be so narrow-minded. Who needed this pompous little sap anyway?

But I didn't move. Couldn't move. Because I *did* need him. I needed this role—any role—to justify the money I kept pumping into my acting career, money we desperately needed to keep food on the table. I'd given up on school as soon as we arrived in West Dallas seven years ago, putting all my energy into working and auditioning, promising each new role would be it, my big break, a chance to get noticed and take my career to its next logical step: Broadway. Maybe even Hollywood.

Both time and money were rapidly wearing thin. I couldn't come home empty-handed.

Tears welled in my eyes, and this time they weren't part of a performance. This was me, Beatrice Carraway, dangerously close to the end of her rope. And it was humiliating.

Mr. Hamilton shifted his hat back and forth in his pudgy hands. "Miss Carraway . . ."

"Please," I whispered. "I'll take any role. Chorus girl, deck-hand, I'll even play a shrub. Something, anything, to get me up on that stage."

He sighed, the smell of old tobacco filling the space between us. "I wish I could help. I really do. You have a pretty enough face, but it just isn't the right look for us."

The right look. Polite words to mask an impolite opinion. I'd been the only one at the audition in handmade clothes rather than store-bought. The only one with a run in my stockings I'd tried to hide with clear polish, the only one with lipstick that cracked rather than glistened under the stage lights.

I'd looked West Dallas. That's what he meant. Next to all the other girls, I'd looked *poor.*

"Come back next time—we're doing *Good News* in May—and I'll see what I can do." He let the hollowness of his sentiment linger for a moment before gently nudging past me and into the hall. I watched him retreat, his rapid scurrying along the darkened corridor reminding me very much of a rat fleeing a sinking ship.

Fleeing *me.* I *was* the sinking ship.

I slapped at my cheeks, taking out my frustration on my mas-cara trails. There was no time to wallow in self-pity, no matter how much I wanted to. I'd failed in my lunchtime endeavor, but I still had to go back to work. It was the only thing left to do.

Hargrave's Café was a plain-looking brick building, unique only in its semicircular shape around a peculiar jog in Swiss Avenue, the busy road that passed directly in front of it. There was nothing that made it stand out from any of the other hundreds of cafés in Dallas. Nothing except that the air above it was clear, its location being several miles from the smokestacks of the Trinity Portland Cement Company, which belched black fumes day and night over my house in West Dallas. Its main clientele were the handsome young men of the Baylor medical college, whose attention I had no trouble getting with a few swings of my hips and flutters of my eyelashes. They were good with tips—important because I was barely making three dollars a week—and even better with good times. In the two years I'd been working here, I'd had several dates, even more necking sessions in the backs of men's cars, and more than enough whiskey-filled parties to make me forget about failed auditions. For a night, at least.

What I hadn't gotten, however, was one to stick around. That, I was hopeful, was about to change. Lowering my head against the brisk autumn breeze, I quickened my pace along the five blocks from the theater to the café, trying to shake off Mr. Hamilton's words by sticking my hand in my coat pocket and pulling out a strip of photos. They were from the booth at Fair Park, taken about a month ago with the newest prospect, Roy, a tall drink of water from up near Wichita Falls, studying to be a surgeon. He had deep-green eyes and thick black hair that always smelled of Brilliantine pomade. He held the door open for me on our first date and bought all my drinks without insisting on anything physical in return—until the next date. He paid for meals, brought me flowers, and always drove me back to the bus stop after our nights out. For six straight weeks, he'd waited for me after nearly every shift. He even told me he thought he was falling in love. And even though he'd gone home to visit his family in Wichita Falls for two weeks, he'd promised to call on me when he returned—and he was to return this evening.

It was on Roy and Roy alone I tried to focus my thoughts as I hung my coat in the narrow hallway leading to the kitchen and pulled my grease-stained apron from the rack. I grabbed my waitress hat from its spot atop the shelf, making sure to smooth my hair—which I'd chopped back into a fashionable bob upon arriving in Dallas all those years ago and had never let grow out

again—under its ugly cardboard frame. Touching up my makeup
in the scuffed mirror beside the coatrack, I plastered on my biggest
fake smile before stepping out into the dining room.

"Hey, Bea, can I get another cup of coffee?"

"Table thirteen needs the check."

"Order up! Special, table five."

The lunch rush was in full swing, and I barely had a chance to
wave to Margaret, my friend, coworker, and fellow West Dallas-er,
before losing myself to the demands of the students, businessmen,
and retirees filling our booths. Tall and slender, with a mouth like a
horse's and a pair of bulgy brown eyes to match, Margaret was no
beauty, but she always covered for me when I was late, shared the
stash of cinnamon candy she kept in her pockets when my breath
smelled of last night's cigarettes and booze, and lent a sympathetic
ear as she waited for my heart to rebound over some Baylor under-
grad who liked to touch but never call. She was engaged to a
mechanic by the name of George, a scruffy, barrel-chested tree
trunk of a man who stood to inherit his father's body shop, so
she cared little for the handsome men who gathered at our tables,
allowing me to have first dibs on the ones who caught my fancy.
In return, I shared my tips with her. Sometimes.

"How did it go?" she whispered as we waited near the order
window for our dishes.

"Mr. Hamilton is an idiot." I thumbed through the tickets on
the counter, avoiding her eyes. "Wouldn't know talent if it jumped
up and bit him on the nose."

"I'm sorry, Bea. I know how much that part meant to you. I
really thought you'd get it."

"It's fine," I replied flippantly, though that lump began to rise
in my throat once more. "There will be other roles."

"Right."

I could tell by her tone she knew the truth. It *wasn't* fine and I *wasn't* okay. Doggone it all. I wasn't as good at faking as I thought. From inside my hurt, a familiar panic rose up, that nagging voice echoing in the deepest recesses of my brain. *Maybe Mama is right—maybe I'm* not *a good enough actress.*

"Listen, Bea, I didn't want to do this now, but—"

"Order up! Tuna melt, cheesesteak on wheat, and BLT on rye, table eleven."

"That's me. We'll talk later." I put the plates on my tray, balancing it expertly in the crook of my elbow, and swept away from the counter. I needed the tips. I needed the distraction. I needed to get myself together before I even attempted to talk to Margaret again.

Table eleven was a group of three med students, each of them dark-haired and strong-chinned, in matching white button-downs with ties of various shades of blue and green. They had textbooks open in front of them, but none of them were studying. Instead, they watched me approach with their food, a hunger in their eyes that had nothing to do with Sal's cooking, I was sure.

"Here you are, gentlemen. Is there anything else I can get for you?"

"How about your phone number?" Tuna Melt asked.

I pressed my lips together and let out a low giggle. "Oh, sugar, you're too late. I've already got a beau." Feeling their eyes linger as I walked away, I gave a small shake of my rear before twisting my head slightly over my shoulder. From this angle, I knew my hair shone and my lips looked fuller. "But come back next week and check again." Their whoops and hollers followed me all the way back to the counter.

What was I thinking? I still had it. I was as good an actress as they came.

Margaret came up behind me, the coffeepot in her hand sloshing dangerously toward the top. Several strands of her frizzy brown hair had come loose from beneath her cap. "Bea, I really need to talk—"

"Order up! Chef's special and a footlong with kraut and fries, table seven!"

I grabbed the plates. "I'm fine, Margie. Really."

"It's not that. It's . . ."

But I'd already walked away. The couple at table seven were clearly on a date, and judging by their complete lack of interest in me or their food, it was going well. Which meant I'd have to work extra hard to make any kind of impression grand enough to get even an average tip.

I kept glasses filled and condiments stocked, flirtations and service a delicate balance I'd perfected. By the time those customers were finished, another batch had rolled in to take their place, and the whole charade started all over again. Reading each table and anticipating which type of waitress they'd tip most kept me almost as busy as collecting orders, clearing dishes, and refilling coffee mugs. And it definitely kept me too busy to finish my conversation with Margaret. But not too busy to notice her doleful glances in my direction, which she quickly covered with weak smiles every time I caught her. By the time the lunch rush was over, I was scolding myself for making her worry so much about me; it was hard enough for her to get tips as it was, let alone when she was walking around with an expression like that.

"Margie, listen." I blinked against the bright sunlight as I stepped outside, wiping my hands on my apron and leaning against the brick wall, which was warm despite the chilly fall air. The last of my tables had cleared out, and I was taking a breather before gathering their soiled napkins and leftover bread crusts.

"I really am fine. I'm disappointed, but there will be other parts. I'll bounce back."

Beside me, Margaret pulled a cigarette out of her pocket and offered another to me. I inhaled gratefully, watching the smoke from our lips swirl together in the early afternoon sun. We stood in silence, enjoying the warmth at our backs and in our lungs. Behind us, we could hear traffic on Swiss Avenue and, faintly, Sal whistling in the kitchen as he scraped down a skillet. The smell of grilled onions and charred meat wafted outside to mix with the scent of soap from Yates Laundry across the street.

The cigarettes were long gone when Margaret finally spoke. "Roy stopped in while you were out."

My stomach fluttered. "He did? He knows I don't get off until three. What was he doing here? Simply couldn't stay away any longer?" I grinned at the thought.

Margie, however, was not smiling. "He . . . he left this." She reached into the pocket of her coffee-stained apron.

A tingle crept through my limbs and down my spine. He'd left me something! He must have brought me a present from Wichita Falls. Some new makeup (I'd mentioned needing some), some sweets, or—dare I even think it—jewelry?

I bent my neck forward to see, trying not to feel too disappointed when the only thing she produced was a folded slip of yellow paper. When she pressed it into my palm, her bottom lip nearly disappeared under the bite of her large front teeth.

My heart pounded in my throat. I didn't like Margaret's face. It was not the face of a woman about to swoon with happiness or jealousy, the way she normally looked whenever I regaled her with stories about Roy. No, the rapid blinking, the fidgeting with her buttons, the lack of eye contact . . .

She was nervous. And I was nauseous.

Bea,

Sorry I missed you. I didn't want to do this with a note but maybe it's for the best. We've had some great times over the past few weeks, and I won't ever forget that night by the lagoon at Fair Park. I've never met anyone like you. You're wild, Bea. Just wild.

But my time at home made me realize it's time for me to settle down. My father reminded me that I've almost finished school, and it's time to get serious about life. As such, I feel that I have to tell you I've become engaged. She's a real sweet girl—the daughter of one of my father's oldest clients—and I know you'd love her if you met her.

You're a good-time gal, Bea, and I know you won't have any trouble finding a new beau. Thanks for putting some flavor in my life. Take care of yourself.

Roy

I reread the words several times, my eyes blurring, stomach twisting. Engaged. Roy was engaged.

"I'm so sorry, Bea. I didn't mean to read it, but he was acting so strange and I was worried . . ." Her words trailed off into a defeated sigh. "I'm so sorry."

I shook my head, barely hearing her. *A good-time gal,* he'd said. Just like with Mr. Hamilton, polite words masking an impolite opinion.

Margaret's arm around my shoulders was gentle enough to finally knock the tears from my eyes. I sobbed into her chest, my mascara dropping black dots onto her pale-pink uniform. Her thin frame was bony but strong, the only thing that kept me from collapsing into a heap on the weed-riddled concrete. "Shh," she whispered against the top of my head. "Shh. I know it hurts. He seemed so kind and good. I thought he was the one for you, too."

She held me until I had no tears left, then convinced Sal to let us leave thirty minutes early; the café was so asleep with the midafternoon doldrums that our absence would surely go unnoticed until the next shift arrived at three. When we removed our aprons, the photo strip of Roy and me fluttered out of my pocket and onto the floor. His smiling face stared up at us like a ghost from the sticky green linoleum. It was Margaret who picked it up, crumpling it into a little ball before throwing it into the trash can with more gusto than necessary.

I leaned on her all the way to the bus stop, listening to her alternate between bouts of sympathetic silence and outbursts of frustration and rage. I stayed quiet, letting her air the usual breakup sentiments in my stead. Letting her grieve over my broken heart and lost love. She was a good friend, after all. And her camaraderie was a better alternative than exposing the truth.

My tears were not for Roy. Not really. My tears were for myself.

I hadn't been enough for Roy, and I hadn't been enough for any of the dozens of men who had come before him. I hadn't been enough for Mr. Hamilton or the other directors in Dallas, just like I hadn't been enough for the pageant judges all those years ago. I hadn't been enough for my teachers, who told me school was wasted on someone who had neither the attention nor the desire to learn. I hadn't been enough for the Browns, who'd fired me as their nanny after only a week, or for Mr. Thompson, in whose candy shop I'd only lasted a day.

I wasn't enough to keep Eleanor fed or Mama off the bottle.

That nagging suspicion I'd carried with me for years was no longer just speculation. These past few years had proven it true.

I wasn't enough. For anyone.

CHAPTER SIX

Nana and Grandpop had passed away within a few short years of our arrival in West Dallas. I tried to tell myself it wasn't due to the stress of having three extra bodies in their home. They'd left us their house, completely paid off and structurally sound, unlike so many others in our neighborhood, but we still struggled to keep the lights on and the heat running. It was situated just over the Trinity River in an area known as the "Devil's Back Porch," which was essentially a slum built on top of a floodplain, where the thick, muggy air mingled with the constant belch of factory smoke to create a putrid, barely breathable haze that seeped into your clothes and dulled your hair. Mosquitoes as big as rodents swarmed in clouds that could block out the sun. Garbage littered narrow dirt streets that turned to mud with the slightest sprinkle, and the stench of sewage was a constant you never really got used to. Among the population, there were vagrants and car thieves, bootleggers and con artists. But there were good people, too. Normal, decent people like my nana and grandpop, when they were still alive, or like Eleanor and me. Eleanor, for sure.

Nevertheless, there was always a sense of disappointment as you crossed the bridge from downtown. That moment when the shiny skyscrapers were replaced by blackened smokestacks, when the pedestrians in suits melted into men and women with dirty faces and even dirtier overalls. Lunch pails hung limply from exhausted hands as workers made the long trudge back to their shanties, while the next shift lumbered tiredly in the opposite direction, toward the foundries and factories that never slept.

Still I was lucky. I had a home—a proper home, built with lumber and not cardboard—a warm bed without fleas, and a job without fumes. Compared to so many others, we Carraways were well-off.

And after seven years, we were still free of Charles Thomas. No matter what my mother said, that was definitely an improvement, smog and all.

He hadn't even come looking like Mama said he would. It wasn't as if he couldn't have found us; there was really only one place to which we could have fled. But rather than a humbled and apologetic man begging us to return, divorce papers showed up on our porch less than six months after we'd left, then an engagement notice in the newspaper for the new soon-to-be Mrs. Charles Thomas not long after. There was no doubt in my mind that Mama, and perhaps even Eleanor and I, were being painted as the villains in all this back in Wingate. We couldn't be saved after all, I guess.

But his pride could.

Margaret left me on the front stoop with a hug, promising to stop by and take me out later, before she scurried off to start dinner for her parents—good practice for when she got married, she always said—in her own house two blocks over.

I pushed in the front door, which was weathered and in desperate need of paint but still kept out the chill. "Eleanor? Mama? I'm home."

There was no answer. It was dim, the autumn sun already sunk low despite the early hour. Dust sparkled in the rapidly fading light.

"El?" I called again. My sister had been allowed to stay in school, bright despite her lack of verbal skills, and would finish her formal education in a few months. She could usually be found on the sofa when I returned from work, nose in a book and pencil in her hand. But the brown tattered couch was empty. Eleanor's pile of schoolbooks lay on the table unopened. Perhaps she was next door cleaning? She was usually able to make a few dollars a week sweeping and mopping the neighboring houses, though Mama wouldn't let her travel much farther for fear of the hoboes that camped down the street. No telling what they'd do to a girl like Eleanor who couldn't speak up for herself—literally.

I dropped my purse on the armchair and pressed farther into the house, down the narrow hallway with its frayed runner and peeling wallpaper. A faint light shone through a crack at the base of the kitchen door. I pushed it open to find my mother sitting at the table, chin to her chest, cigarette dangling from her fingertips. A glass of amber liquid sat in front of her.

"Where's Eleanor?"

My mother's head jerked up, strands of blonde hair falling from beneath the red handkerchief covering her hair. Her face had aged fifteen years in the past five. Once-vibrant skin was now leathery and dull, with permanent scowl lines pulling down the corners of her mouth. There was always an air of exhaustion about her, no matter the time of the day. Her blue overalls were worn at the knees, the knuckles of the hands that rested on them inflamed and cracked from hundreds of hours sewing buttons on men's trousers at a local garment factory. Her hazy eyes studied me with little interest.

"Next door. Mrs. Taylor said she'd give her twenty cents to clean out the upstairs closet and sweep the bedroom. Her mother is moving in with them soon." She took a long drag off her cigarette as she rubbed her forehead with two fingers. "What are you doing home anyway? I thought that beau of yours was coming back into town."

I walked over to the sink without answering, pulling a glass from the cupboard and filling it with gritty water from the tap. I drank it slowly, my mind racing with excuses.

From the table, my mother eyed me through her smoke. "What happened?"

I scraped my tongue with my teeth, the last bitter dredges of sediment rolling around my mouth. "Nothing. He was delayed, that's all."

"You're lying."

"I am not!"

She pulled the hankie from her head, shaking out her hair. Her golden blonde was now brassy and bland. She let out an amused grunt. "Lost another one, eh? What is he? The twelfth? Thirteenth?"

My face began to tingle. "I didn't *lose* him."

"What's the point of going all the way across the river, working at a job for pretty girls, if you can't even snag you a man? Plenty of boys around here with a factory job that will at least keep a roof over your head. It would be one less mouth I'd have to feed."

"I like my job."

She waved a hand dismissively, smoke trailing out from behind it. "Let me guess. You didn't get that part, either?"

I should have been more prepared. I knew it was going to come up. But the pain of Roy's engagement had temporarily smothered the audition failure. My mother's words stabbed me anew, sending a wave of anguish over me so intense it caused me to flinch. I coughed, trying quickly to cover it.

But I wasn't quick enough. My mother tilted her head up, her smile dripping with spite. "Ah. Two for two."

"I turned the role down," I lied, pinching my skirt between my fingers. It was a trick I used onstage to focus attention away from my jitters. Shifting my concentration to the nerves in my fingertips, the coarseness of the fabric, the prickling of my skin.

My mother grunted and smashed her cigarette into a nearby ashtray. "No wonder you didn't get it. You can't even fool your own mother."

The grip on my skirt tightened. My fingernails stabbed through the thin fabric and into my palms.

"You know, we could have bought a whole extra carton of eggs, two bottles of milk, and a loaf of bread if you'd taken an extra shift at the café rather than going to that audition." She pushed her chair back with a squeak, grabbing her glass. "Could have had even more than that if we'd never left Wingate."

The last part was spoken under her breath, barely loud enough for me to hear but bitter enough to assure I'd never miss it.

It always came back to this. It was my fault. Everything was all my fault. My fault my mother had to work twelve-hour shifts at a factory making nine dollars a week, which was barely enough to cover our utilities and groceries. My fault poor, simple Eleanor was forced to scrub toilets for pennies. My fault that we were here, that we were poor, that we couldn't catch a break in this smoky, swampy, bug-infested hellhole called West Dallas. Never mind no one had laid a hand on us since we'd arrived, that our cuts and bruises and scrapes had healed without new ones to take their place.

What hadn't healed was my mother's ego. She'd gone from being a kept woman—abused, yes, but kept—to another nameless, faceless, worn-down factory worker, living for the weekend and the bottle, unremarkable and undesirable, each day simply another few hours closer to the grave.

And it was all because of me. Because my grand plan, my fairy tale, was an utter and complete failure.

I stared after her retreating form as she went out the kitchen door. A slight stumble in her gait assured me the drink in her hand was not her first of the day. My anger went right out with her. I could have followed her, yelled, argued my case. That's how these "discussions" usually unfolded. But I was too tired to fight. And most depressingly, too close to admitting the truth in her claims.

Instead, I heated up some beans, one of only three cans left in our pathetic pantry, and tore off a piece of bread from a hardened loaf on the counter. I ate little, just enough to quell the rumble; Mama's dinner would be liquid, but I wanted to make sure Eleanor had something when she got home. I retreated to the bathroom for a soak—the water tepid and gray but sufficient at removing the smell of grease—then up the narrow staircase and into my small bedroom to change clothes. I chose a dress made of black wool that had worn thin around the collar last year. I'd altered the neckline to a V shape, cutting fringe into it to make it appear more fashionable, and added a splash of white cotton to the opposite shoulder, also fringed, in an attempt to make it seem newer. I fashioned a belt around my waist and slipped into a pair of black heels, the toes covered with a thick layer of polish to hide the scuffs. I was just finishing my makeup—barely enough rouge to cover my cheeks, but my smoky eyeliner more than made up for it—when I heard a car horn. Scribbling a note to Eleanor, telling her I loved her and would be home later, I rushed down the stairs and into Margaret's fiancé's waiting car without bothering to tell my mother goodbye.

The interior smelled of cheap cologne and even cheaper tobacco, but George handed me a flask as we pulled away. "Heard about that college beau of yours. Figured you might need this."

I gave him a grim smile and took a sip, wincing at the welcome burn. "Where we going?"

Margaret squeezed my hand. Her dress was the same shade of brown as her hair, collared and button-up, cinched at the waist with a yellow belt. Her makeup was fresh, her lipstick a shade of red she wouldn't dare wear at work. She looked beautiful. Glamorous, even. For Margaret, at least. "George's cousin is having a little get-together over on Herbert Street. It should be a good time. I know you aren't big on local boys, but—"

"I don't care where they're from," I interrupted. "As long as there's whiskey and dancing and not a Baylor man in sight."

The party was at a clapboard house a few blocks from the campground, where the lowest of West Dallas's population slept in tents and under wagons, if they slept at all, being just yards away from the railroad tracks. As we climbed the steps, music drifted from the open window. Drinks were shoved in our direction within moments of entering the hazy interior. Bodies swelled all around us, men in suits and overalls, girls in nice dresses and patched-up skirts, dancing and drinking, smoking and schmoozing. It was hard to tell one face from another, though I doubted I knew anyone other than Margaret or George anyway. The crowd was a hodgepodge of varying classes of wealth, brought together by booze and music and the allure of the opposite sex.

It was exactly what I needed.

I downed one drink and then another, allowing myself to be swept into the living room, where the meager furniture had been pushed to the edges for a makeshift dance floor. A large wireless sat in the corner, horns and drums and Duke Ellington oozing from its speakers. I laughed and grabbed Margaret's hand, swinging my hips in time with the beat. We moved and shook, giggling and toasting our glasses, until we became separated in the crowd. I closed my eyes, my body tingling with the alcohol and music. My mother, Roy, the audition—all of it melted into the smooth baritone and upbeat piano.

I felt a hand slip into mine and lead me into a twirl before a firm arm wrapped around my waist to steady me. I blinked out of my reverie and into a gaze as deep and gray as a storm cloud, sparkling as if lit from electricity within. The hands belonged to a man. A man with thick dark hair slicked back from his forehead and a crisp gray suit stretched over broad shoulders. He smiled at me, his grin as handsome and strong as it was mischievous. He spun me again and pulled me closer. When he did, his full lips let out a laugh that sprouted goose bumps down my arms and made my insides tremble.

My body knew it, even if my mind didn't. It knew this was the moment my life was going to change forever.

Because that was the moment I fell hopelessly in love with Jack Turner.

CHAPTER SEVEN

NOW

Jack was pale. He had barely woken when I pulled him from the car, his head rolling on his shoulders as his feet dragged across the dry, windswept pasture. I felt as if my right leg would shatter beneath his weight; only recently healed, it was scarcely strong enough to support me, let alone him. And yet we'd made it, half-walking, half-crawling, fully exhausted.

There were no cars in the drive, no lights in the windows. I left Jack on the ground beneath a nearby tree as I went to assess the place. Holding a .45 behind my back, I knocked on the door several times—pounded actually—and when no one answered, I tried the knob, surprised when it moved easily in my grip. I stepped inside, knowing I was being reckless, expecting a gun in my face or an ambush of lights, but all remained calm, quiet, and empty.

The house was sparsely furnished. A quick hobble through the place revealed a shabby kitchen, small living room, and a staircase leading to an upper level my aching leg wouldn't allow me to explore. The house was definitely lived in, yet the air inside felt stale and unused, as if its occupants had suddenly abandoned their domain. It set my teeth on edge.

Or maybe that was just a side effect of the past twenty-four hours.

Whatever the case, we were here, and the place appeared to be unoccupied. If it wasn't . . . well, I would deal with that later. I was in no state to argue with an off feeling. Not in my condition. And most certainly not in Jack's.

Somehow I managed to get him inside and onto the couch. He moaned and curled in on himself before falling still once again. Ignoring the searing pain in my lower half, I limped into the kitchen. Finding a drawer full of rags and towels, I pulled out two and, wetting one, returned to Jack's side. I winced as I removed the shirt I'd fashioned as a tourniquet around his shoulder. It was completely soaked through and, I noticed with rising panic, already starting to stain the fabric of the couch beneath him.

I pressed the wet rag to his forehead before rewrapping his arm with the dry one. He made no more sounds. He was no longer even sweating. I didn't know whether that was good or bad.

I wished, not for the first time, for Alli, a desire that stabbed into my heart with a pain deeper than my own injuries. I couldn't think of her now. It wouldn't do any good. I should focus instead on searching for medicine. Surely a house this size—for a family, no doubt—had some somewhere. Maybe in an upstairs bathroom?

My eyes drifted over to the darkened staircase, and my body was instantly overcome with weariness. I couldn't climb those steps. Not now. Jack desperately needed medicine, but I knew if I tried to take even one more step, I would collapse. I wasn't strong enough for this. Not my body and most definitely not my heart.

Instead, I melted onto the floor in front of the couch, too exhausted even to cry. I managed only to bring Jack's fingertips in contact with my own before every inch of me surrendered to sleep, to the memory of what that day had cost, and to the blackness of a future shattered by gunfire and betrayal.

When I finally awoke, untold hours later, it was to two realizations: Jack had miraculously survived the night . . . and we were not as alone as I'd thought we were.

CHAPTER EIGHT

THEN
NOVEMBER 1929

"You sure you don't want a ride?"

Margaret eyed me sideways as she pulled pins from her hair, letting it fall over her shoulders as she stuffed her cardboard waitress hat into her apron pocket. Her lips were pursed into a thin line, which bulged over her large teeth. "No thank you."

I let out an irritated snort, only halfway disguised as a laugh. "Oh, come on, Margie. It's better than the bus. And it's *free*."

"You know that car's stolen, don't you?" she hissed, her glance not at me but at the dark-haired man sitting at the counter, leafing through a newspaper.

Jack. *My* Jack.

I took a tube of lipstick from my purse and touched up the bright-red color using the scratched mirror. "That's just a rumor."

My eyes flitted out the diner window to a black-and-silver Buick with whitewall tires and shiny wire rims parked out front. It was different from the Ford coupe he had last week. And the Model T he had when we first met. But he had told me he was in the business of transportation: he got paid to take cars from Dallas to Oklahoma for resale. Who was I to argue? He made good money—a single trip could fetch him an easy $100—and he used that money not only to keep himself looking good, with fancy suits and intoxicating colognes, but also to shower me with gifts. No more cheap makeup or threadbare dresses. For the first time since moving to the city, I looked like a city girl.

And not only that, I *felt* like a city girl. Even though he was a West Dallas-er himself, Jack was rising above it. With Jack, there wasn't depression and fatigue and dirt. With Jack, there were parties and dinners and dancing. The drear that seemed to settle permanently over West Dallas, suffocating me, seeping into my clothes and my hair and my lungs along with the factory smoke— with Jack, it had lifted. With Jack, there was light. With Jack, there was hope. With Jack, there was *fun*.

And rumors. But who had time for rumors?

"This is the third time this week he's picked you up," Margaret said, removing her name tag. "You've been seeing a lot of each other."

"I know." She meant it as a caution, I was sure, but I couldn't help the dreamlike sigh in my response. For the past month, my life had practically been all Jack Turner. And I still couldn't get enough.

"Why don't you take a break and come out with me instead tonight? We could go ice-skating in Fair Park. It's cold enough now."

"Margaret, he's already here. It would be rude to blow him off, don't you think?" I smoothed my hair and took a step forward. I'd changed into a baby-blue crepe de chine dress, cinched at the waist and ruffled at the shoulders. It was new, a gift from Jack, and moved like fluid over my body. I couldn't wait to show him how it looked on me. "Tomorrow, maybe."

She grabbed my wrist with surprising intensity. "Bea, please. You need to be careful. George told me there's some stuff going around about Jack. He's already been arrested twice—once for possession of stolen property and another time for breaking into a gas station near Hutchins. And everybody knows the racket he has going with his brother—"

I pulled my arm from her grasp with a forceful burst of air through my nostrils. None of this was new information; Jack had told me himself about his priors, swearing he'd gone straight. Everything else was just whispers from jealous neighbors and overly suspicious lawmen. "The cops hate anyone from West Dallas, especially if they have the nerve to try and pull themselves up out of the muck, like Jack." I lifted my chin. "Let 'em come. He's got nothing to hide."

Margaret's shoulders deflated. "Bea . . ."

"If you're sure you don't want a ride, I'll see you tomorrow. I have the lunch shift. You?"

She shook her head. "Breakfast. But I'll see you when you get here." Her grimace was now a full-blown frown.

"Okay. Well, tell George I said hello." I brushed past her into the dining room, swallowing the smidgen of guilt I felt at abandoning my friend once again. She was only looking out for me, after all. But she didn't understand. She was from West Dallas, sure, but she had George—a steady future with a steady husband, a house and kids and a destiny that didn't rely on tips. It wasn't stacks of money and stage lights, but it was more than I'd had. All

I'd had was a meager-paying job with a heap of failed auditions on the side, as well as a rotating door of well-off men who loved to carouse but never commit. I had ambition. I had *dreams* . . . and I was stuck in the doldrums.

Until now. Until Jack.

Still, I *had* been neglecting her lately. After all, I wouldn't have even met Jack if she hadn't forced me to go to that party. Perhaps I should make more of an effort to spend time with her. And skating at Fair Park *did* sound like fun . . .

But any plans that had begun to form in my head vanished at the feeling of Jack's lips on my cheek, his warm hand on my waist, the smell of his cologne and the soft fabric of his suit as his body pressed against mine in an embrace not entirely proper for my place of employment. "You look amazing."

I felt my cheeks redden. I knew I did, but I liked to hear him say it anyway.

He looked sharp himself, but then again, he always looked sharp. Today it was a fine black suit with a matching vest and a wide gray tie that perfectly matched his eyes—eyes that were now sparkling at me from beneath a black fedora. "Ready?"

Despite not having a single drink, I felt drunk as he led me from the diner, a high matched only by the open-mouthed stares of the Baylor boys whose large tip—an arrogant deposit on the pleasure of my company for the evening—would in fact go unfulfilled.

I snuggled close to Jack in the front seat as we drove away. My dress was beautiful but more suitable for June than November, a minor inconvenience negated by his body heat and the flush of my own skin next to him. He smiled lazily as he drove, one hand on the wheel, the other across my shoulders, keeping me close.

The skyscrapers of downtown glowed like fire in the fading sunlight as we headed westward, the air hazy with dust and smoke.

It wasn't until the car jolted over the bridge, heading across the Trinity, that my intoxication with the moment finally cleared. "Where are we going?" I asked. "I thought we were going dancing tonight?"

"Change of plans," he said simply, glancing in the rearview mirror before gunning the engine and changing lanes.

My body pressed back against the seat with the force of his acceleration. My heart went along with it, my mind racing nearly as fast as the car. What was happening? Had I been wrong? Was Jack simply another Baylor boy, disguised as a West Dallas-er—he'd had his fun and now it was time to move on? I cleared my throat, hoping he couldn't feel me tense beneath his touch. Digging deep into the recesses of my acting chops, I exhaled in an attempt to steady my voice as I let out a nonchalant "Oh?"

"Yeah." The back tires lifted slightly as we crested the hill on the other side of the bridge, sending our bodies into each other. Laughing, he braked enough to squeal around a turn before accelerating again, this time to a normal, leisurely speed. He winked at me—oh, my goodness, was he *handsome*—before turning his attention back to the road. "I want you to meet my family instead."

My mouth opened and then closed and then opened and closed again. No sound came out. Instead, I pressed two fingers to my lips, staring at him.

"Is that . . . is that okay?"

It felt as if wires were pulling up my cheeks; I couldn't have stopped my smile even if I tried. At the same time, inexplicably, tears blurred my vision. No man had ever taken me home to meet his family. No one could be bothered when there was fun to be had. I was Bea Carraway, after all. A "good-time gal." Whiskey and cigarettes and late nights on the town.

But apparently that wasn't all. At least not to Jack.

I blinked my tears away before he could see, nodding my head vigorously as I leaned forward, covering his neck and cheek with kisses.

He laughed. "I take that as a yes?"

Jack's family owned a garage and scrapyard off Borger Street, a half mile from the railroad track and the transient campground. A white clapboard building with green trim and large front windows served as both the office and the family's residence, while two side buildings housed tools and a work area. Immediately behind the buildings, rows of junked cars sat behind a rusted metal fence, a treasure trove of car parts and rattlesnakes.

Jack stopped the car near one of the garages. He grabbed his hat from my lap, giving my knee a quick squeeze. "You ready?"

I clutched his hand as he started to pull away. As my eyes flitted over the house, my beautiful dress suddenly felt itchy and too revealing, my makeup greasy and overdone, my hair limp and dry. "Jack . . ."

He smiled. "They're going to love you, Bea. I know they will."

I clung to his arm as we walked over the hard-packed gravel lot, my low heels twisting on several stray loose pebbles. He'd given me his jacket, but goose bumps sprouted down my arms and legs anyway, even despite the sweat I could feel soiling the fabric under my arms.

He led me around the side, away from the office entrance, and held the door open for me as we stepped inside. The interior was dim, a low fire crackling in the fireplace giving off little heat and even less light. It took a moment for my eyes to adjust. The wooden floor was covered by a gray rug, the same color as the drab walls. There was a sagging couch buffeted by an armchair on either side, all of them covered in pale-green damask fabric, and a coffee table littered with playing cards and several beer bottles. The smell of cigarette smoke lingered in the empty room, mixing with the scent of roast chicken wafting in from somewhere in the back.

Jack touched my back lightly. "Come on. They must be back here."

He led me through a dark, narrow hallway. The smell of meat and the sound of laughter grew stronger, bursting forth like a sudden gale as he swung open the door to the kitchen. Bright light flooded over us, the din of excited voices pausing momentarily, then erupting once more as Jack stepped over the threshold.

"Jack! What a surprise! We weren't expecting you tonight!"

"I was. He told me he was coming."

"Then why didn't you tell anyone else?"

"Forgot."

"Oh, Emmett. Stop it."

A mix of laughter, a rush of bodies. I struggled to keep up with the voices, the faces, the movement. A dark-haired woman with deep frown lines had spoken first, and she was now pulling Jack away from me, patting his cheeks and pushing the hair from his eyes. Her thick, squat body created a barrier between us, forcing me to take a few steps back into the hallway. The second voice had come from a younger man, taller than Jack but with the same gray eyes and dark hair, who remained seated at a table in the corner, laughing, cigarette dangling from his lips. Another man sat with him, identical yet older, with thinning gray hair rather than the shiny black of his tablemate, a pipe in his hand, watching the whole spectacle with lazy bemusement.

"You're too thin, Jacky. Too thin. Too many smokes, not enough sausage." The older woman—his mother, I presumed—propelled him further into the kitchen. The door broke free from Jack's grasp and swung shut behind her—leaving me alone in the darkened hallway.

My frozen smile melted as voices swelled on the other side of the closed door. I stood rooted to the spot, staring at cracked wood. I couldn't make my hands push it back open but neither could I flee. Before I could make a choice between mortification or indignation, the door swung open again and a woman stepped through, a wide smile on her face.

"I am so, so sorry," she said, grabbing my hand and tugging me inside. "Sarah gets a little crazy where Jack is concerned." The woman's shoulder-length auburn hair was pulled back at the sides, her dress a simple pink cotton button-down with flowing sleeves and a turned-down collar. Obviously homemade but done well. She had a smattering of freckles across her nose, pale but full lips, and green eyes vibrant even without eye shadow. I felt self-conscious next to her effortless beauty, but her smile conveyed nothing but warmth. "Come in, come in. You must be Jack's girl."

I nodded. "I'm Beatrice. But everyone calls me Bea."

"Well, Bea, welcome. I'm Alli, Emmett's wife. He's the clown over there. Or I guess I should say, the clown *without* the gray hair. Jack's brother." She gestured with her head toward the table. "And that's Jack's dad next to him. Earl. He'll throw a fit if you call him Mr. Turner." She lowered her voice. "But make sure you call *her* Mrs. Turner. She just started letting me call her Sarah within the last few months—and Emmett and I have been married almost two years."

She squeezed my arm conspiratorially and gave a small laugh, which I returned, feeling the tension in my shoulders start to relax. Mrs. Turner was still fussing over her son, and the other two Turner men were too busy mocking the scene before them to notice me. But something about Alli made me feel safe. And a little less alone.

She guided me toward the table, where I folded myself into

a corner chair. Realizing I was still wearing Jack's coat, I stood to remove it, draping it over the back of my seat and smoothing my dress before sitting down again. It was only after I'd crossed my ankles and gathered my hands in my lap that I became aware of the sudden quiet.

Jack was no longer the center of attention. I was.

Every eye in the room washed over my dress. It was as if the blue fabric were a spotlight shining on me, illuminating my presence for the very first time. I fought the urge to cross my arms over my chest, thrusting my chin upward instead. It was a beautiful dress, and I had every right to wear a beautiful dress, especially one gifted to me. I would not allow myself to feel ashamed.

Or I would sure as anything try not to.

It was Alli who spoke first. "Wow, what a spectacular dress!"

Jack, still held firmly in his mother's grip, grinned. "Aw, it ain't the dress. It's her. Ain't she a knockout?"

"Gorgeous. Even if I owned a dress like that, I don't think I'd look half as good. It suits you." Alli's tender smile made her praise seem genuine.

I felt my cheeks flush.

Mr. Turner—Earl—coughed as Jack winked at me. Beside him, his mother's scowl intensified. I looked away quickly.

"Let me help you finish up the chicken," Alli said, breaking the silence once more. She guided Mrs. Turner back toward the oven, though I noticed it took a bit of force to pry her fingers from Jack's arm. Free from his mother at last, he snatched a slice of bread from the counter, leading to a playful scolding, before settling in beside me at the table, draping one arm around my shoulders. My body relaxed at his touch. It felt like a physical shield from any daggers his family had yet to throw.

Next to him, Emmett took a long drag off his cigarette. A

spirited smile played on his lips as he exhaled a cloud of smoke. "So which one are you?"

I felt Jack go stiff beside me.

"I can't keep 'em straight. Is this Irene? Or Lois? Or wasn't there an Eva in there somewhere too?"

"Stop it, Emmett. You know this is Bea."

Emmett shrugged as he snuffed out his cigarette, that mischievous grin growing wider. "Hey, what can I say? I'm a simple man. I can't keep it all straight. Every other week you're running off with another girl's name on your lips."

Beneath the table, my knees locked together as numbness spread through my limbs. Suddenly Jack's form next to me didn't feel quite so comforting. I shifted in my seat but his grip around my shoulders tightened.

"Aw, shut up, Emmett. You've been pecked in the head one too many times."

Earl let out a large laugh, causing me to jump. "You *both* got pecked one too many times. Worst bunch of chicken thieves I ever saw."

"He ain't much better at stealing cars!" Jack ribbed.

All the men laughed, though the air around them shifted. It was a joke but a raw one. I could tell by the way Emmett's shoulders hunched, the way his mouth contorted with a smile he obviously didn't quite feel.

He took a swig from the brown bottle in front of him. "Those charges were dropped, thank you very much."

"Only because you never actually stole the car. You got caught trying door handles." Jack's handsome mouth twisted into a not-so-handsome smirk. There was a slight bite tinting his jest.

The two men stared at one another, both smiling, yet neither seeming to mean it. Earl's eyes swept between the two of them, then over to me. Before I could look away, he raised his bushy eyebrows and gave a weary shake of his head.

Thankfully, it was Alli, once again, who broke the tension. She placed a basket of bread in the middle of the table. "It doesn't matter. He doesn't do that stuff anymore." She gave Emmett's arm a quick rub. "Right, honey?"

Spell broken, Emmett looked from Jack up at his wife. His smile turned genuine. "Right." He kissed the back of her hand and pressed it to the side of his face.

I softened at the tenderness between them. The familiarity and ease. Maybe one day I'd have a love like that. Maybe even with Jack. I glanced over at him, my heart fluttering.

But he wasn't looking at me. Instead, his eyes were narrowed slightly, his face an unreadable mask as he stared at Alli and Emmett. I quickly redirected my gaze to my lap as a pain began to spread through my chest. I was being stupid. When Jack looked at the love between his brother and his wife, he wasn't filled with longing. His expression spoke many things—irritation, displeasure, maybe even a hint of disgust—but affection for me wasn't one of them. After all, I was just one of many apparently.

I moved my body away from his. This time he let me.

"He never did that stuff," Mrs. Turner called from the stove. "Both of my boys are good boys. Those Dallas cops are crooked. Just looking for any excuse to empty out the slums so the richies across the river feel better."

"Here we go again," Earl muttered under his breath. He sent a sideways grin in my direction.

Alli retreated to the stove and returned with two dishes, one of diced potatoes with onions and another with collard greens. Mrs.

Turner placed a tray of roast chicken in the center of the table. The smell was homey and inviting, my stomach growling despite my heartache.

Alli took her place next to Emmett. "Sarah, would you like me to say grace? Or would you like to?"

"I will. Thank you for offering."

All heads around the table bowed but I stared forward, ice in my veins. I hadn't prayed since we'd left Wingate, hadn't even allowed myself to think about God. I knew the memory of Charles and the trauma of my "cleansing"—the pressure in my chest, the stench of manure, the ripping of my scalp—would inevitably come with it. Even now, all these years later, it took only the quiet murmur of Mrs. Turner's words to bring it all roaring back. Charles's ghost floated in front of my vision, his wicked smile and hurtful words causing a nauseated clenching of my stomach.

A small cough broke through his shadow, my gaze sharpening not on my stepfather, but on Jack's mother, whose dark eyes were narrowed at me, an expression of obvious disapproval plastered across her stern face.

I closed my eyes, as much to avoid looking at her as Charles. The inside of me screamed with both the painful past and the unbearable present.

"Heavenly Father, we thank You for the blessing of this food, for Your provision during these tough years. We're thankful for the nourishment You provide for our bodies and for our souls. Lord, keep us safe in these wicked times. Our enemy the devil walks about like a roaring lion, looking for someone to devour, and his temptations in this place are especially strong. I pray for my boys, for the allure of the devil's lifestyle around them. Save them from those that would lead them away from You, who would offer them nothing but temporary pleasure and an eternity in hell."

My hands clenched. Charles was not just floating in front of me. He was speaking now, speaking through the words of Jack's mother, taunting and mocking my sinfulness, my insufficiency, *me*. The wounded girl inside of me bit back tears while the woman I was now seethed. I should leave. Forget this woman and her judgmental God. Forget Jack and his parade of girls.

I didn't need him. I didn't need her. I didn't need *this*.

And then Jack's hand was on mine, his touch soft and warm and soothing. I didn't want to want it. Yet at the feel of his skin, the blood rushed back into my limbs, and the pounding of my heart retreated from my throat. I no longer heard the pointed, critical prayers of his mother. Instead, like a lifesaver, I felt only Jack.

I stayed quiet during dinner as the men railed about the stock market crash, which had happened just the week before; the agricultural depression, which had been happening for years; and the depravity of the world, which had been happening since the beginning of time. Alli smiled at me from across the table, a welcome respite from the continued glowers of Mrs. Turner, and rolled her eyes as the dinner table conversation floated from unfortunate neighbors to unscrupulous law enforcement, from new Fords to old Chevrolets. The Turner men loved cars almost as much as they hated cops.

"You sit and relax," Alli said after the chicken had been picked clean and the beer bottles emptied. She placed a hand on Mrs. Turner's shoulder as she started to rise. "Let me clean up and bring in the dessert. You've done enough for the evening."

"Nonsense," Mrs. Turner replied, placing her napkin on her plate. "It's too much for one person."

"Beatrice will help. Won't you, Bea?"

Momentarily surprised yet grateful for a chance to escape, I stood quickly, knocking the bottom of the table with my knee and causing all the dishes to rattle. I winced. "Sorry, I . . . yes. Yes, of course I'll help." I gathered my plate and Jack's with shaky hands before rounding the table. "Can I take your plate, Mrs. Turner?"

She turned her head, not answering, but allowing space for me to collect her things. I did so with a subdued sigh and followed Alli, who was carrying the remainder of the dishes to the sink. She turned on the water and handed me a towel. "I'll wash, you dry. I'd hate for you to get splashed and ruin that dress. It really is beautiful." She gave me a kind smile. "I mean it."

I let out a small laugh. "Thank you. I'm glad someone likes it. Besides Jack, I mean."

She ran a plate under the water, lowering her voice so as not to be heard over the sound of the flow. "Don't worry about her. She'll thaw out. Eventually."

"Right." I took the dish from her with a snort, rubbing the towel across it with a little more force than necessary. "How long did it take her to warm up to the others?"

Alli stopped and tilted her head toward me, her eyebrows scrunched together. "Others?"

I put the dried plate on the counter with forced nonchalance, hopeful she couldn't read the very obvious tremble I'd bitten my lip to conceal. "The ones Emmett was talking about," I said thickly. "Irene and Lois and Eva."

She laid a hand on my wrist. "Jack's been on a lot of dates, Bea. But you're the first girl he's ever brought home."

"See, I told you they'd love you."

I laughed, one loud, bitter guffaw. "Are you kidding me?"

Jack put one hand on the seat, straining his head over his shoulder as he backed the car out of its parking spot. "What?"

"Were you even in there? Your mother *hated* me."

He pulled into the road, tires spinning out a little on the gravel before gaining traction. "She didn't hate you! She just doesn't know you yet. She's . . . protective of me. That's all."

I rolled my eyes in the darkness. "Sure."

He chuckled and pulled me closer to him. He smelled of cigarettes and strawberries, Alli's shortcake overpowering the stale beers he'd taken with dinner. He twirled the ends of my hair between the fingers of one hand. "Give her a chance."

"I don't think me giving her a chance is the problem. I think it's the other way around."

"The last few years have been hard on her. She never wanted to move to the city. A country girl through and through. But when cotton prices plummeted, her and my dad had no choice. We had to eat. We had to live. Though some days I think she believes we would have been better off starving than moving into this cesspool of sin, as she calls it."

An iciness crept down my spine. "So she's a believer?" I said slowly. "In God and all that religion stuff?"

"Oh yeah. Used to beat the living tarnation out of Emmett and me, trying to save our souls. We're too big now, but she'll still whack us if our sin gets too big for our britches."

He laughed. I did not. Mrs. Turner was more like Charles than I thought. My heart swelled with pity for Jack but also bewilderment. How could he love a woman like that? Perhaps her "salvation" had never gone as far as drowning.

I swallowed. "But Alli was nice," I said, wanting to change the subject.

The headlights of an oncoming car swept over Jack's face. I was surprised to see his smile gone. "Yes."

"She . . . she really liked my dress."

"I bet."

His tone was flat and measured, a sharp departure from the discussion of his mother. I licked my lips and put a hand on Jack's knee, a move he didn't acknowledge. I cleared my throat. "Is there . . . is there something wrong with Alli?"

"Alli's fine."

Short. Clipped. End of discussion. I could take a hint. I pressed my back into the seat, staring out the window as the slums of West Dallas crept by. Across the river, lights glittered in the sky, the buildings and people of Dallas proper dancing into the night. It felt like a world away.

But for the first time, so did the man next to me.

I felt his body rise and fall next to mine in the dark, a weary sigh from somewhere deep within. "Things have changed a lot since Alli came in the picture. Before she came around, me and Emmett, we had a lot of fun. We were going places, making money, making plans, getting real good at—" He stopped, clearing away his sentence with a slight cough before continuing again. "We were good, is all. Then Alli came in and started spreading her church stuff—"

My breath caught in my throat. *Church stuff? Alli? But she was so . . . nice.*

"—and now Emmett's all goody-goody, doing everything she wants, to heck with me and the business we'd been growing."

"But your ma?" I asked timidly. "Your ma is into that church stuff, too?"

He shook his head. "It's different with her. I can't explain it. All those years of Ma's churchin' didn't do nothing to change Emmett the way Alli has. She got in his head somehow. Won't let church be church and business be business. She . . ."

But whatever she had done would remain unspoken. He

reached into his pocket and lit a cigarette instead, smoke filling the space where his irritation still hung.

"What . . . ?" I hesitated. I didn't want to ask the question. But I had to. For Margaret, for my mother, for all the other rumors and whispers and stares. For *me*. "What kind of business?"

Jack pulled to a stop in front of my house and killed the engine. The silence left by its absence pushed between us, growing larger the longer he failed to answer my question. A car passed by, its headlights washing over both of us—me staring at Jack, Jack staring at the road. His mouth was flattened into a line, the tips of his fingers pressed to his chin. When he finally spoke, his voice was quiet, the slightest hint of a quiver just below the surface.

"I'm not a perfect man, Bea. I've done some bad things, but that doesn't mean I'm bad, neither. I just want to have a good life."

"Jack—"

He turned to me finally and put a hand against my lips. His gray eyes were darkened by shadow but still somehow burned into mine. "But my idea of a good life has changed since I met you. It's more than what I thought, more than what I ever could have dreamed. I . . . I think I'm in love with you, Bea."

My muscles began to tremble as a long-closed-off place deep inside me shattered open. I leaned into his touch, suddenly feeling weak. Everything else around us began to fade. He loved me. Jack Turner loved me.

"I think I love you too," I managed to whisper.

His kiss was deep and passionate, his embrace enveloping me until I no longer knew where he ended and I began. Tears rolled down my cheeks as he caressed my face, my neck, my back, the two of us releasing small, euphoric giggles in between kisses. He pulled me to him, pressing my head against his chest as he stroked my hair. The warmth of his body was a blanket against the cold that had begun to seep into the cab. Pressed against him, I listened to the steady sound of his breathing, felt the gentle rise and fall of his chest as his lips brushed against my forehead. We lay against one another for what felt like hours, unwilling to break the gentle peace binding us to this moment.

But just as I felt myself beginning to doze, safe and secure in his arms, in the back of my head, a small, nagging voice broke through the stillness:

He didn't answer your question.

I pushed it away, snuggling in tighter under Jack's shoulder. In response, his strong arms wrapped tighter around my body, stifling any sort of unease.

I didn't need answers. Because I had Jack. And he had me.

CHAPTER NINE

I was still floating the next day. My body sat on the number seven bus, bound for downtown Dallas and another shift at Hargrave's, but my mind was still in the Buick with Jack, his arms around me, his voice whispering those words in my ear:

"I think I'm in love with you, Bea."

The bus stank of body odor and booze, the tired masses huddled together for warmth against a late-fall chill the pathetic heater couldn't quite mask. The man beside me was asleep; sour breath leaked from his slackened mouth, and what looked to be several days' worth of grime coated his overalls. I scrunched next to the window to avoid smudges on my dress. The day outside was overcast and dreary, yesterday's spotty clouds merging into a solid blanket over the Texas sky.

And yet it was beautiful. The whisper of rain—maybe even

snow!—was glorious, the stench of bodies familiar and comforting, the snoozing man beside me an amusement. Even the factory smokestacks, their thick, black belches visible even from the Trinity River bridge, couldn't bother me today.

Because Jack Turner loved me.

I whistled as I exited the bus and drifted along the two blocks to the diner without noticing the frigid wind.

"Good morning!" I called over the tinkle of the bell above the door. The tables were empty, but a few older customers lingered at the counter, sipping coffee. It was the worst shift. This time of day, the lull between breakfast and lunch, most of the Baylor boys were in classes. I had at least a solid hour before any tips would roll in.

But it didn't matter. Jack Turner loved me. And the quiet would give me enough time to gloat about it to Margaret. She could whisper all she wanted about the rumors; Jack was head and shoulders above any "upstanding" Baylor man. He had a past, sure, but he wanted to change. For *me*. That counted for something. As my best friend, I hoped she could see it too.

I gave a wave to Sal, the cook, as I pushed into the hallway to hang up my coat, straining my neck to find Margaret. She wasn't in the hall or the kitchen. Perhaps she was out back having a cigarette? I pulled on my apron and cardboard hat, giving myself a quick once-over in the mirror, before heading toward the back door.

"Beatrice?"

Mr. Miller stood in the doorway of his office. As usual, the manager's stringy gray hair was slicked back from his forehead, doing his receding hairline no favors. Small watery eyes were hidden behind wire-framed glasses, though they could not conceal the pockmarks covering his cheeks. He was certainly nothing to look at, but he was a kind man, generous with leftover food and jovial with customers and employees alike.

Today, however, there was no trace of his usual smile. Instead, his expression was serious and pained. Red hands clutched one another in front of his large stomach.

"Can I speak to you for a moment?"

He led me into his dim, windowless office. The only light came from a green-shaded lamp on his cluttered desk. A cigarette lay smoldering in an ashtray, filling the room with haze. He gestured to a scratched wooden chair in front of his desk, indicating I should sit.

I did, swallowing a sense of dread that only intensified when he sat across from me and frowned.

"Beatrice, first of all, let me say how much I've enjoyed having you here."

Oh no. No, no, no.

"You're a real hard worker," he continued, "and your smile puts the customers at ease. You're never late, you never screw up orders, and you're usually available to pick up extra shifts whenever we need the help." He cleared his throat. "That being said . . ."

My stomach sank to my knees.

"I'm sure you're aware there's a depression going on. Business just ain't what it used to be. And we're . . . well, I'm sorry, Beatrice, but we're gonna have to let you go."

I'd known it was coming, and yet still, at his utterance, a sudden coldness pierced my core.

"I'll pay you for today since you came all the way into town, and I'd be happy to provide you with a letter of reference if you—"

"But I'm one of the best waitresses you have! You said so yourself!" My tongue finally unhinged from the roof of my mouth, and the words spilled out with a force that surprised even me. "Those Baylor boys—a lot of them come in just to see me. I bring in twice as much business as the other girls."

A blush spread across Mr. Miller's cheeks, turning his pock-marks a shade of purple. "I won't deny you have a certain . . . appeal, especially to our younger customers. But it would be immoral of me to keep you around just because of a pretty face."

"Immoral?"

Mr. Miller bit down on his lip. His small eyes flitted around the room, looking somewhere, anywhere, but at me. When he finally spoke again, his voice was barely above a whisper. "I'm not running a brothel, Beatrice."

I craned my neck forward, eyes widening, and folded my arms over my stomach as if I'd been hit. "Excuse me?"

He scratched at his throat. "You've been going out with a lot of boys. The other waitresses are starting to complain. It ain't right for you to be using your after-hours *companionship* to make more money during your shift. It reflects poorly on this establishment, even if it does bring in more business. Now, I know those kinds of things are permissible where you live, but here in Dallas proper, we have rules and standards to uphold. And with the economy being what it is, we had to make some tough decisions about employees. I'm sorry, Bea. You simply didn't make the cut. But if it makes you feel any better, you weren't the only one."

I swallowed several times. The lump in my throat was trying to gag me, even as the heat in my cheeks began to spread to other parts of my body. "Who?" I already knew the answer, but I needed to hear him say it. "Who else?"

He shuffled papers on his desk, a pathetic playacting of forget-fulness. "Um, well, Margaret, for one. And Gertrude. From the night shift."

I closed my eyes. My heart felt as if it would burst from my chest. Margaret and Gertrude. The only other West Dallas-ers on staff.

Mr. Miller coughed lightly. "Yes, well. Nothing personal, of course. Just business."

Blood pounded in my ears. Nothing personal? The effects of Black Tuesday might have only begun to trickle into Texas, but if it wasn't personal, Mr. Miller would have been begging me to take extra shifts rather than throwing me out on the street. But times were tough, and the people of Dallas were circling the wagons, leaving me, Margaret, Gertrude, and the other West Dallas-ers to fend for ourselves.

"Here's today's pay." He thrust an envelope in my direction without looking. "You can leave your apron and hat here. No need to wash and return. We'll take care of it."

I stared at his outstretched hand. His fingers were trembling. I should take the money and rip it to shreds, cursing him, the diner, and the whole city of Dallas. I wanted to tell him that his food was terrible, his coffee was weak, and his "respectable" Dallas waitresses went on just as many dates as I did—they simply hid it beneath their false modesty and painted-on piety.

But I kept my mouth shut. I didn't know what would come out if I opened it: a bellow or a bawl. Because I wasn't promiscuous but I *was* poor. And to Mr. Miller and those like him, at least morally, they were the same thing.

So instead I snatched the envelope from his fingers and settled for throwing my apron in his face instead. The hat, I momentarily forgot, tossing it out the window and into the street when I saw my reflection in the bus window. I made it all the way across the river, stewing in my own humiliation and hatred, before the tears finally began to fall.

Thankfully, the house was quiet when I got home. I didn't want anyone to see me, much less talk to me. I hoped to slip into the kitchen for a quick bite before retreating to my room, but as

I pushed open the door, I caught sight of my mother packing a lunch of stale bread and hard-boiled eggs for her shift. She froze when I walked in.

"What are you doing here?"

I knew I looked a mess. My eyes burned from crying, and I could feel the dried mascara on my cheeks, the loose bobby pins barely holding my mussed-up hair. Yet my mother did not ask if I was alright. She did not ask what was wrong. She only wanted to know why I was there in the kitchen, disturbing the brief moments of peace she got before starting her long shift at the factory.

Sadness hardened into irritation. I clenched my jaw and brushed past her without answering.

"You got fired, didn't you?"

The sneer in her voice caused me to freeze on the stairs. My fingers curled into balls at my sides.

"What was it this time? Coming in late? Getting sloppy with orders? You steal something?" Her laugh, bitter and callous, prickled my skin.

I spun around, fuming. "I did *not* steal anything!"

My mother lit a cigarette. In this light, the wrinkles lining her cheeks looked deeper, the circles under her eyes darker. Her beauty was now firmly in its twilight; the smile on her lips only made her look uglier. "But you *were* fired, right?"

"There's a depression, Mama. Lots of folks are losing their jobs."

She rolled her eyes.

I should have let it go. But I couldn't. "I'll find another job. Mr. Miller gave me good references. In the meantime, I'll use some of the money I've been saving to get new headshots and go on some more auditions." The idea came to me suddenly, but I clung to it with the ferocity of a life raft in a hurricane. "They're casting for

Diamond Lil at the Majestic, and I've heard there may even be Hollywood scouts there. It's perfect timing, actually. I'll—"

"Over my dead body."

"What?"

My mother gripped the counter, her eyes blazing despite their exhaustion. "I said over my dead body. You'll march right on down to the foundry and apply for a job. Today."

"The foundry?" I stuck my chin in the air, meeting her gaze with a narrowed one of my own. Stubbornness was all that would keep me from panic. "I will *not* be working at the foundry. I'll find another waitress job eventually."

"*Eventually* isn't going to cut it anymore, Beatrice. Going across that river each day hasn't done anything for you, and it sure hasn't done a thing for this family. It's time to stop playing around with dreams and start living in the real world."

The real world. To my mother, the real world meant West Dallas. Scarcity and smokestacks, whiskey and woe. The muddy, dreary hellhole I'd forced my family into . . . then refused to remain in myself, even if only in my head. The lines of shapeless, faceless men and women, their bodies cloaked in shades of gray, trudging through the dirt to another sunless, miserable day inside the factory. Hours upon hours of toil, waiting for the moment they could collect their pennies and escape to their filthy, broken-down homes, trying to forget—at least for a few hours—that the same fate awaited them tomorrow.

Anxiety rose in my throat, tasting of bile. There was no light, no glamour, no fun, no *hope* in the real world. Living there would kill me, just as it was killing my mother.

I shook the threat from my head, feeling the last of my bobby pins come loose. "I won't. I'll go into town tomorrow and find another waitress job. Mr. Miller himself said I had the looks for—"

"Stop it!" My mother's shriek caused me to shrink back, my shoulders hunching up around my ears. "What's it going to take to get it through that thick skull of yours? You can dream and pretend all you want, but you can't ever escape who you really are. The world will make sure of that. It did it to me; it'll do it to you, too." Her last words were quieter, spoken more to herself than me.

"What are you talking about?"

"You think you're the first small-town beauty who fancies herself making it in the big leagues? Before you were born . . ." She closed her eyes, swaying slightly. "I was gonna do something. I was gonna *be* somebody. Then I met Ernest, and we were so young and stupid and in love. I gave it up for him. For *you*. Not that there was much to give up at that point."

For the first time, something like pity began to pull at my heart. I'd known my mother was never truly satisfied with her circumstances, but I'd never imagined her having a life—having dreams—outside of our family. I'd always thought she'd just missed Pa; turns out, maybe her heartache began way before we put him in the Texas soil.

"Ernest thought you'd have a shot at pageants and I agreed, if only because it would give me a taste of that life again, however small and secondhand. But as you got older, I could see it in everyone's eyes. The same look they'd given me not so very long ago. You weren't good enough, Beatrice. Just like I wasn't. Not because of anything we did, but because of who we are." Her eyes met mine. They were bloodshot with just a twinge of sadness beneath that bitter veneer. "It's time to face the truth. You're a West Dallas gutter rat just like the rest of us."

"No." I could barely choke out the words. "No, I'm a—" *A star.* Jack often called me a star. So why couldn't I bring myself to say it?

"You're a nobody, Beatrice Carraway." My mother grabbed her

lunch pail and pointed it at me like a weapon, though her tone had lost its fight. "That pretty little face of yours will wither and wrinkle, your body will grow soft and round, and you'll die without a single soul remembering your name. Same as me. And the sooner you accept that, the better."

Tears sprang to my eyes. I'd been able to remain steadfast in front of Mr. Miller, but I knew it was useless now. Partly because she was my mother. But more so because Mr. Miller's allegations had been false; Mama's, on the other hand, were much closer to the truth.

She pinched the bridge of her nose with knobby, arthritic fingers. "Get yourself cleaned up. You look ridiculous." Pulling a handkerchief from her pocket, she tied up her hair and snuffed her cigarette into an ashtray on the table. "And then get down to the foundry and apply for a job. If I find out you didn't, you can find somewhere else to sleep tonight."

The slam of the door rang in my ears as I slid to the ground and wept until all my tears were spent.

Later that afternoon, while walking the last few dreary blocks back to my home, the sound of a car horn startled me out of my misery. I pulled my chin out of the collar of my coat and looked around. A black-and-silver Buick pulled up beside me, engine idling. Inside the window, Jack's grin broke through the gray of the day—and my mood.

The air inside the car was warm and smelled of Jack's cologne. For some reason, it made me feel as if I would start crying afresh. Thankfully, however, his hands were in my hair and his lips were on mine before I could say a word, distracting me from anything except the feel of his skin, the nearness of his being.

"I missed you," he murmured against my ear.

I wondered if he could smell the foundry on me. Could he tell that's where I'd been? Standing in line with the rest of the desperate masses, signing on the line to sell my day for dimes on the hour.

"I was on my way to your house to see if you wanted to grab a bite to eat. What are you doing out here, so far from the bus stop? It's freezing." He squeezed my hands, the soft warmth of his barely registering against the numbness of my own.

I gave him a wavery smile. "I was . . ." I swallowed, trying to start again. I wanted to be brave, to be strong, to be the happy, bubbly girl he'd fallen in love with, but my strength broke at the sight of him, his kind eyes and tender touch. I burst into tears.

"Bea! Bea, hey, what's wrong?" He pulled me closer, cupping my cheek with his palm. "Shhh. It's okay. Tell me what happened. Did someone hurt you?"

I shook my head, taking big, rasping breaths against my sobs.

"It's okay. I'm here. I'm right here. Just tell me what happened."

In between blubbers, I told him about Mr. Miller and the diner, my mother and her threats, and—most humiliatingly—about the foundry . . . where I was due to start on Monday. He listened intently, his eyebrows rising with each new revelation, his mouth growing narrow and puckered. By the time I'd finished, my cries had become whimpers but my indignity had become a scream.

"I'm not a star." I nearly spat the words. "I can't even be a real lady. I'm just trash from West Dallas, and I always will be. It was stupid to think I could ever be anything else."

"You stop that." His voice was sharp enough to cause me to jump. He gripped my chin, moving my head until it was in line with his. The hardness in his eyes was unsettling. "Now you listen to me, Beatrice Carraway. You *are* a lady. You're *my* lady. And my lady doesn't talk about herself like that, and she sure as anything is not going to be working in no foundry. My lady *is* a star, and one of these days, everyone else will see you the way I do. Do you hear me?"

I gave a slight nod, as much as I could with his hand still holding my face.

"I said, 'Do you hear me?'"

"Yes, I hear you."

He released me. "Good."

"But, Jack . . . what am I supposed to do about the job? About money? About my mother? When she comes home tonight and finds out—"

"I'll take you to Margaret's for tonight. Everything else, just leave to me." He winked as he started the ignition. The engine roared to life, and the car pulled away from the curb with a lurch that did little to settle the butterflies swirling inside my stomach.

CHAPTER TEN

The next morning, I crept inside my house, easing the front door shut. Stepping around the creaky floorboard and into the living room, I spied my sister curled on the couch, a wool blanket over her lap. Morning sunlight streamed in from the window, causing dust in the air to sparkle. "Is Mama home?"

Eleanor glanced up at the sound of my voice. She tilted her head toward the ceiling.

"Asleep?"

She nodded.

"Good. No school today?"

"It's Saturday."

"Oh. Right." I sat down next to her and pulled at the blanket, exposing her knees. Her simple floral housedress was thin and two years too short, a holdover she'd tried to stretch for much longer than she should have. Goose bumps sprouted instantly across her arms, and she yanked the cover back with a giggle. "I guess there's too much on my mind to keep my days straight."

Eleanor tipped her head onto my shoulder, giving me a sympathetic grimace.

"I take it Mama told you?"

She nodded. "Did you get the job?"

I pressed my lips together. "Yes . . . and no. It's hard to explain. But I don't want to talk about it." I gave her shoulders a tight squeeze. "How about breakfast instead? Have you eaten?"

She laughed. "Of course I've eaten. It's ten o'clock."

"Is it really? Golly. What can I say? Margaret's house is a lot quieter than ours. It's easy to oversleep. Especially when you don't have a job to run off to." I ruffled her hair. "How about an early lunch then?"

She grinned.

"That's what I thought. Come on. Let's see what I can scrounge up."

The pantry was sparse—as usual—but I managed to find half a box of dried pasta, which I boiled and mixed with some butter, parsley, and peas. There were even a couple of hard biscuits left over from last night's dinner, which tasted just fine with the last scrapings of strawberry preserves. After finishing and doing a cursory clean of the kitchen, Eleanor returned to her book while I went upstairs for a hot bath. Well, as hot as I could get it in West Dallas. Still, the steam melted away yesterday's tears, and the lavender soap Jack had brought back from a trip to Oklahoma City soothed my dry skin. It also reminded me of his promises the evening before:

"Everything else, just leave to me."

Those words and his lingering kiss as he dropped me off at

Margaret's, disappearing into the night with a promise to call on me today. *"Don't worry about a thing,"* he'd murmured. *"It's all going to be okay."* His assurances had calmed me; Margaret's sympathies had helped me to sleep. But now, in the bright light of day, my anxiety began to swell again.

It was Saturday. I was due to start at the foundry in two days. Sweet whispers aside, I couldn't afford to let this job slip through my fingers. I loved Jack, loved even more how he believed I was a star. But those beliefs wouldn't put food on the table or pay the bill when the electricity started to flicker. For that I needed money. And for money, I needed this job. Plain and simple.

My heart sank as I allowed my body to submerge under the lukewarm water. Would Jack still love me when my skin started to turn gray? When my hair dulled from the constant smoke and I was too exhausted for a night on the town? Would he still see me as his star then?

By the time I'd mustered enough energy to emerge from the tub, the soap had reduced to mere film on the water's surface. Wrapping a blanket around myself, I collapsed onto my bed, trying to release my grief with tears, only to find I had none left. Instead, I slept—a restless, dreamless sleep.

I awoke later, groggy and confused, unsure of the time but surprised to see the sun had dipped far enough into the western sky to spill into my window. I had no idea what time I'd be seeing Jack, but I certainly couldn't let him see me like *this*. If my days with youth and beauty were numbered, I had to make them count. I pulled a dress from my closet, a simple brown broadcloth with raglan sleeves and decorative buttons around the waist and along the collar. I chose a pair of off-white low heels that buckled around the ankle to match the cardigan I threw over my shoulders. My face looked puffy and exhausted, a reality my cheap makeup did little to conceal, but falling asleep with wet hair had enhanced natural waves I was able to slick back with pomade and bobby pins. I clicked down the wooden stairs and into the kitchen. Coffee—even a weak one like the kind we could afford—would hopefully perk up my vigor and my complexion.

I found my sister at the kitchen table, newspaper spread out in front of her. She smiled when she saw me. "You look pretty."

My mood instantly lifted. Eleanor still spoke little, but when she did, you knew she meant it. "Thank you. I'm meeting Jack later. Did Mama leave for work?"

She nodded.

I bit the inside of my cheek, trying to conceal my relief. "Well, I'm going to make a cup of coffee. Do you want one?"

She bobbed her head once and returned her attention to the paper. I ran the water for a couple of minutes to allow most of the sediment to wash from the pipes and grabbed two mugs from the cabinet. "I don't think we have any sugar," I said, peering into the back of the pantry. "Do you know if Mama grabbed any mil—?"

There was a sharp tug on my arm, causing me to lose my grip on one of mugs. It fell to the floor and shattered. "Eleanor!" I shrieked, more out of shock than actual pain. "You scared me to death!"

In response, I received only a face full of newspaper. I jerked my head back as the smell of paper and ink overwhelmed my senses. "El, stop. What?"

The paper vibrated with agitation, my sister's wide eyes appearing and reappearing with each shake. I pried it from her fingers, placing one hand on her arm to calm her. But she was having none of it. Instead, she grabbed my hand and laid it inside the paper, curling my finger to point at a headline near the bottom of the page. Her eyebrows bounced up and down as her gaze shifted from me to the article and back again.

The headline was small, the article a mere blurb beneath a "Breaking News: Evening Edition" banner: "Bandits Steal $100 from Dallas Diner."

The tips of my fingers went cold.

Police are asking the public for help after robbers made off with over $100 from Hargrave's Diner in downtown Dallas last night. Details are limited at this time, but police confirm the diner was closed at the time of the robbery, the burglary only discovered when the morning crew arrived at around 5 a.m. to find the lock on the back entrance blown away by a large-caliber bullet. Witnesses report seeing a dark-colored sedan, possibly a Buick, cruising along Swiss Avenue several times before the diner closed at 10 p.m. Police are asking anyone who may have seen or heard anything suspicious during that time to contact them.

How I managed to keep ahold of the paper, I'll never know. At that moment, it felt like every ounce of energy was being used to keep my heart beating.

Someone had robbed Hargrave's. Right after I was fired. After I told Jack as we were sitting in his Buick. His dark-colored sedan. After he told me he'd take care of it.

The rumors about him pushed in from all sides, louder than his whispered *I love you*s and murmured desire to change. Too loud now to possibly ignore. I wouldn't believe it. I couldn't believe it. I loved this man, and he loved me.

Did he love me enough to steal for me?

Did I love him enough to pretend he wouldn't?

I realized I'd been holding my breath. I let it out with forced steadiness, lowering the paper with hands I hoped my sister couldn't see shake. "That's crazy," I said with fake cheer. "Guess getting let go was a good thing. Crime is going up everywhere, apparently even downtown. Wouldn't want to be walking around there at night anymore." I moved my foot, feeling something disintegrate under its weight. A piece of ceramic. I'd forgotten about the broken mug. "I'll get a broom. I don't want you to cut yourself."

I pushed past her, throwing the paper in the garbage as I did. I made sure not to look at her face. That was the thing about Eleanor: she didn't need words to communicate, which meant she was extra good at reading what others didn't say. Especially me.

"You look amazing. I brought you these, but you don't need them. In fact, you put 'em to shame." Jack pulled a bouquet of yellow daisies from behind his back, tilting his head to his shoulder with a mischievous smile.

I did not take the flowers. They hung between us in his outstretched hand, seeming to wilt with each passing second.

Confusion flickered in his eyes, though his smile remained. "Bea?"

I hesitated a few more seconds, then finally accepted them. They were beautiful. Of course they were beautiful. But their bright-yellow petals seemed defiled, tainted with the stench of something unpleasant. I held them at arm's length.

Jack blinked several times, his bafflement obvious. "Well," he said, clearing his throat. "Should we go then?"

I stood on the threshold of my house, unable to step forward. Eleanor was gone, babysitting at the Pattersons' two houses down, and with Mama at work, it would have been easy to not answer the door when he knocked. But I did. And here he was, looking so handsome in his crisp gray suit, which perfectly matched the shade of his eyes. His face had lit up when he saw me, as if it had been days rather than hours since we'd last seen one another.

There's no proof, I reminded myself. There was no proof he'd done anything wrong. I could go to him. After all, there was no reason to wound him over nothing more than a suspicion.

Right?

Taking a deep breath, I pulled my feet from their concrete encasement and stepped forward. I tried not to tense as Jack's arm wrapped around my waist. He guided me down the steps with a firm but uncertain touch.

But it wasn't the Buick parked at the curb. Instead of the black sedan with whitewall tires, this was a hunter-green coupe, Ford, with a soft top and shiny chrome bumper. The heaviness in my legs returned, causing me to stumble.

Jack caught me by the arm. "Easy there! You okay?"

Nausea rose in the back of my throat. "Yes. I'm fine. I . . . Where's the Buick?"

His fingers pressed into my hip, something I wouldn't have noticed but for my own heightened nerves. He stared at the car; I wondered if it was simply to avoid looking at me. "Ah, that old thing. It was a lemon. Needed new brake pads already. It's in the shop. My pa's gonna fix it up; then I'll take it to Denton to sell. Maybe even across the state line. Folks in Arkansas pay good money for used Buicks."

His words came out rapidly, in one breath, as if rehearsed.

Because they were. I knew they were.

I slid into the front seat, my heart falling as low as my spirits. He got in next to me and moved to start the ignition. "Jack." I put my hand on his arm.

He gripped the steering wheel but didn't look at me.

"Did you do it? Did you rob Hargrave's last night?"

For a moment, he didn't respond. Didn't even react. Then he let out a long, low sigh and dropped his chin to his chest, his shoulders sagging.

It was all the confirmation I needed. Biting down on a sob, I moved to grab the door handle.

"Bea, wait. Please." His hand gripped my wrist, painful and urgent. "Please, will you listen?"

I lifted my other hand, prepared to strike him, scratch him, whatever it took to free myself and avoid looking at his face. But my heart had a mind of its own, and my gaze washed over him before I could stop myself. Tears collected in the corners of his eyes.

"That man hurt you, Bea. I couldn't let him get away with it. He treated you like trash."

"I am trash, Jack!" The words exploded from my mouth, causing him to drop my hand. "Look at me! Look at my house! Look at my *life*! He wasn't telling me anything I didn't already know. I was just too stubborn to admit it before now."

"But it doesn't have to be that way!" He recovered enough to grab my hand again, squeezing my fingers until they hurt. "We don't have to live like this anymore."

"Is that so?" I snapped. "How? By robbing people?" My rage had returned, though I was no longer sure whether I was angrier with him or myself. "No thank you. I'd rather be trash than a criminal." I yanked my hand free and moved toward the door again. "We're done, Jack Turner. Do you hear me? Done." The door handle jammed under my thumb. Frustrated, I kicked at the base until it broke free with a pop. "If you ever come sniffing around here again, I'll call the police. I will. Don't think I won't—"

"I didn't think city life would be this way," he murmured. He stared at his hands, folded in his lap.

I froze, one foot on the pavement outside, the other on the floorboard of the car. The chilly November air swirled around my skirt, bringing with it the smell of dead leaves and molten metal from the foundry.

"Back in Magnolia, on the farm, everybody wore the same clothes, worked the same, played the same. We were poor, sure, but so was everybody else. It wasn't until we moved to the city that I realized that wasn't how the rest of the world worked. In the real world, everyone is different. The real world is a system of haves and have-nots. . . and we were the latter."

Go, Bea. Get on and go. But I didn't. I remained rooted to my seat, images of Wingate swirling before me, of our life before Dallas, both the good and the bad, fading into the reality of the West Dallas street before me.

"I tried, you know? I really did. When I came here and saw how the other half lived, I tried my hardest to achieve it. We were living in a tent at the camp, but I went out for ten, twelve hours a day collecting scrap metal with Pa. 'Rag picking,' he called it. We ate nothing but bologna sandwiches passed out by the Salvation Army until we'd saved up enough money to buy us the house and garage. At first, we didn't bring in enough business to support the mortgage, so I got a job over at Proctor & Gamble, making eighteen dollars for a sixty-hour workweek. That put a little food on the table, sure, but what about everything else?" He shook his head. "What kind of a life is that? Where's the fun? Where's the joy? Where's the money to go out dancing or to a picture show or to take a beautiful woman out to dinner? Ain't a penny I earned that didn't go toward life expenses . . . but not a cent toward actual *living*."

As if on cue, a whistle from one of the factories blew in the distance, mournful and rude, signaling the end of one shift and the beginning of another. I knew it wouldn't be long before we'd see the line of workers making their way home, exhausted and beat down, ready for their bottles and their beds. I shut the door against the sound.

"I even took on extra work as a telegraph boy for Western Union. I lasted less than two weeks. Not because I didn't need the money—I did. But because I couldn't set foot in most of the places in Dallas proper without getting stopped by the cops. What was a guy like me doing downtown? I didn't look right, see, with my ragged suits and worn-down soles. Nobody that belongs in Dallas looks like that. Surely I was up to no good."

I picked at my cuticles, my heart cleaving as I remembered the words of Mr. Hamilton, Mr. Miller, and the dozens of other Dallas-ites over the years. I was pretty enough, sure. Pretty enough to look at, play with, even carouse around town with for a week or two. But I wasn't good enough to make that jump from one side of the river to the other permanently.

Just like Jack, I wasn't good enough for Dallas, either.

"Finally it got to the point where I thought, you know what? If the cops already think I'm up to no good, maybe I should be. At least I could get something out of it. Stealing cars and taking 'em over the border got me a hundred dollars for one night of work. Before I knew it, I was feeding my family and walking into Dallas stores with money to burn. No one knew who I was. Where I'd come from. I fit in. And it felt good, Bea. For the first time in my life, *I* felt good." He turned to me suddenly, his cheeks flushed with emotion. "But it's nothing compared to how I felt when I first met you."

I pressed my fingers to my lips, my heart pounding in my throat. I needed to leave. Before he could say anything more, I needed to go.

"You understand me, Bea. Like no one else. You make me feel . . ." He stopped. Swallowed. Started again. "You are everything to me, Beatrice. Everything. Since we got here, I've spent all my time trying to do something with my life, to *be* something. To be enough for my parents, for Dallas, for the world. But since I met you, all I want is to be enough for *you*."

"Jack." The ache in my chest began to throb. "You *are* enough for me. I love you just as you are. You don't—"

"No." He grasped my hand between both of his, shaking his head. "Don't you see? You deserve more than this life. We both do. And I refuse to accept that this is all there is for us. Don't you want to escape from this place, from these people? From the factories and the discrimination and the misery?" His gaze locked onto mine. "Don't you want more?"

And in his eyes, I saw it. My past and my present, my ambition and my wretchedness—all of it mirrored inside his very soul. Bad circumstances, unfair prejudice, the determination of the world to crush our spirits and our hope. My story was his and his story was mine. He knew. He understood.

Only he was not going to take it lying down.

And for the first time ever, here was someone who didn't expect me to, either.

I pressed my mouth against his with an intensity that surprised us both, smothering that small, worried voice in my head with the warmth of his breath and the softness of his skin. My pulse quickened with equal parts desire and exhilaration. Because it was true: I not only wanted him, I wanted what he was offering.

I wanted more.

And with Jack by my side, there was finally hope of getting it.

CHAPTER ELEVEN

But to get *more*, it turned out we had to start with less.

Less noise, less people, less recognition. Less *Dallas*.

Which is how we ended up outside a darkened service station in Alvarado one chilly night in early February. Only an hour's drive from the banks of the Trinity and the looming Dallas skyline, but it might as well have been another world. There were no lights, no cars, no movement, no noise at all, save for the wind through the dead grass and incessant chirping of crickets. With the faint smell of manure in the air, it could have been Wingate, and I could have been twelve years old again, roaming the pastures aimlessly in an effort to be somewhere, anywhere, but home with my stepfather.

Yet the prickle of nerves creeping down my spine reminded

me it wasn't Wingate. And my sweaty, knotted hands gripping the door handle told me I most certainly wasn't that little girl anymore.

I was a woman. A woman serving as lookout while her boyfriend emptied the safe and cash register inside the Alvarado service station.

This truth, coupled with the sudden intensity of memory, made me feel very big . . . and very small at the same time.

Jack had been downright giddy as we'd set out, caressing my knee as he went over the details of the plan one last time. Seeing the joy in his eyes, knowing I was a part of it—that we were finally taking a stand, making a step toward our dreams—had enhanced my own excitement; the anticipation was electrifying. I'd giggled and kissed his neck as the bright lights of the city faded behind us.

As the *past* faded behind us.

But all of that changed when he got out of the car and the reality of what we were doing pressed in on me as severely as the rural darkness. We were committing a crime. An actual, we-could-go-to-jail *crime*.

"*There's nothing to worry about,*" Jack had promised before leaving. "*I'd never put you in danger. We're safe.*"

I wanted to believe him. After all, there was no reason to be nervous. Not this far out in the country, in a boring little town of barely over 1,000 people, all of whom seemed to be fast asleep, none the wiser to what was happening inside the service station.

Except that I was. Breaking the law might have been old hat to Jack, but it wasn't to me. My vision swam with images of bullets and blood, coppers and capture, not to mention the face of the service store owner—in my mind, he looked a lot like Grandpop, all bushy-eyebrowed and gap-toothed—when he came tomorrow morning to find his hard-earned money missing. It made my stomach churn. I knew what we were doing was necessary, but the harm it might cause—to us or to others—stole a bit of the thrill already wrestling with fear.

The hoot of an owl caused me to jump. Or was it truly an owl? Maybe it was a signal of some kind. Jack had assured me a small-town heist was safer, but in this moment, it sure didn't feel like it. In the city, where it was busy and bright and preoccupied, it was so much easier to blend in. Here, in the dark stillness, I felt exposed; there was no telling who was watching from the shadows.

Goose bumps sprouted along my forearms despite the unseasonably warm evening. Blackness squeezed in closer, inching toward the service station door, where Jack remained inside. What was taking so long? I strained, trying to make out movement inside the large windows covered with advertisements for motor oil and tires, but it was no use. The night was simply too thick.

From a copse of trees beyond came the sound of a branch snapping. Dead leaves crunching. Blood rushed to my head, away from my limbs and into my ears, making it harder to hear. But those had been footsteps. Definite footsteps. I was sure of it.

An animal?

Another rustle in the underbrush.

Pain seized my chest. I found myself unable to breathe. Unable to see. The only things still functioning, it seemed, were my nerves.

And every single one of them was telling me we were in danger.

I had to warn Jack.

But before I could convince my paralyzed muscles to move, he was there, sliding in next to me with practiced, deliberate movements. Jack's face was serious but not fearful, his pace quick but not rushed. He started the engine, shoving a brown sack into my lap. Gray eyes glanced back and forth between the rearview mirror and the windshield as the coupe slid from the parking lot, onto the highway, and into the quiet countryside beyond. Despite my alarm, no one followed us. No one gave chase. Not even the cows in the pastures gave us a second look.

And still it felt as if my heart would never again slow down.

We drove for miles without speaking. Finally, just outside of Midlothian, Jack left the highway in favor of a back road and pulled to a stop beneath a thicket of oak trees between two barren fields. Dust lingered in the air from our tires, creating a sparkling haze in the moonlight. A lazy smile spread across his handsome face. "Open it," he said softly.

So consumed had I been with anxiety during the drive, every ounce of energy taken up with watching Jack's face for signs of danger and the passing landscape for the cops I knew would swarm any minute, that I'd forgotten the canvas bag in my lap.

I looked at Jack. Even in the shadows, eagerness radiated from his face. He pulled my hand to his lips, kissed my palm, and placed it back on the bag.

"Open it," he said again.

With a tremble in my fingers, I undid the flaps. Darkness made it impossible to see the contents. Tentatively I reached my hand inside, where I was met with the unmistakable feel of dry, smooth paper. *Lots* of paper.

Money. The sack was full of money.

All the saliva disappeared from my mouth. Slowly I let my fingers curl around the bills, feeling them give way beneath my touch with an intoxicating crinkle. A chill trickled down my spine that had nothing to do with fear. Because there *was* no fear. Not anymore. There was only the very real, very powerful feel of dollar bills beneath my fingertips.

That . . . and Jack.

Releasing the money, I grabbed the lapels of his jacket and pulled him to me, kissing him. Deeply, passionately, needing to convey all the words my mouth could not say. Recovering quickly from the momentary shock, he twined his hands through my hair and returned the kiss eagerly, only intensifying my euphoria. I had never felt so loved, so powerful, so *alive*. The precariousness and dread of that empty Alvarado parking lot seemed a distant nightmare compared to the exhilaration of success now steaming up the windows of the coupe.

It had been so long since I'd won at anything—beauty pageants, auditions, job interviews, *life*. And now I'd done it. *We* had done it. This man, the one kissing my nose and circling my waist with his hands, had been the missing part, the key to unlock my world. With him, our dreams were entirely possible.

No, I thought, feeling the bag of money press between our bodies as he kissed me again. Not just possible. With Jack Turner, our dreams were inevitable.

CHAPTER TWELVE

Yet the harsh reality of life in West Dallas stubbornly refused to conform to the new world Jack and I had created for ourselves that February night. The money we'd secured was enough for one night out—just one—once we'd paid off our bills, put a dent in our families' outstanding debts, and secured a few weeks' worth of food for our pantries. We'd gotten away scot-free—not even a whisper about the robbery reached the tongues of the city—but the thrill of the escapade was quickly smothered by the gloomy skies, stench of poverty, and ever-present drain of daily expenses that soon left Jack and me right back where we started.

More robberies were necessary, not only to keep the bills paid, but also to keep us from succumbing to the melancholy that lingered over the city, as real and tactile as the smoke from the factories. A hardware store in Grandview, a refinery office in

Arlington, a service station in Grand Prairie, a café in Katy, among others. Always in and out, Jack on the job, me on the lookout. And we'd gotten away every time. We were a good team, Jack and I. Untouchable. Unstoppable.

And soon . . . uninteresting.

Don't get me wrong. The money was nice. Nothing earth-shattering, but it was keeping our families out of the red. An unfettered escape was even better. But I'd been surprised by how quickly the initial intoxication had worn off. The high of the first heist was never quite replicated, the thrill always tainted by the knowledge that whatever loot we secured wouldn't be enough to last more than a few weeks and most of our nights would still be spent on the wrong side of the river.

Moreover, our transgressions just seemed too . . . *easy*. Where was the bounty? The chase? The accolades of ill repute? We didn't want to get caught, of course, but it bothered me that no one even seemed to notice. Dozens of bandits graced the front page of the *Dallas Morning News*. But not us. We'd done no more than make the blotter. Each of our crimes produced indifference rather than indignation; it was hard to maintain the romantic appeal of being an outlaw when the law itself couldn't be bothered to put up a fight.

These murmurs of discontent grew louder with each subsequent heist, but I didn't dare voice them to Jack. I was too afraid of hurting his pride. Most of all, though, I was too afraid of hurting *us*.

But no matter how hard I tried to smother them, by early April, those whispers had become an all-out scream.

Maybe it was the weather, too hot and muggy for this early in the season. Maybe it was because our last payday had run out even quicker than normal, with Jack's mother needing medication for an ulcer and Eleanor needing a new pair of work shoes. Or maybe it was because I was spending my evening playing lookout in McGregor, a backward village with more cows than people, once again far from the lights of the Dallas skyscrapers. Far from *any* lights, save for the blink of a lonely railroad signal next to the tracks. The dull yellow reflected off the side of the depot. On, off. On, off. Each time it flashed, it seemed a little more sluggish. Just like my pulse.

There was no danger. No risk. Just like all the ones before. The best kind of job. And also the worst.

I felt invisible. Restless. And mind-numbingly *bored*.

I drummed my fingers on the dashboard, feeling my simmering bad mood starting to rise.

This was ridiculous. We didn't need a lookout. Not here. And I was *sick* of just sitting in the car every place we went. Perhaps a more active role was the answer to my tedium. I couldn't crack a safe but I sure as anything could hold the money bag. I moved to open the door, intent on entering the depot and demanding Jack allow me to help, only to have it yanked from my grip of its own accord. It was the first shot of adrenaline all night, and I let out a small scream despite myself.

"Shh! What are you doing?"

"I was going to—"

"Scoot over. Let's get out of here."

Jack slid in next to me, pushing me over to the passenger side as he started the engine. Keeping the lights off, he eased out of the parking lot and headed north out of town. McGregor lay sleeping behind us, not a single soul witness to our escape. It wasn't until the faint lights of the main square had faded entirely that Jack felt secure enough to flip on the headlights and gun the engine, his

Ford coupe—this one bought legally—fishtailing on the gravel, struggling to gain traction as it carried us into the night.

I leaned into Jack. He was quiet, but then he was usually quiet after a job. I'd learned not to ask questions until he was ready—and *ready* meant he started talking first. He needed to mentally replay each operation, ensure every string had been tied, every detail tidied. So I let him think, careful to give him my presence but not my postulations until he was good and ready to hear them.

But this silence went on longer than usual. He kept both hands on the steering wheel rather than one arm draped around my shoulders and eyes glued to the road, his mouth pressed into a thin line. His muteness stretched past Whitney and Hillsboro. It only inflamed the bad mood I was trying to shake. I thought perhaps this tension would carry us all the way back to West Dallas, but then he pulled into a motor court outside Lovelace. The new roadside cottages were a modern luxury we'd only recently been able to afford; it seemed glamorous to play house for night, with a kitchen, sitting area, and bedroom, the small cabins offering a privacy neither of us could ever hope to achieve in our parents' homes, especially after an escapade when we wanted to count our loot and celebrate. Normally I welcomed the uncommon splurge.

But tonight . . . tonight felt different. Tonight I worried Jack was thinking the same thing I was. That the motor court would give us an escape—if only momentarily—from the West Dallas slums from which it seemed we'd never truly be free.

"There's a diner across the street," I ventured after he'd backed the car next to our cabin. "Says it's open all night. Do you want to go grab a bite?"

"Later."

"But—"

"I'm tired, Bea," he snapped, pushing open the car door. "I just want to go inside and get some sleep."

"Okay. I'm sor—"

He slammed the door and disappeared inside the darkened cabin, not waiting for me to follow.

I gathered my skirt with sweaty hands. This was very unlike Jack. My Jack, the gentleman, always held doors open for me, allowed me to enter buildings first. He'd even carried me over the threshold our first night in a motor court together, the two of us collapsing on the floor in a fit of giggles at the sheer absurdity of it. My heart panged at the memory. But then, just as sharp, another emotion welled up inside my dejection: anger.

We were in this together. I would not allow him to shut me out. Or treat me as anything less than his lady and his partner.

His star.

My low buckle-style heels clicked on the stone steps as I stomped up to the cottage and pushed open the door. "Now you listen here. I—" I stopped, my words choked by the sight before me.

Jack sat on a sofa against the far wall, head in his hands. He didn't look up when I entered. Above him hung a painting of the desert—New Mexico, perhaps—which seemed to glow in the weak light of a tableside lamp. On the narrow coffee table in front of him, he'd laid a small cloth bag. His black suit coat was tossed over the side of a wingback chair in the corner near an unlit fireplace.

"Jack?" I ventured.

He didn't look up.

I struggled to hold on to my irritation. I was mad—I had every right to be mad—but he looked so small sitting there. Too small to be my Jack. Too small to bear the brunt of my anger. I slipped off my shoes and sat next to him, tucking my stockinged feet beneath me. "What's wrong?"

He rubbed his forehead with one hand, gesturing half-heartedly to the table with the other. "Count it."

I hesitated before grabbing the sack. Reaching inside, I pulled out a stack of bills, counting under my breath as I laid them on the table. "Sixty dollars," I said finally.

"Sixty dollars," he repeated.

I frowned. It was less than we'd hoped, but not bad. More than I used to make at the diner in two months.

But it wasn't exactly a roaring success, either.

I crossed my arms. "Alright, so we're no Pretty Boy Floyd."

"Pretty Boy Floyd? We're not even a Bradshaw. He ain't in the papers like Floyd but at least he's raking in the dough. Supposedly he's the one who hit up that bank in Hobart last week. Got away with at least three grand."

"Yes, but—"

"We don't have the money *or* the fame, Beatrice. We're so small-town, we aren't even worth the ink or bullets it would take to try and stop us."

I swallowed the lump in my throat. My deepest insecurities, spoken by the lips of the man I loved, hurt way worse than when they simply rattled around inside my heart. "Now," I tried, grasping for a line, "that isn't true. We've made the papers."

"They didn't even know our names," Jack scoffed.

"That's a bad thing?"

"Why am I talking to you about this? You don't understand."

"How do I not understand? Tell—"

My words were snipped by Jack's hand slamming on the table. "For pete's sake, Beatrice. Would you stop it? You're giving me a headache."

His shout cut through the air between us like a sudden cold breeze, tingling my skin. Jack had never yelled at me before. Never even raised his voice. But that wasn't what bothered me the most. It was his tone. As if he were an adult and I a child.

As if he were better than me.

I pressed my back into the lumpy couch cushion and gathered my elbows at my sides, staring at my clenched fingers in my lap.

But then Jack's hand was on my face, his tone awash in regret as he stroked my cheek. "I'm sorry, Bea. I didn't mean that." He scooted toward me, pushing against the icy bubble between us. "Please, forgive me."

I resisted his attempts to pull my body onto his.

"Beatrice, please. I shouldn't have spoken to you like that. You don't—"

"No, you shouldn't have."

Although I still refused to meet his gaze, I felt him sigh. "It's not you. It's me. I just . . . I can't help feeling like . . . like this is a waste of time. How are we ever going to get where we want to be with this?" He released my face and swung a limp hand over the table. "I mean, is sixty dollars even worth the risk?"

I followed his gaze. Beneath his disapproving glance, the pile of bills did look smaller somehow. Dirtier.

A part of me was still in shock, still angry over his words and his condescending scowl. But another part of me couldn't help but sympathize. I understood what he felt because I felt it too. The lack of attention and meager rewards almost felt like an insult.

Like no one cared.

Like we weren't even good enough to be criminals.

My heart broke, not only for myself but for Jack too. "Okay. We're not Pretty Boy Floyd," I repeated slowly, measuring my words. "But may I remind you, Pretty Boy Floyd was just arrested while *we* are still cozied up together on the outside. I'd say not being him is a good thing." I gave Jack what I hoped passed as a persuasive smile.

He pressed his head against my shoulder and rubbed my knee with his thumb. His body deflated, though I wasn't sure if his relief came from my rationale or because he realized he'd been forgiven for his outburst. "You're right. Of course you're right. I'm being stupid."

He remained in that position as minutes ticked past, time during which I knew that he—like me—was still staring at the loot in front of us. As the seconds passed, the limp bundle of bills seemed to shrink, mocking us with its insignificance.

Jack exhaled, slow and steady. I could tell he was going to wallow. "I just—"

I pressed my lips against his with enough force to dissolve his protests. I didn't want to hear it. Couldn't hear it. The disappointment in his voice, the defeat—it would only serve to validate my fears and inflame that restless itch.

Jack and I were all right. We weren't rich or famous, but we were in love. We were free. And though we weren't where we wanted to be, we were much better off now than when we'd started. We *were*.

So why didn't it feel like it?

As I snuggled up beneath Jack's chin, the beginnings of his stubble scraping against my face, I realized it was a question to which I already knew the answer. It was because simply staying afloat would never be enough to suffocate the nagging voice inside my head. The one that had grown louder with every rejection from pageant judges, casting directors, Dallas elites, and Baylor boys.

From my own mother.

You're not good enough. You're not pretty enough.
You are not enough.

Jack shifted beneath my touch. I knew he could feel my muscles tense, my chest constrict. "Bea? Are you okay?"

I sat up. His brows were furrowed, full lips pulled downward into a frown. Gosh, I loved him. I loved him so much. I wanted nothing more than to shove these feelings of inadequacy out of the cocoon we had been weaving around ourselves. We were *safe*. No praise but no peril. We could shake those chips off our shoulders and walk off into the sunset. Well, maybe not the sunset. But the point was we would be together. Be happy, if only we'd just try. And yet as I placed my palm against his chest and stared at my reflection inside his stormy gray eyes, I knew we couldn't. Not really.

Because even though I'd won the battle tonight, tomorrow was another day. And those same doubts would rise yet again to greet us with the morning sun. Jack's insecurities . . . and my own.

"Maybe . . ." I paused. Exhaled. "Maybe you're right, though. Yes, we're doing okay. More than okay, especially compared to most people. But maybe we can be more than just okay. Let's not just get even—let's get *ahead*."

"Bea?"

"Let's get enough money that your parents' mortgage isn't just caught up, it's paid off. Let's make it so my mother and sister don't ever have to work again. Enough money to buy anything we want. To buy all the *time* we want. To make people sit up and pay attention."

Jack straightened, wrapping his arm around my waist to keep me close. Close enough that I could see the fire reignite inside his eyes. "What are you saying?"

"I'm saying we can show the whole world we don't need any Mr. Millers, Mr. Hamiltons, or any other Dallas-ites to decide who we can or can't be."

Jack's lips parted slightly, the corners just starting to curve upward before he pressed them against mine roughly. "We could travel," he murmured. "Go to New York or Hollywood. Somewhere they'd recognize your talent. My shining star in her rightful place."

My pulse began to race as my childhood dreams, which had grown hazy and distant with disappointment and disillusionment, were yanked into sharp focus once more. Sharp, *attainable* focus.

He tucked a strand of hair behind my ear as he kissed my cheek, my nose, my neck. "Or we could buy a house. Anywhere you want. We could fill it with beautiful things, spend our days in leisure, wrapped up in each other, never to be bothered by the police or poverty ever again. People would know our names, and no one would ever look down on us. They would envy us. 'Boy, they have it all,' they'd say." His mouth brushed my ear, sending shivers down my spine. "It would be me and you, Bea. Not a care in the world for us. For our families. For our children."

I jerked my head back, the fluttery feeling from my stomach rushing through my limbs. "You . . . you want kids?"

A blush spread across his cheeks. "Of course. I want all of that. The house, the kids. Most importantly, you. Me and you. Forever."

My head swam with images. An elegant two-story house with a terrace covered in ivy. A backyard with a garden and a tire swing. Jack pushing a blonde-haired, gray-eyed girl with a carefree giggle into the sky. Me, on break from my sold-out performance onstage, lounging on the porch with my sister, emptiness banished from my soul for the first time in my life. No smog or melancholy, no empty tummies or strife.

A life no one would have ever believed I could achieve.

Tears welled up in my eyes. "That's what I want too, Jack. More than anything in this world."

He kissed me gently. "Are you willing to do what it takes to get there?"

I nodded, equal parts excitement and anxiety causing me to quiver beneath his embrace.

"Good. Then let's get a bite to eat and a few hours' rest. Tomorrow we'll head back home."

"To do what?"

He buttoned the top button of his shirt and straightened his tie, grinning. "To bring in reinforcements."

CHAPTER THIRTEEN

Reinforcements, as it turned out, meant Emmett. And Emmett, it seemed, was none too happy with the proposition, a sentiment he made clear time and time again on the long, hot drive to Cisco, a modest-sized town between Dallas and Abilene. Jack had spent two weeks scoping out various targets within a three- to four-hour radius of West Dallas and had decided the First National Bank of Cisco to be the perfect hit: large enough to promise a big payout but small enough to avoid a substantial police presence. Most importantly, it was far enough from the city to avoid any recognition from the Dallas coppers, who already had it in for Jack. Distinction, not detention, was the name of the game.

"I'm telling you, Jack. If Alli finds out about this . . ."

"She's not going to find out about it!" Jack's eyes flickered to the rearview mirror, where he met his brother's gaze momentarily before returning his attention to the road.

"But I promised her." He leaned forward and draped his arms over the back of the seat. "I promised her I was done with all this stuff. I've gone straight. I *promised* her, Jack."

"And how's that promise working out for you? Look at Bea. Look at that scarf. Don't it bring out the color in her eyes? Don't it make her look like a lady? Show just how much she's loved?"

I blushed and put a hand to the cornflower-blue silk draped around my neck. A gift Jack had given me two days earlier right before dinner and dancing at the Baker Hotel capped off by a moonlit walk through Fair Park. My heart fluttered at the memory of his kisses and romantic words.

"Tell me, Emmett," Jack continued, interrupting my daydream. "When's the last time you bought Alli a present? When's the last time she had a night out on the town or even just some flowers?"

I kept my eyes forward, but I could feel Emmett deflate behind me, his indignation paling next to his shame.

"She doesn't need all that material stuff. She told me so."

Beside me, Jack gave a slight shrug. "Alright. If you say so. But how about this—when's the last time you had the energy after a day at the factory to sit and have a conversation with her? A *real* conversation, not just about work or her day?"

"We read our Bibles together every night," he said stubbornly.

"Bible reading," Jack muttered under his breath. "Charming."

Stomach clenching, I gave Emmett a small smile. Religion aside, it was sweet to think of the two of them lying in bed, Bibles in their laps, fingers intertwined. Jack's and my relationship was so different—wild and passionate and intense. I'd never known such quiet intimacy. I wondered what it was like.

"Well, your Bible isn't going to put food on the table or put a roof over the heads of all the kids Alli wants to have. I'll tell you that much."

Emmett's breath came out in one long sigh, spilling the scent of old tobacco into the air. "That's why you get this one job, Jack. Just this one. We split the money and trickle it in, never speaking of it again, especially not in front of Alli. For all she knows, I got a raise. You understand me?" He waggled one finger near Jack's face. "Just this one job."

Jack swatted it away with a laugh. "Sure, Emmett. Whatever you say."

Cisco's bank was a two-story brick building right on the town square. I didn't like the idea of robbing someplace in the middle of town; it created too many obstacles to a clean getaway. I liked even less Jack's plan to rob the bank in broad daylight. Darkness was one of the keys to our success, and he was throwing our best ally out the window. But banks, he argued, were different than stores or cafés. All the money was secured in a vault at night, a vault we had zero chance of entering. It had to be done when the bank president was there.

And Jack knew the president's schedule to a T, since he'd been scoping out the building for the past five days.

At exactly eight thirty, he pulled the Chrysler to a stop in front of the building. The car was the second of two stolen vehicles we'd used on the trip (Jack's own car feeling too risky), the first one from Dallas, the second from Gordon, with plates we'd swiped in Olden. His eyes scanned the sidewalks as he killed the ignition. It was gray and drizzling. Storms from the night before lingered as a miserable mist, which worked to our advantage as it seemed to be keeping most pedestrians indoors.

"Let's go over it again." He turned in his seat to face both his brother and me. I couldn't help but notice the sweat on Emmett's forehead.

"The bank president arrives at precisely eight forty-five each morning. The one security guard doesn't arrive until nine, when the bank opens. We have fifteen minutes to get in, get the money, and get out before he shows up and the place starts filling with customers."

Emmett nodded, biting at his lips.

"Bea, the car must be in the road and running by the time we exit. This isn't like the other times when you sat quietly at the ready. You have to be in the driver's seat, foot over the pedal. You got it?"

I bobbed my head. We'd gone over it a hundred times, yet I still felt a sense of exhilaration every time he said it. I'd only driven a handful of times and certainly never done so with the prospect of bullets flying through the air or police sirens wailing. But Jack believed in me, so I had no option but to believe in myself too. Even if it made my pulse race, muscles twitch, and breathing hitch.

This was no McGregor Depot, after all.

A dark-blue Buick roadster pulled to a stop around the corner of the building. I tried not to think of the man who emerged—gray-haired and black-suited, obviously well-off—as a person with a family and feelings, but rather an obstacle to overcome, one more thing to be conquered on the way to our dream. He was merely a symbol of a cruel world designed to keep people like Jack and me underfoot.

The silence that filled the car after Jack and Emmett left was excruciating. They'd taken the air with them, and I had to force breath from my lungs. The windows of the bank were dark. I had no idea what was happening inside. The car keys slipped in my sweaty fingers as I tried to start the ignition, and it took several tries before the engine finally sputtered to life. I backed from the parking spot and idled in the street, the seat beneath me vibrating with impatience as I stared at the door, willing Jack and Emmett to hurry.

Two women emerged on the town square to my left, umbrellas overhead, with two large dogs who were pulling at their leashes, oblivious to the rain. They glanced at me as they passed.

I sat idle but not quiet, the engine continuing to rumble.

A worker stepped from a café just ahead, placing a signboard advertising the day's specials—green chile stew and roast beef on rye—under an awning. He squinted in my direction.

The engine seemed to grow louder, as if feeding off my apprehension.

Come on, Jack. Come on.

A man in a cowboy hat sprang up out of a nearby truck. The holster on his hip and swagger to his step reminded me very much of a Texas Ranger or, at the very least, a rancher with whom you didn't want to tangle. He walked toward me, hat pulled low.

By now, the engine was screaming, begging me to move.

Cisco, which just moments before had been deserted, was now crawling with people. And all of them, it seemed, were looking at me.

"Jack," I said aloud, my voice quivering, hoping against hope that somehow he'd hear me. "Hurry."

And then Jack and Emmett burst from the bank, several cloth bags in their fists, guns in the air. Elation swelled, as powerful and intoxicating inside my blood as whiskey, before my mind had a chance to register the gunshots. They rang out from nowhere and everywhere, as a shrill alarm wafted from the still-open bank door. There was a horrific explosion behind me, which caused me to shriek and press on the gas, even as Jack and Emmett were still trying to get inside the vehicle. I slammed on the brake, accidentally killing the engine.

"Bea!" Jack screamed. "Go! Go!"

I forgot every driving lesson I'd ever had, stepping on the clutch, the gas, the brake, unable to remember which was which. The sound of gunfire increased, and I became aware of Jack's gun, mere inches from my head, shooting through the back window, which was no longer covered in glass.

Sirens screeched. They seemed to be coming from every building on the square. A uniformed security guard was running up the sidewalk, his workday beginning a few minutes earlier than planned.

"Bea! Go!"

By some miracle, I finally managed to press the right pedal. Jack nearly flipped into the back seat as the car lurched away, bullets whizzing through the air beside us. My scarf—my beautiful new silk scarf—was yanked from my throat by the wind.

A fine drizzle coated the windshield, obscuring my view. I scrabbled with the wipers, pressing every button and pulling every knob until I found the right one. The view cleared, but it did not improve the situation. The street suddenly seemed to be filled with cars, blocking my path. "Which way?" I shouted. "Which way?"

"There!"

I jerked the car in the direction of Jack's thumb. Stores and cafés faded into houses, which disappeared into wheat fields. The bullets ceased, but the sirens never seemed to lessen; my ears rang with their howls long after we'd made it into the countryside and turned down several narrow dirt roads to nowhere.

"Jack, where are we? Where—?"

"Stop," he said sharply. "Just stop. Let me drive."

I pulled over on the muddy shoulder, climbing over him as he slid into the driver's seat. For the first time since he'd gotten in the car, I got a good look at him. His face was ashen, his hair askew.

Sweat had soaked through not only his shirt, but his jacket as well. His eyes locked with mine and he grabbed my hand. "Are you hurt?"

I shook my head. The euphoria that had surged through me earlier curdled in my veins, feeling like the first twinges of a hangover. But I wasn't shot. And that was something.

He glanced in the rearview mirror. "Emmett, you alright?"

Emmett lay sprawled on the back seat. His eyes were closed, his breathing heavy. Two large cloth sacks were clutched to his chest. "I think I wet myself," he said, not opening his eyes. "But I'm alright. Let's just get out of here."

Jack started the car—much quicker than me—and pressed on the gas. The car pitched but didn't move. He stepped harder. I could feel the wheels rotate beneath us, and yet we remained stationary. My stomach dropped as Jack swore and stomped on the gas again, to no avail. The ringing in my ears was fading, but the sirens were not. In fact, they were getting closer.

"We're stuck," he said unnecessarily. "Come on, we'll have to run for it."

All sorts of objections rose in my throat. It was raining. I was in heels. We were in the middle of nowhere. But none of it mattered. Not compared to being arrested. Or killed.

Jack grabbed my hand and dragged me out of the car after him. My T-straps sank immediately into the thick, saturated ground. I yanked as hard as I could but my shoe remained firmly entrenched in the mud. In the distance, a chorus of dogs began to bark. I had no choice; I'd have to continue in nothing but my stockings.

The three of us ran through an overgrown field. The sharp stalks poked the soles of my feet, drawing blood, but Jack refused to stop. We ran and ran, crossing wheat fields and pastures, crawling under fences and dodging stray cows, the constant rain both a blessing of cover and a curse that slowed our progress. My lungs burned, my legs ached, and I was chilled to the bone from my soggy clothes. But whenever we paused, the sirens were there. Once or twice, we even heard voices. The entire county, it seemed, had learned of our crime and was mobilizing to find us.

The sun was high in the sky, though still muted by clouds, by the time Jack finally allowed us rest. We were next to a creek, swollen with the recent rain, the muddy waters racing back toward Cisco and everything we were trying to leave behind. I sat beneath a gnarled oak tree, examining my bruised and bloody feet as Jack paced, looking for a place to cross.

"It's over, Jack," Emmett said. He had one arm outstretched, braced against a tree, the other clutching the bags of money to his waist. "I can't run anymore. We have to stop."

"We're not stopping," Jack spat, spinning around angrily. "We've come too far."

"It don't matter how far we go! Those coppers ain't never letting up."

"We just have to get to the next town and get a car. Get a car and get back to Dallas, lay low for a while. It'll all blow over."

"It ain't blowing over! We shot at people! We mighta killed—"

"We didn't kill anyone!" He rushed toward Emmett, jutting out his chin and pulling back his shoulders. He thrust his face directly in his brother's. "Stop talking like that. You're scaring her."

"I'm not scared," I said quietly, wrapping my arms around my knees. My body let out an involuntary shiver nevertheless.

Jack's rigid posture deflated as he looked at me. He retreated from his standoff, crouching before me and taking one of my hands in his. "Bea," he whispered. "Bea, I—"

But he was cut short by the bark of a dog. Several dogs. And voices, growing louder by the minute.

His grip on my fingers tightened as his eyes went wild. "Go."

He pulled me to my feet with enough force to cause me to stumble. "You have to go."

"Jack."

He pushed me toward Emmett, who caught me roughly. "Take her. Across the river. You've always been a strong swimmer."

"But, Jack, I—"

"Just get her out of here. Now."

My mind struggled to keep up with his words, his actions. By the time I realized what was happening, Emmett was dragging me toward the rushing waters, stuffing the bags of money inside his shirt. "No!" I screamed, fighting against his grip. "No! Jack!"

Jack remained where he stood, his face twisted with anguish. "Get as far away as you can. I'll lead them away."

"Jack!"

But then the frigid waters of Sandy Creek stole my breath and my words. Emmett struggled against the current but kept a firm grip around my waist. Even so, we were several hundred feet downstream by the time we finally reached the other side. And Jack was nowhere to be seen.

"Ja—" I started to wail, but Emmett's large hand clamped across my mouth.

"Let him be. We have to move."

"But Jack!"

"Jack's the only chance we got at getting out of here. You go screaming for him, we'll *all* get caught. Now let's go!"

He pulled me along after him. My frozen muscles barely functioned as we stumbled blindly through a field littered with dung. Another cloud burst overhead, adding insult to injury as we trudged forward. Behind us, we heard an upswell of voices and a few rounds of gunfire, the shrill bark of bloodhounds and my own ragged sobs punctuating the deafening silence that came after.

CHAPTER FOURTEEN

The knocking would not go away.

No matter how hard I pressed the pillow over my ears, no matter how high I pulled the covers, the knocking would not go away.

I didn't understand why someone didn't answer it. My mother was at work, sure, but where was Eleanor? Since I'd returned home a week ago, I'd retreated to my room, as much hiding out as I was mourning, emerging only to use the bathroom or pick at an occasional meal left outside my door (by Eleanor, no doubt—no way my mother would entertain such coddling). They knew I didn't want to be disturbed, so why were they allowing this incessant knocking to continue?

Emmett and I had escaped by stealing a Model T from a farmhouse outside Morton Valley, which we ditched for a Chrysler 52 in Mineral Wells, where we also stopped for a change of clothes.

We abandoned that car when we reached Fort Worth, preferring to take a combination of buses back to West Dallas. We didn't speak. We hardly even looked at one another. The weight of what we'd done—and more importantly, who we'd left behind—was too heavy to sustain a relationship we'd barely begun. A discarded newspaper on a bus stop bench gave us temporary elation—Jack was wounded but alive!—that plummeted when we read the list of charges that kept him in an Eastland County jail. No mention of our names—Jack had never been a snitch. He alone was facing time for robbery, fleeing the scene of a crime, and attempted murder for the hail of gunfire he'd loosed.

He'd finally gotten his name in the paper. But it sure didn't feel like a victory.

When we parted at the bus stop in West Dallas, it was with a brokenhearted hug, during which Emmett discreetly deposited a stack of bills into my pocket. I shook my head violently and tried to give it back, but he retreated, protesting as loudly as possible without drawing attention. I persisted. In the end, the only thing that convinced him to finally take it was my threat to burn it the moment I returned home.

No amount of money could make up for the loss of Jack. Or my future.

I faked a lovers' quarrel as an excuse to retreat to my bedroom, though I knew my mother would eventually find out the truth of Jack's arrest, either from the paper or from Dallas's incessant gossip. I didn't care. Let her think what she wanted, judge him—and me—all she wanted. I didn't have the energy to fight. She'd never liked Jack, though whether it was him or simply my own happiness she disliked, I wasn't sure. Besides, she might have had her suspicions about where I'd been getting all this money—even the best makeup girl at Daisy's, the fake job I'd conjured for myself, couldn't possibly bring in more than Mama made at the factory each week—but still she took the bills without question.

I told Eleanor nothing of what had happened, but I felt as if somehow she already knew. She was the only one allowed in my room, as she never asked a single question, instead holding me whenever the full force of my grief overtook me, wailing and weeping until I was sick, then wailing and weeping once more.

And not just for Jack's predicament, but also for my own role in putting him there. The bank heist might have been his idea, but I was the one who'd planted the seed. Pushed him for bigger. Better. No matter how I tried to frame it, I was not innocent.

Now Jack was paying the price.

So I wept. And once all that misery was finally spent, I slept. For hours—days, even. Because only in my dreams could I be with Jack. So I slept. And slept and slept and slept.

Until now. Until this knocking that would not go away.

"Eleanor!" I hollered. "Can you get the door?"

Nothing but silence. And knocking.

"Mama!"

My second shout was feeble; I knew full well no one would respond. If someone was going to answer it, they would have done so by now. And whoever was at the door didn't seem to be giving up. It must be something important.

Blood froze in my veins as my head cleared. The police. It had to be the police.

I sprang from my bed, my heartbeat throbbing in my ears. Or was that still the knocking? I couldn't tell. I pulled on my robe and crept down the staircase, pressing myself against the walls to avoid being seen. A blurry shape was visible through the opaque glass window. I sank to my knees, crawling over the dirty floor to the side window like a cat on the prowl. In the space between the windowsill and the bottom of the curtain—I didn't dare move it even an inch—I could make out the edge of a skirt.

A teal skirt, covered in small brown polka dots. Most assuredly *not* a policeman's uniform. Or any kind of man at all.

I hadn't realized I'd been holding my breath until the force of its release. I stood and pulled open the door with liquid muscles.

Alli Turner stood on my doorstep, one fist raised in midknock. Her mouth pressed into a tight smile at my appearance. "Beatrice. Hi."

She was the last person I expected to see, the last person I *hoped* to see, other than the police. I'd been complicit in involving Emmett, in making him break his promise to her as if it were nothing. This woman who had been so hospitable to me. The weight of my selfishness tugged at my heart, and though her face was not unkind, shame burned in my cheeks as if I'd been slapped.

She wore a short-sleeved dress with a square neckline, her auburn hair tucked beneath a wide-brimmed raffia hat, and sensible, well-worn low heels that buckled at the ankle. If I hadn't been so flustered, it would have made me self-conscious about my own appearance. I was in a pink threadbare nightshirt, barely covered by my equally threadbare white robe. I couldn't remember the last time I'd showered. There was no telling what my greasy hair and makeup-less face looked like.

Too long had passed between her initial greeting and an appropriate response, and still I found myself at a loss for words. Somewhere in the distance, a faint melody of horns and pianos drifted from someone's open window. I recognized Fred Waring and His Pennsylvanians—"Little White Lies."

The universe had a funny sense of humor sometimes.

"Are you going to invite me in?"

I moved aside to allow her entrance, closing the door behind us to block out that cursed, guilty song. My tongue felt heavy as I finally managed to squeak out, "Would you . . . would you like a cup of coffee?"

"Yes, please."

I led her through the dim living room and into our small kitchen, where natural light streamed from the open window. After the darkness of the room before, it seemed too harsh, like a spotlight. But not the ones they used onstage. More like the ones cops used to find guilty parties.

"We don't have any cream," I said, not having to try very hard to sound sorry. "There may be a little bit of sugar, though."

Alli took a seat at the table. "Whatever you have is fine."

I kept my back turned to her, busying myself preparing mugs and heating water. Silence filled the kitchen, so loud and forceful I felt as if my ears would burst from the strain. She seemed to be waiting for me to speak first.

Which I wouldn't. Couldn't, actually.

Finally she sighed. "Jack is okay. In case you were wondering."

I turned to find her staring at me. She had removed her hat, and her hair had fallen around her shoulders, glinting like copper in the slanted sunlight. To my surprise, however, her eyes were not narrowed in anger or betrayal. Instead, they were ringed with sadness.

"Sarah and I went to see him. Well, I drove her and she went into the jail. She was too upset to drive herself, and Earl couldn't afford to close up shop for the day. Jack was only allowed one visitor, so I sat outside, praying the visit wouldn't upset her even more. I don't know if her heart could have taken it otherwise."

I placed a steaming mug in front of her, which she acknowledged with a slight nod, and sat down across from her.

"He was shot in the shoulder, but the bullet went straight

through. Clean, he said. And the docs had taken real good care of him. According to him, it still hurts, but it's healing."

I lifted my eyes toward the ceiling, hoping gravity would force the tears back in. It was good news, of course; oftentimes it was an infection that killed, rather than the bullet itself. But thinking of Jack in a cold jail cell, alone and in pain, was almost more than I could bear.

"He swore he was done with this kind of life. That he was going to use this time to turn over a new leaf and start fresh. And he . . . he asked about you," she continued. "Wanted to make sure you were doing okay, that the cops weren't bothering you because of your connection to him. He wanted to make sure you knew where he was and what had happened . . . since you were at home with your sister that night."

I clenched my fingers around my mug.

"He wanted his mama to know you had nothing to do with it. That you were a good girl and you might need some looking after until he's able to get out. Which, I'll be honest, Bea, is looking like it might be a while." She took a sip, her eyes remaining steadfastly on me. "Although possibly a little less now."

I tilted my head to one side.

"Emmett turned himself in yesterday."

I was lucky my mug was firmly planted on the table. Otherwise, it would have been in a thousand pieces on our dusty floor.

Alli hesitated a moment, studying my reaction. Or nonreaction, which might have been just as telling. She took another sip before speaking again.

"It took him a couple of days to confess to me what had happened, where he'd been, what he'd done. Not that I didn't have my suspicions, of course. Coming home looking like he did." She closed her eyes for a moment as if remembering. I saw it in my mind's eye too, though I gripped the sides of my chair, trying not to betray the memory. "And then we got word about Jack. There was no hiding that he already knew. He showed me the money and he . . . he . . ." Her voice wavered. "He was on his knees, beating his breast with shame. He begged me for forgiveness, begged God. He was physically ill with the guilt, unable to look me in the eye, pulling away from my touch as I tried to console him." She was crying openly now, no longer trying to fight it. "He would have put on a sackcloth and covered his head with ashes if I'd let him. He had tried so hard to change, to repent from the past. He slipped up—just once—and look at what had happened. He'd let me down, he said, but more importantly, he had sinned against God."

The seat squeaked as I shifted. *God.* Once again, Charles's face swam before me, his words echoing inside my head. That familiar shameful pang about the person I was—the wicked, sinful person I'd been told I was—pierced my heart.

"We cried together, prayed together, sought the Lord's guidance and will. I didn't want Emmett to do it; he didn't want to do it either. But we both felt God telling us the same thing. We couldn't move forward, have the life together we'd always wanted, with this hanging over our heads. Not just the fear of being found out—even though we knew Jack would never squeal—but the wall that would forever be between us and God. We couldn't have a true relationship with Him if we didn't deal with this first."

I rolled my tongue around my mouth, dumbfounded.

"The police in Cisco were so impressed. They took his statement—that he'd been present and participated in the robbery of the First National Bank with Jack . . ." She paused, glancing at me as if waiting for me to say something.

But I sat as blank-faced as possible as the ramifications of her words rolled in my head. Emmett had turned himself in. But he hadn't betrayed me either. He'd promised Jack to look out for me, and he was doing it even from inside a jail cell. I was grateful, humbled . . . and more than a little ill at ease.

Eventually she continued. "After they'd finished taking the statement, they said they'd never had anyone turn himself in before. Or return stolen money, minus what he'd used for clothes and transportation, of course. They believe he'll get a softer punishment. Possibly a year, maybe two."

Her tone was casual, throwaway, but my reaction was swift and almost visceral. Like being stung by a wasp or bit by a rattler. "And you're okay with that?" I sputtered. "What about your life? The family you wanted to start? You're just going to sit around and wait on him for two years because you think it's what *God* wanted you to do?"

Alli straightened in her chair. Her eyebrows furrowed together. "Of course. I love God. I love Emmett. And I love that he's doing the right thing. For him and for God. It's the only way to move forward with a clean conscience. For *all* involved."

Sweat dampened the fabric under my armpits. I pulled my robe tighter around my body. She knew the truth. She knew I was there, knew I was a part of it. Maybe Emmett had told her. And now she wanted me to go to the police too. Just the thought of those cold metal bars slamming shut sent shivers down my spine. I couldn't go to prison. My reputation would be in tatters. I'd never get another legitimate job, on the stage or otherwise. My mother would be scorned. And Eleanor! Sweet Eleanor. I didn't even want to think about what my absence—no, my *incarceration*—would do to my sister.

In my mind, I felt Charles's hands again, heard his commands to confess, to repent. I felt the water in my lungs, the burning in my limbs, the cruel and harsh finger of God in the form of my stepfather.

I loved Jack, but going to jail would not set him free. Nor would it magically make me feel better; in fact, more than likely, it would only make things worse. For everybody. No matter the enormity of my guilt, my aversion to any notion of divine forgiveness was bigger. No, I would not go to jail. Especially not for Charles's God. Or Alli's.

"Well, that's good news," I said thickly. "For both of them."

Her shoulders slumped as she let out a long breath of air through her nostrils. When she met my eye, it wasn't condemnation I saw. It was disappointment.

And that hurt worse than her anger ever could.

She stood suddenly, the scrape of her chair an echo in my tiny kitchen. "Well, I guess I should be going."

"I'll walk you to the door."

"I can see myself out, thank you." She placed her hat back atop her head, tucking a loose strand of hair behind her ear, and took a step toward the hallway.

"Alli . . . wait."

She turned, eyebrows arched in expectation.

I wanted to tell her everything. To tell her I was sorry but also to defend myself. Tell her the robbery had been planned and executed by Jack, that my confession wouldn't make much difference anyway because I was only the getaway driver. I wanted to explain all the reasons I couldn't go to jail and to assure her it was okay, that I was done with that life too. To beg her to please forgive me, to not hate me, to understand.

But instead I said nothing.

After several moments, her face broke into a small, sad smile. "I'll be praying for you, Bea. You take care of yourself." And then she turned and disappeared out my front door.

I stared down the hallway for what seemed like hours, the

memory of her final expression lingering long after she'd gone. Then I gathered the empty mugs from the table and placed them in the kitchen sink. I'd clean up later. Before my mother returned, if I remembered. I didn't have the energy to listen to her complain. But for now, I retrieved the newspaper from the counter and retreated to the living room, black marker in hand. I spread the help wanted section out on the coffee table.

I didn't need any sort of religious repentance or God's forgiveness. I didn't need God at all. I could prove to Alli—to everyone—that I could move forward on my own. I'd find a job, save every penny, and when Jack got out in a few years, he'd find me waiting on him, my foot firmly planted in the future I'd already begun to build for us. We'd grab on to those dreams we'd whispered about in the motor court not so very long ago and never look back. I could do it. *We* could do it.

Yes, work was what I needed. For money, for salvation, for distraction. Because maybe Alli didn't hate me. But I hated myself enough for the both of us.

CHAPTER FIFTEEN

NOW

It was only the squeak of a floorboard, but it was enough to send me straight up from my spot on the floor, eyes wild, .45 gripped in my sleep-numbed fingers.

The light was dim and gray, early morning from what I could surmise, and I struggled to find anything among the shadows. The gun shook in my hand as I swung it around the room. There had been a noise. I was sure of it.

A moan of agony escaped my lips as my body fully transitioned from asleep to awake, a deep, intense stab reminding me of my barely healed injuries. Pain shot through my hip and down my right side, severing my breath; my legs buckled beneath me, and I gripped the couch to steady myself, catching a view of Jack through black-spotted vision.

Jack.

He was pale and slack-jawed, eyes closed, unmoving. *Unbreathing.*

I fell to my knees, ignoring my own torment, and dropped the gun as I seized his arm. "Jack," I tried to shout but my throat was too dry. "Jack, wake up." I squeezed his hand, but he did not squeeze back. Hot tears bubbled up, a product of grief and uncontrollable fear.

He couldn't leave me. Not now. Not here.

The makeshift bandage on his shoulder was saturated with blood. I pressed two fingers roughly against it. But still he did not stir. Clenching my jaw, I laid a palm to his bare chest, leaving a smudge of red on his white skin, and closed my eyes, willing his chest to expand and contract beneath my trembling hand.

And then, somehow, miraculously it did. I held my breath, begging for it to be real and not my own hopeful stupidity, and watched as his flesh rose and fell once again with nearly imperceptible movements. I let out a grateful sob as I pressed my face into his side, pulling his fingers to my lips, my cheek, my forehead. They were cold and flaccid, and they did not respond to my touch . . . but they were still alive.

Behind me, the floorboard creaked. This time, I knew I didn't imagine it. I scrambled to my feet and spun around, only remembering the .45 after it was too late.

A woman stood in the doorway leading to the kitchen. Her thin frame was outfitted in a simple cotton nightdress, its color muted and indistinguishable in the dim light. Brown hair was pulled away from her face in a high braid, though several strands had escaped during sleep, giving her a frazzled, almost-comical appearance. Her face, however, was anything but funny; with her pressed mouth, sunken cheeks, and protruding eyes, she radiated a deep terror. I didn't know if it would force her to run from me or at me.

We stared at one another, her eyes moving from me to Jack and back again, while I tried to subtly listen for any other movement at the top of the stairs. This woman didn't scare me necessarily. If there was a husband somewhere, however . . .

"Please," I managed finally, dropping my shoulders. "He's . . . he's hurt. We need help." I took a step backward, holding up my hands and nudging the gun discreetly under the couch with my foot. "We mean you no harm. We didn't intend to break in but—"

The woman walked forward with unexpected confidence, stopping my words in my throat. She knelt in front of Jack and placed a hand on his forehead. "He's dying." Her voice was not unkind, but it broke me just the same. I'd known he was in bad shape; hearing it from a stranger's mouth, however, made it more real.

"Can you . . . can you help him, Miss—?"

"Rose," the woman interrupted, shifting her eyes from Jack to me. "My name is Rose. You're already in my house; you might as well call me by my first name."

My throat burned as I tried to swallow. "I'm . . . Eleanor." It was the first name that came to my mind, and I regretted it immediately. I didn't deserve to use my sister's name. It felt as if I were soiling it by speaking it aloud. But it was too late to go back now. "And that's . . ." I glanced around and spotted a tattered Agatha Christie paperback on the table. "Quin," I finished. Such a glaring, obvious lie. I tried to cover it by adding quickly, "Do you have any . . . ?" *Bandages. Medicine. Surgical skills.* Every possibility dissolved on my tongue. She was a simple farmwife. This was a simple farmhouse. There was nothing this woman could do besides call a doctor or the police. It was essentially the same sentence either way.

But Rose merely stood and disappeared up the stairs, reappearing a moment later with a bundle of rags, one bottle of pills, and another of clear liquid, as well as a glass of water. "I don't have much in terms of extra fabric," she said, "but these were my late husband's shirts. It's better than nothing."

I tried not to react, even though her words washed over me like warm water. *Late husband's.* So there was no one else. We were safe. For the time being.

She forced a pill into Jack's mouth, then tipped his head back to allow water and gravity to do their job. I watched the vein in his throat throb under the strain. Satisfied, she turned and offered the glass to me. It was painful as it went down; I was so parched it was as if I had forgotten how to swallow.

"What happened to him?"

I held the water in my mouth, truth and falsehood battling inside my heart. It was with no small amount of shame that I allowed the latter to fall from my lips: "Car crash."

Jack let out a small groan as she shifted him, removing the blood-soaked T-shirt I'd fastened around his wound only hours before. The skin beneath was stained with blood, the jagged flesh around his injury bright and grotesque —and very obviously not from any car accident. But Rose continued her work without missing a beat, cleaning the area with another rag and the clear liquid, which I now understood to be some type of alcohol.

Weariness overtook me again as I watched, the feeling of relief tinged with the ominousness of delaying the inevitable. I sank into a nearby armchair and rubbed at my eyes. Jack had fallen back into stillness, not even flinching as the alcohol bubbled into his wound. If possible, he looked even thinner and paler. Were those really the same strong arms in which I'd rested so many nights? I lowered my eyes, not wanting to look at him.

The squeak of a floorboard pulled me yet again from myself. I looked up just in time to see Rose returning from upstairs. She held something small and brown in her hand. As she knelt in front of Jack once again, I closed my eyes; I couldn't watch her futile attempts at healing anymore.

But then I heard a familiar crinkle. Opening my eyes, I saw her still sitting at Jack's side, though she was no longer tending his wound. Instead, the small brown object now lay open upon her knees. A book. A Bible. She ran a bony hand over the pages, her lips moving silently but passionately.

Praying. She was praying.

Iciness flooded the pit of my stomach, and I gripped the arms of the chair, trying to stop the tremors. I pressed my eyes shut.

I couldn't watch that, either.

CHAPTER SIXTEEN

"Now, the Westovers are coming for dinner Monday night, so I'll need you here early to clean."

"Yes, Mrs. Russell."

"Cynthia's dress will need to be pressed and mine—the purple one with the lace collar and bell sleeves—will need ironed as well." My employer snapped one long manicured finger. "In fact, I think I'll send those home with you tonight. I know tomorrow's your day off, but it's a lot of work and I don't want you to fall behind."

"Yes, Mrs. Russell."

"Give me a moment and I'll grab them."

"But my bus—"

She cut me off with a wave of her hand as she moved toward

145

the stairs. "Nonsense. It will only take a minute. And besides, there will be another bus."

I watched her float up the wide carpeted steps, her long yellow georgette dress billowing out behind her. Ruffles cascaded from her shoulders to her waist, where a jeweled belt accentuated her slender figure—and perfectly matched the bracelets on her wrist. Her cream-colored heels barely registered a sound as she ascended.

Quietness was a sign of class. Only a poor person's shoes made noise.

Sure enough, by the time Mrs. Russell returned with the dresses, insisted I put them in garment bags, and gave an "Oh, would you please fix Cynthia a bedtime snack before you go?" I had missed my bus and had to wait twenty minutes in the stubborn early September heat for the next one. Twilight was creeping in when I finally arrived home. The darkness and grubbiness was still always a shock after a day spent in the Russells' Dallas palace. I needed to make more of an effort. The place wouldn't be so bad after a good, thorough cleaning. But after twelve hours of sweeping and dusting and scrubbing upper-class toilets, I simply had no energy to lift a finger for my own.

"Bea?"

"Yeah, it's me." I dropped my purse on the coffee table and hung the dresses on the coatrack before making my way to the kitchen. The windows were open, letting in the ever-present stench of sulfur from the factories. It wasn't helped by the smell of boiled cabbage and corned beef on the stove. Eleanor stood beside it, stirring with one hand, a book in the other. I gave her a tired smile. "What are you reading?"

She held it up. *The Mysterious Affair at Styles*.

"Agatha Christie, huh? Thought you weren't into mysteries?"

She shrugged. "I finished all the Oz books from the library. And I couldn't read *Dr. Dolittle* again."

I sat down at the table and pulled off my shoes. There was a hole in my stockings; my littlest toe was raw and red. I tried to tuck it back inside, but it popped right back out again. I sighed. Fantastic. Something else to mend.

Eleanor set a bowl in front of me with an apologetic grimace.

"Thank you. I'm starving." I took a bite to appease her, even though it burned the roof of my mouth. The cabbage was bitter, the corned beef salty, and the broth watery and flavorless. But it *was* food, made with love by my sweet sister, and its warmth stuck to the sides of my stomach. I gave her a smile. "It's good."

She let out a small laugh. Ladling herself a bowl, she sat down across from me.

"Mama at work?"

She shook her head.

"Oh, please don't tell me she's out with *him* again."

Eleanor scrunched her nose as she took a spoonful of stew. She swallowed with a curl of her lip and then nodded.

"Ugh. That's the third time this week. Does she even *work* anymore?" Jack had been in Eastham for five months, but despite the lack of funds rolling in from our *extracurricular activities*, my mother had refused to go back to double shifts at the factory. She claimed she couldn't, though we all knew it was simply because she *wouldn't*. Instead, she'd leaned in to her old standby: man hunting. I didn't mind *too* much. For the most part, it kept her distracted and out of my hair. She'd been too busy lately to throw around *I told you so*s about Jack, berate me about the pennies I put aside every few weeks for my next set of headshots (even though I hadn't had the energy or the heart to search for auditions in months), or criticize how haggard I was starting to look (though if I spent even a cent on makeup, she'd go through the roof). Though none of the men had been as wealthy as Charles Thomas, none of them had been as big of jerks, either.

Until this latest one.

Sylvester Hobbs owned a pawnshop at the corner of Comstock and Beatrice, a source of endless, inappropriate jokes every time he saw me: "Lotta traffic on Beatrice today. Even a few cars, too. Ha!" His jokes were as sleazy as his appearance. His thinning brown hair was always slicked back in a way that showed too much of his wide forehead and protruding ears. He reminded me very much of an overgrown rat in looks and in mannerisms, a sentiment his small watery eyes and twitchy mouth only served to enhance. I didn't like how he talked to me. I didn't like how he looked at me. And I certainly didn't like how he bossed my mother around like he owned her and our house.

I took another bite of stew and shook my head. "What does she see in that guy?"

Eleanor rubbed her thumb and first two fingers together in the universal symbol for money.

I sneered. "He doesn't have *that* much. And if he does, it's because everything he sells in that stupid shop is stolen. But no money in the world would be worth that man touching you."

My sister laughed. We finished our dinner in contented silence, and I helped her clean up the dishes before seeing her off to her study group. Three days a week, she traveled across the river to take a secretarial class, and on Saturdays, she met with some of the ladies in her class to practice and compare notes. She'd won a scholarship that paid for half her training, and I made it a point to fill in the gaps left from her nannying work with anything I could spare from my own, despite her protests. This was her ticket to a steady, decent-paying job, and I would do anything it took to make sure she finished the course. She was excelling, even with her stunted verbal skills, which was a testament not only to her brains but to her determination and drive.

Most days, it felt like the only thing stopping my star from fading completely was the spark it got from helping my sister ignite her own.

The house felt too empty after she'd gone. I gathered up the Russells' dresses and carried them into the kitchen. It was work I could do tomorrow, but if I did it now, I could truly enjoy my day off. It felt subversive, a way to stick it to Mrs. Russell, who obviously wanted to ensure I was working even when I wasn't working. I pulled Nana's old board and cast-iron presser from the pantry, placing it on the stove and lighting one of the gas rings. It was a tedious process, especially for garments as large as these dresses. The iron cooled quickly and would have to be reheated several times to ensure maximum sharpness to the folds. Luckily, neither dress was too terribly wrinkled; it wouldn't take long, and I would still have my Saturday night.

As if Saturday nights even meant anything anymore. I had no money, a boyfriend locked in Eastham Prison Farm, and Margaret, my lone friend—besides my sister—was married and engulfed in her newfound role of wife. No, Saturday nights were definitely not what they used to be. There were a lot of things lacking in my life, but I'd say *fun* was the thing I missed most of all. Perhaps even more than Jack himself.

Pressing the dresses took a little over an hour. By the time I finished, the sun had sunk completely, draping most of the house in shadows. I retreated up the stairs and into my room, flipping on the dim table lamp beside my bed and hanging the dresses from my closet door to ensure they remained wrinkle-free. Pulling a stack of envelopes from their hiding place under a loose floorboard, I removed the top one from beneath the rubber band holding them together.

My star,

    Why haven't you written? I understand it's hard for you, that you don't know what to say or even how to go on in this state of limbo, but your words are the only thing keeping me going in this place. The darkness here—the things I've seen, the things I've heard—is trying to drown me. I need you, Bea. Please write, even if it's just to tell me about the weather.

    At first, I was sad when I found out Emmett wouldn't be joining me here. I thought it would be nice to have an ally and familiar face, and I was almost angry when I found out he was heading to the Walls instead. But now, now I'm glad. Yesterday, I was one of five chosen to restrain the legs of another inmate while he got "the bat." The name sounds drab but the thing itself . . . the man had wounds all over his body when the guard finished. And we had to stand there and watch, hold the poor fellow still while the guard whipped him to a pulp.

    How's a man supposed to recover from that? And I'm not just meaning the one who was beat.

    I kept thinking to myself, "What if that had been Emmett?" I still can't believe he turned himself in, though I guess I should be thankful since it brought my sentence down to two years. But I couldn't bear to think of him seeing or doing the things I'm faced with every single day. I don't even want to tell you about them—and the worst of the things, I don't—but I can't keep it all bottled up inside. I'm scared, Bea. I'm scared every day. And not just for my body. For my soul.

*The field work is hard. The food is terrible. The nights
are restless and short. But it's the other things that bother me
most. The things that happen in private and in plain view
of all. The things the guards let slide and the things they
encourage. Things I would never taint your sweet heart with
knowing. All I can say is that, even after only a few short
months here, I feel somehow less human.*

And maybe that's the point.

*But that's why I need to hear from you, Bea. I've told you
before, I don't want you to visit me. I know that makes you
mad, but someone like you—so pure and so perfect—I don't
want you anywhere near this place. And as much as I want
you to wait for me, I understand if you find someone else,
as long as he treats you like the star you are. But please, can
you write me? I need the warmth of knowing we've touched
the same paper. That there is still good in this world and her
name is Beatrice Carraway.*

Please, Bea. I need you.

All my love, always and forever,

Jack

A familiar ache spread across my chest. I wasn't sure why I did
this to myself, reading his letters over and over again. The pain he was
enduring, the loneliness, the unspeakable savagery. It cut me to my
very core. How quickly his hope and defiance had faded, and how fast
despair and desperation rushed in to take their place. Even though I
hadn't physically seen him in months—he'd expressly forbidden me
from visiting him, and when I'd attempted to do so anyway, I'd been
shocked by his refusal to see me—I felt witness to his deterioration
as the hopelessness in his tone grew with each new letter.

He'd written me eleven times since he'd arrived at Eastham. I'd written three. It had been over a month since my last attempt.

It wasn't that I didn't care. It was the opposite really. I cared too much. I loved Jack with every fiber of my being, and the agony of his current condition—not to mention my own culpability in it and my impotence to do anything about it—was unbearable. My words wouldn't fix his state. And anyway, what would I say? Moaning about my boredom, my mother's creepy boyfriend, my menial job would be insensitive considering his alternative. Painting a false positivity would be dishonest, and perhaps even worse, he would either see right through and feel betrayed by my lies or else grow more depressed at the life he was missing. I could reassure him of my love, which had not waned, but even that somehow felt deceptive.

Because I didn't know how much longer I could hold on. I missed him. Every single day, his absence hit me anew, like a wound ripped open with each sunrise. My love for him was as real as the day I'd last seen him, running through the fields to lead the cops away from me. But the torture and misery of a life lived without him, unable to move forward and yet powerless to move back . . .

I felt stuck. It was painful to think of leaving him. But some days, it seemed even more painful to stay.

I reread Jack's letters to feel close to him, to cling to our connection. But they never made me feel better. Sighing, I tucked the letter back in its wrinkled envelope, slipping it under the rubber band and placing the entire stack under the floorboard. My mother didn't know I was still communicating with Jack, and I planned on keeping it that way. I couldn't bear to hear her snide remarks. I could bear even less being forced to answer questions about our relationship and our future—a future now as hazy and stagnant as the ever-present West Dallas smoke.

I crawled into bed and wrapped the blanket around me. I needed to shower, to brush my teeth, to change out of my itchy wool uniform. Needed even more to call up Margaret and beg her for a night out on the town. Instead, all I could bring myself to do was switch off my light, swallow the heaviness in my heart, and slip into a deep, restless sleep.

The sound of glass breaking woke me minutes or perhaps hours later. Darkness pressed in, my eyes straining as my mind struggled to catch up. Blood pounded in my ears. The house was silent. Had I dreamed it?

But then, from downstairs, more glass. I froze. Was someone breaking in? My mother loved to joke there was nothing worth stealing, but I knew West Dallas's ruffians could sniff out a source of possible income from a mile away. Shoot, they'd even steal Nana's old cast-iron presser if it meant a few coins from the salvage yard.

And I *had* left the iron sitting on the counter to cool. In full view of the window. Oh *no*.

A rock dropped into my stomach. Eleanor. I had to get to my sister.

I slid from my bed with bated breath, pausing after each step across the threadbare rug, and eased open my door. After only a moment's hesitation, I leapt across the hallway and into Eleanor's open doorway in an attempt to avoid the squeaky floorboard that separated our two rooms. I landed with a soft thud. My entire body tensed. I waited to hear footsteps on the stairs signaling I'd been found out.

There was nothing. But there was also nothing in Eleanor's room. She wasn't home yet. Thank goodness. She was safe.

My relief quickly faded as I heard another noise below my feet. I spun around, eyes scanning for something I could use as a weapon. I wouldn't rush into battle, but if the battle came to me . . .

Unfortunately, Eleanor was the least violent person in the world. The only thing I could find was a book—a thick, heavy dictionary. I positioned myself just inside her doorway with it, trying to will my heartbeat out of my throat long enough so I could hear. And hear I finally did. Voices. A man and a woman.

My mother and Sylvester Hobbs. Drunk, from the sound of it. And arguing.

Sighing, I put the dictionary back on Eleanor's desk and shuffled to my room, not bothering to avoid the creak in the hallway floorboard. I could only hope Sylvester would give up and storm out quickly; I was too tired to listen to a long fight like the last one they'd had. That one lasted nearly two hours before he finally walked out and slammed the door with such force, it cracked the corner of the front picture window.

I lay back down in bed and pulled the pillow over my head. It muted their voices. Not entirely but enough. I was just starting to slip back into a dream when a scream cut through the air. I sat bolt upright, clutching the blanket to my chin. The scream came again, this time louder and more insistent. My mother. And not angry this time, but in pain.

I flew down the stairs before logic had a chance to grab hold, bursting through the kitchen door with a shout. I squinted against the bright light. My mother sat on the floor, one hand holding her cheek. Drops of bright-red blood oozed out from between her fingers. Above her, broken beer bottle in hand, stood Sylvester. His chest heaved beneath an unbuttoned collar and skewed tie. The entire room smelled like alcohol and sweat. Neither registered my appearance, so focused were they on each other, until I stepped between them.

"You need to leave."

Sylvester blinked. A malicious smile spread across his face as his eyes finally cleared. "Well, look who it is."

"You need to leave," I repeated, trying to swallow the quiver in my voice.

He smoothed back a few loose strands of his greasy hair. "We was just talking."

"Looks like it."

"Beatrice, I'm fine." Behind me, my mother struggled to her feet. I grabbed her arm to help, gasping as a large gash revealed itself on her cheek. She had been slashed from mouth to ear, and blood poured from the angry, gaping wound. Not fatal but serious. The rest of her flesh was white, her forehead drenched with sweat.

"Mama!" I grabbed a towel off the nearby counter and pressed it against her cheek, moving her own hand to hold it in place. She winced with pain but did not fight. I narrowed my eyes at Sylvester. "Did you do this?"

He shrugged. "She shouldn't have been dancing with that other feller. I done warned her."

"I wasn't!" Something between a scream and sob erupted from my mother's lips. "He grabbed me, and I tried to push him away. Honest. You know me, Sylvester. It's only you. Just you—"

"Shut up!" he roared, throwing his arms in the air and startling both of us. My mother's grip on me tightened as I tried to pull her backward, away from his erratic swing. He raised the mouth of the broken bottle to his lip, narrowed his eyes at the lack of libation, then let out a chuckle when he realized his own absurdity.

He swayed as he returned his attention to us. "You ain't just been dancing. I know that. I hear the stories." His words slurred yet lost none of their menace.

"Sylvester, I swear—"

I squeezed my mother's arm, cutting off her words. "Get out of my house."

Sylvester's eyes bulged momentarily before he threw his head back in a loud, foul-smelling laugh. "You're a pistol, Beatrice. A real pistol. That's what I like about you." His glassy eyes crawled over my body. "I'll tell you what. I'll leave . . . if you dance with me."

Inside my stockings, my toes curled. I pulled my arms to my sides while keeping a firm grip on my mother.

His smile was hungry, his twitchy mouth wet and glistening with saliva. "Aw, come on. One dance and then I'll go. Your mama danced with some other feller, so I get to dance with you. Tit for tat, right?"

I felt my mother suck in her breath. Her nails dug into my forearm. But I didn't dare look at her. Not when Sylvester Hobbs appeared ready to pounce.

He took a step forward. "Come on, sweet thing. One little dance." He was close now. So close I could smell the tobacco on his breath, see the brown stains on his teeth, feel the heat radiating from his large, sweaty body. He rolled his tongue around the inside of his mouth, making a horrible, nauseating squishing sound.

When he stretched a hand forward to graze my collarbone, I didn't think. I didn't hesitate. I simply reacted, pulling my knee upward in one swift motion and connecting with his groin. His eyes rolled back in his head as he fell to his knees in front of me. I yanked the broken bottle from his hand and aimed the jagged end near his nose. "Get out of my house."

He stumbled backward, one hand shielding his face, the other clutching his lower half.

I pressed the bottle against his cheek hard enough to draw blood. *"Now."*

He half walked, half crawled down the hallway and to the front door. Curse words poured from under his strained breath. I kept the broken bottle against his back, only pulling it away when he was over the threshold. Then I lifted my foot and kicked as hard as I could, sending him flying down the front steps, before slamming the door and locking it behind him. Leaning my back against the wood, I held my breath, hoping he wouldn't try to come back in; the element of surprise was all I had. I'd be no match against his full fury.

Thankfully, after several tense minutes, I heard the scrape of his feet as he attempted to stand. Peering out the window, I could make out his hunched, stumbling shape dragging himself down the street and into the dark.

Only then did I exhale. Peeling my depleted form away from the door, I went back to the kitchen to check on my mother.

I found her at the table, a fresh towel pressed to her cheek. The old one was wadded into a crimson ball on the floor. I sat down beside her. "Let me take a look at it, Mama."

To my surprise, she recoiled, yanking her arm from under my touch. "Don't you dare."

"Ma, I know it's going to hurt, but I think you might need a doctor. I need to see—"

"Don't touch me!" she shrieked, pushing away from the table with such force, her chair fell backward.

My hand flew to my chest. "Mama?"

Black eyeliner had smudged above her cheekbones, giving her eyes a hollow, shrunken look. Within the eyes themselves, however, there was fire. "You ruin everything for me! Everything!" She clutched the side of the table and leaned forward until her face was inches from mine. Her breath reeked of whiskey. "Anytime I get a good thing going, you muck it up."

"What?" I sputtered. "Sylvester was *not* a good thing. You're probably going to need stitches."

"It's one small cut! One stupid fight, one tiny little scrape. What's that compared to the money he brings in, the security he can offer?" Even as she said this, the first traces of red were beginning to seep through the towel.

Small cut, indeed.

"And you went and chased him away!" she continued. "What would it hurt to have given him what he wanted, Beatrice? One little dance just to keep him happy."

My mouth fell open. My insides began to cramp. Surely she wasn't serious. "He didn't just want one little dance. You know that."

"Sylvester is *my* boyfriend!" she screamed, wincing as her wound opened further beneath the force of her wail. When she continued, she was quieter. "He's mine. All he wanted was a dance. Who do you think you are to insinuate otherwise?"

I pinched the bridge of my nose in disbelief. "Mama—"

"And it's not just Sylvester. We had a good thing going in Wingate with the pageants, until you grew out of your cuteness and everyone realized just how little talent you actually had."

I flinched as if I'd been struck. But either she didn't see or she didn't care.

"And then Charles! *Charles.* You ruined that with your sass and stubbornness."

"Charles tried to kill me!"

"Charles tried to *save* you! Save all of us! But it wasn't good enough for you! Nothing is ever good enough for Beatrice Carraway, especially if it involves placing another person's happiness above her own." Blood dripped from under the towel, landing with a silent plop on the floor below. "Even that boyfriend of yours."

My body stiffened.

She gave a nasty smile, made even more wicked by the smudge of blood near her lip. "Got himself locked up, rotting away, while you're out here, sitting pretty. You ruined him too. And you don't even care."

"Stop it." My eyes burned with unshed tears. "It's not true."

"Charles saw your wickedness, and that's why you made us run. Because it was a little too close to the truth. But all you've done since is prove him right. You're worthless, you're selfish, and your very soul is rotten." She swayed slightly. "You're no good, Beatrice. For anybody."

I fled then. Tears rolling down my cheeks, I burst from our house and into the darkened street, giving only a passing thought to Sylvester still lurking somewhere in the shadows. I ran without seeing, rocks poking my stockinged feet. I saw no one and no one saw me. Jack had said I was a star but he was in prison, broken, helpless, and alone, and in this moment, I was only a ghost. Or maybe I simply wanted to be.

Ramshackle houses melted into cardboard camps. The glow of campfires and peals of distant laughter wafted into my ears from those who had less, and yet somehow *more*, than me. I slowed to a walk momentarily as I passed the encampment, contemplating the homeyness of these "homeless" camps. I was romanticizing them, of course; the people within were unwashed, hungry, possibly drunk, and perhaps even criminal, but it was a testament to my despair that I could see nothing but how rich they looked at that moment, gathered together in their tents and shacks, sharing stories and songs around a fire. Safe.

I could join them, I thought. *Cast off everything and start fresh.* My mother wouldn't miss me. Eleanor would, of course, but she'd be better off. In the long run.

But even then, I'd find a way to ruin it. Just like I'd ruined everything—and everyone—else.

I walked on aimlessly. Dried tears began to crack on my cheeks, eyes burning from the exertion. A few cars rolled past, bumping over the hardened dirt streets, but otherwise it was quiet, the poverty and hopelessness a blanket that smothered West Dallas and muted it from the rest of the world. I paid little attention to where I was going; I had nowhere *to* go, and everything looked the same. After a few mindless turns, I didn't even know where I was anymore. So it was a surprise when I found myself where I did. Or maybe not a surprise at all.

I hadn't been here since before the arrest. In this light, the white clapboard storefront was gray, and the trim I knew to be green looked black. The large front office windows were darkened, but the faintest of lights glowed from the depths. Mr. and Mrs. Turner were inside, I knew, probably gathering around the dinner table. Reading the paper, smoking cigarettes, chatting about the weather, the price of wheat, the latest game between the Dodgers and the Phillies, and wondering if Dallas would ever get a team of its own. I wondered if they talked about Jack or Emmett. Wondered if they talked—or even thought—about me.

I walked up to the side of the building and placed a hand on the wall. A flake of paint came off on my palm. I stared at it for a moment before sinking to my knees in a fit of fresh sobs. What I wouldn't give to go back to that first night, even with Mrs. Turner's sourness. To Jack's smile and Alli's kindness and Emmett's laugh. To the warmth of the kitchen and the richness of the food and the sense of belonging and family made complete by Jack's touch and his words. The first confession of his love and my own. Before the world had pressed in, when it had still just been Jack and me.

The only time things had ever been good—when *I* had ever been truly good or at least seen that way—was when it had just been *us*. Jack and me. Together.

And now he was gone. Because of me.

My tears intensified. I wanted to go inside. To be in the place where Jack had lived, breathe his air, touch his clothes, try to connect with him, the old him, the Jack he'd been before the robberies and Eastham. But I couldn't. Not only would I look insane, but Mrs. Turner was no fan of mine. She probably blamed me for what had happened to her sons, and not without merit. But still I pressed myself up against the side of the building, as if the remnants of Jack's presence would somehow flow through the weathered boards.

"Beatrice?"

I scrambled to my feet, slapping at my cheeks. Gravel crunched beneath footsteps as a woman approached. For a moment, I considered running. But then Alli Turner materialized out of the darkness. In the dim light, I couldn't tell if her Hooverette-style dress was black or navy blue. All I could really see was the white-trimmed pockets and ruffled sleeves. Her hair was pulled back from her face in two braids that merged behind her head. A large lumpy *something*—which I later determined to be a wicker basket—hung from her forearm.

"Beatrice," she repeated. "That *is* you! What are you doing out here?" She paused for a moment, and I knew she was taking in my tearstained face and lack of shoes. "Are you okay?"

It was the kindness in her voice that did it. No judgment, no criticism, not even a hint of aversion. Just genuine, loving concern. It was more than I deserved, especially from her. I began to sob once more.

The basket dropped to her feet and her arms were around me within seconds, the smell of lilac enveloping me as she pressed my head into her shoulder. "Shh, Beatrice. It's okay. It's okay."

"No, it's not," I hiccuped. "I miss Jack. I . . . I can't do this without him. I'm so tired of being strong and doing this on my own. I can't make it two years. I can't make it one more day. I need him. I need us. I need . . ." But my needs and my words collapsed under the weight of my sorrow.

Alli held me as grief racked my body, strong and steady against my trembles. She smoothed my hair and rubbed my back, speaking gentle hushes into my ear, just as I imagined a real mother would do. A mother who was not *my* mother.

After several minutes, she pulled away slightly, her green eyes locked on my own. "Why don't you come home with me?"

I tensed under her grip. "I couldn't. I—"

But she talked over me. "Nonsense. My apartment is only a couple of blocks over. I was here dropping off some soup for Sarah. I know it's late, but she hasn't been feeling well ever since . . ." She coughed and picked up her basket.

I knew what she'd been about to say. Since Jack. Since Emmett.

"Anyways, I had some left over, and it's too much for just one person. It will spoil before I can eat it all."

The tightness spread from my chest to the back of my throat. She was alone now too. Her husband was in jail, where I should have been. Why was she talking to me as if that wasn't true?

"Let me leave it inside and then we'll go back to my place. What you need right now is some hot tea and a good night's sleep."

"Alli . . ." Her kindness was almost unbearable, needling my guilt from its hiding spot beneath my sadness.

"I won't take no for an answer. I mean, what kind of person would I be if I let a woman walk home in the dark alone?"

"But you were walking alone."

She let out an amused burst of air through her nose. "True." She tilted her head back and forth as if considering. "But I, for one, am at least wearing my shoes."

CHAPTER SEVENTEEN

I awoke the next morning in a fog, back stiff and muscles weak. My throat ached. It felt as if every ounce of moisture had been leeched from my body. Bright sunlight blinded me when I managed to rip my eyes open, the lids puffy and swollen together, and it took several minutes for me to remember where I was.

The lumpy brown couch. The orange-and-yellow wool blanket. And on the wall just above me, a simple wooden cross.

The events of the night before came flooding back. My mother, Sylvester, the fight, her words. Her horrible, truthful *words*. Fleeing from one pain only to collapse inside another outside Jack's house. The unexpected solace of Alli's embrace. I glanced down, pinching the worn fabric of one of Alli's nightshirts in between my thumb and forefinger. She'd given me clothes and food and a place to rest. Most importantly, she'd given me silence; she hadn't pried, hadn't meddled, hadn't even really spoken. She'd simply tucked me onto her couch and let sleep take me.

But I was awake now. And I needed to leave before she could offer me any more undeserved kindness.

I slipped out of her nightshirt and back into the itchiness of my uniform, realizing with an internal groan just how soiled it had become. I'd have to spend the day cleaning it before returning to the Russells' tomorrow. I pulled on my stockings (even more holey now than before and, more than likely, beyond repair) and was just starting to tiptoe toward the door when I heard a key in the lock. I froze midstride.

Alli stepped inside. She wore a dark-green taffeta dress with capelet sleeves and a narrow brown belt. The pleated hem landed midcalf and swung like a bell when she moved. A large brown bow rested near her collarbone, its rich chocolate color the same hue as the slouch-style hat atop her head. She smiled when she saw me. "Good morning, Beatrice."

I wrapped my arms around myself. "Good morning. You . . . look very pretty," I managed.

She raised and lowered one shoulder in a *this old thing* gesture. "Thank you. It's the nicest dress I own. The only thing, really, that hasn't been mended or repurposed a hundred times. Emmett bought it for me on our honeymoon. I thought it was too much, but he insisted. Said it could be my church dress. So, you know—" she held up the Bible in her hand as if in explanation—"church."

Of course. It was Sunday. And Alli was into all the Sunday morning *stuff.* Suddenly the need to escape was even greater than before. I cleared my throat and took a tentative step forward. "Thank you again for the hospitality last night. But I really need to be going."

"Are you sure? You're welcome to stay. I'm getting ready to fix lunch." She removed her hat, pulling out a few pins and letting her hair fall down over her shoulders. "I didn't want to wake you this morning by clanging around in the kitchen before church. So I am absolutely starving now. You must be too."

"I really have to go." But at that moment, my stomach growled loudly in the ultimate act of betrayal. I pushed my hands against it, trying to stifle the noise.

Alli laughed. "Come on. Let's eat."

I followed her grudgingly into the small kitchen, where sunlight streamed in from a square window above her sink, causing dust in the air to glitter. "What time is it?"

"Almost noon. You were exhausted."

I sat down at the small two-person table that sat flush against the wall. Noon. I wondered if my mother was worried about me or even cared where I was. Probably not. Eleanor might. But she also might have assumed I'd gone to Margaret's. If Mama had cleaned up the blood and broken glass in the kitchen, that is. I hoped she had.

Alli plucked a small package from her icebox. "Bologna okay?"

My stomach let out another audible growl.

"I'll make you two," she said, winking. Her kitchen looked smaller this morning than it had last night but no less pleasant. A row of neat white cabinets with a wood-burning stove and chest-high icebox. No frills, no extravagance, save for the light-blue curtain in the window and small potted lavender plant on the sill, which gave the room a slight, but pleasing, floral scent. The walls were covered with the same drab paper as the living room, and the floor was dark wood, scratched and scuffed but hidden for the most part by a rug the same color as the curtains.

This room—the entire apartment really—was sparse and

obviously poor. Nevertheless, there was an air of abundance here I hadn't experienced anywhere else in West Dallas.

"Did you sleep okay?" Alli was asking over her shoulder. "That couch has a loose spring that can be a doozy if you move in the wrong way."

"It was fine. Thank you. Again."

She put a plate in front of me—sure enough, with two sandwiches—and sat down in the other chair with her own. I lifted one to my lips but stopped when I noticed her head was bowed.

Praying. She was praying.

I bit the inside of my cheek as I waited for her to tell me to bow along with her, to berate me before God the way Charles had done with his mealtime prayers. Instead, she remained silent, her head dipped to her chest. Then she lifted her gaze and gave me a smile before grabbing her sandwich and taking a big bite.

I did the same, slowly, averting my eyes as I chewed. She'd prayed silently. There was no show, no rebuke, no grasping for control. Just Alli and her God, quietly, reverently, privately.

Somehow it unsettled me even more than Charles's prayers used to do.

"I wish I could offer you more," she said, swallowing. "With Emmett gone, I've had to stretch things a bit further than normal, even with only one mouth to feed now. Though I take anything I can spare over to Sarah, more to check in on her than to feed her. Nowadays, I eat more bologna sandwiches than I care to admit." She chuckled. "But I try to mix it up. Fried bologna, pickled bologna, bologna casserole, bologna salad. Emmett's going to be blown away when he gets home with just how many ways you can use bologna."

She laughed again, but I didn't see what was funny. "How do

you do it?" I asked, my tone more bitter than I intended. "With Emmett . . . away, I mean?"

"Sarah and Earl help, of course. I do some bookkeeping for them at the garage, and they pay me what they can. Plus I make a little money on the side, doing some nursing jobs in the neighborhood."

"You're a nurse?"

"Not formally trained, no. But my mother was a nurse, and I learned a lot from her before she passed away. Most people here can't afford to see a doctor for every cut or fever, so they call me. I know enough to help with simple remedies or first aid. They pay me what they can, sometimes with money, sometimes with food or other goods." She gave a shake of her head. "It's crazy, actually. I've learned so much over the past few months. Skills I never would have had the time to master if things weren't the way they are."

The way they are. This woman was finding a silver lining even in her husband's incarceration.

"But the biggest thing keeping me afloat," she continued, "is my faith."

Bologna solidified in my stomach.

"The church provides so much. Food, funds, even the occasional handyman work when I need it. And God . . ." Her words fell off into a smile. "Well, He provides everything else."

"Except a husband," I muttered under my breath.

Alli paused midbite. "What was that?"

I should have let it drop. Finished my sandwich, passed on my thanks, and moved on with my day. Alli had been kind to me. Her faith—as foolish as it might have been—wasn't hurting me in any tangible way.

So why in the world did I feel so suddenly, inexplicably *angry*?

"I don't understand you." I dropped my sandwich onto my

plate. "This whole God thing. It doesn't make any sense. How in the world could you choose to love a God that has condemned your husband? How could you choose *Him* over Emmett?"

Alli's eyes widened. "Bea, what—?"

"This God you're raving about—you do realize He hates stealing and drinking and any other number of things we do? Considers those who do them wicked, I believe it says in the Bible. Hates them. That includes your husband." *And me.* "We can never be good enough for Him, and yet He doesn't help—He sits up there and judges us, sentencing us to hell when we're just trying to do what we need to do to *survive.*" My voice was getting shriller, but I found myself unable to stop it. "How could you possibly love a God like that? One who made your husband go live in a dank, dirty cell, away from his wife, all to appease His view of right or wrong? A view, might I add, He has the luxury of forcing on us even though He doesn't have to live in the same vile, unfair world we do."

"Bea—"

"That isn't love. Not a God worth loving and definitely not a God who loves you."

Even though it was high noon, I swore I heard crickets outside the window, so loud was the silence left behind by my rant. But it felt good. Good to finally be honest, show Alli how I really felt, the person I truly was.

Maybe now she'd stop being so nice to me.

Across from me, Alli swallowed her bite with a loud gulp, as if the bread in her mouth had gone dry. She placed the remainder of her sandwich on her plate and wiped the crumbs from her palms before leaning forward, elbows on the table. Her gaze didn't flinch from my own. "I don't know who's been telling you about God, but He doesn't *hate* people, Beatrice. It's not in His nature. He loves us. He *is* love, in fact. He loves us so much, He sent His Son to die for us so we wouldn't *have* to be condemned, even though, you're right, we are wicked."

"So you agree—"

She held up her hand, silencing me. "I agree we are all wicked. Maybe we don't all steal or kill or whatnot, but we all do and say things that go against the holiness God desires for us. But that does not mean we are condemned to hell. It only means we need saving."

In an instant, I was back in Wingate, my head beneath the filmy waters of the trough, Charles's hot breath in my ears.

"No one can save us," I managed, my words thick with the memory.

Alli leaned back, crossing her arms over her chest. "You're right. I can't save Emmett any more than you can save Jack. Or yourself. No one can. Only Jesus."

Again, Charles's words clouded my ears. The smell of manure, the chill of the water, the intense pressure in my lungs. I sank in on myself, drawing my elbows to my stomach.

"Beatrice? Are you okay?"

I shook my head, trying to force Charles back into the box I'd kept him in. "I'm fine."

And suddenly her warm hand was on mine. I looked up to find her arm stretched across the table, her lips pressed together in a sad smile. "Jesus loves you, Beatrice. I don't know what you've done or what's happened in your past to make you think otherwise, but I'm here today to tell you the truth: He loves you. And it's a love you can't outrun or outsin. He knows every thought you've had, every word you've said, everything you've ever done—and yet still He loves you."

I hated her words. They were stupid and fantastical, the longings of a child or the musings of the deluded. Painful and lovely all at the same time, it was everything I didn't want to hear and had been waiting to hear my entire life. I wanted her to be quiet and keep talking at the same time. Most of all, though, I wanted to leave. Because if I didn't leave right this second, I was going to start crying . . . and once I started, I didn't know if I'd be able to stop.

Alli squeezed my hand. "Beatrice."

"I was there." The words fell from my lips. I don't know why I said them. As soon as they were out, I wanted to take them back. But the pain of releasing them was buoyed by relief, as if the weight on my heart had lifted. Alli tilted her head as I pulled my hand away. "That night with Emmett and Jack. I was there. I was part of it."

The skin above her lips expanded as she held in a breath. "I know," she said finally. "Emmett told me. But he made me promise not to say anything. Jack went to prison trying to protect you, he said. He didn't want that to be for nothing."

"But don't you hate me?" *And doesn't your God?* "Your husband is sitting in a jail cell while I walk free. I had all these reasons for not turning myself in, but when it comes down to it . . . it's not right. That I escaped punishment and they didn't."

"I wouldn't exactly say you've escaped punishment, Bea. Would you?"

Her tone was kind but the truth in her words cut. I'd spent so much time hating myself for walking free that I'd built a prison of my own guilt. I'd been working myself ragged, not allowing myself to experience any little bit of joy. I'd told myself I was doing it for Jack, to give him something good and straight to come home to after his sentence, but really I was doing it for myself. To earn the forgiveness I'd sworn I didn't need for crimes I'd refused to admit out loud.

Until now.

"What you have to understand is Emmett's confession was about more than that night. There are crimes in his past—crimes he'd gotten away with, at least in the eyes of the law—that his heart was still struggling with. He came to faith when he met me, and although he believed in Christ, it was still hard for him to accept His forgiveness. It's one thing to say the words; it's another to feel them in your heart."

I stared down at my lap. I hadn't realized I'd been picking my cuticles. Drops of blood lined my thumbnail.

"He didn't give himself up for me. He didn't even really give himself up for God. He did it for himself. Accepting responsibility and facing consequences was what he felt was needed to finally clear the space in his soul to truly let God in. Breaking down that wall of guilt he'd built." She paused. "Beatrice, will you please look at me?"

I took a deep breath. Raised my head.

Alli's arm was stretched across the table between us, her fingers open as if waiting for my own. But I couldn't bring myself to accept the invitation. After a moment, she pulled it back and rested her chin in her palm.

"When I showed up that day Emmett turned himself in, I didn't do it because I was mad at you or wanted to see you punished. I did it because I have seen firsthand what happens when you let unconfessed guilt take root in your soul. I didn't come see you because I hated you; I did it because I care too much about you to see you fall into the pit Emmett is struggling to crawl out of."

I pressed my fingertips to my eyelids, trying to hold back tears. It was all too much to take in. Charles had spent so much time attempting to beat the wickedness out of me. Heavy-handed discipline was the only way to save my soul and appease his horrid version of God.

And then . . . then there was Alli.

Alli, who told me she couldn't save my soul, but her God could. That it wasn't my wickedness keeping me from Jesus, but my own brokenness. And most astoundingly, that it wasn't punishment that would bring me back to Him, but love . . . love He freely and willingly gave.

I wondered how two people could both claim to know Jesus and come up with completely different views of Him. I wondered how their servitude could take such vastly different forms. Most importantly, I wondered who was right.

"Can I pray with you?"

Her question shocked me out of my own mind. I shook my head violently. I wasn't ready for that. Wasn't even sure I *wanted* that.

"Okay, okay," she said quickly. "Can I pray then? Not out loud, just to myself, while you sit here with me?"

I finally met her eyes. There was no reproof in them; in fact, they shimmered with tears just as my own did. I gave her a shaky nod.

And so we sat there, the two of us holding hands as Alli lifted her silent words to a God I wasn't sure how to take. All I knew was that I felt less alone in this moment than I had since I'd last seen Jack, and the despair that hung like a cloak over my heart, while still there, felt lighter, as if the lining had been removed for the spring.

When she finally led me to the door, I found myself inexplicably promising to return soon. What was even more inexplicable was that I actually meant it.

CHAPTER EIGHTEEN

The eraser was bitter in my mouth. I pulled it out, spitting tiny pieces of rubber into my fingers and wiping them on my dress. It was an old one, cheap red cotton with tiny white blooms, that I'd retrimmed with black tulle from a worn-out scarf to create ruffles around the gathered sleeves and side pockets. I'd gotten handy with my sewing abilities since starting at the Russells'. So handy, in fact, that Mrs. Russell no longer ordered out a seamstress but brought her garments to me . . . and paid me an extra ten cents for every piece of cloth I mended.

I wiggled my pencil in the air. *That* was something I could tell Jack. He'd be proud of my new skills and resourcefulness for sure.

I've gotten quite good at sewing. Mrs. Russell now uses me exclusively for all but her fanciest alterations. And my own dresses? I can take the most boring housedress from the Sears and Roebuck catalog—even the horrid cheap ones with the itchy fabric—and turn it into something spectacular using scraps of fabric lying around the house. I know you're picky, but I may be so good you'll even let me tackle some of your suits when you get out.

I paused, pencil poised over the paper, then erased the last sentence. I didn't want to remind Jack of his suits, not when I knew he'd been forced into T-shirts and jeans or, worse, jumpsuits for the past year. And when he got out, who knew what use he'd have for the suits anyway? More than likely, he'd be off to factory work and the suits sold for extra money. Shaking the taste of rubber from my mouth (I'd once again absentmindedly stuck the eraser between my teeth), I started a new paragraph:

I got a letter from Margaret last week. She and George are doing well and really enjoying Austin. It was a heck of a blow when George's father's body shop went under, but he's found good work at a dealership there. She said the money was enough they were hoping to be able to order a house soon—you know those kits you can get out of magazines? George is going to build it himself, and Margaret hopes he gets it done before the baby arrives. She thinks it's a girl, but George swears up and down it's a boy. I guess we'll find out who's right in about four months!

Speaking of babies, I have good news. I got a role in a play! It's only a small role in a Summer in the Park production of Sir Arthur and His Knights next month. I'm "woman with a

*baby." It doesn't pay a cent, and I'm only in three scenes, but
I'm onstage again! Oh, Jack, I wish you could see it. But I
know you will see the bigger roles that will surely come my way
now. When you get out, your star will blow you a kiss from the
bright lights of a real stage, my love. Can you picture it?*

I paused again, debating. Did the last paragraph sound too
happy? I mean, it was hard *not* to be; this was my first successful audition in years, and I'd snagged it only two weeks after Alli
had finally convinced me to start trying again. Not that I'd mention anything about Alli to Jack. Our friendship was one of many
details I always left out of my letters.

I glanced at the Bible on my desk, the one Alli had given me
and I'd slowly begun to peruse, hesitant but curious. *That* was
another thing I never spoke about to Jack. He made no secret of his
feelings about Alli, how her religious nonsense had led to Emmett's
unnecessary surrender and suffering when Jack had been willing to
take the fall for all of us. I couldn't imagine his response if I told
him I was dipping a toe in those same waters.

Or his response if he knew that, while I still wasn't 100 percent
sure I'd found God, I *had* found a friend. And outside of Eleanor,
she was the truest, most patient, and kindest friend I'd ever had.

But honestly, I couldn't imagine a lot of things about Jack
nowadays. He'd been in prison for a little over a year, a full thirteen
months since I'd last seen or touched him. And while I could still
picture his face—his eyes, his lips, his smile—could still remember
the feel of his skin and the strength of his arms, that Jack felt more
like a memory. And not just because of the absence of his sight,
his touch, his smell, but because my Jack, the one I loved, was not
the one writing the letters I received twice a month from Eastham
Prison Farm.

My Jack was sensitive; prison Jack was coldhearted and cyni-cal, reporting on the beatings (and worse) of fellow inmates with a callousness that hardened a little more with each letter. My Jack was demure, wanting to do his time and get back home to me; prison Jack was confrontational and bitter, telling me stories about how he challenged guards and doubted he'd ever actually be set free. My Jack wanted to marry me and start a family; prison Jack spoke nothing of the future or life on the outside. His whole world—his thoughts, his friends, his ambitions—rarely ventured outside the concrete walls or barbed wire fence. Alli confided in me that he'd stopped writing his parents. And though his letters to me continued, albeit less frequently than they had in the past, they sounded more like aggrieved diary entries than expressions of love and longing.

Which is why I wrote enough for the both of us. I was scared for him, for the person he was becoming . . . and for the fact that it was my fault. Over the past eight months, Alli and I had spoken a lot about guilt and forgiveness. While my heart felt as if it were healing slowly, the pain and disgrace of Jack's incarceration—and Emmett's—left a wound all this Jesus talk hadn't quite reached.

So I'd gone from too few letters to perhaps too many. But no matter how negative, how disillusioned, or how embittered his words, I made sure to fill mine with light, with love, and with assurances of our eventual happiness. It was a delicate balance, staying positive without sounding overly content, and the result was often rewritten several times over and full of glaring omissions I felt distressed about cutting out.

Because the truth was I *was* content, for the first time in my life. Things weren't perfect. I wasn't rich. I wasn't famous. In fact, in many ways, life was still downright hard. But somehow I felt a kind of tranquility I'd never experienced before. We didn't have much, no, but Eleanor and I had a safe place to live and food to eat. I had a decent if not glamorous job. I was even acting again, even though the roles were small and the lights dim. I was doing it because I enjoyed it, not because it was a means to an end. And it was all because I had a friend—a true friend—who loved and encouraged me . . . and who was trying to introduce me to a way of living that was bigger than myself.

But not in the ways Jack and I had always imagined.

Which meant it was a nuanced contentment I couldn't share with the man I loved.

I signed off the letter with my usual *I love you*s and promises to write again soon and spritzed the paper with a hint of Bellodgia by Caron, a French perfume Mrs. Russell had given me as a Christmas present. It made me feel exotic, even in my frumpy maid's uniform, as if I were hiding a secret beneath the ugly black wool. I hoped Jack liked it as much I did; he never mentioned it, but I sprayed it on each letter all the same.

"El?" I slipped the paper into an envelope and dropped it in my purse. It was only four; Mrs. Russell had let me off early, owing to a charity dinner they had that evening. If I hurried, I'd be able to catch the Saturday evening mail pickup while I was out. "El, I'm heading over to Alli's!"

My sister popped her head in my bedroom. "Market?"

"I can stop by on my way home. What do you need?"

She tilted her head back and forth, thinking. "Potatoes? Chipped beef over fried potatoes for dinner?"

"Oooh. Sounds delicious. How about I grab some bananas for pudding too? If they have any, that is."

"Bea, rent is due—"

I pulled a dime from my pocket, a gift from a skirt alteration I'd done for Cynthia Russell yesterday, and grinned. "My treat."

She nodded and rubbed her hands together like an excited toddler, causing me to giggle.

"I'll be home by six. I'm just stopping by to drop off this book she let me borrow." I held it up.

Eleanor squinted at it. "Dorothy L. Sayers?"

"They're poems," I said, shoving it into my bag. "Alli thought I'd like them."

"Did you?"

I smiled. "Yeah. I did." I grabbed a cardigan off the back of my chair. "Anyway, I won't be gone long. I don't want to miss your day off. They're so few and far between now, Miss Secretary."

Eleanor blushed and looked down at her feet. I was embarrassing her, I knew . . . but I also knew she liked it. She was proud of what she'd accomplished, as she should have been. She'd finished secretarial school in December and scored a job at an advertising agency downtown, filing paperwork and taking shorthand—telephone duties were left to someone else. It was a steady, Monday through Friday, eight-to-six job with excellent pay, which she supplemented with babysitting jobs on the weekend, simply because she loved kids. That in addition to my work at the Russells' meant that, while we weren't rich, we were well-off enough to afford our own place.

That's right. Eleanor and I had moved out from under Mama's roof and into our own two-bedroom apartment beside the Trinity River. We were still in West Dallas, but we were far enough from the factories to allow for clearer skies. The roads here were paved and did not turn to muddy creeks when it rained, and—best of all—there were no drunk boyfriends of Mama's showing up on our doorstep at all hours of the night.

We were safe. No, Eleanor was safe, and that was the most important thing. We had a good thing going. Not easy. Not perfect. But good.

The early May sun was warm on my skin as I left our apartment. So warm I left my cardigan tucked over the top of my purse. I was just in time to grab the bus. As it ventured deeper into West Dallas, the pinks and yellows of trees in bloom along the banks of the river faded into the familiar drab grays and browns of the slums. The blue of the sky disappeared beneath the usual smoke, blocking the sun and causing a chill that forced my cardigan around my shoulders after all. But it didn't bother me. I was too busy thinking of Alli, of the promise of warm coffee and even warmer conversation, followed by an evening of delicious food and board games with my sister. When the bus stopped, I exited and paused by the nearest mailbox, the unsettled feeling that always accompanied thoughts of Jack vanishing into the dark recesses along with the letter.

I climbed the steps to Alli's apartment, giving three swift knocks on the door.

There was a murmur of voices, breaking off just long enough for Alli's giggly command to come in.

I pushed open the door, pulling her book from my purse as I did. "It's me! I just stopped by to drop off your . . ." The volume fell from my hands with a thud much too loud for paper on carpet.

"Hey, Bea. Long time no see."

Emmett grinned up at me from his seat on the couch. Beside him sat a dark-haired man with a familiar, expectant smile.

Jack.

CHAPTER NINETEEN

Alli hugged me first. "Isn't it wonderful?" she breathed in my ear. She smelled like lilac, and I noticed as she pulled away that she was wearing her church dress, even though it wasn't Sunday. I smiled but my tongue remained frozen to the roof of my mouth.

Emmett was next. His embrace was strong and swift, more like a brotherly squeeze than an actual hug, the damp fabric under his arms warm and moist against my upper arms. "It's good to see you," he said with a laugh. "Were you surprised? We wanted it to be a surprise."

I nodded, feeling dumb. Why couldn't I speak?

And then he and Alli stepped back as if parting the sea, leaving Jack and me alone in the middle. The late-afternoon sun slanted through the window, casting an orange pall and adding to the dreamlike atmosphere. Was it really him? Was he really here?

His hair was longer, and it wasn't slicked back in its usual style. Instead, a stray lock fell across his forehead, brushing the tops of his eyebrows. His cheeks were hollow and covered in a fine layer of stubble. Dark circles ringed the skin around his eyes. That million-dollar smile was still on his face, but it was unfamiliar. Older. He twisted his fingers in front of his abdomen as his gaze flitted between me and the floor.

He was Jack . . . but he wasn't. And somehow these few feet between us seemed a bigger distance than the two hundred miles to Eastham ever had.

The floorboard creaked. Alli. Alli was still here. Her presence snapped the tight coil around my nerves, and I took a step forward, freeing Jack to do the same.

Within seconds, his arms were around me. My rigid muscles struggled to respond. He felt different, sinewy rather than muscular, and his hands lacked the confidence they'd once had. It was as if they were soiled, and he was unsure where to put them without polluting me. Even the texture of his clothes—a rough white T-shirt and jeans rather than the smooth fabric of a suit—felt awkward. I forced my hands to his shoulders, narrower now, and gave them a quick pat before taking a step out of his embrace.

He met my eyes for only a moment before looking at the floor, but it was long enough for me to see the damage I'd done. The ways I had disappointed him. This was not how either of us had pictured our reunion. He was supposed to be different; I was supposed to be different. And not in the ways we actually were.

Tension filled the space between us, pressing against the very walls, until at last, Emmett cleared his throat. His voice echoed with forced cheer. "Let's have a drink!"

Alli disappeared into the kitchen and returned with two bottles of beer and two glasses of ginger ale. I pretended not to notice Jack noticing me. I'd never turned down a beer with him. When we clinked our drinks together, he looked only at Emmett.

The four of us settled into the small living room, Alli, Emmett, and Jack on the couch, me in a chair brought in from the kitchen. Alli rubbed the back of her husband's head and gazed at him with stars in her eyes as he sipped. Emmett kept one hand on his beer bottle, the other firmly around Alli's waist. His fingers pinched the fabric of her dress as if to continuously remind himself she was real. Jack, on the other hand, sat pressed against the far side, his knees turned away from his brother's, eyes in his lap. He picked at the label on his drink.

My ginger ale grew warm in my palm. The need to fill the silence suddenly became more powerful than my desire to remain quiet. "How . . . how are you *here*?" I managed.

Emmett laughed. "Well, we didn't break out, if that's what you're meaning."

I shook my head. "No, of course not."

"Parole! We made parole! Both of us, if you can believe it." He gave Alli's hip a squeeze. "Rumors had been floating up through the grapevine for months. Apparently Governor Moody had done a tour of some of the prisons a while back, and he was so offended by what he saw—how overcrowded everything was, no food, no beds, no medicine, that kind of thing—he ordered an immediate review of all cases to see what inmates met the 'rehabilitation' requirements for release, even if they hadn't yet fully met their sentence. 'Course, then he got ousted by Sterling, and everyone thought that was the end of it. But lo and behold, my name came up and—" he lifted his bottle in a mock salute—"here I am."

"It was God, baby. All God." Alli nuzzled her face in his neck. "His blessing for your doing the right thing." She kissed him tenderly.

On the other end of the couch, Jack shifted. Our eyes met momentarily before he looked away again. But not before I saw the look of pure loathing on his face.

"I am surprised they let you out, though," Emmett said after breaking away. He hit Jack playfully on the knee with the back of his hand. "I heard rumors all the way over in Huntsville about you. Mouthin' off to the guards, gettin' in fights. How in the world did you get paroled with that record, Little Brother?"

"Because I was one of the few there who hadn't killed anybody."

His words landed like a cement block. For the first time, Emmett's smile left his face. We'd all known the types of people Jack had been around at Eastham, far different from the sorts housed with Emmett in Huntsville. But it was different hearing it come from his mouth, so matter-of-fact. From outside the open window, the sound of children playing in the street below wafted in, their giggles and delighted screams almost obscene in the taut silence.

"Well, I still say it was God," Alli said, trying to break the mood. "God and your mama. All those letters she wrote to the governor—one nearly every single day—for *both* of you. She never knew if he was actually reading them, but she never stopped trying. Never gave up hope."

"And neither did you." Emmett's smile returned as he looked at his wife.

Alli shook her head. "I wrote a few. As many as I could muster. But your mama? She could fill a book."

The two of them giggled. Jack did not. And neither did I. I hadn't written a single letter to the governor. I should have, told Alli I would . . . but I never did. Maybe it was because of my own guilt. Or maybe because I simply didn't know what to say and never felt my opinion would truly matter. Or perhaps, if I was being honest, it was because I didn't want any more attention put on me by anyone in government or law enforcement than was necessary. For all my words and promises to Jack, I hadn't really upheld my end. He'd gone to jail for me, and for what? The fire of hope was never something I'd even let smolder, let alone truly burn.

And maybe that was why Alli was in her lover's lap while I was halfway across the room from mine.

"I need to get some air." Jack stood and placed his empty bottle on the floor with an aggressive thud.

I winced as the door slammed behind him. It felt like a slap. A public goodbye he was too wounded and too polite to speak. I blinked back sudden tears, placing my lukewarm glass of still-full ginger ale on the coffee table. "I . . . I have to be going any-way," I said thickly, pulling on my cardigan even though sweat had soaked through the back of my dress. "I promised Eleanor I'd run to the market before dinner."

"Oh, stay!" Alli said, jumping up from her spot and grabbing my hand. "I was going to make some chicken. The kind with the lemon juice Emmett loves. There will be plenty. Stay and celebrate with us, Bea."

I shook my head and tucked my purse under my arm. "I wish I could, but I promised El. Saturday nights are our nights, remember?"

"She's invited too!"

I shook my head again, more vigorously this time. The tears were close. It wouldn't be long and I'd be sobbing. "I can't. I have to go."

"Okay, if you're sure . . ."

I gave her a quick one-armed hug, making sure to keep my face turned away. "Welcome home, Emmett. I'm very happy for you.

For both of you." I pushed my way toward the door, thankful the apartment was so familiar. My vision was too blurry to see clearly. "Let's get together soon."

"Are you sure you—?"

Alli's question was cut short as I crossed over the threshold and down the steps. Outside, the warm breeze did nothing to stifle my tears. Instead, it served as a release, and as I leaned against the brick facade, my sobs came out in long, choking rivulets. Jack had been away for over a year, but it was only in this moment that he truly felt gone.

I'd thought I was moving forward in an attempt to make things better for us. What I'd failed to consider was, just because I was going one way didn't mean Jack was following. In fact, he couldn't. I hadn't even invited him along for the ride. It shouldn't have been a surprise that now, here in the flesh, he was a stranger, and I only someone he used to know.

And yet it was. A brutal, heart-wrenching surprise.

"Bea?"

I jumped at the sound of his voice, dropping my purse as I ripped myself from the side of the building. He picked it up and held it out to me. As he took in my tears, his face crumpled briefly before hardening back into its uncomfortable mask. Our fingers brushed as I took the purse, that old spark flaring momentarily and causing unexpected chills to sprout over my arms. He snatched his hand back quickly, stuffing both hands into his pockets. He'd felt it too. I knew he had.

And yet he'd still pulled away.

I straightened, swallowing another round of weeping. "It was good to see you, Jack. I'm really glad you're home."

He gave a slight nod.

"I . . . I have to go. Eleanor's waiting."

I forced myself to take a step past him. And then another. And then another. *Just get to the bus stop. Hold it together until the bus stop.*

"Bea?"

Against all rationale and reason, I turned around. Jack remained where he was, his silhouette framed by the falling twilight. He looked even smaller out here, more a boy than a man, and even though his face was hidden in shadow, I had the distinct impression he was frowning.

"Will you take a walk with me?"

I knew I shouldn't. But I loved him still; it took a broken heart to show me just how much, despite everything. And for the burdens he had carried for me over the past year, I owed him. More than a walk, for sure, but it was only a walk he was requesting. So I found myself falling in step beside him.

The children from earlier had retreated into their homes for dinner. The street was empty save for a few rumbling cars and elderly couples out for a stroll before the ruffians emerged for their mischief. At our feet, the sidewalk was littered with vegetable peels, brown-stained saliva, and empty bottles. The smoke from the factories merged into a gray tapestry above us, almost comforting in its familiarity, the smell of coal and exhaust a reminder of days gone by. Of us in this place. Before.

We walked in silence for several blocks. Birds twittered from a nearby tree as Jack paused to light a cigarette. "Want one?"

I shook my head.

He exhaled slowly and began to walk again. "Did I ever tell you about the day I arrived at Eastham?" He let out a bitter laugh as he answered his own question. "Of course I didn't. I wouldn't've." He took another drag. "It's out in the country, you know? These rolling hills, all green and yellow, like something out of a painting.

And the Trinity River goes right by there. Can you believe it? The same river you and I crossed every day flowed right past the prison. It made me feel better when I saw that. Thinking maybe you saw the same water I did. Like we were still connected somehow."

I dug my nails into my palms, resisting the urge to reach out and touch him.

"Anyway, the bus pulled up in front of the building that first day, and the guards were barking at us to get off and line up. So we did, me and seven other men, all dressed in these scratchy gray uniforms I swore were crawling with fleas. We lined up in front of the bus and this guard—this big beefy guard with this bright-red mustache—he walks up and down the line, staring at us, spitting tobacco out of the side of his mouth every few feet. When he gets to me, he grabs his baton and smacks me across the face."

I stopped, my hand flying to my mouth, but Jack continued to walk. After a moment, I hurried to catch up. He was still talking.

"'I don't like the look of you,' he says. Now, I didn't look any different from any of the other guys, but for some reason, that guard didn't like me. My nose was bleeding. My eyes were watering so much I couldn't open them. And you know what he said? 'Run.' He wanted us to run out to the fields and get started with our work. Never mind we'd just gotten there. Never mind I couldn't even *see*. He wanted me to run. And when I didn't, he hit me again."

Despite the warm night air, a coldness spread through my limbs. I rubbed at my arms, feeling the fabric pill under my fingers. I couldn't bring myself to look at Jack.

The fresh scent of tobacco told me he'd taken another drag. "I could hear the others running. The gravel crunching, you know? So I tried to follow. I really did. But I couldn't open my eyes, and I tripped. There was this big ditch along the side of the road, filled with stagnant water and mosquito eggs, and I fell right in. The water wasn't cold but the shock of it made me feel like I couldn't breathe. And I couldn't see well enough to pull myself out. The ditch was only four feet wide but when you're blind and disoriented, it might as well have been the ocean. I thought I was going to drown."

My mind flashed to that long-ago horse trough. The stench of dirty water, that intense, burning pressure in my lungs. I could still smell it. Feel it. As if no time had passed. Yes, I knew all too well that particular brand of terror.

But somehow it hurt even worse to learn that Jack now knew it too.

He threw his cigarette down on the ground, scuffed it out with his shoe, and immediately lit another. I pretended not to notice his shaking hands. "I didn't, of course. The guard pulled me out and called me every name in the book for ruining my clothes. He made me strip down right there in front of everybody and walk inside naked to get a new jumpsuit. And then I still had to run out to the fields and work. So the first time I walked inside Eastham, I was naked as the day I was born, being jeered at by prisoners and guards, a whole mess of people I couldn't hardly see but I could hear. Oh, could I hear. I still hear them. To this day."

We'd arrived at Fish Trap Lake, a makeshift park in the middle of West Dallas that was little more than a sunken floodplain. Moths fluttered around a flickering streetlight that illuminated a cast-iron bench beneath it. Jack sat down and put his elbows on his knees, one hand holding his cigarette, the other rubbing his forehead.

"I thought it couldn't get any worse after that. But it did. Ten-hour workdays, seven days a week, out in the field. The calluses and sore muscles were bad, but it was the sunburn and mosquito bites that really got me down. Made it so I couldn't sleep, not that sleeping shoulder to shoulder with other inmates in crowded rows of bunk beds allowed for much rest anyway. But it didn't matter how tired you were—when the guards came in with their guns each day at 4 a.m., you better get your behind up or else. There were bullet holes in the concrete above our heads to prove it."

The cigarette in his fingers dropped ash on his shoe. He didn't seem to notice. Or else care.

"We were allowed ten minutes to eat our food, if you could even call it food. A cup of water and a crust of bread. Maybe a withered turnip or piece of rotted meat, cooked until it was leather to kill the germs. But when you're that hungry, you'll eat anything they put on your plate. Anything."

I thought back to my meager dinners at Mama's house. How I'd complained about navy beans or cabbage stew. I wrapped my arms around my waist, feeling instantly guilty.

"Even then I could have managed, though. Hard work and terrible food?" He rolled his shoulders. "That's nothing. We had that stuff on the farm when I was growing up. No, that wasn't it. It was the *people*, Bea. The guards would beat us for no reason. Random beatings kept people scared and scared people are easier to control. Turns out my beating on that first day was standard procedure—they always picked one Joe to rough up first thing so the other newbies would fall into line. I just happened be the unlucky Joe." He shook his head. "And the other prisoners? They were even worse. You couldn't trust anybody. Every day, someone was getting stabbed or attacked or . . ." His eyes flitted over to me but quickly returned to the ground. "Or worse." His last words were a whisper.

I didn't know what he meant by *worse*. I didn't want to know. His tone told me enough.

"Men would hurt themselves. To get out of field work or get a couple days in the infirmary, away from the dorms. They'd cut off fingers or toes just to get a break. The most desperate would cut off a hand or a foot in hopes they'd be too maimed for farm-work and get a permanent transfer to Huntsville. I thought it was insanity when I first heard about it. But after a few months . . ." He craned his neck this way and that as if trying to shake the images from his mind. "Six months in, there was a day I was on wood-chopping duty. I had the ax in my hand. It was like the devil himself was sitting on my shoulder telling me to swing. But there weren't no angel on the other side telling me not to." His hands clenched, dropping his cigarette to the ground only half-smoked. "Only thing that stopped me was the guard blowing his whistle for lunch. It was like I broke out of a trance. I dropped the ax and my hands were shaking. I would have cried if I didn't think I'd get beat for it. I'd never felt the darkness like that. It was like . . . it was like it was *inside* of me, Bea."

He turned suddenly, causing me to jump. Shadows cascaded over his face from the dim streetlight above our heads. "I'd never been so scared in my life. But it didn't stop. Every single day was a fight to keep the darkness out. Every. Single. Day. And I'm . . . I'm so tired. I'm so tired of fighting." He took a long, ragged breath that echoed inside his lungs. "I just . . . I need you to know how much I love you, Bea. Never stopped loving you. I still want to give you the world, but something inside of me is broken now. I . . . I don't feel like I have anything left to give. Even myself."

And then Jack Turner collapsed into sobs.

It was the first time I'd ever seen him cry. In the past year, while I had been growing stronger, healthier, and more whole, this dynamic, dazzling, confident man had been reduced to a child. Any awkwardness vanished; all I could feel now was his despair.

I slid across the bench and wrapped my arms around his shoulders, pulling his head to my breast and running my fingers through his dark hair. His body heaved with months of built-up tears. And when he finally summoned the courage to hug me back, his grip was so desperate, I couldn't stop tears of my own from dampening his crown.

When I felt his breathing slow, I tilted his face up toward mine. For the first time in over a year, Jack's beautiful gray eyes met my gaze and held it. They were red and exhausted, not from crying but from the ruin he held deep inside. A damaged, defeated ruin for which I was to blame.

Without thinking, I leaned forward and pressed my lips against his. It took a moment or two before he responded. Then, beneath my hands, his body melted with relief; he leaned into me, his hands curling through my hair.

"Bea . . . ," he whispered before his voice was choked once again by sobs.

We hugged and kissed and cried and then hugged and kissed and cried again, longing, liberation, and lament washing over us in waves. Nearby, frogs croaked and crickets chirped. The smell from the foundry mixed with the scent of incoming rain. Several trucks rumbled down the street, grinding their gears as they groaned toward home. But Jack and I saw and heard nothing. The outside world faded as we fell headfirst back into each other, each kiss and touch familiar and exotic at the same time.

After several minutes of this, he shocked me by pulling away. I made to protest but he held a finger to my lips. I could taste tobacco on his skin. With his other hand, he cupped my chin. A line appeared between his eyebrows. "I can't go back there, Bea. Ever."

"You won't," I said, pulling his hands from my face.

"But . . . I don't know how to do this." He rolled his eyes toward the light overhead, then back to me. "A house, kids, money. Life without . . ."

"You have me," I said firmly. "That's all you need for now. The rest, we'll figure out. We'll do it the right way this time. Together."

He pulled me close, and I buried my face in his neck. There was no expensive cologne or aftershave now. Just Jack, the very essence of his being. I breathed deeply, marveling at the feeling of newness as I drew my fingers over his chest. Different, but still my Jack.

I pushed down a surge of momentary conviction. I was different too, but not in a way I could explain to Jack. I thought of the hours with Alli, poring over her Bible, debating and discovering. Those afternoons were what had given me strength to get through our time apart, started to heal me from the broken little girl I'd been when Jack and I had first met. What would he think of me if he knew the truth? Would he still want to be with me if I was like Alli? I couldn't lose him, not again, not so soon. But even more unsettling was the thought of what would happen to him if he lost me.

The darkness, he'd called it.

I felt Jack sigh, content. I ran my finger over his collarbone. I wouldn't tell him. Not yet. Alli had won over Emmett in spite of his past, purely by her prayers and her gentleness. I didn't have her faith yet, but I *had* been living straight for several months now. I could show Jack how to do it, support him and love him as he figured it out, like Alli had done for me. We could move forward and figure it out together.

That was the key word. *Together.* Jack and I were together. And nothing would ever tear us apart again.

Long ago, he had saved me from the darkness of a cruel, unloving world; now it was my turn to save him.

CHAPTER TWENTY

THEN
OCTOBER 1931

A few orange leaves dotted the hood of Jack's Model A. As I climbed inside, I noticed they were the exact same color as the patches of rust along the baseboard. I thought it was charming, a nice coincidence that enhanced the beautiful fall colors now starting to speckle the otherwise-colorless landscape. But I also knew better than to say anything to Jack. He found the rust a lot of things, but *charming* definitely wasn't one of them.

I rolled down my window as he walked around the rear of the car to his own side. "Thanks again for dinner."

Alli placed on a hand on the sill. "Anytime. It's so good to see you. It's been too long."

I chewed the skin on my lip. There was nothing malicious in

194

her tone, but I felt guilty all the same. It had been over a month since the last time we'd gotten together. We'd made it all the way through dinner without her bringing it up. "I've been busy. Work."

She winked and let out a small laugh. "Right. Work."

I smiled. Work *had* been taking up a lot of my time. Mrs. Russell had reduced her number of household staff by half; the Depression wasn't just for poor people anymore. She'd kept me on, and while I was very thankful to still have a job, my workload had increased tenfold. It wasn't uncommon to be putting in twelve- or fourteen-hour days just to get everything done. So yes, work had been taking up most of my time, for sure.

But Jack had been taking up the rest.

"I understand," she said, squeezing my hand. "You've had some lost time to make up for. We all have." She glanced over her shoulder as Emmett emerged from their apartment, lighting a cigarette and walking toward Jack. When she looked back at me, her eyes were shining. "For what it's worth, I'm proud of you, Bea. Of both of you. It's not easy to make a fresh start."

A fresh start. Was that what we'd done? On paper, yes. Jack had been helping at his father's garage, making minimal money but an honest living. I'd held a steady, decent-paying job for almost eighteen months now; between the two of us, it was more than enough to pay the rent, put food on the table, and keep water, heat, and lights running through the apartment that was Eleanor's and mine in name but in which Jack lived all but officially. There were fewer nights out dancing and drinking than before, fewer material gifts, and more nodding off while listening to the radio, but we had love. We had each other. We had the whole future ahead of us.

We'd made our fresh start. So why didn't it feel like it?

From the other side of the car came the murmur of voices. Jack and Emmett stood with their backs to us, heads lowered, talking in hushed tones. Even from here, I could see the rigidity of Jack's posture, the stiffness in his hand movements. Emmett put a hand on his brother's shoulder, only to have Jack shrug it away. Emmett took a step back and held up his hands; when he turned, our gazes met briefly and he pressed his lips together in an irritated grimace before lowering his eyes once again and saying something to Jack I couldn't hear.

I turned back to Alli, who seemed not to have noticed the exchange. "Thank you," I said with false brightness.

"By the way . . ." She lowered her voice. "Are you still reading the Psalms?"

I glanced through the windshield at Jack as my stomach clenched. He still had his back turned and gave no indication he'd heard. "Yes. Kind of. As much as I can."

It was Alli's turn to grimace, though hers was more sad than irritated. When she spoke again, her tone was gentle. "I understand you've been busy, and we haven't had the time to get together like we used to. I just want to make sure . . ."

"Make sure what?"

She paused. "You don't have to be ashamed of it, you know?"

"I'm not!" The force of my protest served to only highlight its dishonesty. "I'm . . . I've had other things to do. I had that play over the summer and then work and more auditions. And Jack, of course."

She put her hands in the pockets of her sweater, wrapping it around her like a blanket. "Jack," she repeated. Somehow she'd heard everything I left unspoken behind the name: I couldn't read the Psalms with him around. Five months after his release, I still hadn't been able to bring up my close relationship with Alli. My weekly chats and studies with her were now down to once a month, if that. But it wasn't that I was ashamed. Or rather, it wasn't *only* that I was ashamed. It was that, with Jack in my life—our new life, full of work and rent and grown-up responsibilities—there simply wasn't room for anything else.

And so the God I'd been investigating for the past year had been put on a back shelf, along with Alli's friendship and her dusty Bible. In the fullness of Jack's presence, it didn't bother me; it was only in her company that my conscience truly began to prickle.

That's why, despite my yearning for those days we once shared, it was so much easier to just stay away. Out of sight, out of mind.

Though Alli was never truly either.

Jack slid into the seat beside me and started the engine, which groaned and sputtered before finally roaring to life. "You ready?"

I nodded. Before we could pull away, however, I felt Alli's hand on my arm. "Come back anytime, Bea. You are always welcome here." She squeezed my wrist gently. "Always."

I gave her a smile I hoped passed as genuine. As we pulled away, Jack drew me close to him. The heat of his body washed over me as I snuggled under his shoulder. The spot where Alli had held on, however, felt the warmest of all.

"Thank you for taking me to dinner," I said, kissing his cheek. It was stubbly; he hadn't had a chance to shave after work before going over to his brother's. "Though I know you would have rather gone to Giovanni's."

"Well, *this* dinner was free." He grunted, but a smile played on the corner of his mouth. "Even if it meant I had to share you."

I giggled and kissed him again. "Alli has been bothering me for weeks to come over for dinner. I'm glad we went. It was fun."

"Fun." He gave a single nod, though I noticed his smile was gone. Instead, his lips were folded into a tight line.

My mind flickered back to the exchange I'd witnessed beside the car. It had been heated, that much was obvious, though it seemed as if Emmett had backed down from the fight. Whatever it had been, I knew better than to touch on it. "Their new radio is nice," I said instead. "With that shield grid speaker, the sound was crystal clear. Felt like the Boswell Sisters were right there in the room with us."

"There something wrong with our radio?"

His body had gone rigid, his tone cold. In trying not to say the wrong thing, I'd somehow said something even worse. "No," I stuttered. "No, of course not." Our old Magnavox with the horn speaker popped and hissed constantly, making it hard to hear the notes . . . but there was no way I was going to bring that up now. "I could dance with you to nothing but a train whistle," I added, leaning forward to kiss him once again.

He jerked his head sideways, out of my touch. "He makes more money than I do, Bea."

I sat back, wounded and confused. "I didn't—"

"I'd buy you that radio if I could."

"I know that. But I don't need *things*, Jack. Just you." I tried to meet his eye, but he continued to stare forward, his expression unsettled and annoyed. Whatever Emmett had said had put him in a mood. One of his sulking, slighted fits that had become more common over the past month. My mind raced with things to say, events of the evening on which to comment, ways to lighten the air, but everything I came up with felt wrong. I sighed and settled back in my seat. There was a gap between us now. The frayed interior of the seat was visible between our bodies, but he did not move to pull me back to him.

We drove in silence over the rutted dirt of Harston Street. Belching black smoke from the foundry was visible even in the fading daylight. The slight chill in the air had become colder as Jack accelerated; I rolled up my window as the car picked up speed.

He shifted gears roughly, sending gravel spraying and causing the car to jerk . . . and sending me into the dashboard. I touched my cheek, smarting.

"Sorry," he muttered under his breath.

I crossed my arms over my chest. That was the thing about Jack's bad moods. He was never content to keep them for himself; he had to make sure they spread. And he was usually successful.

Suddenly Jack let out an angry swear and the car slowed. It took me a moment to register the wail of a siren swelling around our vehicle. It cut abruptly as we lurched to a stop. A nondescript but all-too-familiar black sedan pulled up behind us. My vexation melted into dread.

We were getting pulled over. Again.

Jack rolled down his window. The scrape of the policeman's shoes echoed as he walked toward our car. His journey seemed to take hours, and it felt as if he relished the anticipation his slow arrival could bring. Enough time for us to fret. Enough time for the neighbors to peek out their windows. Enough time for Jack to get angry and give the copper an excuse—any excuse—to finally bring him in. Over eighteen months since his last crime, and Jack's name was still on everyone's lips

But not in a way that was doing us a lick of good.

"Mr. Turner," the officer said, removing his hat as he peered into our window. His face was ruddy and round, a thick blond mustache over his fat top lip. "What a surprise."

"Surprise my rear," Jack replied through gritted teeth. "Don't you act like you didn't know it was me."

The cop laughed, causing me to shift uncomfortably in my seat. It was never a good thing when coppers laughed. "Now, now. I had no idea. I was out patrolling and happened to notice a speeding car. That's all."

"I wasn't speeding!"

The cop gave a shrug, and I noticed a baton hanging from his right hand. My stomach dropped to my knees. *Please, Jack,* I begged silently. *Please keep your mouth shut. For once, don't talk back.*

"That shower of rocks you sent up back there tells me otherwise."

Jack's hands clenched around the steering wheel. "That was just loose gravel and a bad transmission, and you know it."

The cop clicked his tongue. "Oughta be more careful with your driving, especially with a lady present." He ducked his head, trying to get a better look at me. I shrank back against my seat. "What is this, the third time you've been pulled over this month?"

"The fourth." His tone was deep, threatening. "And yet here I am. Ain't been able to pin nothing on me yet, have you?"

My heart went sluggish as the smile finally left the officer's face. "Watch it, boy. Just 'cause we ain't got the evidence, don't mean you're innocent. We bide our time long enough, and one of these days you're gonna slip up again."

"Bide away," Jack growled. "I'm clean."

Two pairs of eyes peeked from behind the curtains in the house to my right. I knew they weren't the only ones. I felt the veins in my forehead begin to pulse against my skin. Why couldn't people mind their own business? Why couldn't people just leave us *alone*?

"This your car?" the cop asked after a long, tense moment.

"You know it is."

The officer took a step back and appraised the vehicle with a sneer. "Yeah, you're right. I should've known. A car this junky ain't worth stealing."

Jack's knuckles went white.

"Until the next time, Mr. Turner." The cop replaced his hat and strolled away, whistling softly as he swung his baton at his side.

Jack waited until the sedan was completely out of sight before starting the engine, which wheezed and groaned again, impervious to the effect its noises had on the driver. When finally it began to hum, he slammed it into gear a little harder than necessary and pressed on the gas, sending another shower of rocks into the air. A small act of defiance that gave him only a passing satisfaction before the black look returned to his face. The cop might have been long gone, but his presence remained between us for the rest of the drive back to my apartment.

Still not speaking, he threw his jacket on the couch and disappeared inside our small kitchen. I heard the clink of ice as he poured himself a drink. I was glad Eleanor was babysitting at the Youngs. I hated when she saw Jack like this; she never said it, but I knew every time she looked at me during one of Jack's moods, she was seeing my mother.

He was sitting at our small table with his back to me, an already half-drained glass of whiskey in his hand. I hesitated at the doorway, considered giving him his space, but pushed my way inside instead. I dragged a chair from the opposite side of the table directly next to his and pulled his hand into mine.

He placed his drink on the table with a *thunk* and rubbed his forehead with his free hand. "I'm tired, Bea."

"Come to bed then. Let's get some slee—"

"I don't need sleep. I need . . ." He shook his head and sighed. "I have walked the line for months, not sticking even one toe out of place, but they still won't leave me alone. It isn't fair. Not to you, not to me. How's a man supposed to make a clean future when the coppers keep rubbing his nose in the dirt of the past?"

I pressed his hands to my lips, my heart aching. "I don't know, baby. I don't know. We just have to keep trying, that's all. Eventually they'll stop."

"Will they? It sure doesn't seem like it." He downed the rest of his whiskey in one gulp, wincing at the burn. "And it isn't just the cops. It's everybody. I can't get a decent job around here. They all know Jack Turner, the criminal. Doesn't matter what I say or do. I'm not that man anymore, but no one can see it. No one *believes* it."

"I believe it."

He gave me a tired smile. "I know you do." He kissed me softly on the cheek before rising and pouring himself another drink. He did not return to his seat; instead, he leaned against the counter and swirled the amber liquid inside his glass. "Emmett said he might be able to get me a job," he said after a moment.

"What? Where?"

"Where he works. At the United Glass Company. As a glazier."

A shot of elation rushed through my veins. "Really?"

"He said his preacher gave him a good character reference, and he might be able to convince him to give me one too." He took a sip. "If I start going to church."

"That's wonderful! This—"

"I told him there was no way on earth I was going to step into a church to be judged by a bunch of goody-goodies and grovel at the feet of some preacher."

My body slumped as if tied down with weights. All happiness evaporated. "Jack . . . why? It could—"

"I spent an entire year of my life prostrating myself at the feet of men who thought they were better than me. I refuse to do it here on the outside."

I chewed the inside of my cheek. This was my chance, though I wasn't sure exactly what to say. I walked over to him, wrapping him in a hug he only half returned. I waited until I felt him relax under my arms before finally daring to speak. "But maybe . . . ,"

I said softly. "Maybe it doesn't have to be about that. Maybe . . . maybe it's not about people but about God?"

Jack's response was quick. I let out a small cry of shock as he pushed me away. It was as if he'd been scalded. "What did you say?"

I hunched my shoulders. "Well, Alli . . . Alli said—"

He let out a bitter laugh, interrupting me, and shook his head. "I can't believe I didn't see it before. She got to you, too, didn't she? Alli. First my brother, now my girl."

"Jack . . ."

"Is that what you've been doing over at her apartment when you go? Reading the Bible? Praying? Talking about God?"

The way he said it—so snide, so arrogant. It was as if he were speaking to a naive child.

"Let me tell you something, Bea. Alli can spout off her pretty words all she wants, but she doesn't understand. She never went to bed hungry, never cut holes in her shoes to try and make them fit long past their intended wear. Her daddy was a traveling preacher, her mama a nurse; they weren't kings, but she sure wasn't picking fleas out of her hair neither. She's not like us. And she may think she 'rescued' Emmett when she swooped in, but she's done nothing but torture him, making him think he has to choose between feeding his mouth and saving his soul."

A physical pain pressed on my chest. "I don't think that's it."

He took another swig of his drink, slamming the glass on the counter behind him and making me wince. "You don't think that's it? Take a look around, Bea! You think God cares about us? You think a good, loving God would allow the rich to get richer, the poor to get poorer, and the depravity of a place like Eastham to go unchecked? What kind of a God creates a world like this, then judges a man for doing the things he has to do to survive it?"

Iciness flooded my core. He was wrong. Charles had been wrong about God, and now Jack was too. Or was he? His words made sense, his bitterness pulling my own from the depths in which I'd hidden it away. It *wasn't* fair. Any of it. Living outside the law had brought its own troubles, but playing by the rules hadn't improved our situation much either. We had each other, yes, but we also had unpaid bills and empty pantry shelves. Bone-deep exhaustion and unspoken dissatisfaction. Alli didn't know what it was like. Emmett had a steady job with no suspicious bosses underfoot, no coppers stopping him at every turn. Religion was all fine and dandy until real life stepped on your toes. If God was so good, why did trying to do things His way bring so much misery?

My fragile faith—a faith I'd tried so hard to find, to grow, to nurture—seemed to wither under the frost of his truth.

"Jack."

He brushed past me, ignoring my tears and outstretched arms.

"Jack, where are you going?"

He grabbed his jacket from the sofa, not looking at me. "I'm sleeping at my parents' house tonight."

Nausea seized my stomach. We hadn't spent a night apart since he'd been released. I couldn't bear to think of sleeping in my vast, cold bed without him. "Jack, please."

His only answer was the slamming door. I sank to my knees as sobs racked my body. The sound of Jack's car faded into the night. He had left, but I wasn't really alone. In his absence, the doubts and distrust that had plagued me since childhood—the ones Alli's teachings had tried to soothe and dispel—resurfaced in full force, throwing into disarray everything I thought I'd learned and overcome in the past few months. That God, the one she'd tried to tell me about, seemed so far away.

Or maybe He'd never really been there to begin with.

CHAPTER TWENTY-ONE

I crumpled the yellow paper and threw it in the rusted garbage can next to the bench before climbing the steps to the bus. I'd gotten off work an hour early—which meant I had to be at the Russells' an hour earlier tomorrow—to come downtown and get the cast list for *Cinderella*. Since my turn in the King Arthur play in June, I'd been so consumed with Jack's homecoming I hadn't had time to audition.

But I had time now. I hadn't seen Jack in three weeks. Calls, visits, and letters went unanswered. I made two trips to Alli's, looking for comfort and answers, but Emmett's presence there—even when he wasn't actually present—was too painful, Jack's absence heightened by their striking physical similarities and stark spiritual differences. All of Alli's prayers and Bible verses fell on a hardened soul. I didn't want words; I wanted *Jack*.

God felt lost to me, and Jack even more so. The only thing I had left was work . . . and the stage. Impulsively, and as much to ease Eleanor's worry over my melancholy as to distract myself from my grief, I'd thrown myself into an audition for the title role in an amateur production of the little cinder girl, part of the holiday series at Fair Park. I was perfect, I thought—a natural beauty hidden beneath years of hard work and servitude. I *was* Cinderella, minus the godmother . . . or magic . . . or Prince Charming. The role was hefty for a relative nobody on the drama scene, but I had nothing to lose by auditioning.

Except my last shred of hope. Because the role had gone not to me, but to Shirley Albertson, a proper Dallas-ite with platinum hair and legs for days. She'd completed her entire audition without a single stumble (probably because she didn't have a work schedule to interfere with rehearsing), and her outfit had been an expensive chiffon dress altered to *look* poor. Not actual poor like my own belted wool frock.

So that was that. Another failure. Another dead end.

As the bus rumbled across the Trinity, swollen and angry with recent rain, I wondered how I was going to tell Eleanor. She'd been so hopeful for me, so sure of my success—we'd read the Cinderella story so many times, and she assured me no one could play her like me. The only feeling worse than my own defeat was knowing I'd have to bring my sister down with me.

My feet sank into a puddle as I exited the bus, adding insult to injury. Thick brown mud covered my toes, the icy water nearly to my ankles. I grimaced as I pulled them free. The cheap, worn leather would take hours to dry; more than likely, I'd be putting on soggy shoes for work tomorrow morning, even if I got them next to our weak heater straight away. If the heater was even working.

It was with no small amount of self-pity that I pushed myself through the apartment door, slipping off my soaking shoes on the tattered rug near the entrance. But the room was warm, and the smell of coffee and baking bread a welcome respite. "El? Are you here?"

"Here," came her voice from the kitchen.

I peeled off my stockings—also soaking wet—and dropped my purse on the couch before moving further into the apartment. Swallowing heartache, I plastered my best audition smile on my face, intent on staying positive as much as possible for my sister's sake. "Hey, El. How was your—?"

I stopped. Eleanor's face was white, her lips twitching with words her mouth was unable to speak. I rushed toward her and pulled her tightly clenched fists into my hands. "What happened? Are you hurt? El, take a breath. Just breathe. Tell me what happened."

Her lips continued to move but no sound came out. Eleanor struggled with her verbal skills most when she was upset or overly stressed. Even I, the person with whom she was most at ease, found it hard to break her free from herself when she got too worked up.

I guided her to a seat at the table and did a quick examination. I couldn't see any physical injuries. A rapid glance over the kitchen revealed no outward signs of distress or accidents. A small relief.

"You need to breathe, Eleanor. Take a breath. Don't try to talk. Just breathe."

My sister trembled. Her eyes remained focused on me, a panic swimming within them that she was trying desperately to convey.

I tried to smile despite my own rising alarm. "It's okay. I'm here. Just breathe."

Her chest rose and fell slowly. She pressed her knuckles into my palms as she licked her lips. "Ph . . . ," she started, then shook her head. "Phone," she finally managed to croak.

"Phone? Did someone call?"

She nodded. "Jack. Jail."

I gripped her wrist, though my fingers had gone too numb to feel her skin. "What?"

"Jack. Jail," she repeated.

"He called you? From the jail?"

She nodded.

"When?"

"Hour. Two hours."

"What did he say?"

"Arrested."

My heartbeat went sluggish. "He was arrested? When?"

"Night. Last night. Car."

I closed my eyes as a rock dropped into my stomach. "Stealing a car."

She nodded. Tears dripped down her cheeks.

My chest ached as I pulled her toward me. She wasn't crying for Jack; she was crying for me. For the pain she knew I'd feel when I found out . . . and the fear of what lay behind it. "I wasn't with him, Eleanor. I promise. Jack and I, we . . ." We what? My sister knew we'd had a fight and he hadn't been around in the last few weeks, but I hadn't told her much beyond that. "But," I said instead, "I know he didn't do it. Jack's straight now. He's got a real job and everything. He's done with all that. He told me. He's innocent."

I didn't know whether I was saying it more for her or me.

I pulled away from her, keeping my hands on her shoulders and trying to catch a gaze she wouldn't quite meet. "I have to go down there, though. I have to make sure he's okay."

She let out a large sigh, though from disappointment or defeat, I wasn't sure.

"Are you okay? If I leave, will you be okay?"

She hesitated for a moment before nodding, still not making eye contact.

It felt wrong to leave her, but it would have felt even worse to stay. I pulled on fresh stockings and low heels that looked out of place with my uniform but were mercifully dry and hurried out to catch a bus back across the river.

The Dallas County jail, mere blocks from the riverfront, was a misleading structure. Its ornate facade looked more suitable to host fancy dinner parties than serve as a holding ground for Dallas's undesirables. The aura was only enhanced by the castle-like appearance of the Old Red Courthouse next door, complete with turrets and gargoyles. How could something so pleasing to the eye hold so much grief and sorrow?

It was twilight by the time the bus dropped me off on Main, and a light rain had started to fall once again. My heels were not designed for running but run I did, until I stumbled just two blocks from the entrance. Landing on my rear on the cold, wet concrete, I realized the problem: one of my heels had snapped off completely, leaving a large, gaping hole in the sole of my shoe. I cursed and smacked it against the sidewalk in frustration. I couldn't catch a break. But then again, neither could Jack. If I had to go into the jail and beg for his release in my bare feet, that's what I would do.

"Bea?"

I looked up, shielding my eyes from the drizzle. For a moment, I thought it was a dream, a trick of the streetlight and my water-logged brain.

"What are you doing down there?"

It wasn't until his hand pulled me into a standing position that I fully believed what I was seeing. Jack. Not in jail but here in front of me, dark circles around his eyes but an incredulous smile on his face.

The last three weeks vanished. I wrapped myself around him and kissed him full on the mouth, tears springing to my eyes. After a moment's hesitation, he returned the kiss, his fingers twisting through my damp hair.

"What are you doing here?" he asked when we broke away.

"I was coming for you. I hopped on a bus as soon as I heard and . . ." My rapid-fire words melted away. "But . . . you're not in jail. What are—?"

He shrugged. "They let me go. Had to. Not enough evidence to charge me."

"But what did—?"

"They say I stole a car. The one I was driving. I tried to tell them it was a clunker and I was taking it to my pa's garage, but you know the coppers." He scowled momentarily, then shook his head, twisting his mouth back into a smile. "It doesn't matter. Are you hungry?"

"Starving actually."

"Me too. There's gotta be a diner nearby. Let's get out of this rain."

We found a dingy restaurant on Elm, no name on the door but an Open sign in the window. The floor was sticky and the air smelled of burnt grease, but it was warm, dry, and the coffee was fresh. A bored waitress took our orders—two burgers and a shared side of fries—as Jack bummed a cigarette from a grumpy-looking busboy. The lamp over our heads cast a sickly yellow glow into our back booth, showcasing the dark stubble on Jack's cheeks and highlighting bloodshot eyes that struggled to look at me. The relief at our reunion had quickly settled into awkwardness.

"Jack . . ."

He reached over the table and grabbed both of my hands in his. "Don't, Bea. You don't have to say anything. I've been an absolute mess without you. I'm sorry."

It took every ounce of self-control I had not to climb over our plates and into his arms. "I'm sorry too, Jack."

"You've got nothing to be sorry for. I'm an idiot. You're the best thing that's ever happened to me. I don't know why I do the things I do. My mouth—"

"I love your mouth."

He let out a guffaw, causing the few other customers to glance in our direction. He lifted a hand in an apologetic wave. "Ah, Bea," he said with a shake of his head. "I love you. I hope you know that."

"I love you too."

He grinned and took a large bite. Mustard squirted out the side of his bun. "So what have you been up to while I was being dumb?"

"Work. You know how it is. And . . ."

His face fell as I told him about the audition, about Shirley and her waves, her flawless makeup and eloquent lines.

"I'm sorry, Bea," he said when I'd finished. "Those people . . . they're so blinded by their own arrogance, they couldn't see talent if it slapped 'em in the face. You're a star. You know it, and I know it. And one of these days, everyone else will know it too."

I let out a short burst of air through my nose. "I don't know, Jack. It feels like it's never going to happen. Maybe it's not meant to be." I swirled a fry in ketchup, swallowing a lump in my throat. "I . . . I want to be honest with myself. With you. Yes, I want those dreams, the ones we talked about, sure. But when it comes down to it, I want you more. Just you. Just us. Living a real life. Together. Like we were trying to do before . . ."

Jack reached across the table and took one of my hands. The lamp over our heads created a halo above his crown. "I want that too, Bea. More than anything. I really am sorry about the whole Alli thing. I was . . . angry. About a lot of things. But I overreacted, and I'm sorry."

"I'm sorry too. I shouldn't have hidden it from you. I knew how you felt about Alli and her religion stuff, but she helped me a lot while you were gone. I wouldn't have made it through without her."

"I know. And I'm grateful for that, no matter how else I feel about her." He rubbed his thumb inside my palm. "But . . . the thing is, I'm not Emmett, and you're not Alli, and I don't want us to be. They got their thing and we've got ours. If you want to read a Bible and pray and do all that religion stuff, that's fine . . . but I need you to understand that's not me. I need you to love me for *me*, not for some man you're trying to change me into."

"I do love you, Jack. *You*. All of you, every piece of you, just the way you are. I . . . I just want us to be happy. For *you* to be happy."

"I am happy."

"Are you?"

I hadn't meant the question to be so heavy. But something in the air suddenly shifted. Jack dropped my hand and looked at the ceiling.

"With *you*, yes. But if we're going to be completely honest with one another . . ." He took a deep breath. When he spoke again, his voice was barely above a murmur. "I did steal that car. The only reason I got off so clean was my prison buddy Ralph covered for me, claimed it was his, forged up some real quick papers to prove it."

I closed my eyes. "Jack . . ."

His hand clenched around mine, so hard it caused me to wince. "I had to. I know I told you I wanted to go straight, and I do. But it's not working for me. My reputation is killing any chance I've got at a decent-paying job, and there isn't any way to get ahead without money. I figure, if the cops are gonna harass me, might as well live up to my name." He held up a finger to my protests. "It's only for a couple months. No robberies, no guns, just transporting cars across the border. Couple hundred dollars a pop. And I'll save every penny. You'll see—by this time next year, we'll be married with a real nice house."

I shook my head, pressing a hand to my lips.

"Bea, please. This world, these people . . . they're never gonna let us be. Never gonna let us rise above the gutters from where we started. Don't you see that? Look at those coppers, stopping us at every turn. Look at your auditions. You've got more talent in your little finger than the rest of those girls do combined. But it doesn't matter. The only thing those people care about is where you came from . . . and making sure you stay there."

I felt my cheeks go hot. My eyes began to blur.

"Don't cry, Bea. Not over them. They're not worth it. They're hypocrites. The whole lot of 'em. They like to pretend they're better than us, not just financially but morally. And yet their entire lives revolve around judgment and prejudice. Yes, okay, I stole a few cars. But how else am I supposed to make ends meet when everyone has already decided I'm not good enough to do anything else?"

There was a charge in the air after his question, both dangerous and affirming. We'd been trying. God knew we'd been trying. Even Jack, who cared nothing for religion, had attempted the straight and narrow. For me. *With* me. And yet no one—not the cops, not the Dallas elite, not even God—seemed to care. Or even wanted us there.

And still . . .

"I can't lose you," I whispered. I raised my head, meeting his gaze. "Jack, I can't lose you again."

He rose and slid into the booth next to me, wrapping his arm around my shoulders. "You won't. I'll be careful—I promise. I'm *not* going back to jail. I'm not going *anywhere*." He tilted my chin upward, his eyes searching mine. They were red-rimmed and exhausted, but the need in them was greater than their fatigue. "All this is just a means to an end. And that end is *us*, Bea. I'm doing this for *us*. Because no one will ever love you more than I do. I can promise you that."

I leaned into him, trying not to cry. I didn't want Jack to be in harm's way, didn't want him to risk his life or his freedom for me or anyone else. And yet I was sick of feeling defeated, deficient, and defective. Tired of working myself to the bone trying to meet the world's standards, only to have the bar raised farther and farther out of reach. Tired of feeling less than. Tired of feeling worthless.

And tired of seeing the man I loved feel the same.

In the dim light, Jack's eyes shimmered with unshed tears. "Please say you love me too. Please say you'll stay with me."

My stomach churned, fear and fire burning in equal measure. I didn't want this. For all the progress I'd made over the past few years, this would be like a freight train pushing me backward. But what good was going forward when the only thing that lay ahead on this path was an impenetrable brick wall?

No, I didn't want this. But I wanted Jack. Most of all, I wanted everything the world said people like Jack and I couldn't have.

"I'll stay until the end," I murmured against his lips. Our shared tears made them salty and wet. "Until the very end. Because no one loves you more."

CHAPTER TWENTY-TWO

"Bea . . ."

I jumped up from the chair in which I had been dozing. My stiff muscles and injured leg screamed in protest, but I ignored them. They didn't matter. Nothing mattered.

Because Jack was awake.

I fell on my knees beside the couch, grasping his cold hand in my own. The merest flicker of his fingertips, weak and lethargic but alive, brought tears to my eyes. I pressed my other hand against his cheek. The scratchiness of his beard tickled my palm. His eyelids fluttered several times before opening a slit. His mouth once again breathed out my name: "Bea."

"I'm here, Jack. I'm here."

Glassy eyes rolled around his head, struggling to find me amid the haze. "Bea . . ." His face contorted as his mind caught up to his body. "It hurts."

My chest constricted. I tried not to look at his shoulder, the makeshift bandage saturated with dark blood. The woman—Rose, I reminded myself—had changed the strips of cloth twice, binding them as tight as she could, but though the bleeding had slowed, it still hadn't stopped.

"I know, baby. I know." I pushed a stray lock off his forehead. Sweat beaded on his pallid skin. Looking around, I grabbed a washcloth from a nearby end table; it was only partly damp but still cool, and it would have to do. I pressed it against his head, amazed at how quickly his fever penetrated the fabric.

"Where are we?"

"At a farmhouse somewhere in . . ." My words trailed off as I realized I didn't know. Oklahoma? Texas? New Mexico? "We ran out of gas, and this was the only place for miles. There's a woman—" I paused and glanced around. There had been a woman, but I didn't know where she was now. I'd dozed off after she'd given me a bit of salted beef and a hunk of day-old bread, and I had no idea how much time had passed since then—minutes, hours, days. Perhaps she had fled. Perhaps she was on her way back with the police at that very moment. Fear prickled the back of my neck and I rolled my shoulders, trying to stem it. It didn't matter; it wasn't like either of us could run. All I could do now was keep Jack still.

I stared down at his limp fingers as I continued. "There's a woman. She's helping us. Helping you."

Jack fumbled his way up his chest with his free hand until his fingers found mine. Gripping my wrist, he pulled my hand from his cheek with surprising strength. "No," he said hoarsely, his voice collapsing into a pained, raspy wheeze. He swallowed noisily and licked his cracked lips. "You have to leave."

"Jack—"

"You have to leave." Despite the weakness in his voice, his eyes were clear for the first time. "Take the car—whatever car you can find—and go."

I shook my head violently. "You're not strong enough. We're not going anywhere."

"Don't be stupid!" He winced, but his agony did nothing to quell his fervor. "I'm not going anywhere ever again. I'm . . ."

Dying. Only he didn't say it. Couldn't say it. Or perhaps I simply wouldn't allow myself to hear it.

"Get yourself out of here," he said instead. "Now."

He didn't react as a tear dripped from my cheek onto his hand; I wondered if he could even feel it. "But . . ." My closed throat barely allowed the words to pass. "We said until the end."

"Don't you get it? This *is* the end," Jack's face crumpled. He closed his eyes, perhaps hoping I wouldn't see his anguish, but it was too late. "I don't deserve it, Bea. I don't deserve to have you here as I go. Not after everything . . ." He let out a low moan and twisted his head back and forth as if the pain in his mind was worse than the pain in his body. "What I've done. To everyone. To you. To Emmett." Another moan, this one louder and more desolate. "Emmett . . ."

My shoulders curled over my chest. I wanted desperately to embrace him but knew I couldn't. And not just because of his wound. We were bound by grief but separated by guilt. My love for him was fierce, overwhelming, real . . . but it wasn't enough to comfort him. And it wasn't enough to erase the consequences of what we'd done. "Jack," I whispered through my tears.

At the sound of my voice, his eyes widened, clear once more. But in place of despair, there was anger. "I said leave!" he yelled. With supernatural vigor, he pushed at me, causing me to topple backward off the couch. "Go!"

I landed with a thud. Intense pain shot up my injured leg.

"Get out of here! Leave!" Jack flailed on the couch, his howls shrill and guttural.

I pulled myself to my feet with an anguished sob. Tears blinded my eyes as I pushed my way into the kitchen, Jack's screams echoing through the house.

And my heart.

"Leave! Leave! Leave!"

Consumed by my own misery, I failed to notice the black shape that materialized in front of me until it was too late. I ran into it, causing both the shape and myself to fall backward. My already-aching legs felt as if they shattered all over again. I pressed my hands to my face, willing myself to breathe through the blinding pain.

"Josephine!" came a shout. "Josephine, are you okay?"

The black spots slowly faded from the corners of my vision, revealing Eleanor sitting across from me on the kitchen floor. No, not Eleanor. It couldn't be Eleanor. Eleanor was grown. This girl was young, no more than ten, dressed in a pale-blue flour sack dress, short brown hair pushed back under a headband. She was seated across from me on the kitchen floor, her eyes wide with fear and awe.

Not Eleanor, I told myself, trembling. *Josephine.* The woman had called her Josephine. Still, the resemblance was uncanny. Enough to make my heart stop beating.

We sat frozen on the ground, staring at one another in shock and fear, albeit for very different reasons. Suddenly Rose appeared.

Her lips pressed together in a grim expression as she helped the girl to her feet. "I thought I told you to stay upstairs," she hissed. "What are you doing down here?"

"I . . . I heard shouting," the girl answered meekly. "I wanted to see—"

"Ain't nothing for you to see! You get your behind back up those stairs!" Rose's voice was stern, but the pat she gave the child was gentle.

With a wide, longing glance over her shoulder, the girl disappeared up the servants' staircase.

Rose stared after her, making sure she was really and truly gone before running her hands over her face and turning her attention to me. "Well, it appears you've met my daughter."

CHAPTER TWENTY-THREE

"Bea? Bea, are you listening?"

I jumped, causing lukewarm coffee to splash onto my dress. "Ah, shoot!" Brown liquid began to seep across the green fabric, turning the pattern of small pink flowers gray. I pulled at the black buttons, peeling the fabric from skin already starting to chill.

Alli pressed a towel into my hand. "Here. Use this."

I gave her a grateful—and embarrassed—smile. "Thanks."

She settled down across from me, tugging a shawl back around her shoulders. "Do you want to borrow one of my dresses? The heat in here is . . ." She wiggled her head and rolled her eyes. "Emmett can't figure out what's wrong with it, but there's no money for a repairman. We get by with blankets and such, but you'll catch a cold real quick in those wet clothes."

"No, it's fine. Thank you." Truth be told, I *was* cold, but I didn't want to put her out any more than I already had, especially when I was in her apartment, drinking her coffee, eating her food, and not even really paying attention to her or our Bible lesson.

"What's up with you today? You seem . . . distracted."

Distracted. That was a nice way to put it.

I gave Alli my best audition smile, fluttering lashes that felt as if they weighed a million pounds. "Just tired. I've been really busy."

"You can talk to me about it. I . . ." She dipped her chin. "I know about Jack."

"What about Jack?" Even I didn't believe the innocence in my tone.

"Bea."

I closed my eyes and sank back into my chair, the rickety wood making a rude squeak nearly as loud as my sigh. "How?"

"He was here two days ago. With that friend of his. What's his name—?"

"*Ralph*." The word came out like a spit. Ralph Schultz. Jack's old prison chum and the newest member of our operation. I didn't like anything about the man. Even his name.

"Yeah, Ralph. They had a few drinks with Emmett while I read in the other room. I couldn't hear what they were saying, but the mood definitely seemed to shift the longer they were here. The murmurs became forceful, and that Ralph man . . . it sounded like Jack had to stop him from shouting several times. Even from my spot in the bedroom, I could tell he was drunk. He knocked over my coatrack on his way out."

I clenched my jaw. So now it wasn't only my apartment Ralph disrupted when he was drinking.

"Emmett came to bed in a huff. He apologized and said he

wouldn't let that man into our place again. He even—" She stopped, the corners of her eyes crinkling as if she were in pain.

"What?"

"He even said Jack was bordering on not being welcome here anymore. Not if he was gonna bring that kind of riffraff around. Or continue to pester Emmett about joining his . . . business."

I pinched the bridge of my nose and let out a long exhale. "I'm sorry, Alli. I had no idea he was trying to bring Emmett into the fold. I'll talk to him."

She tilted her head. "Are you in the fold?"

Though her words were not unkind, I turned my body sideways to shield myself from their impact. The thin pages of the Bible in front of me—my own, a Christmas present from Alli—fluttered with my movements.

I'd known she'd find out. Eventually. What started as a once- or twice-a-week trip out of town to deliver stolen cars across state lines had quickly evolved into a full-time gig, which was why Ralph—and now apparently Emmett—had been roped into the game. I'd quit my job at the Russells'; there was no time, and we didn't need their pennies when we were bringing in dollars. But more important than the money was the joy we'd found again. The thrill. That feeling of being masters of our own future, of spitting on that invisible line that separated the haves and the have-nots.

I wasn't ashamed of what we were doing. It was righteous in its own way.

And yet for some reason, I couldn't quite look Alli in the eye.

She scooted her chair closer to mine and placed a hand on my arm. It was icy, but I didn't pull away. Even though we were the only ones in the apartment, she still lowered her voice when she spoke. "You're playing with fire, Bea. Tongues are wagging all over town. Jack's name is out there, and it isn't just friends who are hearing it. He's getting bold, he's getting stupid, and he's gonna get caught. It's only a matter of time. You have to be careful. 'Whoever walks with the wise becomes wise, but the companion of fools will suffer harm.'" She gave my wrist a light squeeze. "Proverbs 13:20."

I jerked away from her, feeling heat rise under my collar. "Jack is no fool."

"That's not what I—"

"You don't know what it's like!" I snapped. My anger was sudden and vehement.

"What *what* is like?"

The evenness in her voice irritated me. "To be told *no* at every turn. To struggle and strive and try with every fiber of your being . . . and still have people look at you like you're worthless."

"I don't look at you that way."

I rubbed my forehead with my fingertips. "You just don't get it. Everybody loves you, Alli. Even Mrs. Turner—and she hates everybody. You have a wonderful marriage, steady money, and you're happy. Jack and I . . . we want those same things. We just . . . have to go about it a different way."

"But that's the thing, Beatrice." She reached out a hand to touch me again, but I did not reciprocate. With a slight frown, she pulled her hand back into her lap before continuing. "I *understand* wanting those things. The need for love, security, acceptance—it's inherent in all of us. But the way you and Jack are going about it? You think it's going to give you everything you want, but it's only going to lead to heartbreak. God—"

"God doesn't have anything to do with it. He's not down here in the mud. He doesn't understand what it's like—doesn't understand *me*—the way Jack does."

Alli closed her eyes. Raised a hand to her chest. It was as if I had punched her. And that only made me angrier.

"What are we supposed to do, Alli? We tried God's way. Your way. It didn't work. I know Jack's no saint, but neither was Emmett when you first met him. Why should I be expected to walk away from the man I love when you didn't?"

"Jack and Emmett are very different people."

"What is that supposed to mean?"

She fiddled with the thin gold band on her finger. "I met Emmett because he came to one of my father's revivals. He was fed up with the life he'd been living, all the stealing and constantly looking over his shoulder, waiting for the other shoe to drop. No matter what Jack thinks, I didn't force Emmett into anything. He *wanted* to change. Wanted to get his life right. It was a journey we decided to go on together. It hasn't been perfect, and it hasn't been easy. But the only reason we have any kind of happiness in this wretched place is because we made a commitment to keep going down this path side by side. One that leads us toward God and not away. One I thought you wanted to take, too." She lowered her voice. "But one I know for sure Jack doesn't."

Her words were quiet, but they doused me like a cold shower. She was right. In all the months I'd been meeting with her, Jack had never once asked about our studies. Never once risen to the conversations in which I'd attempted to engage. He had zero interest in that part of my life. He'd made clear whatever Alli and I did together was *my* thing. It was tolerated as long as it didn't interfere.

And it didn't. Because what we were doing was justified; we were just trying to survive. To balance the scales and get what the elites were hoarding for themselves. The wealthy and the upper class, they were criminals, not us. Besides, Alli had told me God loved me no matter what. It was how I reconciled our business with my Bible study. I could have both.

I *could*.

Yet all these things I'd told myself splintered under the harsh reproof my friend—someone who claimed to love me—should not have presumed to speak. In only a few short sentences, Alli had pulled a curtain on the bright lights of Jack's and my enterprise, giving length to shadows of doubt that had only been creeping along the edge. I balled my hands into fists and pushed myself away from the table. Anger felt an easier burden to bear than the fear threatening to overtake me.

"I should have known," I spat. "You're just like the rest of them. All those church people going around, telling people we're all the same, all sinners . . . then casting stones at anything you see as wickedness."

"That's not what I'm saying at all."

"What about that story you were telling me? The one with the woman caught in adultery."

"Beatrice—"

"All those religious people, ready to put her to death because of some law in their holy book. Because she wasn't good enough for their standards." Charles swam up in my memories once again, his critical stare and self-righteous abuse. When I spoke, I spoke to Alli, but my words were directed at them both, "You were the one who told me how Jesus called out the hypocrites. How he didn't condemn that woman, He simply *loved* her." My face felt hot, my eyes blurry. "Why can't you do the same?"

Alli's face was so wounded, I almost apologized. Almost. But I wasn't sorry. I might have hurt her feelings, but she had poked that seed of conviction in my heart. And that was way worse. So instead, I strode from the kitchen, grabbing my coat from the back of her sofa, and stomped to the door.

"Beatrice, wait, please."

I spun around, a snarky remark on the tip of my tongue, only to find Alli right behind me, my Bible in her outstretched hand. Her shawl had fallen, exposing one bony shoulder, and tears glistened in her eyes.

"No, Jesus didn't condemn that woman. And I'm not condemning you. But that's not how the story ends, either."

I narrowed my eyes, hoping she couldn't see my lip begin to quiver.

"'Jesus declared, "Go now and leave your life of sin."' John 8:11." She paused. "Loving a person—truly loving them the way Jesus does—doesn't mean you ignore sin. God *is* love; therefore, any encouragement that steers you onto a path away from Him is unloving. So we love with truth, even if it's painful to hear." She exhaled, long and slow. "That's what I'm trying to do. I care about you, Bea. I just . . . I don't want to see you hurt."

I didn't respond. I couldn't. Instead, I left her standing there with my Bible, escaping into the January night, where the air felt coldest on my empty hands.

The apartment was quiet when I returned, Eleanor still at her babysitting job two floors below. Momentarily, I thought about joining her, but my sister was way too good at hearing words I didn't speak. I couldn't risk it. So instead, I dropped my purse on the kitchen table and walked down the short hallway to my bedroom. I snapped on the light.

"Hey!" came a voice. "What? Who?"

Jack sat up in my bed, rubbing his sleepy eyes. He was clad in a white undershirt and black pants, wrinkled from sleep, and his dark hair stuck up at odd angles. Crease lines crisscrossed his cheeks where his face had been pressed into the sheets.

I'd never seen a more beautiful sight.

I kicked off my shoes and rushed to him, pulling the blankets back over us as I squeezed under his arms. I felt his chest deflate with a contented sigh.

"There's my girl," he murmured. "Where you been?"

"Out." The simplicity of the word betrayed its heaviness.

He yawned. Wrapped an arm around my waist in a gentle, satisfied squeeze. "Well, I'm glad you're home."

"We need to go bigger." I didn't plan the words. Or maybe I did. Either way, it felt like they had been hovering on the edge of my consciousness for months; my argument with Alli hadn't formed the decision, but she had given me the courage I'd needed to release it.

Outside my window, a truck rumbled by, its engine sputtering and coughing in the frigid air. The wail of a baby on the floor above floated down through the boards of the ceiling. And ever so faintly, horns wafted from someone's wireless. A Bing Crosby song or perhaps Guy Lombardo—from here, it was hard to tell.

Yet despite all of these nightly noises, silence stretched on after my words, louder and more tangible than anything else in the room.

After what seemed like an eternity, he finally spoke. "What?"

Though cocooned by the blankets and Jack's warmth, my entire body trembled. "I'm done with West Dallas. Done with all of this. I want to get out of here. For good."

He sat up. "Where is this coming from? What do you—?"

"Does it matter? I just want to get out of town. Get enough money to go. As far as we can as fast as we can. Whatever it takes."

"You know I'll do anything for you. Anything at all. But I have to know . . . are you sure about this? Absolutely sure?"

Yes. No. I wasn't sure of anything anymore except my need to run. Toward our goal. Yes, that's what it was about. It wasn't about running away from Alli and her God. It was about running toward something. Something I knew to be true. The *only* thing I knew to be true. Jack. And our future together.

"I'm sure."

"Well, alright then." When he kissed me, he smelled of sleep and cigarettes. He smelled of *home*. "Whatever you say, my star."

I stared into his eyes, hoping to see myself in them. But the shadows were too great, and I saw nothing but darkness. "I love you."

"I love you, too." He gave me a wink. "In fact, no one loves you more."

I wrapped his words around my heart as I burrowed under the blanket next to him. But despite his heat and the radiator on the wall finally coughing out a trickle of warm, dry air, the iciness in my core continued to needle at me long after the tendrils of winter had been pushed to the edges of the room.

CHAPTER TWENTY-FOUR

Jack wasted no time heeding my request. Two nights later, I found myself in the passenger seat of a Ford Model A coupe—presumably stolen, though I didn't bother to ask—heading west out of Dallas to a destination unknown. All I knew was it was in Fort Worth, which Jack had confided was one of his new favorite haunts. Close enough to home to allow a relatively easy back and forth, but far enough away to avoid the ever-persistent Dallas cops.

I tried not to think about what Alli had said about Jack's name being out there, and not only among friends. I tried not to think about Jesus' command to sin no more or Alli's warning about carousing with fools. I tried not to think about either of them, period. All I wanted was to think about Jack.

From the back seat came a scratch and the nauseating scent of menthol. Ralph Schultz insisted on smoking Spuds, rather than regular old Lucky Strikes like everybody else. Another thing to hate about him.

I shot a sideways glare over my shoulder, which he seemed to misunderstand in the semidarkness of the evening. He waggled his eyebrows, an obnoxious, unattractive thing for any man to attempt, but it was even worse on his sweaty, piggish face. "Nervous, sweetheart?"

I let out an annoyed *humph* and crossed my arms over my chest, not answering.

Jack laid a comforting hand on my knee. Passing headlights illuminated the mischievous grin playing on his lips. "Beatrice has nerves of steel. She's the backbone of this whole thing. I couldn't do anything without her."

I gave him a grateful smile. I hoped it was true. Needed it to be true.

Jack glanced in the rearview mirror as he pulled off the highway and onto a side street. It was properly dark now, the winter sun tucked away hours earlier than what was comfortable . . . unless you were bent on no good. Which we were.

Fort Worth was sleepy compared to the hustle and bustle of Dallas. The midnight streets were practically empty. But to my surprise, Jack steered the car south, away from the downtown area and its plethora of stealable vehicles, into the more rural outskirts. As we drove on, the streetlights became fewer and farther between, casting us deeper into shadow as the lights of the business district began to fade behind us. There were only a handful of buildings now and even fewer cars.

"Jack," I said quietly, "where are we . . . ?"

My question trailed off as he killed the headlights and pulled the car into an empty lot. The crunch of gravel under the tires turned soft, and we came to a stop on grass near the back corner, farthest from the road. Through the darkness, I could see nothing but the outline of scraggly trees amid miles of nothingness. Beside me, I heard the scrape of fabric as Jack shifted, though it was impossible to see him in the moonless night.

"You ready, Schultzy?"

There was a brief, intense flash of orange as Ralph lit another cigarette. "One more smoke, Jack. Steadies my hand."

I felt Jack rather than saw him, a warmth on my arm that did little to curb the goose bumps.

"This is it, Bea. You still in?"

I nodded, thankful the darkness covered my tremble. "I'm in. But . . . for what? There's nothing here."

I felt gentle fingers on my chin, turning my head around. In my apprehension, I hadn't noticed the squat brick building across the street. It was set far back from the road and surrounded by a metal fence. There was a lone security light outside but no cars, no signs, no indication whatsoever of wealth, goods, or treasure within. Even so, whether it was because of its murkiness or its mystery, the place radiated danger.

And excitement.

"Jack, what is this place?"

From the back seat came Ralph's nasal, condescending guffaw. "Geez, Jack, you ain't told her yet? How she's supposed to help when she don't even know what we're after?"

"Shut your mouth, Schultzy. We all got our parts to play. And for her own safety, Bea requires as little information as I can get away with telling her."

"I want to know," I said. "I want to know what we're doing. Everything we're doing."

Once again, Jack's hand was on my cheek. I could only vaguely make out his shape, though he was mere inches in front of me.

The smell of his peppermint gum was strong, overpowering even the blasted menthol wafting from the back seat. "You have to trust me, Bea. This is the first stop on our road outta West Dallas. But for now, the less you know, the better. It's for your own protection. In case we get caught."

My heart leapt into my throat. The sudden, powerful memory of Cisco made it difficult to speak. "You think we're going to get caught?"

His lips on mine, warm and dry. "Not with you here."

And then we were out of the car and into the chilly air. My sweat evaporated instantly, sending a shiver deep into my bones. We crossed the street and slipped through a hole in the fence that Ralph cut easily with a tool he produced from a bag I hadn't even realized he was carrying. Jack held my hand as he led the way to the rear of the building, and though I noticed a slight quiver in them as we ran, I wasn't sure if it came from his fingers or mine.

There was a single black door on the back side of the building, secured with a padlock, which Ralph once again had no trouble removing. Before following him inside the darkened interior, Jack kissed me, then lit a flashlight, reminding me what to do if I saw or heard anyone approach. Two short whistles if the threat was coming from the front, one long one if it was coming from the back. This would help them plan their escape. I, on the other hand, was not to wait but to make a break for it. I was supposed to pull the car around and give them three minutes—only three minutes and not a second longer—before driving away.

Don't wait. Over and over again Jack reiterated these words. My safety came first. The most important words of a plan I had no intention of following, no matter how many times I nodded in agreement.

My exhilaration plummeted along with the temperature the

moment Jack left my sight. I stood pressed against the chilled brick, peering around the corner every ten seconds at a road that remained mercifully empty. Wind whistled through the nearby trees, screams in a silence so heavy it felt like quicksand. There was an energy carried by the breeze, and it wasn't just anticipation. Something felt off about this place. I shuffled from one foot to the other.

What was taking so long? It felt like hours since they'd gone inside. What *was* this place? What were they doing?

Jack, where are you?

Just when I'd decided to go inside and see for myself, his hand found mine, pulling me from the wall and across the gravel lot to the fence line. My mind raced; my heart jumbled. We were through the fence, across the road, and back in the car before I even realized what happened. The thud of heavy bags in the back seat, the rumble of the engine, and we were on the highway, putting miles between us and that building, that darkness, that danger.

High on adrenaline, nothing and everything was funny as the lights of Fort Worth faded behind us. Nestled into the crook of Jack's arm, I could feel his whole body shake, releasing tension along with boyish chuckles. Even Ralph's hyena-like howls from the back seat didn't irk me as much as they normally did.

We had done it. We were free. We were safe.

Eventually our giggles faded into contented silence. Even though he was sure we hadn't been spotted and it would be hours before the robbery was discovered, Jack kept to the back roads to avoid any patrols. Better to not be seen at all. The thirty-minute drive stretched into two hours, but none of us really seemed to mind. Jack and Ralph rested in a successful job; I rested in Jack.

I didn't even realize I'd dozed until I was awoken by the slamming of a car door. I sat up, wincing at my stiff neck. We were back in West Dallas—that much I could tell from the familiar lit skyline in the distance. But it was farther away than it should have been, the Trinity not yet in sight. I twisted around in my seat, searching for Jack and Ralph, both of whom had exited the car. We were in an empty lot, once again across from a large brick building, only this one was brightly lit and belching smoke from towering stacks. The sign out front read Texas Portland Cement & Lime.

Jack and Ralph were moving toward a Model A sedan parked nearby, each with a large bag hefted over his shoulder. As I watched, Ralph opened the rear door and deposited one of the bags inside. Beside him, Jack put the other bag on the ground, bent toward it, and removed two objects from its depths.

Two long, slender objects.

Even from here, even from my limited experience, I knew. They were guns.

My mouth went sour. Jack tucked a gun under each arm, shook Ralph's hand, and began walking back to the car. I turned around quickly. The car shook slightly as he opened and closed the trunk, and when he finally slid back in next to me, his hands were empty once again.

He smiled. "You're awake."

"What was that place?"

"What place?"

My stomach hardened. "The place we robbed, Jack. What was it?"

His smile vanished. "Come on, Bea. I already said I didn't want you to—"

"Tell me."

"It was an armory, okay? A Texas state armory."

My stomach lurched as if he had just pressed on the gas, though the car remained idle. Every town in Texas had an arsenal, a collection of state-owned weapons held for its militia in case of local emergency. They were coveted targets for thieves. Thieves much more notorious—and violent—than we were.

"Jack."

"You said you wanted to go bigger. And to go bigger, we need bigger guns."

My mind flashed once again back to Cisco. To the sound of bullets whizzing past our car, shattering our window. To the one that pierced Jack's shoulder, the one he was lucky to have survived. And to the ones he had spent, which miraculously spared their targets—and spared him a murder sentence.

Guns were a part of this life. I understood that. But I'd seen what just a couple of .45s and six-shooters could do. There was no telling what Jack had found inside that armory. What "improvements" he'd thought we needed. Or what kinds of damage they could inflict.

"I never said I wanted to hurt anybody."

"We won't." Jack turned from me and started the car. Gravel flew out from beneath the wheels as he peeled from the lot. "As long as nobody gets in the way."

I shifted in my seat and tugged at the collar of my dress. It suddenly felt itchy. With each turn of the car, the knot in my stomach tightened. Neither of us spoke during the drive; my words would be insufficient and besides, Jack's were more than enough. But it still didn't stop the prickle of resentment from creeping up my spine, stop apprehension and frustration from competing against each other in my chest. This was what I'd wanted, yes. But I hated that Jack felt he possessed the sole authority on how it should be done.

When we finally arrived back at the apartment, I didn't even wait for him to shift into park before I exited. I strode to the front door without a backward glance. Before I could step into the building, however, Jack's hand was on my arm, his tug hard enough to make me let out a soft cry of pain.

He pulled my face inches from his, so close I could see the stubble starting to break through on his cheeks. His lips were cracked, and his red-rimmed eyes flashed with anger. "This is exactly why I didn't want to tell you where we were going. I knew you wouldn't like it. Well, go ahead and pout all you want, but let me tell you this: if the coppers close in, we need to be able to protect ourselves. I need to be able to protect *you*. I've said it once and I'll say it again: I am not going back to prison, Bea. And I sure as anything won't be letting you go there either."

He didn't stay with me that night. He didn't even kiss me good-bye. Instead, I climbed the stairs to my apartment alone, counting the small blessing that Eleanor was still asleep when I let myself inside. I crept to my bedroom and shut the door behind me, pushing on the upper right corner to avoid the telltale creak. I sank onto the mattress. I wanted to bury myself in my bed and sleep for weeks. Instead, I winced as something hard dug into my back. Sitting up, I pulled the object into my lap, squinting at the note taped to the front, written in Eleanor's small but immaculate hand:

Alli dropped this off for you.

My Bible. Alli had brought me my Bible.

Feeling as if I'd been burned, I stuffed the book under my bed, shoving a few boxes in front of it for good measure. I inhaled several times trying to steady my breathing. How dare she bring this back to me. I'd made it clear how I felt about her and her God—I wanted nothing to do with either of them anymore.

I'd burned those bridges, and there was no going back now.

I forced myself to lie down, willing sleep to come. But my brain would not empty. It swam from Alli to Jack and back again, with uncertainty and with fear. But mainly it wrestled with the things he'd said, those words I hoped against hope meant something other than what I knew deep down to be true:

Jack Turner was prepared to die for me.

He was also prepared to kill.

CHAPTER TWENTY-FIVE

Sweat dripped down my back as I stared across the street at the pale stone facade of the First Bank of Cedar Hill. It was plain and unassuming, one large square window in the front, a single wooden door to the left, hidden beneath a decorative archway. The sky above was a blinding shade of blue, and a pot of flowers sat near the entrance, purple pansies blooming in the early spring heat and adding a splash of color to the otherwise-drab concrete thoroughfare.

An ordinary day. But not for long.

"I don't like this, Jack. I don't like this at all."

He scooted closer to me. He had removed his suit coat, and I could see perspiration dampening the fabric of his button-down.

His face, however, was calm. "It has to be you, Bea. My face is too well-known."

"Then let's get out of the Dallas area. Go someplace farther away."

He shook his head. When he did, a piece of dark hair fell across his forehead; he did not push it away. "No, this place is golden."

Ralph leaned forward from the back seat, stinking of body odor and his nauseating menthols. "Quick cash and a quicker get-away. Those are the rules, Beatrice."

He was right, of course. The bank was only a few blocks from the highway. Cedar Hill was large enough for the bank to hold significant money, but small enough to keep its citizens sleepy and unprepared for a robbery. It was an opportune crime, one Jack assured me we'd be crazy to pass up.

But for all the boxes this job checked, the two it didn't were the riskiest: it was less than fifteen miles from my apartment and less than ten from the prowling Dallas police officers, who were getting more aggressive by the day. We'd always drawn a line between where we slept and where we played; while Jack swore we were over that line, the margin for this one was too razor-thin for comfort.

Not to mention it was another daytime robbery. The last time we'd attempted a job like this, Jack had ended up at Eastham.

"But sending me in? Jack, I've never been in a bank before. I don't belong there, and everyone in that place knows it. Banking is a man's world; a woman sticks out like a sore thumb, especially a woman like me." I gestured at my dress. It was pretty, store-bought and not homemade, with a V-neck bodice and dropped waist, pale green with navy-blue accents. The nicest one I owned, and yet still, somehow, not nice enough. For a bank, at least. It felt too flashy and modern. I had no hat, no gloves, no sensible jewelry.

In short, I looked like a woman better suited for Saturday night than Monday morning.

"What are you talking about?" Jack waved away my reservations. "You're a knockout in that dress. A real lady."

I couldn't explain that Jack's version of lady and the bank's were not the same thing. There was no point. Bigger risks, bigger rewards, we'd decided. Jack needed me. And we needed this.

Taking a deep breath, I exited the car, shielding my eyes from the sun as I crossed the packed dirt of Cedar Street. My legs were wobbly, a fact not improved by heels, and my ankle twisted twice on loose rocks before I made it to the sidewalk. I wanted to look back, to get one more reassuring smile from Jack, but I knew I couldn't. His instructions were clear.

I reached for the door, only to be startled when it opened of its own accord.

"After you, ma'am." A red-haired man in a crisp three-piece suit extended his arm, holding the door open from the inside.

"Th-thank you," I stuttered, managing what I hoped was a smile as I stepped inside. He dipped his chin and exited behind me. The bank lobby was cool, dim, and cavernous, with deceptively high ceilings and a wooden floor that echoed with every step. To one side was a long wooden table covered in slips of paper. Ahead, a stone counter topped with bars, which separated the balding, overweight teller from the customers.

At a little past eight, there were only six people inside the bank, not including me. The teller; another worker behind him, suited and giving off an air of importance—the president, perhaps?—three customers; and one security guard.

All men. All staring at me.

Every instinct told me to run. Instead, I lifted my head high and met their gazes, trying to mimic the way I'd seen Mrs. Russell behave when talking to her cook. I stepped into line behind an elderly gentleman holding a cane. He narrowed his eyes at me briefly before turning back around and facing the teller. A cough, the shuffle of feet, the crinkle of paper. A return to business.

I bit down on the tiniest hint of a smile. My pulse began to quicken, that old familiar thrill propelling the fear from my veins. Step one had been successful. I was in.

I kept my head forward but allowed my eyes to flit around the room. The security guard stood by the far end of the counter, smoking a cigarette. He looked to be in his midthirties, tall but lanky. He might be a fast runner, but in a fight, he'd be no match strength-wise for Jack. The gun holstered on his hip, however, might be a problem. But Jack had two Browning automatics in the car, and Ralph had two more. In a gunfight, the guard's small pistol didn't stand a chance.

In a gunfight. How I hoped it wouldn't come to that.

I let my eyes wash over the teller's box. The partition was thin, and the teller himself was fat and red-cheeked. He wouldn't put up a fight if there was a barrel in his face. And the fancy pants behind him? Even from here I could see his knock-knees and thin arms. All the money in the world couldn't atone for his feebleness. And his feebleness was the only thing standing between Jack and the vault door behind him.

"Ma'am?"

So concerned with my mission, I hadn't realized it was my turn. The teller's brows were furrowed with obvious annoyance. "What can I do for you?"

My mouth felt dry. When I pried my lips apart, they made an awful sucking noise. "I . . ." The word came out as a squeak, and I coughed, trying to right it. "I'd like to open a new account, please."

That's all I had to do. Pretend to want an account, then bow out, claiming to have left my purse in the car. Delicately. Womanly. Nothing to cause suspicion, nothing to raise eyebrows. Just a foolish, forgetful, *innocent* woman.

He raised his chin, appraising me. Beads of sweat collected in his neck rolls. "Where's your husband?"

"I beg your pardon?"

"Your husband. Women can't open accounts on their own. They need a man's signature. I apologize, but I thought that was common knowledge."

Nausea rolled in my stomach. Having never had a bank account, Jack knew nothing of the etiquette or rules. He'd sent me in here with the express purpose of avoiding attention. He didn't understand that my very presence was curious; the request he'd had me make now turned it suspicious.

"My . . . my husband is at work," I managed, folding my hands over one another in front of me in an attempt to hide my lack of a wedding band. "We're new in town and he sent me in here to set up our accounts."

"And just where did you move from where it's proper to send a lady into a bank unaccompanied?"

Behind him, I saw the bank president's eyes shift upward. He glanced in my direction with a questioning tilt of the head. I took a step backward, clammy hands gripping the sides of my dress.

"I . . ." Words fizzled on my tongue. *Chicago!* my mind screamed. *New York! Washington!* Any number of big cities would perhaps be more progressive and, more importantly, anonymous. *You're a star, for pete's sake. Use your skills!* But my acting brain failed me, my confidence withering under the severe, cynical stare of the teller. "Very well. I shall return with my husband."

I forced myself to stride from the lobby with a confident, practiced gait, making sure to keep my trembling hands clenched in front of me, well out of sight. I was unsure if I'd even spoken the words out loud or, if I had, if I'd spoken them loud enough for him to hear. All I knew was my heart was in my throat and no matter how many laps I took around the block—again, Jack's instructions—it refused to retreat, even after I'd finally slid back inside the car, out of breath and drenched in sweat.

"Go." I gestured wildly. "We have to go. They know something's up."

Jack's face fell. He grabbed both of my hands, stilling them. "What happened?"

"No women," I said breathlessly. "Women can't open accounts. They started asking questions. They know. They *know*. We need to get out of here, Jack."

Ralph's damp hand gripped my shoulder. "How many guards? How many tellers?"

"Just one. One of each. But it doesn't matter. We have to go. It's too risky."

There was a pause after my words, a moment too long and a hair too still. A delay in which the men's eyes met and I knew Jack, for the first time, was questioning my judgment.

"One guard," Ralph murmured. "One teller." He turned from me, his tongue exploring the inside of his pockmarked cheek as he focused his attention on Jack. "We came all this way."

"All this way?" I squeaked. "We're fifteen miles from home!"

"We've got the Brownings," Jack said softly. "One guard is no match for four Brownings."

"No violence." I hated how desperate I sounded, how pathetic and childlike my voice was. "I don't want any violence."

He placed a palm against my cheek. But rather than comforting, his touch felt cold. Condescending. "There won't be. Not with one guard and four Brownings."

"Jack, please. We're going to get caught."

"Caught?" He winked and let out a small, cold laugh. "Come on, Bea. This is how legends are born. And you forget: I'm Jack Turner. Ain't a lawman in Dallas been able to snag me yet."

Jack's confidence sent a shiver down my spine. But this time, it wasn't from excitement.

They were gone less than ten minutes. But rather than Jack's smug smile, it was a barrage of gunfire and the wail of a siren that signaled their return. Jack shoved me from the driver's seat and stepped on the gas, fishtailing away as bullets rained down from every direction.

"They're shooting at us!" Ralph shouted from the back seat. "The townsfolk are shooting at us!"

At that moment, my window exploded, sending a torrent of glass shards across my arms and torso. I screamed, flinging my hands to my face. Thousands of needles ripped at my skin. Jack pushed me down onto the seat just as another bullet shattered the side mirror. The car lurched. He pressed harder on the accelerator, but the sirens behind us never seemed to get farther away. Jack kept one hand on my head, pinning my face to the seat cushion as the rest of my body twisted and slid with each sharp turn. Several pops, closer now—Ralph was returning fire. I could see nothing but the fabric of Jack's pant leg, blurry through my watering eyes, could feel nothing but the hum of the engine and the rapid lefts and rights as he tried to lose our pursuers.

I don't know how long they trailed us. I don't know when the sirens finally faded and the bullets ceased. Huddled beside Jack, I retreated inside myself. There was a great weight upon my chest, like dirty water from that trough all those years ago. I felt cold; my soul was being pulled down, down, down . . .

"Bea! Bea, are you okay?"

Suddenly there was light. And Jack, shaking me. His face was white, his hands clammy. When he pulled them away, there was blood on his fingertips. I blinked, trying to process. *My* blood. I was bleeding.

"Bea, oh, my goodness." He pulled me toward him but I had no energy to return the embrace. "Are you hit? Are you—?" He bit off his question cleanly, like the snip of a pair of scissors.

I patted my body with trembling hands. Every inch of my arms was covered in gashes. The fabric of my dress was ripped, revealing more wounds across my chest and stomach. I put a hand to my face, feeling wet stickiness above my brow. With a small cry, I pulled a shard of glass from the skin above my eyebrow, a gush of fresh warmth cascading down my temple.

I was bleeding. I was in pain. But it was only glass. All those bullets had missed me. Missed *us*.

Jack ripped off his shirt and pressed it to my head. "You've got fifteen minutes," he said flatly. "Fifteen minutes and we're gone, with or without you."

I blinked, confused. But his words apparently weren't directed at me. From the back seat came the rustle of movement and the slamming of a door.

Ralph.

Jack let out a shaky sigh. "Thank goodness you're okay. I couldn't . . ." He stopped, shook his head, and seized my wrist. "It doesn't matter. We have to go."

I winced as he pulled me toward the door. The veins in my head throbbed. Black spots floated at the edges of my vision. I stood woozily, leaning on Jack for support. Through my haze, I could make out bricks. Familiar bricks. My apartment. "Go?"

Arm around my waist, he half led, half dragged me up the walk. "Pack a bag. We have to go. Get out of Dallas. Now."

Clarity slammed into me like a tidal wave, dulling my physical pain behind a veneer of rising panic. I wrenched out of his grip, swaying slightly but holding my ground. "I can't just *go*, Jack. What about Eleanor, my—?"

He grabbed my arm. His eyes were wilder than I'd ever seen, darkened by a shadow that grew from within. "The guard recognized me, Beatrice. He'd heard the stories, seen pictures from cops trying to pin every burglary in a fifty-mile radius on me. He knew me. He said my *name*."

"But—"

"And he saw you too, remember? The cops will be here in no time at all. We have to go. *Now*."

Bile rose in the back of my throat, bitter and acidic. Or maybe that was just my own horror. Yes, I'd wanted to leave West Dallas. But not like this.

I followed Jack into the building on numb legs, ignoring the bloodstains left on the door handle as we pushed our way into the apartment—and right into my sister.

"Oh!" She was dressed for work in a sensible brown seersucker dress with a wide white collar, brass buttons disappearing into her pleated skirt just below the waist. Her hair was up in a tight bun, revealing a face so lightly powdered it might as well have been nude.

Shame squeezed my heart. I'd always been the pretty one. Not a brag, just a fact. But in this moment, my plain-Jane sister was the most beautiful Carraway by leaps and bounds. And not just because of her appearance.

"Bea! I thought you were at work! I was . . ." Her dark eyes, initially sparkling with delight, fell as she fully took in my face, my arms, my legs. Her cheeks paled and her mouth began to twitch, shock and concern stealing her words.

"El . . ."

Jack brushed past us both, pulling me into the apartment and leaving Eleanor standing in the hall, open-mouthed. After a few seconds, she followed, closing the door behind us.

"I'll grab some food," he said, stepping up to the window and peering nervously down at the street. "Go get some clothes. I have a couple suits in your closet. Take them all." He closed the curtains, casting the room in a dim, ominous shadow, and hurried to the kitchen.

I stared after him for a moment, struggling to process his words. Everything seemed to be moving in slow motion, a dream where nothing connected, nothing made sense. Only Eleanor's hand on my shoulder felt real.

"Bea, what . . . ?"

I smiled at her. It was fake and ridiculous; blood dripped from my forehead and onto the carpet below. I lifted a wad of fabric— Jack's shirt, I remembered vaguely—and pressed it to the wound. "I'm okay. Really. It looks worse than it is."

Her gaze flitted over each cut, each red drop. As it did, her grip on me tightened. I could feel her panic, see the dread spreading through her body. Once again, her lips began to twitch. She was losing her words.

Me. Her sister. Her protector. I was the one making her lose her words.

And it was only in that moment I truly took Jack's command to heart. I wanted to take her with me. That had always been the plan. But that plan had gone down in a hail of gunfire. I needed to go. Not only to protect him or myself, but to protect *her.* I couldn't have her involved in this. Sweet, innocent, *good* Eleanor. I needed to get as far away from her as possible in order to keep her safe.

The realization seared me like a hot iron, both tearing at the remains of my heart and spurring me into action. I wrenched from her touch and ran to my bedroom, pulling Jack's suits and a handful of dresses from my closet. Yanking a suitcase from the top shelf, I stuffed them all inside, making a stupid and irrational decision to include my jewelry and makeup bag too. I wanted to grab everything in my room, all my books and pictures, trinkets and memories, and yet I refused. Doing so would mean I didn't plan on coming back. But this wasn't forever. It *couldn't* be forever. Right?

Eleanor stood in the doorway, shifting back and forth on her heels, still holding her purse. As if it were a normal Monday and she was waiting for a bus. Only her face—pale and convulsing in involuntary tics—showed any difference.

"Listen to me, El. I need you to go to work today. I know you probably feel like that's impossible, but I need you to go. For me. Go to work and do your job like everything is fine. That's very important, Eleanor. You have to act like everything is fine." I grabbed a pair of black boots—worn at the toe but flat and practical—and shoved them into the case. "When you get off work, don't come back here. Go to Mama's." The words gagged me, burned in my throat. "I know you don't want to, but it's—"

"Houston."

I spun around, her croak as loud as a shout. "What?"

"Houston," she repeated.

"Mama's in Houston?"

She nodded. "Tony."

Tony was my mother's new boyfriend. We'd only met him once, and that had been enough. He was dark and hairy, and he smelled like garlic. But he was loaded with money from some Italian restaurant he owned on the other side of the river, and for my mother, that was all that mattered.

I sighed, the tiniest cloud of tension releasing from my lungs.

Their absence was the first thing to go right all day. "That's great. Better than great. You won't have to worry about them." I flung one of Jack's belts into the suitcase and closed the lid. "Stay there for a few days. You'll be safe. And, El?" I turned. She stood in the doorway, twisting her hands in front of her waist, her eyes as big as saucers. This time, it was me who struggled to say the words. "If the police come, you haven't seen me. You've been at Mama's the whole time, watching the house while she's away. Okay?"

Eleanor's already-gaping mouth fell wider. And then, in a gesture as stoic as it was absurd, she closed it again . . . and nodded.

Self-hatred rose up inside me, bigger and more powerful than even my guilt. Eleanor wouldn't be able to lie to the police. More than likely, she wouldn't be able to speak at all. And the fact that I was asking her to felt like a new layer of filth on my soul that I'd never be able to wash clean.

"Bea?" Jack's voice from the other room. "We need to go!"

I grabbed the suitcase, the soreness in my arms screaming from its weight, and pulled it from the bed, only to have the contents fall in a heap on the floor. Consumed by my own condemnation, I'd forgotten to latch the lid. Cursing under my breath, I gathered everything into my arms and shoved it back inside. As I did, a cut on my hand knocked against something hard half-hidden beneath my bed and buried under now-wrinkled dresses. I yanked it out with a small yelp.

My Bible.

My fingers tingled as I gripped the spine. It was as if heat radiated from thin pages. *Alli.* What would Alli think when she found out? What would she do? Her face swam in front of me, kind smile and joyful laugh, the warmth of her hand on mine during her gentle prayers. The words of warning she'd given about Jack now seemed prophetic. I had thought I couldn't possibly feel any more pain, but at the thought of her—of our afternoons together—a fresh wave of anguish swelled within me.

"Can you tell Alli . . . ?" Tell Alli what? What could I possibly have to say to her? "Tell Alli . . ."

"Bea! Let's *go*!"

Using a cough to stifle my cry, I shoved the Bible into the suitcase. The clicking of its latch was as loud and permanent-sounding as a gunshot. I half carried, half dragged the bag across the floor, stopping where my sister still stood in the doorway. Her body was stiff under my touch as I hugged her, breathing in the scent of her soap, her shampoo, *her*. It wasn't until I tried to pull away that she finally hugged me back, the strength in her arms communicating feelings her mouth never could.

My blood left patches of crimson on her dress, an image I knew would forever be burned into my memory. A stain neither she nor I would ever be able to get out. "I'm sorry, Eleanor. I am so very sorry."

They weren't the right words. They weren't enough words. And yet they were the only ones I had. As we pulled away from the building, tears blurred my eyes and I wondered if they would be the last ones I ever spoke to her.

CHAPTER TWENTY-SIX

Jack ditched the car in Abilene, removing the plates to ensure it was untraceable, and stole a black Ford Model A coupe that wheezed when he tried to accelerate over thirty. In Sweetwater, we repeated the process, only this time it was Ralph who managed to snag a Plymouth to carry us over the New Mexico state line. We stopped only for gas, only in the most isolated outposts and only when it was absolutely necessary.

By nightfall, the mood inside the car was tense and silent, the stench of body odor and cigarettes making my empty stomach churn. Jack kept a firm grip on the steering wheel despite eyes that were red-rimmed and glassy. Ralph was stretched out across the back seat, snoozing with his hat over his eyes. Jack had made a half-hearted attempt to snuggle with me as we'd left Dallas, but somehow I'd found myself on the other side of the seat, head resting in the crook of my arm, before we'd even reached Eastland. He had not pulled me back to him, and I had not volunteered. Instead, I sat pressed against the passenger door and found my own eyelids growing heavy in the approaching twilight. But I didn't want to sleep. Despite the grim reality, it was my dreams I feared the most.

But as mile after mile of nondescript wasteland crept past my window, my body won out and I gave in to a fitful rest. A loud bang and sudden jolt awoke me only seconds later, or so it felt. My head, still tender from its myriad of cuts, throbbed where it had smacked the dashboard. My eyes, gritty from sleep, blurred from the pain.

Beside me, Jack let out a string of curses before exiting the car with a vicious slam of the door.

I pushed myself back up on the seat and rubbed at my face. My fingers came away red with fresh blood. One—or more—of my wounds had reopened. *Fantastic.* I grabbed the bloody remains of Jack's shirt, which had been flung onto the floorboards, before stepping out of the car myself.

The front end of the Plymouth lay half-buried in a dune. On the smoking hood lay the remains of a fence post along with a couple of strands of barbed wire. There was a large crack in the left side of the windshield; one of the headlights was now nothing but a mess of splintered glass, the shards glinting in the few remaining rays of light still visible over the flattened plain.

Jack stood with his hands on his hips, chin raised to the sky. His nostrils flared with the force of his measured breath.

Ralph appeared behind me, one hand pressed to his nose. Blood trickled out from between his fingers. His swears came out garbled and nasal but dripping with venom.

"Now look what you've done!" he snarled at Jack. "I told ya we shoulda stopped in Seminole—"

"We had to get out of Texas."

"And go where? You ain't even told me where we're going! I'm starting to wonder if you know yourself. Tell me, Jack: where *are* we going?"

"We had to get out of Texas," he repeated.

Ralph attempted a snort, which was cut short by a yelp. I wondered if, in his anger and injury, he'd noticed what I wished I hadn't: Jack didn't answer the question.

"Then you shoulda let me drive! I done said you was getting tired, and getting tired means getting sloppy. Now look where we—"

"*I* drive. You knew that when you signed on to work for me."

"*With* you." Ralph spat a wad of blood onto the ground. "I work *with* you. Fifty-fifty."

There was a challenge in Jack's silence, one I knew Ralph felt if only for the slight deflating of his shoulders as the quiet dragged on. I pressed the rag against my forehead, trying to become invisible. Not that Jack seemed to even be aware of my presence. He was too busy staring at Ralph, his gray eyes a dangerous shade of black.

But when he finally spoke, his tone was calm. "I drive."

The simplicity of his words carried a weight and power that could not be argued with. Especially not beside a deserted highway in a stolen car as night settled in. Rather than debate, Ralph tied a bandanna over his dripping nose and moved to the front of the car, where he attempted to push as Jack slid back into the driver's seat and tried to restart the engine. But no matter how many shoves and punches, no matter how many curses and pleas, the Plymouth refused to return to life.

As the final twinges of purple sky faded to black, Jack let out one last string of swear words. "It's no use." He stepped out of the car and gave the door an angry kick. "It's too dangerous to stick around here any longer. We need to get going."

I pulled at my fingers, shifting from one foot to the other. "And go where?"

But Jack was already taking our bag from the trunk. "There was a farmhouse a few miles back. There's bound to be a vehicle there we can pilfer." He removed a long screwdriver from the side pocket and busied himself detaching the Plymouth's license plate. "And if there's not, we keep walking. We can't be more than ten miles from Hobbs. There are plenty of cars there."

A weariness sank into my body, deeper even than the physical exhaustion. My adrenaline was long gone. The bank in Cedar Hill, the chase, the look on Eleanor's face as we left . . . it didn't seem possible it had happened only that morning. I was sure I'd been awake for days, maybe even weeks, and yet when I looked down, I was somehow still in that same dress, with the navy accents and dropped waist. Only the rips and bloodstains peppering the pale-green fabric made it all real.

My legs felt like lead. The prospect of walking—ten feet or ten miles, it didn't matter—seemed impossible. No, not impossible. *Intolerable.* I just wanted to go home.

But I didn't have a home anymore. By now, the cops had probably closed in on the apartment; I could only hope Eleanor had taken my instructions and fled. More than likely, they'd gone to Jack's parents' place, maybe even Alli and Emmett's too. My stomach clenched as I pictured Alli's face, falling further and further as the cops explained why they were there.

If I'd had the strength, I would have cried then, though I wasn't sure who the tears would be for. All I knew is they wouldn't be for me. I didn't deserve them.

Jack dropped the plate into the bag, where it clanged as it

connected with the others we'd removed, and refastened the latch. "You're gonna need to take this," he said, thrusting the bag at me in the dark.

"Me?"

"It's either that or the guns, Bea. You wanna carry the guns?"

I hated the arrogance in his tone, the way I was sure it was accompanied by a sneer, even though I couldn't see his face. I hated the way he dropped the bag at my feet and started walking, not even bothering to see if I—or Ralph—would follow, because in his hubris, he knew we would. Most of all, I hated that even though I hated all those things, I followed anyway. What other choice did I have?

We cut across dead fields and windswept pastures, careful to avoid the road lest we encounter any gun-toting civil patrols or bored rural deputies. My low heels were soon filled with dirt, which I made the mistake of complaining about only once. Ralph's annoyed expression as I emptied my shoes was nothing compared to the daggers in Jack's eyes. His insistence we hurry seemed born more out of paranoia than actual threat; there wasn't a soul for miles, unless you counted the irritated cows and disgruntled mules. The "farmhouse" Jack had seen turned out to be nothing more than a dilapidated barn, empty and out of use. I wanted to suggest we stop and catch a few winks there before continuing but knew my appeals would be as wasted as the landscape in which we found ourselves stranded.

We reached the outskirts of Hobbs in the still-dark early morning hours, thirsty and exhausted. My feet were blistered and my arms rubber. When Jack left me by a sagging cottonwood in an overgrown park near the water tower, I should have been furious. Maybe even terrified. Yet there was no room for anything but overwhelming fatigue. As he and Ralph disappeared into town under the cover of a moonless sky, I fell asleep, the scratchy bark at my back as comfortable as the most luxurious down pillow. I was barely conscious of them returning, of the idling of an engine, of Jack's arms around my waist and the soft fabric beneath my body. The last thing I remembered was the sound of a car door slamming and the crunch of gravel beneath tires as I drifted into a deep and mercifully dreamless sleep.

CHAPTER TWENTY-SEVEN

I awoke to the feel of Jack's hand stroking my hair, though at first I couldn't muster the strength to open my eyes. Everything on my body ached. My arms, my legs, my feet. But it was my face—my tender, throbbing face—that truly brought the truth rushing back in. My painful body could have been the result of a hard day's work, sweeping and scrubbing the Russells' large house. But the cuts on my face . . .

"Bea."

Jack's voice was gentle and sweet, his touch delicate. But still I couldn't bring myself to open my eyes. And it wasn't just because of lingering exhaustion.

My body screamed in agony as he pulled it close to his; I wanted to press in and pull away at the same time. "Bea, you've been asleep for almost eighteen hours. You need to drink something. Eat something."

Eighteen hours. My eyes fluttered open in sudden fear. "Where . . . ?" My question dissolved into coughs. My mouth was dry, my throat on fire. "Where are . . . ?" I tried again.

"Shh. Don't try to talk. We're okay. We're safe." Jack gave a small smile. The shadow was gone from his eyes, but a weariness remained just below the surface. "We're at a motor court outside Carlsbad. We switched the plates off the V-8 we took in Hobbs with the ones from Abilene and backed it into the garage attached to the cabin. It's not foolproof, but we're over four hundred miles from Cedar Hill. It'll buy us at least a few days."

I blinked, trying to digest his words as my body began to process feelings outside of its own soreness. Cool sheets under my fingertips, a soft pillow under my head. The smell of soap on Jack's skin, the smoothness of a new shirt. I let my hands travel down my body, shocked to discover a cotton nightdress where ripped satin had once been.

"I changed your clothes," Jack said as if reading my mind. "I wanted to get you in the shower, but you could barely even stand. I thought it best to let you sleep."

The room was simple, small, and dim. The lamp on the nightstand was unlit, curtains drawn over both windows. I had no idea what time of day it was. The walls were wood-paneled, but the drab was broken up by several paintings hung throughout, most of them uninspired desertscapes filled with cactus and sagebrush.

Jack's arms gripped me tighter. I could feel the rise and fall of his chest, the hitch in his breath before he spoke again. "I . . . I'm so sorry, Bea. I've been a beast. All I could think about was getting you somewhere safe. But that doesn't excuse my behavior. I pushed you too hard, and I'm sorry." He buried his face in my neck. "Please forgive me."

I wanted to. I was still too tired, still in too much pain to fight. But it didn't escape my notice that he apologized only for the way he'd treated me during our escape, not for the bungled robbery I'd warned him against. The one that had brought us to this place to begin with.

The one that had cost me my sister.

I stiffened under his touch.

He pulled his head back to look at me. "Bea, I'm sor—"

"Why didn't you listen to me?" I shifted myself out of his embrace, trying to pretend my wounds didn't scream in agony as I did so. "I told you that bank was too risky."

He rolled onto his back and closed his eyes as he sighed. "I know you did. But we got away—"

"Got away?" I shrieked. I felt a cut on my cheek open back up under the force, but I did not lower my voice. "Look at my face, Jack! Look at . . ." I gestured wildly to our surroundings.

"What's wrong with this place?" he asked, propping himself up on his elbows.

"Nothing except for the fact we are using it to *hide from the law*!"

He pushed himself off the bed, causing the whole thing to shake. "I got you out of West Dallas, didn't I?"

"I didn't want it like this!"

He threw his hands in the air. "Then what, Beatrice? What is it exactly we were supposed to do? Ask the bankers for the money politely over a nice cup of tea?"

I felt my skin flush. For all the ways Jack made me feel golden, he was equally as gifted in making me feel stupid and immature.

"We scored over a thousand dollars in that robbery. A thousand bucks! Would I prefer we'd gotten away scot-free? Of course. But now we've got a pretty little chunk of change to start us on this new life. The one *you wanted*." He raised his eyebrows at me in a pointed and almost-accusatory glare.

I pulled my arms and legs toward my core. "But what about . . . ?" I hated the tremble in my voice. "What about your family?"

"They'll be fine. They didn't have anything to do with this, and pretty soon the cops'll have to leave 'em be. But we'll send them some dough, make sure they're taken care of."

"And Eleanor? She was supposed to come with us."

For the first time, I felt the air in the room soften. Jack sat down beside me. His hand hovered over my skin as if searching for a place to touch that wasn't covered in cuts. Eventually he settled for my knee. "I know, Beatrice. And I'm sorry. It just didn't work out that way."

Didn't work out that way. As if it had been a game of chance that led us to this point and not Jack's arrogant choices.

Or my own rash ones.

"But we'll send her money too," he was saying. "Everything we can spare. She'll be fine." He rose and kissed me on the forehead. "Ralph should be back with breakfast soon," he said. "There's a diner across the street, and I thought he would be the safest bet to send inside. I couldn't stomach any more bologna or potato chips. Are you hungry?"

The conversation was over. The account settled. In Jack's mind, money solved everything. And I suppose, in my mind too. Except for this. Because what Jack couldn't understand—and what I couldn't explain—was that it wasn't money Eleanor needed. It was *me*.

Or at least, the old me. The me who wasn't a fugitive. The me whose presence wouldn't put her in danger.

But that person didn't exist anymore. And so I let it drop too.

Jack disappeared into the main part of the cabin while I show-ered in the white-tiled bathroom with flowered wallpaper that had begun to bubble in a few places. The porcelain in the tub was chipped in several places, revealing the cast iron underneath. But the water was hot, and I stood beneath the spray until it was pain-ful. I was filthy: my skin, my hair, even under my nails. The heat massaged my muscles but reopened cuts on my face, arms, and abdomen. Rivulets of brown and red cascaded down the drain.

I stayed in the shower until the water grew cold. Stepping out, I dug through my suitcase until I found a light-blue housedress, simple cotton with pink ribbing around the collar and arms. I topped it with a black wool cardigan. Plain. Boring. Every bit the picture of an ordinary housewife, should anyone come knocking. I was just getting ready to sit down at the smudged mirror and have a go at my tangles when I heard a door slam. The smell of sausage and potatoes was powerful enough to penetrate the closed bedroom door, and my hair and makeup were instantly forgotten.

The rest of the cabin was much like the bedroom, wood-paneled and dim, curtains pulled across two large windows that looked out onto a gravel parking lot. The main area consisted of a living room and kitchen. Yellow linoleum floor throughout, though a shaggy brown rug covered most of the ground beneath the coffee table and sagging couch, the cushions of which were in such disarray, I surmised it had served as Ralph's bed. In the kitchen, there was a sink, an icebox, a stove, and a small oval-shaped table, currently covered in greasy paper bags, the smell from which was even stronger and more intoxicating out here.

I was suddenly hungrier than I'd ever been in my entire life. But to my surprise, Jack and Ralph were not digging into the bags. They weren't even pulling out plates and silverware. They were, instead, standing side by side next to the sink, their noses buried in a newspaper. Engrossed, they didn't even register my appearance or raise their heads at the crumpling of the bag as I pulled a flapjack from its depth.

Not bothering to see if there was syrup or butter, I took several quick bites. My stomach rolled, rebelling against the pancake's richness, and I took a deep breath, using every ounce of willpower I had to keep myself from scarfing down the entire thing and making myself sick. I forced myself to count to twenty, and when the food stayed safely down, I devoured the rest and reached for a second, pausing only for a small sip of coffee.

"Woo-hoo!"

The sound of Jack's holler caused me to jump. I dropped a piece of sausage, which I retrieved swiftly from the floor and wiped on a napkin.

"Look at this, Bea! Look!" Jack shoved the newspaper in my face, so close the words blurred. I pulled my head back until the print finally came into focus.

In bold black and white, front and center on the front page, was the headline:

Dallas Desperado Strikes Again!

Jack Turner, also known by locals as the Dallas
Desperado, robbed a bank in Cedar Hill on Monday,
making off with over $1,000 from the First Bank's
vault.

I frowned. "The Dallas Desperado? Who calls you the Dallas Desperado?"

Jack grinned, rolling his shoulders. "No idea. But I like it." He pointed to the paper. "Keep reading!"

Turner and an as-yet-unidentified second man entered
the bank shortly after 8 a.m. on Monday, brandishing
weapons and demanding cash. Fearing for his life, the
bank president, Mr. S. J. Arnold, entered the vault and
handed its contents to Turner as the second man held
the lone guard and several patrons hostage. A shoot-out
ensued, however, when another patron, Mr. Abraham
Phillips, entered the building and, seeing the robbery
in progress, pulled a pistol from his coat and began
firing. Turner and his companion returned fire and fled,
though not before striking two patrons and the security
guard, all three of whom are expected to make a full
recovery.

My back went rigid. The half-chewed sausage in my mouth
suddenly tasted putrid. I felt foolish to not have realized. I'd been
there; I had heard the guns being fired. And yet seeing it now in
black and white, the truth somehow felt more real.

"You shot a man," I said quietly.

Jack stretched his neck to one side, rubbing at it with the hand
not holding the paper. "It was just the security guard."

"And two patrons."

He let out an exaggerated burst of air through his nostrils,
clearly irritated. "So? They're all going to survive. It says so right
there. Besides, you said yourself they treated you like garbage when
you were in there."

"That was because I was a woman in a man's place, not
because—"

"It doesn't matter, Bea. It doesn't matter because *we* don't matter to them. Or have you forgotten that already?"

Ralph made a grunting noise in assent. I dipped my chin to

my chest and said nothing, returning my attention to the paper in Jack's hand.

Turner and his companion escaped in a V-8 with a blonde-haired woman police have identified as Miss Beatrice Carraway, also of West Dallas. The Salacious Sheba is believed to be Turner's romantic partner as well as his scout, as eyewitnesses place a woman matching Carraway's description inside the bank just moments before the robbery.

So there it was. My name in print. Finally. I even had a handle to boot. My pulse began to throb inside my ears.

The Desperado and his Sheba are wanted in connection with several other robberies, including ones in McKinney, Plano, and Cleburne, as well as numerous auto thefts throughout the Dallas area. Any information leading to the capture—

Jack pulled it away before I could read any further. "What an article! Front-page center, in a newspaper over four hundred miles from Dallas! But that isn't even the best part. Look!" He pointed to another article, this one smaller and toward the bottom of the page.

Oklahoma Sheriff Shot; Pretty Boy Floyd Wanted

"We're a bigger story than Floyd!" Jack was positively giddy. "Look at the size of our headline compared to his!"

Jack's spirits were through the roof. Mine, on the other hand, felt torn in two. He was right: we *were* a big story. Big enough to warrant attention outside Texas, maybe even outside of the entire Southwest. Perhaps folks in Chicago and New York were reading our names. The money was wonderful, yes. But more importantly, people were finally starting to pay attention.

It felt electrifying. Vindicating. But it also felt very, very sobering. Because it brought with it one simple, now-undeniable truth: I could never go home to Eleanor again.

"You shoulda heard the folks at the diner talking." Ralph paused long enough in his gleeful dancing to pull a container of fried potatoes from one of the bags. He stuffed a handful into his mouth with dirty, fat fingers. "Whole doggone place was jawing about us. The beginning of the end, they're calling it. Another regular Joe fightin' back against the system." Pieces of potato squished between his brown teeth as he spoke. "Those crooked bankers are getting what they deserve. Give the money back to the people, where it belongs!"

Jack leaned close to me. "We're heroes, Bea." His breath in my ear was warm, yet it sent chills down my spine. "They love us."

Both he and Ralph settled down at the table, pulling mounds of food from the bags. Eggs, pancakes, sausages, potatoes, and toast. They divided the food, piling their plates as if they hadn't eaten in days, which of course we hadn't. But now I found myself nowhere near hungry.

Because another thought had weaseled its way into my mind. The thought of Alli sitting down to read the paper. Of her seeing my name—not just my name, but the name they'd made for me. The Salacious Sheba, as if I were some crime-fueled promiscuous kitten. Of her seeing how all her Bible lessons and prayers had been wasted on me.

I shouldn't have cared. But for some reason, I did.

I chewed on a rubbery bite of eggs, more for something to do than because of any real desire. "It said we were wanted for robberies in McKinney and Plano," I said, trying to shake Alli's face away. "I've never even been to those places. Have you?"

Jack shook his head.

"So they're blaming us for crimes we never even committed. Doesn't that bother you?"

"Of course not. People need someone to root for, need a David against the banking Goliaths. And they can't give headline space to every Tom, Dick, or Harry who robs a bank. Better to condense it all into one recognizable hero. Better yet if that hero is me. *Us.*"

Ralph held up his coffee cup in a mock toast, which caused a flush to creep up my body. Here he was, celebrating our "victory," thinking he was Jack's equal, a champion and idol for the masses. But he wasn't even named in the article; no one knew who he was, least of all the police. *He* could pack up and go home anytime he wanted. Yet here he sat, relishing a criminal career to which he was only minimally tethered.

I didn't need another reason to dislike Ralph. But that smug, satisfied smile on his greasy lips brought me dangerously close to slapping him silly.

Rather than having to look at his piggy little face a second longer, I pushed back my chair with a rude squeak. "I'm going to lie down," I mumbled. "I'm still tired."

"Good idea, honey," Jack called as I retreated toward the bedroom. "You rest up. Ralph and I will get to work, planning our next move."

I froze, one hand on the doorframe, and turned slowly. "Next move?"

Jack remained in his chair, though he had stretched out his legs and relaxed his posture into a satisfied, almost-lazy slump. He was grinning. Those full lips were now tinged with ominousness I hadn't seen before. "Of course. That money will eventually run out. We'll have to get more. And we can't keep our fans hanging now, can we?"

I gave him a weak smile and closed the bedroom door. My stomach churned as I pulled the sheets over my head. The murmur of soft voices from the kitchen was as chilling as the police sirens I'd heard only a few days before. Jack and I were stars, the Dallas Desperado and his Salacious Sheba. For the first time in my life, people knew my name. They loved me. I missed my sister, but for the most part, I had everything I'd ever wanted, all my dreams come true. The bright lights were now shining directly on me.

Why, then, did the future feel so dark?

CHAPTER TWENTY-EIGHT

NOW

"I thought you said there was no one else in the house."

I stared at the empty stairway, the memory of the little girl's wide eyes burned into the back of my mind. Rose's daughter, Josephine.

Not Eleanor. Josephine.

Rose offered her hand and pulled me to my feet. "I said there was no husband. I never said there was no one else in the house."

I rubbed my hands over my face. The last—what? Twenty-four? Forty-eight?—hours had been a blur. I honestly didn't know *what* she had told me. And even then, heaven knew I was in no position to judge her for lying or telling half-truths.

She gestured toward the kitchen door. "He alright?"

Jack was quiet now, but his words still hung in the air, as

loud and painful as when he'd first shouted them: *"Get out of here! Leave!"*

The shock of running into Rose's daughter had pulled me from one misery to another, but the agony of Jack's words now came back full force. He had never pushed me away like that. And to do it now, of all times . . . I could only shake my head in response to her question, not wanting to betray the truth.

"I'll go check on him," Rose said quietly. "There's a bit of cold sausage in the icebox and a few slices of bread. Help yourself."

My stomach was sour and knotted. The last thing I wanted was food. But it felt wrong to refuse her. And besides, I had nothing else to do. Jack had told me to leave, but where could I go? I was injured. I was wanted by the police. I couldn't go home. I couldn't go *anywhere*. And yet he had made it clear I shouldn't—couldn't—stay here. Feeling defeated, I grabbed a piece of bread and sank into a chair at the table. I was just so tired. So very, very tired.

"He's sleeping again."

The sound of Rose's voice caused me to flinch, and I nearly lost the hunk of bread in my hand. I squeezed it a little too hard with shaking fingers, crumbs from the dry crust falling like dust onto my dress.

"His fever has spiked. I gave him some more medicine but I don't know if it will help. Time will tell." She sighed. "Do you want some coffee?"

"Yes. Please."

As she busied herself with the pot, I glanced out the small window above the sink. The sun was shining. Warm yellow rays fell across the faded linoleum floor, and I could see the orange and red hues of a thicket of nearby trees. The clucks and caws of chickens rose up faintly in the distance. "What day is it?" I ventured.

"Friday," Rose replied without turning around. "You've been here three days."

Three whole days. Could it really have been that long since . . . ? But no, I didn't want to think about that. "And where is *here*?"

This time Rose did turn around. Her brow was furrowed, lips pressed into a line. "Thought you said you were in a car crash. You were driving around, but you don't know where you were?"

My stomach dropped to my knees, taking with it the few bites of bread I'd managed. *Shoot*. My brain scrambled for an excuse. "It was a, um, surprise. From Ja—Quin. He was taking me on a trip, but he wouldn't tell me where we were going. It was our honeymoon."

"Oh?" Her eyes flickered to my hand.

I hastily shoved it into my lap, trying to conceal my bare ring finger. "It was lost. In the crash." There was enough truth in the lie to allow me to meet her eyes, though the ache in my chest made me want to fold into myself.

"I see." She placed a chipped blue mug on the table in front of me and settled into an opposite chair. "Well, I don't know where he was takin' you, but where you ended up was just outside Enid, Oklahoma."

I took a sip. The coffee was bitter but warm, the comfort of familiarity spreading throughout my body almost instantly. I leaned against the back of the chair and held the cup close to my face. Steam washed over my cheeks.

"I lost mine too, you know." She tapped her ring finger against the side of her mug. "Though it happened to me when I was help- ing my husband birth a calf." She shook her head and laughed. It was the first time I'd seen her smile, and I was surprised how pretty and youthful it made her look. "We searched every square inch of that barn floor, but it was no use. Pretty sure that mama spent the rest of her days carrying a gold band inside her." She laughed again and this time, I, too, managed a slight chuckle. "I didn't miss it too much when Harold was still alive, but now that he's gone . . . well, sometimes I wish I still had it. Just as a reminder."

"How did he pass?" I wasn't sure why I asked. It was too personal a question, especially considering the circumstances. But at least it was steering the conversation away from me and my supposed honeymoon.

"Influenza. Three winters ago."

"I'm so sorry."

She waved a hand. "Don't be. Ain't your fault. It was just his time."

My mind went to Jack, mere feet away. Bleeding. Suffering. I didn't want it to be "just his time." It was too soon. We had so much more we wanted to do, plans for a life and a future . . . plans that didn't work without him.

But if I was being honest, plans that didn't work with him, either.

I bit the inside of my lip, tasting blood. I would not allow myself to think of that. Not now. "But don't you miss him?"

The skin around her dark eyes crinkled "Of course I miss him. Every day I miss him. Things are hard without him here, and Josephine has had to grow up way sooner than I'd ever have wished just to help keep us afloat. But things would have been difficult even if Harold hadn't passed. Life is just hard, Eleanor. No matter what."

Trying not to shudder at the mention of my sister's—*my*— name, I turned my eyes from Rose to her small, drab kitchen. Peeling white paint on the cabinets, a dip in the floor from what I guessed was a rotten spot in the foundation, a pantry with more empty shelves than full. Memories began to swim in front of me.

Of beauty pageants and talent shows, of running through the fields in Wingate and the muddy streets of West Dallas. Of full whiskey bottles and empty bellies. Sixty-hour workweeks and barely paid rent. Feelings of rejection, hopelessness, defeat. Yes, life was hard. Everywhere, it seemed, life was hard.

And then there was Jack. His handsome face, strong arms, whispered promises of a future—a better future, a future so close and yet now further away than ever. All we'd ever wanted was everything.

And it had left me with nothing.

I blinked back tears. It was all so unfair. "But didn't you ever want more?"

Rose's calloused fingers pulled the mug from my grip and squeezed my trembling fist. "Of course I did. I wanted a lot of things. But Harold gave me the one thing I didn't even realize I wanted above all those other things: love. And not only from himself. He introduced me to a perfect love, one bigger than us, one that outlasts even death." She tilted her head to one side. "He introduced me to Jesus."

Even though we were sitting, my stomach lurched as if I'd been walking down the stairs and missed the last step. I looked down at my lap and swallowed several times, unable to speak; the thickness in my throat was choking me.

The perfect love of Jesus. Deep down, I knew it was what I, too, had been looking for all along—not Charles's fire-and-brimstone version, but the real, true Jesus. The one Alli told me about, the one I'd come so close to seeing myself. That hole in my heart? Nothing had ever been big enough to fill it, no matter how hard I tried. Not my hopes and dreams. Not even Jack. But according to Rose, the love of Jesus was big enough. He'd covered her grief, the heartache of her own life.

But after everything I'd done, was the perfect love of Jesus big enough to cover pitiful, imperfect me?

After a long silence, Rose sighed. "I bet you could use a nice warm bath. I could heat up some water for you. Does that sound alright?"

I nodded, still not looking at her.

"Let me clear these dishes, and I'll get things set up for you. Might even have some clean clothes for you to wear, though I'm guessing they'll be a mite big for your skinny frame."

I listened rather than saw her clean up, too focused inside my own head and my own heart. The intensity of my regret and longing was surprising, an actual physical ache that spread to every nerve.

"On second thought," Rose said from the kitchen sink, "let's hold off on the bath."

I looked up at her, confused by the fear bubbling up beneath her steady tone. "Why?"

"Because three police cars just pulled up in front of the house."

CHAPTER TWENTY-NINE

We stayed in Carlsbad for three more days before moving on to a motor court near Tucumcari, then another near Shamrock. We stuck to back roads and night driving, avoiding highways and large cities. Every time we moved, we switched cars and plates; the only thing that stayed the same was the driver. Ralph no longer challenged Jack's authority. That first newspaper article—and the dozens that followed—solidified his status as the leader, not only in Ralph's and the public's eyes, but in his own. There were no more power struggles. There was only the "Dallas Desperado and his Salacious Sheba," leaders of the "Turner Gang," a laughable misnomer I found was quickly turning into a reality.

Because it was no longer just Jack and me. It wasn't even just me, Jack, and Ralph. No, as Jack's reputation grew, so did his followers. We picked up Mick in Clovis. A former jail buddy of Ralph's, he couldn't have been more than sixteen, red-haired and covered with an equal amount of freckles and pimples, but he impressed Jack by shooting the cap off a bottle of Coca-Cola while standing on one leg with an eye hidden behind his bandanna—all this even after several rounds of cheap whiskey. He'd been following us around ever since.

There was also a man named Louis and his buddy Eugene—better known as Slick, though I wasn't sure why—who joined us for a quick robbery of the First National Bank in Plainview to replenish our cash supply. They didn't follow when we made our escape to Childress—too large a crowd led to suspicious eyes, according to Jack—but so enamored were they to have taken part in a crime with the great Jack Turner that they promised their services again whenever they were needed.

There were others too, various acquaintances and small-time crooks more than happy to join in for a day or a week to assist with a crime or two in return for the fame and glory of being associated with the Turner Gang. Their presence reduced my involvement once again to getaway driver or lookout. Sometimes I even stayed behind completely. It should have bothered me; the thrill of the escapade was now only secondhand. It didn't, though. Clothes, jewelry, candlelit dinners with expensive wine—Jack more than made up for my reduced role with over-the-top romantic overtures and gifts. For the first time in my life, I was a kept woman. A lady. A star. And no longer just in Jack's eyes.

It was a much easier part to play when I was kept off our twisted version of a stage, my lines confined only to the papers.

And every crime made the papers, no matter how small. Jack forced one of his cronies to buy an extra suitcase just to store the clippings. It didn't matter that we hadn't pulled off a major heist since Cedar Hill, mattered even less that most of the crimes credited to the Turner Gang occurred nowhere near the places where we actually were. Jack's name—*my* name—was in print and on the lips of seemingly every person across the country. And despite the sometimes-heinous things being attributed to us, the overwhelming public sentiment was positive. Curiously, the only ones actually *against* us were the law.

However, the law could never quite keep up. As such, it was no longer the police who kept me awake at night. It was *myself*. The absurdity of my present circumstances and the willing part I played. Despite the excuses and all the ways I tried to mentally separate myself from the goings-on around me, I was still a part of it . . . an active and compliant accomplice.

Yes, the battlefield of my mind and heart deprived me of sleep. But it was more than that. It was Eleanor. Alli. Even Mama. I longed to reach out to them, to let them know I was okay, to tell them most of the things they were reading about me weren't true. It seemed important they separate truth from sensationalism, though I didn't understand why. No matter what, I was still a wanted woman. A person who had let them down, hurt them, and yearned for nothing more than a forgiveness not deserved.

Wichita Falls. Stephenville. Killeen. A tour of Texas with a rotating cast, motor courts and the occasional campout, robberies of convenience and stolen cars. The days and weeks began to blur together. When Jack woke me up with a deep kiss one gray morning in the third month of our life on the run, I didn't even know where we were.

"Good morning, beautiful," he breathed into my neck. "My Bea. My star."

I kept my eyes closed but gave him a sleepy smile. "What time is it?"

"It's early. Mick and Ralph are still asleep in the other cabin."

That was another thing. We'd gotten enough money to afford our own cabin, no longer having to share with any stragglers following us in any given week. It was a small blessing. I could cling to the stubborn fantasy that we were a normal couple on vacation while Jack had the peace of mind of appearing less suspicious with only a woman in tow rather than a group of often rough-looking men.

I yawned. "Then why are *we* awake?"

"Because I couldn't wait any longer to give you this." He pressed a small black box into my hand.

Suddenly I was no longer sleepy.

Jack opened the lid, revealing a beautiful diamond ring tucked into the red-velvet interlay. I gasped, causing his smile to grow wider. "I sent Mick to go get it for me. I wanted to get you a crown. One crusted with jewels and gold, fit for the queen you truly are. But I figured you might like this more." He pulled the ring from the box and held it up. The diamond sparkled brightly, even in the dim morning light. "Marry me, Bea. None of this means anything without you. I need you by my side always. Until the end."

My head swam. Even though I was lying down, I felt as if I might faint. The events of the past few weeks, months, years floated away. *This* was what we'd been working for, what all that other stuff had been leading us to. Jack and I together, a future, a life with a house and kids, love and laughter. We'd weathered the hard stuff, made some mistakes, but now it was here. It was finally time to start living the dream we'd always imagined, putting this nightmare of crime and cronies behind us.

"Be my wife, Beatrice Carraway. Please."

"Do you mean it? Do you really mean it?"

He cupped my chin with his hand. "Of course I mean it. I've said it all along: No one will ever love you more."

"No one will ever love you more," I whispered back. Tears began to stream down my cheeks.

"Is that a yes?"

I nodded, too choked up to speak, and we both started to laugh when he slipped the ring on my finger. I watched it sparkle before pressing into Jack and losing myself in his kisses. In that moment, the Dallas Desperado and Salacious Sheba melted into nothing at the reality of the soon-to-be Mr. and Mrs. Turner, together and finally free.

CHAPTER THIRTY

We left our cabin in Victoria a few days later and headed for a farmhouse outside Waco, near a little town called Prairie Hill. Surrounded by gently rolling fields of wheat and barley, the homestead was isolated but comfortable, situated on a hill just high enough to see the highway in the distance—and anyone who might venture down it. The owner was a friend of Mick's, an old chum named Billy who'd dabbled in petty thievery but, unlike Mick, had never gotten caught.

I enjoyed the farm. It was a nice change of pace from motor courts. I spent the first three days there simply walking the fields, breathing in the smell of dirt and hay, listening to the whistle of the wind through the stalks and the gentle grunts and clucks from the livestock. It made me think of Wingate—Wingate before Charles—a simpler, black-and-white time before the world became all messy shades of gray. My heart ached for those days, for Eleanor. The grief was so intense, it stole my breath; it felt as if my heart was actually tearing in two.

After that, I didn't allow myself to think about the past anymore. I focused instead on the future.

One cloudless afternoon, I wandered through the pasture, watching the sunlight glint off my diamond ring. The air was warm. As I reached up to wipe a bead of sweat from my brow, my fingers brushed against the puckered skin above it. The cuts from our robbery at Cedar Hill had faded into small scars, most of which I could conceal with makeup, though the one over my eye remained prominent no matter what I tried. But it didn't really matter. Not anymore. My stage dreams seemed a lifetime ago, a rapidly fading fantasy considering the reckoning any publicity might bring. A painful realization, yes, but now I had bigger plans. *Better* plans.

No, my life wouldn't be filled with bright lights and movie screens, but I would still have a *life*. A real life with real love. A family. We had enough money to settle down, take on new names. I could dye my hair. Jack could grow a beard. Once things cooled off enough, maybe we could even convince Eleanor to come and stay with us, Alli and Emmett to visit. Because in the future I was painting in my mind, they would forgive us. They *had* to forgive us once they understood we had done everything out of love. I could see it—me serving drinks in my plain country housedress, Jack removing gloves as he came in from the field. The image made me smile and almost laugh out loud—Jack pushing a plow, dirt stains on one of his fancy silk suits—but maybe he'd do it. For me. For us.

I was still chuckling when I arrived back at the wraparound front porch. I paused to pick a piece of dandelion fluff from my navy-blue skirt, tilting my head at the sound of voices from inside the house. Jack's for sure. But he wasn't alone. And it wasn't just Mick and Ralph with him.

I sighed, my heart wavering between irritation and apprehension. What riffraff had found us now? And *why*? The Dallas Desperado was retiring.

Smoothing my hair, I pushed my way into the house. The room was a haze of smoke. The bitter smell of corn whiskey hung in the air, mixing with body odor and, faintly, Jack's cologne—I could pick that out anywhere. Six men sat in the living room, sprawled on the couch and various chairs: Jack, Ralph, Mick, Billy, and two I'd never seen before. One was sharp-nosed and as thin as a beanpole, with spindly arms and legs to match. His pants were too short, revealing several inches of dingy gray sock between his jeans and scuffed-up boots. He glanced at me quickly from behind shaggy blond hair and returned his gaze to his hands, where a limp cigarette dangled between his first two fingers.

The other man was a beast. Barrel-chested and thick-necked. His sausage fingers were curled around a glass of clear liquid I knew wasn't water. He had a head full of thick dark hair, which looked as oily as his squashed face. The stub of a cigar hung from red lips, weaving a curtain of smoke that obscured his eyes. But it didn't matter that I couldn't see them; I could *feel* them on my skin. And unlike his companion, he did not look away.

Jack smiled at me, but Mick was the only one who moved. "Miss Bea!" His voice cracked; adolescence was long since past, and I wondered if his voice would ever fully mature. I got the sense he was never truly comfortable in my presence, but it manifested itself in overeager manners, which was quite alright with me. He sloshed his drink as he stood and gave a slight stumble before righting himself. "Welcome back."

I smiled at him—only him—and replaced my hat on the rack. "Thank you, Mick."

"You want a drink?" Jack waggled his glass in my direction. His smile was lazy, his eyes bloodshot. He was drunk.

I pressed my lips together and tilted my chin. "No thank you."

"Finest corn whiskey in all of Texas," Ralph said from the couch. His face was even redder than normal. Alcohol-induced sweat beaded on his forehead.

"I said, 'No thank you.'"

Sensing my very obvious irritation, Jack jumped to his feet, his frame of mind sober enough to place his glass on the coffee table before taking a step toward me. He kissed me on the cheek. The smell in the air was intensified on his skin, and I nearly gagged. He put an arm around my waist, ignoring my rigid posture. "Bea, this is Lester—" he gestured to the blond-haired pole in the wingback chair—"and Clarence. We call him Clay."

The ogre in the recliner tipped his cigar, still not taking his animallike eyes off me.

"They were at Eastham with me," Jack continued. "Just got paroled. So they came for a visit."

A chill crept up my spine at the mention of Eastham. I remembered Jack's release, his brokenness, and his stories. If these men had been in Eastham, then they'd been immersed in the darkness too. And at least in Clay's case, I wasn't sure they'd been as successful at escaping it.

Jack turned slightly so his back was toward his companions, his face inches from mine. "Do you think you could fix us up something to eat? We have some leftover chicken, I think, and a few slices of bread. Billy has some vegetables in the cellar, too."

I fought against a sneer. I wanted absolutely nothing less than to serve those men. I would gladly feed Jack and Mick—Billy too, for his hospitality. Even Ralph because . . . well, Ralph was obviously here to stay. But these two newcomers . . . more than any of the other cronies we'd picked up along the way, something about them put my teeth on edge. Especially Clay, who still stared at me over Jack's shoulder. I wanted those men gone. Now.

But if serving them dinner would speed the process, then dinner it would be.

I gave Jack a tight smile and saw his body relax. He kissed me on the cheek again. "Thanks, Bea. You're the best."

The men remained quiet as I made my way to the kitchen. Even with my back turned, I could still feel Clay's eyes. It was a relief when the door swung shut behind me, releasing both my tension and the men's now-hushed conversation.

The chicken from last night was in the icebox. I pulled it out and examined it. I really didn't think there was enough left for seven people, even if I took only a bird's share. I hoped there were plenty of vegetables; I'd probably have to get by on bread and green beans tonight. Stepping outside, I yanked open the heavy wooden door leading to the root cellar and retrieved the first few jars I could find in the dark before hightailing it back up the stairs—Billy had said rattlers weren't uncommon down there—and to the light of the kitchen.

The voices from the other room had grown louder again, though still too muffled to make out the words. I busied myself with the wood-burning stove, popping lids off jars and searching through cabinets for any bit of seasoning Billy might have on hand. There was no more evidence of this being a bachelor's place than in the kitchen.

The door scraped behind me as it opened. Jack, I presumed, wondering when the food would be ready. He had no sense of how long things took, especially when he was drinking. "I've only just started," I said. "It will be a little—oh!"

I had spun around to find not Jack, but Clay. In the kitchen. Staring at me.

Instantly, the hair on my arms stood on end. The cigar was gone from his mouth, clearing the smoke and making his face truly visible for the first time. There was a scar running from his brow to the corner of his mouth. Purple and puckered against his flushed skin, it curved below his bottom lip like a fishhook. His eyes were sunken, so dark his pupils seemed to disappear within their depths, and his flat nose looked as if it had been broken often, healing a little bit more crooked each time. Now that he was standing, I could see just how tall he really was—easily over six feet—his arms and hands covered with thick dark hair that matched his head.

He rolled his tongue around his mouth before finally speaking. "I'm going to the bathroom."

I straightened my spine. "It's over there." I gestured with my chin to a small washroom off to the side.

He gave a slow nod but did not take his eyes off me. He didn't move toward the bathroom either. Instead, he ran a fat hand over his chest, sticking two grubby fingers beneath his suspenders. "So you're the famous Salacious Sheba."

I took a step backward, only to feel the handle of the oven dig into my hip. "That's what they say."

"Those papers don't do you justice." He was in front of me now. His hand twitched at his side as he smiled, revealing a row of brown teeth. "They said you was pretty. But you ain't just pretty. You're a goddess, a picture of everything a woman should be." He closed his eyes and leaned forward.

I tensed, but he did not touch me. Rather, he took a deep breath, inhaling my scent. My skin crawled. Somehow I felt even more violated than if his hands had gone under my clothes.

He let out a long, low moan. "It's been so long since I've been with a woman."

My hands shook behind my back. But in their trembles, I felt something smooth and hard brush against my palms. The skillet handle. As discreetly as I could, I wrapped my fingers around it.

His eyes opened. I froze. He grinned, leaning closer. He smelled of garlic and moldy cheese. "Is it true what they say? About how you ain't just Jack's girl? How everyone that joins the gang—?"

And then three things happened at once. I lifted the skillet from the burner just as Jack's sharp voice cut through the kitchen and Clay stepped firmly out of my strike zone.

"Clay!"

Clay's hands went instantly to his pockets.

Jack stood in the doorway. His eyes flashed back and forth between Clay and me.

"I was just going to the bathroom," Clay mumbled.

"The bathroom is over there." Jack pointed with his half-empty glass. "Or you can go outside behind the tree. Either way, there's no reason for you to be in the kitchen."

Clay dropped his chin but not before I saw a roll of his eyes. He bit down on his bottom lip as he moved past. His body brushed lightly across mine. He gave me a sideways glance—a wicked smirk hidden from Jack's view—before stepping out the back door. The crunch of his footsteps echoed as he disappeared into the rapidly fading daylight.

Jack rushed over to me. "Are you okay? What did he do?"

Despite my relief, my body remained stiff and on edge. I felt polluted. Dirty. And not just because of Clay's touch.

It was his words. His disgusting, perverted insinuations.

"Did he hurt you?" Jack cupped my face in his hands, trying to meet my eyes.

But all I could do was look at the floor. He had; he most definitely had. But not in the way Jack meant. Clay's vile suggestion filled my mind, drowned any words I could have spoken to make Jack understand. He hadn't hurt me physically, but his humiliation had ripped open every insecurity I'd ever had.

How many others thought those things? How many men had joined up for a chance at the famous Salacious Sheba? I wasn't a star; I was a toy, a prize, a plaything. A wicked fantasy for every degenerate man from here to Oklahoma.

Nausea rose up in my throat. I pushed Jack away with both hands.

"Bea? What—?"

"I want those men out of the house."

"Bea—"

"Now!"

The murmurs from the next room stopped. Even Jack winced at my shrill, panicked scream. But when he looked at me, there was something other than love and concern in his eyes: annoyance.

No, not just annoyance. Defiance.

"Bea, we're in the middle of—"

I didn't stay to listen. I couldn't bear it. To hear him tell me no or make excuses. To choose his cronies over his fiancée. Instead, I rushed from the kitchen and up the stairs, burrowing into in the scratchy quilt as I gave myself over to sobs.

Rather than follow me up the stairs, I heard Jack return to the front room. The sound of laughter and the men's conversation lasted well past midnight, when my heartbroken tears finally gave way to sleep.

CHAPTER THIRTY-ONE

That night, I dreamed of Clay. Of his scarred face and sour breath. Of his disgusting words, which coiled around me like a snake. The dream was so vivid, his presence so palpable, I jumped when a real hand materialized on my back.

"Whoa." The hand was snatched back. "It's me. It's only me."

I sat upright, aware that it was Jack and not Clay but scooting away from him all the same.

"I brought you some food. I know it's late, but I thought you might be hungry. There wasn't any chicken left but there's bread and green beans. Billy even managed to find a jar of strawberry rhubarb preserves." He grinned as he waggled the plate in front of my face.

My stomach let out a betraying rumble but still I did not take the food.

Jack's smile fell. He set the plate on the nightstand with a weary sigh. "Bea—"

"Are they gone?"

"Who?"

I narrowed my eyes. He was attempting to lighten the mood, and it only made me more irritated. "You know who."

"They're asleep in the barn. Satisfied?"

I wasn't. He'd done what I asked, but only barely.

"What's your problem anyway? You never had an issue with the guys before. Did Clay do something? Did he touch you?"

Memories of his words bubbled up, choking me. *"Is it true what they say? About how you ain't just Jack's girl? How everyone that joins the gang—?"* He didn't have the chance to finish. He didn't need to. The accusation was so appalling, I couldn't bear to bring it past my lips. I knew Jack would be outraged. I thought about the robbery in Cedar Hill and Jack's callousness at the shooting of innocent people. There was no telling what he would do to someone who, perhaps, deserved it. My concern was not for Clay but for Jack; I couldn't bear the thought of him becoming a murderer. He'd walked too close to that line before.

But more disturbing than the thought of him caring too much was the possibility he wouldn't care at all. My mind floated back to his expression when I'd demanded the men leave. That aggravated, haughty look in his eyes.

My mouth felt dry as I realized I honestly didn't know how he'd react. And that was even more upsetting than Clay's vulgarity.

"Why are they here?" I said instead. "I thought we were done with all that."

Jack leaned back on the bed away from me. "What? Why would you think that?"

I crossed my arms over my stomach, all my reasoning evaporated by a single look. "Well, the ring. And . . . we were doing this for us, right? To get enough money to settle down somewhere comfortably. I thought we were going to lay low for a little while, then go back and start—"

"Go back?" Jack let out a condescending snort. "Why would you want to go back? You were the one who said you wanted to get out of West Dallas."

"I don't mean back to West Dallas. I mean back to before. With the money we have saved up, we can go back to just me and you. To the life we talked about. The house, the kids—"

"I ain't ready for that. There's too much . . ."

"Not ready?" I tried to swallow but found myself unable. My tongue felt too big for my mouth. "Jack, we've proved our point. Gotten our glory. Don't you think it's time—?"

"I'm on the verge of something big, Bea. Bigger than big. Bigger than you, than me, than anything we've done before."

An odd tingle slid down my back. "What are you saying?"

Jack didn't look at me. Instead, he picked at a piece of lint on the quilt. "You remember my stories about Eastham, don't you? The horrible, animal ways they treat people? Well, Clay and Lester . . . let's just say things haven't changed. But I have." He finally looked up. His pupils were dilated, turning his gray eyes black. "And now I finally have a chance to do something about it."

My heart began to pound. "Jack . . ."

"It isn't only the outside world takin' notice, Bea. Word spread inside those prison walls too. Skinny little nobody Jack Turner is now the Dallas Desperado, stickin' it to the coppers and bigwigs at every turn." He thrust back his shoulders. "The regular folks out here might love us, but it's nothing compared to the feelings of those still stuck inside Eastham. Out here I'm a hero; in there, I'm a god."

I shifted. It had been weeks since I'd dared open my Bible, even longer since I'd prayed. Despite the harsh words with which Alli and I parted, the memories of my afternoons with her were still painfully tender. For all Jack's and my successes, there was something to the quiet intimacy of those meetings, a hole our fast-paced lives, public adoration, and newfound prosperity couldn't keep filled.

My anger at her had faded. Now there was only deep, aching longing.

Longing . . . and shame.

Shame that was easier to deal with when my Bible was kept hidden at the bottom of my suitcase.

But even after all those weeks away, I still felt the conviction of Jack's statement. I didn't really know God. Wasn't sure if I even liked Him. But although my faith was immature and scant, I knew for sure there was only one God. And His name wasn't Jack Turner.

Yet I was just as guilty of treating him as such as everyone else. And not just him. But myself. *Us.*

"They need rescued," he was saying. "They need a savior. They need *me.*"

My stomach rolled as the realization of what he was planning washed over me. "Jack, please don't do this. It's too dangerous. You're going to get yourself killed."

He shook his head, a lock of dark hair falling over his forehead. "I have to, Bea. Too many people are counting on me—"

"*I'm* counting on you. I am! All these plans we've built for ourselves, they don't work without you. Please don't do this. Please, let's just . . . go." I squeezed his hand.

He didn't squeeze back. "You could really give all this up? Just like that? We're *famous*, Bea. People love us. How can we just walk away from that?"

Fresh tears welled up in eyes I had thought were spent. "Because the only thing that means more to me than all that is you. I don't care about other people. I just want *you* to love me."

He wrenched from my grasp and stood, throwing his hands in the air. "Come on, Beatrice. Don't be like that! You know I love you! Haven't I proved that to you with all those dresses in your suitcase? Those shoes on your feet? Didn't I prove it with that ring you wanted?"

Instinctually I looked down. The diamond on my hand still sparkled, but in that moment, it was no longer beautiful. It felt heavy and harsh, a burden too big to carry. Because if Jack thought my love for him was only about the things he could give me, then I had failed him just as much as I had failed myself.

I opened my mouth to try to explain this to him, only to be cut off by his hands on my cheeks. He gripped my face, staring deeply into my eyes with such an intensity I had to fight the urge to look away. "I love you, Beatrice Carraway. I meant what I said when I asked you to marry me. I still want all those things we talked about—the house, the kids, the comfortable life. Most of all, I want you by my side forever and always, until the very end. No one will ever love you more." With a thumb, he wiped a tear from my cheekbone. "But I need you to understand that this has to come first."

I closed my eyes, another ripple of grief seizing my chest.

"I have a reputation I need to fulfill, wrongs I need to make right. And I can't have my own girl standing in the way." He kissed me gently. His lips were dry, tasting of cigars and whiskey. "Whoever isn't for us is against us, Bea. Please don't be against us. Please don't make me choose."

When I opened my eyes, he was gone. The cheeks he had touched grew instantly cold. Even the spot where he'd laid his lips seemed to tingle from their absence. But it was my heart that felt the chill the most.

Because now I understood: I needed Jack. Jack, on the other hand, needed revenge.

CHAPTER THIRTY-TWO

THEN
AUGUST 1932

The day dawned foggy and gray, ominous by any standards, not just for those planning a massive jailbreak at one of Texas's most secure prisons.

The old me would have told Jack to wait. The time wasn't right; the fog was an unnecessary risk. But something had shifted in our relationship. A fracture now splintered the past from the present. Old Jack and Bea from New Jack and Bea. New Jack wouldn't take kindly to being told how to run his crime, and New Bea would never venture to do so. I was in too deep to allow that fissure to become a full break.

Jack and me until the very end. And on a morning like this, it felt as if that would happen sooner rather than later.

The job itself was not complicated. Dangerous but not complicated. Lester and Clay had told Jack their old unit—Camp 1—was
assigned to cutting wood and clearing brush near a back road on
the edge of the prison farm property. There was a bridge nearby
surrounded by overgrown weeds and cattails—a perfect place
to hide a couple of .45s, a feat already accomplished earlier that
morning by Ralph and Clay. Two of their mutual friends on the
inside would grab the guns when the guards weren't looking and
use them as leverage to break free. Jack, Lester, Clay, and Ralph
would be watching from the bridge and provide additional fire.
Once clear, the gang and seven freed inmates—predetermined by
Clay and Lester, though Jack claimed to know them too—would
retreat to a spot on the other side of the bridge, where two cars
would be well hidden, and drive to a safe house Jack had already
set up with some acquaintances outside Crockett. That's where I
would be waiting.

At least that was the original plan. The fog changed all that.

"Jack, I told you, I don't think I can do this."

I sat on the edge of the bed in our motor court bedroom outside Midway, watching Jack clean and load a variety of firearms
on a blanket on the floor. There were more guns than I'd ever seen
before, and I knew he had to have hit up more armories without
me than I'd realized. He snapped a clip into place before sighing
and turning to look at me.

"You *can* do this. You've driven getaway dozens of times before.
And I'm not even asking you to drive this time. All you gotta do
is honk the horn so we can find the cars in the fog. What's the big
deal?"

I wanted to laugh. Or at the very least, gesture to the absurd
amount of weaponry lying in between us. *That!* I wanted to
scream. *That is the big deal!* This was different from the others.

Jack had always gone on with a "shoot only when shot" dogma; this time, I *knew* he meant to shoot first. It wasn't just the guns. It was the intent and mentality of the man behind them.

"Why can't someone else honk the horn? You've got four men—"

"And I'm gonna need every one of them in this fog."

"But the guards . . ."

"There's more of us than there are of them. We have more firepower, and we have the element of surprise. Plus," he added, winking, "I'm the Dallas Desperado, remember?"

There it was again. That overinflated sense of invincibility. It was going to get him killed. And maybe me along with it.

"But, Jack—"

"Look, if you're so worried about it . . ." He thrust a small pistol in my direction. "You won't need it, but maybe it will make you feel better."

I stared at the silver object in his outstretched hand. The smart thing would be to take it. It *would* protect me, after all. But at what expense? Would I really pull the trigger, knowing I could end someone's life?

"For all who draw the sword will die by the sword,"

My breath caught as the verse came from somewhere deep within. How had it remained in my mind, resurfacing *now*, of all times?

Jack stared at me, those gray eyes bloodshot and swimming with impatience. And yet I still could not bring myself to take the gun.

He sighed, dropping his arm with exaggerated fatigue. He moved to the bed beside me and cupped my chin in his hands. They smelled of oil and metal.

"Nothing is going to happen, Beatrice. I need you to believe that." His brow wrinkled slightly. "Don't you trust me?"

I fought back tears. Oh, how I wanted to. What I wouldn't give to go back to a time when I trusted him completely, when it was him and me versus the world, back before the world wedged itself between us.

I would do almost anything to bridge that gap. But I would not kill.

At least that was what I could think as I was sitting in this warm room, staring into the eyes of the man I loved. Who knew what would happen if faced with the barrel of a gun pointed at me or pointed at Jack? And that's why I could not allow myself to touch a weapon. Not even now.

Instead, I leaned forward and kissed him. Even with the distance between us, his lips were warm and familiar, comforting. The only comforting thing in this world.

He gave me a small smile when he pulled away, still so handsome despite the gauntness of his cheeks and hollow areas beneath his eyes. He laid the pistol back on the ground with the others, then checked his watch. When he looked at me again, the smile was gone. "It's time."

The drive was less than an hour, one Jack had practiced and repracticed over the last few weeks. I'd accompanied him on many of these runs, wanting to spend time with him, hoping against hope to change his mind. Every curve, every hill, every scraggly tree and overgrown pasture was as common to me now as the muddy streets of West Dallas.

But we'd never done a run in the fog.

Nothing looked familiar. Nothing looked visible, *period*. We might as well have been in Indiana or New York for all the good our planning had done. We would be doing this job blind. I only hoped the inevitable bullets would get as lost in the fog as we were likely to do.

By the time we arrived at the agreed-upon hiding spot, we were already late, the denseness severely impacting Jack's speed. He was cursing under his breath as he backed the V-8 coupe into its place beneath a sycamore. Ralph followed a few minutes later. Lester and Clay emerged from the back seat of the second car to arrange weapons as Jack busied himself switching out license plates. The fog made it highly unlikely anyone had spotted us or would be able to identify the plates as ones they'd seen in Midway or along the road (though we'd only passed two other cars, it being barely after daybreak), but Jack was taking no chances. He'd change the plates now and again when we got to the safe house.

I stood nearby, arms folded across my chest.

Jack finished with the plates, looked at his watch, then swore again. "We gotta go," he hissed. "Now. We were supposed to be in place by 6:30. It's 6:42." He gave me a quick, rough peck on the cheek and a squeeze on my forearm that bordered on painful. "You know what to do."

And then he was gone. The fog swallowed him and his companions as they ran away, leaving me alone in thick, heavy nothingness.

As I stood next to the car, gripping the open door, clouds pressed in on me from all sides. There was no wind. There were no birds. There was no anything. The fog obscured my view and muffled all sound. Though I knew the nearest town was less than ten miles away and Jack only a few hundred feet, I soon felt as if I were the only person in the world, suspended and floating in a terrifying, surreal nightmare.

A branch snapped somewhere in the distance. Every nerve in my body tingled. The metal frame grew slippery in my hands even as I stifled a shiver.

I spun around but could see nothing. My breath came in short, panicky bursts. I felt dizzy, as if I would either vomit or faint. Or both. *Help.* The word never passed my lips, but it was as loud as if I had shouted. There was no one around to hear, yet my heart continued to plead: *Help me. Help me, please.*

It was a prayer. I was praying. Praying to a God I'd rejected in favor of a man who'd become a god. However, in this moment of deepest trepidation, it was not Jack Turner I was thinking of. It was not Jack Turner I was asking for help.

It was Him.

Would He listen? Would He even care?

Help me. Help me. Help me.

I attempted another deep breath, feeling my lungs expand and contract, expand and contract. The seconds ticked by. I had no idea how long Jack had been gone. I focused on my breaths, counting them off inside my head, listening for the signal while trying to keep my mind fixed on unspoken prayers to which I hoped God was listening.

And then there it was: the distinct *pop-pop-pop* of gunfire. In the fog, it seemed both miles away and somehow right next to me, so loud I jumped, biting my tongue hard enough to draw blood. My mouth filled with an acidic, metallic taste.

Jack had said to wait for gunfire. When I heard it, I was to press the horn for ten seconds, release it for ten, then press it again. I was to do this over and over until the men reached the car.

I raised a shaky hand above the horn and hesitated. If I honked, my presence would be revealed, my part in the breakout sealed.

Pop-pop-pop!

More gunfire. Louder. Overlapping. More than one gun now.

Who was I kidding? I was in this whether I honked or not. I punched at the horn, wincing at its shrill, ear-shattering whine. Ten seconds I held, ten I released. Over and over I repeated this action, my body growing more chilled with each passing blast that Jack did not reappear.

Honk!

Pop-pop-pop!

Honk!

Pop-pop-pop!

All around, cracks of gunfire were drowned out by the absurdly cheerful horn of the V-8. Just as I was beginning to think I'd hear nothing but these awful, horrible sounds for the rest of my life, there came a shout:

"Bea!"

A blur of shadows, a surge of bodies, and I was pushed into the car. My head smacked the side glass as someone else pushed in roughly beside me, causing my head to swim. There were arms and legs and the intense smell of sweat and gunpowder. Then the engine roared to life beneath us and we thrust forward blindly into the fog.

Black spots clouded my vision as I struggled to right myself. There was a man in my lap, his black- and white-striped uniform stained gray and brown. An inmate. His head was shaved, scalp nicked in several places, and there was a deep gash across his nose. He seemed to be, incredulously, sleeping. Eyes closed, body slumped against mine, his weight was like a bag of sand that merely absorbed my shoves rather than yielding to them. I put a hand beneath his stomach, attempting to get some leverage, but recoiled when my fingers encountered something warm and wet.

Blood. The man was bleeding. No, I realized with sudden horror. He wasn't just bleeding. And he wasn't sleeping. He was *dead*.

I opened my mouth to let out a scream, but it was cut off by a sudden swerve of the car, which caused the dead man to slide further, burying me beneath his lifeless body. Fighting for breath,

I kicked and punched against it—*him*, I tried to remind myself; it was still a him, even in death.

The stench of bodies, the jumble of shouts, the roar of the engine. There was too much noise and not enough air. The corpse in my lap blocked my view of everything but the side window. I had no idea how many men were inside the car, nor even if Jack was the one driving. Who else was dead? The swell of voices was far from jubilant, the tension in the air another passenger in the already-crowded cab. If we hadn't been hurtling down the road at a speed I could feel rather than see, I would have turned the handle and thrown myself out the door. I was drowning in a sea of panic that wasn't just my own.

No matter how fast we drove, no matter how far we traveled, the sound of gunfire remained. It ebbed and flowed but never ceased, and soon the unmistakable whine of sirens joined in. My body swayed and slid as the driver maneuvered this way and that, but the ominous sound of our pursuers seemed to float on the fog itself, as ever-present now as it had been when we pulled away from the prison farm boundaries.

My stomach began to roll from the nerves, the smell, the spreading warmth of the man's blood. Saliva collected in the back of my throat. "Jack . . . ," I tried to croak.

And then there was a horrific crunch, and I was free. Intense pressure spread through my arms and chest momentarily before the shattering of glass released me once again. I was flying. The air around me was gray but cool, and though my mind strove to communicate the danger at hand, my lungs knew only the sweet inhale of fresh oxygen. They took several grateful breaths before another thud covered my body in excruciating pain, and everything went black.

"Beatrice, wake up. You have to wake up."

Jack's voice reached me from somewhere in the darkness, but I didn't want to go to him. The moment I'd heard it, I'd been wrenched from my numbness, and now waves of agony rushed over me. I didn't want to feel this. I wanted to retreat again. I wanted to sleep.

But try as I might to withdraw into the dull nothingness, I was awake now. And so was my pain. I leaned over and vomited into the grass, the torture of this violent movement causing me to collapse into the pile of my own sickness.

"Beatrice. Oh, my . . ."

Jack's face swam in front of me. His skin was gray and ashen, the beginnings of a bruise swelling the skin around his right eye. Sweat beaded above his upper lip, where a large cut slashed him to the base of his nose. At least I think there was a cut; at the moment, there were three Jacks, and his heads were all mixing together.

"We have to get out of here. Can you walk?" He slid an arm under my back and tried to lift me.

Sharp stabs of agony shot down my leg, causing me to scream.

Jack clamped a hand over my mouth. His three sets of eyes swung around wildly. I began to fade again, but from somewhere far beyond the haze, I thought I could still make out the sounds of gunshots and sirens.

Darkness pressed in. Pain flared again, and I realized Jack was carrying me. My eyes rolled around, vaguely recognizing the V-8, its front end smashed into the wooden support beam of a bridge. All four doors were open, and a set of black- and white-striped legs dangled from the rear passenger door, unmoving. A series of questions flickered briefly inside my mind—*Where are the other men? Where is the other car?*—before fading.

I floated in and out of consciousness. I have no idea how far Jack walked, only that every time I awoke, I was still tucked in his arms. Until finally I wasn't. I awoke to grass under my fingers, to shouts and gunfire. Panic wrestled with physical pain, but I was unable to move, unable to yell, unable to stay awake. Then Jack's arms were back. He was carrying me again. My head drooped on his shoulder as nausea swelled once more, but nothing came up. I simply didn't have the strength. Black metal, rubber tires—a car—a lump of fabric near the trunk. A face. Blue, unblinking eyes, blood darkening the dirt beneath their gaze. And then I was losing consciousness again, barely aware of the spray of gravel sent into the air as Jack sped away.

CHAPTER THIRTY-THREE

I awoke to the smell of crackling bacon. Survival kicked in, and my tender stomach roared at the thought of food despite the lingering nausea and throbbing nerves. My eyelids were gummy and stiff; when I finally managed to open them, I found I was in a bed. Flowered cotton sheets, blue-and-white quilt. The room was sparsely furnished but bright and airy, with two windows, both of which were open, allowing the lace curtains to flutter in the breeze. There was a small desk, a wooden nightstand, and in the corner, a pale-blue armchair, occupied by a slumped, dozing body. Long hair lay draped over the face, obscuring my view.

Red hair.

A new pain welled up inside me, but this one didn't start in my leg. "Alli," I tried to whisper. But my throat was so raw, my words collapsed into a fit of coughs instead.

At this, Alli's head snapped up, her eyes widening in concern. She rushed to my bedside and lifted a glass of water to my lips. It burned as it went down, churning inside my empty stomach and threatening to return. Alli held the glass and waited, watching me. When the nausea subsided, I gave a small nod, and she lifted the glass to my lips again. This time, it went down smoother.

She gave me a half smile. "Better?"

I nodded.

She replaced the glass on the nightstand and clasped her hands in her lap. "How's your pain? I brought some medicine." She held up a bottle of small white pills, shaking two into her hand and passing them to me. I took them without asking what they were. "You need something stronger, but Jack said absolutely no doctors, so . . ." She sighed. "I honestly don't know what he expects me to do."

Her words only made minimal headway inside my brain. I couldn't get past her presence. "You're . . . here," I said simply. My lips felt heavy from disuse.

She let out a small, airless laugh. "I'm here."

"How?" It wasn't the question I wanted to ask, but it was the first one that came.

"Emmett and I were out for a walk one evening, and this man approached us, asking for a cigarette. As Emmett fished around in his pocket, the man lowered his voice and told us his name was Billy and he was a friend of Jack's. He said he didn't dare go to our apartment for fear of coppers, but he was sent to tell us you were injured and Jack needed us. He slipped us a piece of paper with this address, and then he was gone."

"Where are we?"

"Wichita Falls. Jack had a friend who was able to rent this apartment for him for a few weeks. He couldn't risk motor courts or camping in your condition. You needed stability, and he needed a garage to hide *his* car." She rolled her tongue in her mouth after the last sentence, as if it tasted bad. Both she and I knew Jack's car—whatever car it was at the moment—wasn't really his. "This place had it all, and a network of acquaintances nearby to ensure relative safety. At least according to Jack."

My stomach sank. The events of the last few—what? Weeks? Days? I had no idea how long I'd been out—came flooding back. The breakout, the gunfire, the chase, the crash. The bodies. They all swam in my head, memories of that morning blurring the line between dream and reality. Who was dead? And how many? And the cops. The *cops*. They'd never stop, not now. Not with a prison break or a trail of corpses.

And now Alli was a part of it all.

Despite my dehydration, somehow hot tears welled up in my eyes. "Alli, you shouldn't be here. It's not safe for you." I tried to sit up, but my lower half screamed with the movement. "Jack should not have dragged you into this. You need to leave. Now."

Alli put a hand on my chest, pushing me gently back onto the mattress. "Shhh. Shhh. Don't try to get up. You're not strong enough." I relented, if only because of the intensity of my pain. "And Jack didn't drag me into anything. I mean, what else was I supposed to do? I have a little bit of medical training. You're my friend, and you needed help. So I came. End of story."

But it wasn't the end of the story. Not even close. Shame bubbled up inside me, and I felt my cheeks redden. After all the ways she'd tried to reach me, save me, help me find God.

After all the ways I'd rejected both of them . . .

Still she came. And her kindness was a bigger burden to bear than if she had left me to my own consequences. Because I deserved this pain; what I didn't deserve was *her*.

"You don't understand," I said thickly. "The cops. Jack—"

"Jack is fine. He's in the other room with Emmett. We were able to bring some groceries, and they're making breakfast."

I shook my head. It wasn't Jack's physical well-being for which I was concerned. Hazy snippets of memory had floated up. A lump of fabric next to a car. Fabric with hair . . . and skin . . . and blood. A body.

I knew without knowing. Jack had killed someone, maybe even more than one. The car now stowed away in the garage was stolen at the expense of another person's life.

That person's life for Jack's. For mine.

A groan passed my lips, weak and tormented. I couldn't bear to look at Alli. I tried to roll away, but my moan turned into a scream that collapsed into a whimper.

"Bea, don't. Don't move." Alli put a hand on my shoulder, so warm it seemed to burn, and pressed me gently onto my back. "You have a broken leg, maybe even a broken hip. It's hard to say. You need a doctor. I don't have the skills . . ." She rubbed her forehead with her fingertips. When she saw me watching, she managed a tight smile. "It's fine. You'll be fine. Do you want some breakfast?"

I shook my head even though I did. As stupid as it was, I felt as if denying it would somehow make up for everything else I'd done wrong. A nonsensical, inadequate punishment, as if rebuffing my stomach would cure the ills in my soul. Pathetic.

But Alli only smiled and brushed the hair from my forehead. "Get some sleep, then. I'll try to keep the boys quiet. Sleep is the only thing that will help."

Alli was wrong about a lot of things. She didn't need to come, she most certainly had other choices, and I was nowhere even close to being her true friend. Even her assertions that she couldn't do anything to help me were wrong; her very presence, though convicting, was the purest thing I'd experienced in a long time.

But she was right about one thing: sleep *was* the only thing that would help. In my sleep, I could escape from myself and pretend that none of this was real. And so it was to sleep that I retreated. And it was where I remained for a very long time.

CHAPTER THIRTY-FOUR

I drifted in and out, awaking every so often to find pills in my mouth, barely registering the bitterness on my tongue before they were washed down with a splash of water. I had no idea how long I slept or whether it was my injuries, the medication, or even my own lack of willpower to face the truth that kept me in my slumber. All I knew was when I finally awoke enough to register any sort of actual awareness, it wasn't Alli but Jack who was by my side. He lounged in the bed next to me, reading a newspaper, long legs stretched in front of him. The cut above his lip had faded into a pale-pink line, and the bruise around his eye was now an ugly but less shocking shade of green. I winced at the pain and stiffness in my leg as I reached for him; it was muted under a layer of medicine but still potent enough to snag my breath.

Jack lowered the paper and smiled. "Hey. You're awake." He

pulled one of my hands to his lips and kissed it. "How do you feel?"

I shook my head, waiting for the pain to subside enough to talk.

"Do you need something?" He reached across me—causing me once again to moan in agony—and grabbed the pills on my nightstand. "It's these, right? How many does Alli give you? Two? Three?"

He obviously hadn't been an active part of my care.

But he was here now. He dropped two white capsules into his palm and paused a moment before tipping the bottle and releasing a third. He placed them in my mouth and lifted the glass to my lips, grimacing as I swallowed. "Better?"

The effect of the medicine was instant, and I felt my eyelids growing heavy again. This time, however, I fought against sleep. My need for answers was stronger than drugs, though I wasn't sure for how long. "Alli . . ."

"She and Emmett drove to Burkburnett for supplies. Hoping to find some more medicine for you, along with some food. We can't move you yet, so we couldn't risk any runs here in town, even though I feel like the heat's off, at least for the moment. We've been here over a week without even a whiff of the police. As long as we lay low and keep our noses clean, we should be okay for a while, long enough for you to heal up at least." He glanced at my legs, which were covered in a blanket. Perhaps I was still delirious from the medicine, but I swore I saw him cringe. "Anyway, if that means going on a longer run for supplies, we go on a longer run."

I didn't point out that *he* wasn't the one having to go on the longer runs. Instead, I licked my lips, which felt dry and cracked under my hairy tongue. "Jack, what . . . what happened?"

He laid the newspaper on his lap and crossed one leg over the other. He didn't look at me when he spoke. "The fools chose to make their move right during a guard shift change. So rather than three guards, there were six. They swore they didn't know, that the guards always changed shift at eight rather than seven, and they had no idea those other bulls would show. And even then, their arrival was masked by the fog. Couldn't see them coming until they were already there." His upper lip curled as he shook his head. "I guess it doesn't really matter. Whether they did or didn't know, it doesn't change what happened."

He paused. The medicine pulled at me, and though his hesitation told me I probably didn't want to hear the next part, I wished he would hurry and say it anyway.

"Joe—one of the inmates—panicked," he said finally. "Walked right up to one of the guards and shot him in the stomach."

I closed my eyes as my chest sank toward the mattress. I wished it would swallow me.

"All hell broke loose from there. We heard the gunshots and started returning fire. You couldn't see anything. I had no idea who I was shooting at. The noise, the confusion . . ." He rubbed at his temples. "I shot at everything and nothing until I ran out of ammo. By that point, I could see inmates running past me. I heard the horn, and I started running too."

My fingers tingled with the memory of the horn beneath my hands. Of all the cloudy, indistinct moments of that day, the feel and sound of that horn was still crystal clear.

"When I found the car, there were eighteen prisoners all clambering to get inside. There were only supposed to be seven. I think in the madness, all the inmates—even the ones who weren't in on the plan—just fled. Some of them heard the horn and figured they'd take a chance. But there wasn't enough room. Not nearly enough room. The V-8 seats five; at most we could have squeezed seven or eight. Even with two cars, there was no way everyone would fit inside. People started pushing and shoving; then Clay brought out his gun. And all this time, bullets were flying and guards were closing in. We were making so much noise, they knew exactly where we were. So I left. It was my car, my breakout—let the others sort out what they could. I was getting us out of there. There were nine of us in the car, though I don't know how we all fit. The last thing I saw was Clay aiming his gun at a group of three inmates as we pulled away."

From the recesses of my mind came the image of a man— a corpse. His blood on my hands, his weight a suffocating, lifeless blanket over my body. I pressed my fingers to my eyes, trying to clear it away.

"The fog was so thick. I couldn't see a thing. I was trying to drive by memory, but the next thing I knew, there were coppers right on my tail. I have no idea how they mobilized so quick or even how they found us in all that haze. I tried everything I could to lose them, but then I was lost too. Everyone was shouting and pushing. I couldn't see. I couldn't concentrate. And then, I don't know . . . one minute we were driving, and the next we weren't. The bridge came out of nowhere."

He paused again, reaching over to interlock his fingers with mine. "I must have gotten knocked out or something. All I know is when I woke up, the car was empty, save for two men who were already dead. From the crash or bullets, though, I don't know. The main thing was I couldn't find *you*. The fog was still heavy, and now I had a swollen eye and splitting headache. You musta flown over a hundred feet. I don't know how you're still alive." For the first time in his story, something like regret flavored his tone. "I . . . gosh, Bea, I'm sorry. I never should have asked you to come along."

He pulled my hand to his face and pressed it against his cheek.

I didn't speak. I couldn't speak. And it wasn't because of his story. It was because I noticed for the first time not what was there, but what wasn't.

My ring. The ring Jack had given me. It was gone. Another victim of his ambition and recklessness. It wasn't just about the diamond, though. No, my bare finger seemed a symbol of something so much bigger.

I'd known the plan was risky, begged not to go. But he hadn't listened. Now my ring was gone. More than that, people were dead. I didn't know if I'd ever walk properly again. And all he had to say for it was *sorry*.

"How did you get me here?" I tried to keep my tone even. I felt disgusted and angry. But the story wasn't finished; there was one more thing I needed to know.

"I carried you as far as I could. Until I found a car."

"You found a car."

He dropped my hand and rolled his eyes. "Come on, Bea. You need me to say it? You know I stole it. That's what we do. We do what has to be done. Should I have just left you to die? Don't get all high-and-mighty on me now."

"Did you kill anyone?"

The question hung in the air between us, so long I wondered if I'd even spoken it out loud. As the seconds ticked by, the gentle throbbing in my heart became full-on stabs. Neither a lie nor the truth would make me happy, and yet I silently begged him to say something—anything—just the same.

He stood suddenly, dropping the paper onto the mattress and stuffing his hands into his pockets. He looked right at me, those soft-gray eyes now the color of steel. "Not that I know of."

I pressed my hand—the one he'd only seconds ago been holding—against my stomach and dropped my chin to my chest, no longer able to look at him. Though neither response would have truly satisfied me, now I knew which was worse. Because for the first time since I'd met him, the love I felt for him was no longer enough to fill the gaps between his words and actions. Between us.

The crack dividing us had just become a chasm.

He cleared his throat. "I'll let you get some sleep. Alli says that's the best thing for you." He leaned forward as if to kiss me on the mouth, hesitated, then brushed his lips lightly over the top of my head instead. "I'll bring you something to eat when they get back. If you're awake, that is." He patted my shoulder as if I were a puppy and then disappeared out the bedroom door.

I didn't breathe again until I heard it latch. Hot, wet tears rolled down my cheeks. In my drug-induced delirium, images from that morning mixed with a shadow of Jack's face, the barrel of a gun, the bloodstained dirt beneath lifeless eyes. I leaned forward to vomit, but there was nothing in my stomach to expel. My body screamed with the force of impotent heaves. I clutched at the quilt, waiting for the spell to pass, and felt something smooth and dry crinkle in my palms. Jack's newspaper.

I pulled it toward me, my eyes struggling to focus on the swimming black ink. On the front page, in bold print, was the headline:

Dallas Desperado or Dallas Dummy?

I blinked. A picture of Jack, his mug shot from his time at Eastham, next to a jumble of words. I rubbed at my eyes before continuing:

Jack Turner, the infamous bandit known as the Dallas Desperado, bit off more than he could chew Monday

when he attempted a mass breakout from Eastham
Prison Farm, near the town of Midway in southeast
Texas. Under the cover of thick fog, Turner and his band
of thugs attacked a unit clearing brush and chopping
wood near the Trinity River. Several of the inmates were
armed with guns believed to have been supplied by
Turner.

I skipped down the page, not wanting to relive it all. Not again.
The article was long and detailed, from what I could gather, with
quotes from supposed eyewitnesses while maintaining that the fog
made actual events impossible to confirm.

The attempt was ultimately in vain, as all escaped inmates
were either recaptured or killed, including recently
paroled convicts Lester McCreary and Clarence Nash,
both of whom are being held in the Houston County Jail
awaiting trial on new charges. Ralph Schultz, a known
member of the Turner Gang, was found shot to death
along County Road 148.

Another wave of nausea crested in my stomach. As much as I
disliked Ralph, it chilled me to think of his violent end. I focused
my eyes toward the end of the article.

Prison Manager Lee Simmons and Dallas County
Sheriff Smoot Schmid are said to be livid over the brazen
attack, which resulted in the death of prison guard
Clifford Paul. An uninvolved civilian, Mr. Gregory
Ferrer of Madisonville, Texas, was also found shot along
a rural road nearby. The car he was driving, a navy-blue

Chevrolet Cabriolet, is missing. It is believed Mr. Ferrer
was in the wrong place at the wrong time and became
another one of Turner's victims.

There it was. The truth I'd known, the one Jack wouldn't
speak. Mr. Gregory Ferrer. Did he have a wife? Children? A name
connected to a whole life, gone in flash. For me. For Jack.

There couldn't be two lives less deserving of the salvation he'd
unwillingly provided.

The stupidity and recklessness of the Dallas Desperado
has reached a new level of depravity with the gangland
hero crossing the line from a modern-day Robin Hood to
a cold-blooded lawman killer. A $1,000 reward is being
offered for the capture of the Dallas Dummy as well
as his Salacious Sheba, though reports differ about her
involvement in the crime.

My head swam, and not just from the medicine. One thousand
dollars. It was a fortune, the largest reward I'd ever seen offered for
a criminal. No one could resist that kind of money, not even Jack's
so-called friends. We were truly on our own now.

If there is a silver lining to be found, it is that the tragic,
amateurish breakout has revealed the humanity of the
mythical Jack Turner. For all the romance and media
obsession, Turner has shown himself to be nothing but a
barbaric killer, selfish and incompetent and unworthy of
his status. Authorities have promised not to relent until he
is captured or killed, an outcome they assure the public is
imminent.

I threw the paper on the floor. I didn't want to read any more.

Jack's rashness hadn't just cost the lives of the people around him; it had cost him the love he'd so desperately craved, the publicity I was just as guilty of relishing. All the bloodshed was for nothing. We were nobodies again. Worse than nobodies even—we were *despised*.

And now we were being hunted with the full force of the law. The end was coming.

I allowed the medicine to finally take me, no longer wanting to see or feel anything. But as I drifted back into darkness, one final thought stabbed at my heart: of all the love we'd lost, it was the one between us I mourned the most.

CHAPTER THIRTY-FIVE

My leg and hip began to heal; my heart unfortunately did not.

The imminent arrest didn't come. Two weeks, three weeks, four went by and still no lawmen came. Every passing day was filled with dread. Despite my bedridden state, Jack insisted I dye my hair. I nearly cried as my blonde locks disappeared beneath the cheap brown coloring. It was only Jack's annoyance that kept the tears in their place when Alli removed the towel and revealed my new look. He'd grown a beard. Emmett had shaved his head. Even Alli had cut her long, beautiful hair into a bob. We were all making sacrifices. *For you,* his look plainly said. Because I was taking so long to heal. Because I wasn't yet strong enough to stay on the move like we needed to be doing.

So I didn't allow a single tear to break free. Not then, at least.

I saw more of Alli than Jack. He came to me each day with an obligatory kiss and superficial query as to my state. He did not linger; he rarely even sat down. Alli said he was busy, but I knew that, like me, he was a prisoner inside this apartment. The risk of recognition was too big even with his altered appearance. How busy could he be? But her lie felt different from Jack's. She was trying to protect me; he had been trying to protect himself.

Not that I really wanted his company anyway. I didn't know what to say, even less how to feel, in his presence. I longed to touch him but also recoiled at the merest glance. My heart swelled when he was near, but the source felt distant, as if encased in memory, and I knew it was the past—that time and that Jack—to which my emotions truly clung. I'd promised to stay with him until the end, but it felt as if the end had already come and gone.

What hurt most of all was the truth in this sentiment I could see in his eyes, too.

Alli, on the other hand, was faithful and warm. She waited on me hand and foot, bringing me food and medicine, helping me to change and wash when I couldn't yet rise from bed, and when she'd assessed me as at least semi-healed, forcing me to move despite the pain. With her help, I sat up again. Using her strength, I stood. When I begged off walking, claiming the pain was too great, she reappeared the next day with more determination—and a cane. With her resolve and prayers, I went from immobility to two steps, from two steps to ten, and eventually I could make it from one side of the room to the other. My muscles were weak, my bones stiff and warped, but I could walk. And even if it meant the cane would be with me for the rest of my days (no matter how long or short they might be), I would never take that ability for granted again.

During these times, we would talk. The argument we'd had the last time I saw her, the truths she'd spoken and I'd refused to believe, the person she'd thought I was and the me I'd always been inside . . . all of those things were our constant companions, bigger even than my physical pain or the ever-present paranoia of a coming reckoning. Yet it was a subject never broached. We spoke instead of home. According to Alli, Mama had been in contact with Mrs. Turner every so often to ask up on me. But as the women had little information to pass along, and even less in common, the relationship was more about mutual concern than actual friendship—though I was sure Mama's concern had less to do with my well-being and more to do with the attention she was receiving from the press. Her *woe-is-me* stories were a big hit from Dallas to Detroit—another victim of the Salacious Sheba, and one for whom the public's appetite was insatiable and sympathy abounded.

If I hadn't been so terrified of the letter being traced, I would have written to the press myself and set the record straight. She was no more a victim than I was.

It was stories about Eleanor, however, I craved the most. She was still living in our apartment, still holding down her secretary job, which was a relief, considering her association with me. Alli stopped by to check on her once a week, and though Eleanor had a hard time speaking around her, a certain level of peace and familiarity had begun to settle over their visits.

"Mainly," Alli told me one day as she was brushing my hair, "we sit together and read. I think she's lonely more than anything else. I get the sense it's hard for her to make friends."

I picked at a hangnail, imagining my sister alone every night in our small, dark apartment. I was disgusted with myself for a lot of reasons, but in that moment, none of them were bigger than what I had done to Eleanor. I was the one person in the world she trusted and counted on . . . and I had abandoned her.

Alli paused and I got the sense, not for the first time, that she could read my mind. When she pulled the brush through my hair again, it was gentler, more for the motion than the actual task. "She isn't mad at you, you know. She's scared for you. And honestly, I think she just misses you."

I chewed the inside of my lip, glad Alli was behind me and couldn't see my face. I knew she was trying to help, but her words only made me feel worse. Eleanor *should* hate me.

I sure did.

That night, there weren't enough pain pills left in the world to put me in a sleep deep enough to avoid dreams about my sister.

Outside the apartment, the unbearable summer heat faded into the more tolerable but still-uncomfortable warmth of a north Texas fall. Per Jack's instructions, we kept the curtains drawn, but there were days I managed to hobble over to the window and peer outside. On one particular morning, I discovered that, by moving the curtains just a hair, I could feel the sun on my face without exposing myself to any prying eyes. Our apartment was above a garage, and from my vantage point, I could just make out the tops of the trees in the scraggly forest behind us. Elm, I thought. The leaves were beginning to turn from green to yellow. The sky above them was blue and cloudless, so bright my eyes hurt. So much color in the world beyond these drab walls. Would I ever experience it again?

Alli walked in. She was clothed in a plaid housedress, blocks of blue, yellow, and white crossed with black lines. The white embroidered flowers around the square neckline were yellowed with age. Her hair was pinned back at the sides; though it had been weeks since she'd cut it, I still wasn't used to seeing her bare neck. She smiled and held up a tray. "Breakfast?"

"Yes, please."

She placed it on my lap, removing one of the plates for herself, and sat on the corner of the bed. I surveyed the sausage, toast, and sliced apples and decided on a bite of the thick buttered bread first, chasing it with a sip of coffee sweetened with a spoonful of sugar. Alli was always thoughtful like that.

Across from me, she chewed an apple, staring into the space between the curtains. "Beautiful day."

"I bet."

The words came out more bitter than I intended. Alli paused in her crunching, obviously noticing but saying nothing. I took another sip of coffee and cleared my throat, wanting to change the subject but finding myself with nothing else to talk about.

Alli put her plate on the bed next to her. "You don't have to stay here, you know."

"I know." I could move about the apartment now. I was strong enough. But trading one set of walls for another wasn't exactly the freedom for which I was longing. Still, I knew Alli was trying to stay positive. So I was determined to do the same, if only for her. "I might take a walk around the living room later. You told me I had to do—what was it?—at least three hundred steps a day?"

She chuckled. "We're up to five hundred now."

I shook my head with mock exhaustion. "You're killing me."

"But you're walking."

I smiled. "Yes, I am."

But to where?

My smile faded as the question bubbled up from my heart, painful and sharp. Was this to be the rest of my life? Walking from one room to the next? Never feeling the sun without a pane of glass between the rays and my skin? Never breathing in fresh air, the scent of earth and rain and springtime flowers? Never feeling

322 || THE GIRL FROM THE PAPERS

the wind in my hair as we drove down the highway, hearing the laughter of children as I strolled through the park?

Never again seeing my sister. Never feeling the touch of a man who truly loved me. Never knowing when a knock at the door would be the end of it all.

Stuck. Stagnant. Suspicious. Until the end of my days.

Melancholy settled over me, heavy and dense enough to make my shoulders sag beneath its weight. I put the plate on the floor beside me, no longer hungry. I wanted Alli to leave so I could take a few more pills and retreat into sleep.

She, however, remained stubbornly on the edge of my bed, head tilted and mouth pressed into a line. "You don't have to stay here," she said again, quieter this time.

"I already told you I'd take my steps," I snapped, instantly feeling guilty at my tone.

But my ugliness bounced off her with minimal effect. Instead, she lowered her chin and raised her eyebrows, those bright-green eyes pleading and almost fearful. "That's not what I meant." She glanced over her shoulder at the closed door. It was silent; I wondered if Emmett or Jack was even awake yet. They'd been up late playing cards, from what I could hear. She turned back to me. "You could leave."

The shock of her statement caused me to laugh out loud— a cold, harsh guffaw that surprised even me. "And go where?"

"Home."

I shook my head violently. "No way. That's the last place I could go. The cops are probably watching my apartment every hour, day and night. I show up there, and they'll be knocking on my door within minutes."

"And so what if they do?"

My mouth opened and closed several times, letting out sputters rather than coherent words. The absurdity of her question caused me to bristle. If they showed up, I'd be arrested, of course. Locked in jail for who knew how long. The throwaway nature of her comment, as if going to jail were no big deal, felt cruel, especially coming from the lips of one so God-loving as Alli. Indignation quickly replaced my incredulity.

But then I looked at her. And the expression in her eyes was anything but callous. In fact, tears collected in the corners.

"Beatrice, we can't go on like this forever. Emmett needs to go back to work—it's a miracle he hasn't been fired yet. And the manhunt for you and Jack . . ." She shook her head. "They're never going to stop looking for you. Not with the dead guard—"

"Jack didn't kill that guard." I didn't know why I felt it important she know that. Jack was a killer, plain as the nose on my face. But I couldn't bear the thought of him being accused of taking a man's life in which he hadn't been the guilty party.

"The police don't care. He was there. The breakout was his idea. Whether he pulled the trigger or not, in the eyes of the law, he's guilty. It's only a matter of time before they find us. And when they do . . ."

Jack's words echoed in my mind. The night he'd robbed the armory, when he looked me in the eye and tried to make me understand why he needed the guns. It was for protection, he'd said. For him and for me. In case the cops closed in. *"I am not going back to prison, Bea. And I sure as anything won't be letting you go there either."*

The bread hardened like a rock in my stomach.

"Emmett's been talking to Jack, trying to get him to understand. There's no winning this time. Emmett thinks if you guys give yourselves up, go willingly, the cops might agree to give you both a little leniency. I don't know how much because of the . . .

severity . . . of the crimes, but any little bit would help. Anything to avoid more bloodshed."

I shook my head. "Jack will never go for it. He'll never go back to prison. Never surrender. He told me so."

"But that doesn't mean *you* can't."

Her quiet words seared me. Of all the scenarios I'd imagined, I'd never once pictured myself walking away from Jack. Despite everything—the things he'd done, the lies he'd told, the ways in which he'd disregarded and disappointed me—I'd made a commitment. In a broken, painful, irrational way, I still loved him. And a world without him wasn't one in which I wanted to live. Wasn't one in which I knew *how* to live. Who was the Salacious Sheba without the Dallas Desperado?

"I couldn't," I whispered. "I couldn't leave him, couldn't go to jail. We have to be free."

"But even outside a cell, will you ever truly be?"

My breath caught in my throat. I knew she wasn't just talking about a life on the run. Safe house after safe house, a never-ending chase. She was talking about my very *soul*. The prison I'd built out of my own shame and rejection, its bars solidified by the choices I'd made and damage I'd caused to those around me. Inside or outside of jail, it was those shackles I'd never escape.

I sat back, arms crossed against my stomach. My throat was too tight to allow a response. After a silent moment, I felt Alli's hand on my leg. Though I didn't look up, I knew she was staring at me.

"He hasn't left, you know," she murmured. "Do you remember the story of the Samaritan woman at the well?" She didn't wait for me to answer before continuing. "Much like with her, He knows everything you've done. Those things in the open and in secret. And yet, remember, He did not flee from her, nor did He recoil in disgust. Despite everything she had done, He still offered her living water. 'A spring of water welling up to eternal life.'"

My cheeks went hot. I hunched my shoulders around my ears.

"That offer still stands to you, Beatrice. No matter how far you run or how many walls you build, He's still right there. Offering His grace. All you have to do is look up."

I waited until I heard the door click behind her before allowing myself to release a deep sob. I knew the story she was talking about. And somewhere deep inside of me, I hoped what she was saying was true.

Yet I was still too ashamed to lift my eyes.

CHAPTER THIRTY-SIX

My dreams that night were restless, full of shouting and sirens. I flip-flopped in my bed, trying to ignore the throbbing in my hip, but the noises never abated. Instead, they grew louder and more insistent. More real.

"Beatrice! Wake up!"

The light in my room was gray and pale. Early morning. Yet, despite my waking, there were still shouts. And Alli. No, not just Alli. A terrified, white-faced Alli. Shaking me with an urgency that sent stabs of pain through my leg and chills through my heart.

"The cops are here, Bea. We've been found out. We're surrounded."

"What? How? When?" The questions tumbled from my mouth even though I didn't really expect—or need—an answer. The specifics didn't matter. The end was here, and with it came a sense of unadulterated horror . . . and unexpected relief.

It was over. One way or another, it was over. And it was the scariest, most freeing realization I'd ever felt.

I sat up and swung my legs over the side of the bed, ignoring their protests. "Where's Jack?"

As if in answer to my question, both he and Emmett burst into the room. Jack was in black slacks and a white shirt, several buttons in mismatched holes as if it had been thrown on in a hurry. His hair stuck up at odd angles, and though a thick dark beard covered him like a mask, from the wild look in his bloodshot eyes, I knew he was frowning. He pushed past both Alli and Emmett to reach me, kneeling before me and taking my hand in both of his. For the first time in weeks, I didn't flinch at his touch.

His eyes searched mine. "This is it, Beatrice."

I nodded shakily. "What's the plan?"

"Emmett says we should surrender. He thinks it's the safest bet and might even allow for some leniency in our sentences." He glanced at his brother, who gave a quick, defeated nod, before turning his attention back to me. "I don't believe him. I don't want to go back to prison. But . . ." He gestured weakly to my legs.

I looked down at them. Even from a sitting position, it was obvious my right leg had healed crooked; it bowed in all the wrong places.

"We made a promise, Bea. Until the very end. I won't leave you." He laid a hand on my cheek. "So it's up to you. What do you think we should do?"

My heart swelled with this small glimpse of the old Jack. I wanted to tell him what I knew he hoped to hear: that we could do it—flee, escape, return to the glory days, and prove all the naysayers wrong. But the fact was I couldn't run. Even if I'd wanted to . . . which I found I didn't.

I looked from Alli to Emmett and finally to Jack. I leaned

forward and kissed him. It was the first kiss I'd initiated since the accident, the first one with any emotion behind it. Because I knew, no matter what happened, it was the last. Underneath the scratchiness of his beard, his lips were still the same, and at their touch, thousands of memories and emotions swam back, more powerful than the present fear. The way things used to be, the way things could have been. But instead, there was only this.

The end. In more ways than one.

I pulled away, lips tingling with the finality of the moment, and nodded. "It's time, Jack."

He let out a long, heavy sigh. His body went slack as he pulled from beneath my touch.

I'd let him down. And if I thought he truly still loved me—*me*, not the Salacious Sheba—I would have believed I'd broken his heart.

Behind him, Emmett uncrossed his arms and took a deep breath. "Okay. I'm going to go out first. I'll keep my hands in the air so they see I'm unarmed, shout out my name, tell them my wife is inside, and explain to them you want to surrender. I'll tell them Beatrice is injured and needs assistance. Then, Alli, you come out too. Remember to keep your hands in the air. Give them no reason to suspect treachery."

Alli closed her eyes and dropped her head. I could tell she was praying under her breath. I might have done the same if all my energy hadn't been focused on keeping the contents of my stomach in their place.

"Once we're both safely outside and the cops' guns are lowered, Jack, you exit, also with your hands in the air."

A prickle crept up my spine. I would be left in the apartment to face the police on my own. What if they didn't believe I was unarmed? What if they didn't care? A phantom gunshot pierced my chest, and I had to press a hand to my breast to assure myself it wasn't real. I felt as if I would faint.

Emmett held out a hand to his wife. She took a step toward him, then paused, turning back and wrapping me in a tight, desperate hug.

"It's going to be okay," she whispered. "It's going to be okay."

I didn't believe her. But I squeezed her back anyway. It was an inadequate thank-you for the kindness and bravery she'd shown, neither of which I deserved or could ever repay.

Then she and Emmett were gone, leaving Jack and me alone with the enormity of our decision.

"You should get dressed," he said quietly. "There are press out there. I don't want pictures of you in your nightgown splashed across the front page."

I grabbed my cane from the bedside and hobbled to the dresser, selecting a navy-blue polka-dot wrap dress with a white shawl collar. I didn't feel respectable, wouldn't be treated as respectable, but I could look respectable. I pulled it on with substantial effort, still unable to put much weight on my right leg unassisted. Jack didn't offer to help. Instead, his eyes remained focused on the closed door, his head cocked as we waited for the sound of Emmett's voice. I was fully dressed and back on the bed next to Jack before it finally came:

"My name is Emmett Turner. I'm Jack Turner's brother, and I'm coming out unarmed to discuss his surrender."

A fresh sheen of sweat broke out across my forehead. No going back.

The sound of Emmett's voice became muffled as he exited, and Jack and I moved to the living room to better hear. Alli stood by the door, her body visibly trembling. But there were no gunshots. Not even the returned shouts of the police. Just Emmett's baritone, growing fainter as he walked toward the police and away from the safety of the apartment.

When it was her turn, Alli stepped through the front door without hesitation, though she did give me one last mournful glance over her shoulder. Summoning every ounce of courage I could muster, I gave her a brave smile. And then, just like that, she was gone too.

I took a shaky breath. Two down, two to go. All I could do now was wait for the police to come.

But Jack, as it turned out, was not content to wait. As soon as the door clicked shut, he grabbed my arm roughly, startling me. I dropped my cane. "Let's go," he hissed. "Now."

"What?"

"I told you I wasn't going back to prison." His voice was gruff, his eyes as feral as a coyote's. "And I ain't letting you go there either."

My mind went numb along with my limbs. His words didn't make any sense. "But you told Emmett . . ."

He tugged my arm, trying to yank me upward. My weak leg twisted, causing my body to collapse into his. Grunting, he wrapped his arms around me and pulled me back upright. He began half dragging me toward the kitchen. "I needed to get him and Alli out of here. They'd never let us run."

"Run? Jack, what are you—?"

My question was cut off as he swung open the door at the back of the kitchen. The one that led down to the garage.

To the car.

Blood flooded into my ears, pounding against the side of my head. "No!" I thrashed my arms against him, trying to break free from his grasp. "I don't want to go! I don't want to run anymore!"

My open palm connected with his cheek, startling him, but not enough to release me.

"Stop it!" he shouted. "Don't you get it? I'm trying to save your life!"

I continued to wrestle as he lifted me from the ground. He carried me down the stairs, his arms pinning my own to my sides. I wriggled and squirmed, feeling myself growing weak as every nerve in my leg and hip screamed. Jack threw me on the front seat of the car and slid in next to me. I kicked at him with my one good leg, which he dodged easily, grabbing my injured one instead and making me yelp. Tears sprang to my eyes as my body deflated. The pain was too intense, too all-consuming and paralyzing.

I heard the engine roar to life beneath me; then Jack pushed on the gas and the car lurched forward. With a sudden rush of daylight, we burst through the garage door into the world beyond.

Instantly, a hurricane of gunfire erupted all around us. Metal on metal as bullets connected with the body of the car, echoing throughout the cab with terrifying ferocity. One—or more, I couldn't tell—hit the windshield, splintering it. Jack let out a yell, but still he drove on, though I had no idea how he managed to see through the fractured glass. I winced at every crack, every ping, every shout but managed to pull myself upright enough to see out the window.

Five police cars sat on the front lawn of the apartment—which was painted blue, an odd, insignificant fact that lodged in my brain despite the horror unfolding all around us—with at least twenty cops spread out, all with pistols or long-barreled rifles pointed directly at our car. My eyes swung around wildly, searching for any sign of Emmett or Alli in the madness.

I found Emmett just in time to see him stagger forward,

a bright-red spot spreading against the stark white of his T-shirt. He fell to the ground as Alli reached him, her body crumpling beside his as her hands pressed to her mouth in a horrified wail.

The scream was so loud and bloodcurdling, so horrendous, that it wasn't until we were safely out of range of the gunfire that I finally realized it hadn't been coming from Alli's mouth. It had been coming from my own.

CHAPTER THIRTY-SEVEN

For the first time, I didn't care if we got caught.

The coupe maneuvered this way and that, Jack Turner doing what Jack Turner did best—running. My body slid and twisted with each hairpin turn. The tires beneath me thumped over pavement, then gravel, then pavement again. Jack's eyes flickered constantly from the splintered windshield to the rearview mirror, his face ashen but his movements smooth and practiced. And while the gunfire had ceased, the sirens never did, and I knew we weren't out of the woods yet.

But my heart did not thud. My breath did not catch. That familiar panic did not bind my movements or harden my stomach. Rather, an overwhelming sense of grief seeped into every fiber of my being, draining what little energy I had left and leaving me in a puddle on the front seat, detached and indifferent to everything happening in the pursuit behind us.

Emmett was either dead or severely wounded. For all I knew, Alli was too; I'd seen her drop, though it was impossible to tell whether it had been from a bullet or her own anguish. Maybe it was both. Even worse was that being dead was a best-case scenario. Left alive, they were now in the hands of the police and, for all intents and purposes, accomplices to our getaway. The truth of the matter was never considered when it came to the hunt for the Dallas Desperado.

But the truth mattered to me. And the truth was Jack had betrayed them. He had betrayed us all.

My arms ached where he'd pinned them, the memory of his roughness not just in my mind. As the car slid around yet another turn, I noticed red marks on my upper arms, deep and angry, already threatening to bruise. Fingerprints of the man I once loved more than even myself. Tears blurred my vision. I didn't fight them. Rather, I welcomed them—anything to avoid looking at the stark reminders of reality. To avoid looking at *him*.

I don't know how long we drove. I didn't even know which direction we were traveling. I didn't care. The last tie to normalcy had been snapped, and I was floating, untethered, toward a reckoning I was no longer sure would come from without. As the sirens faded and our speed decreased, I knew we'd escaped once again, but freedom from the law meant I'd have to face consequences of my own making. I could no longer make excuses. I could no longer play pretend. The end did not justify the means because the end *was* the means. We were not the heroes in this story. We were the villains. And because of us, people were dead.

People I loved. Maybe even more than I loved Jack. Certainly more than he loved me. And as daylight waned and we bumped along a back country road, the wretchedness of that understanding built a wall between us I knew would never again be breached.

It was early evening when Jack finally pulled the car to a stop.

The sun had begun its descent into the western sky, turning the high clouds multifaceted shades of orange and pink. Just like the day before. And the day before that. As if the world was the same as it had always been.

"Bea." It was the first word he'd spoken to me in hours, the voice I'd known so intimately sounding foreign in the silence of the now-still cab.

I remained pressed against the front seat, my face buried in my arms. My hip and leg were stiff and aching. I longed to stretch, even more to sleep. But misery kept me bound where I was, unable to move but—most especially—unable to look at Jack.

"Bea, I . . ."

I pressed my shoulders up around my ears. I didn't want to hear his reasons for what he had done. His apologies meant nothing. But it wasn't either of these things he was offering. Instead, his words choked my anguish, replacing it with a fear that froze me to my core.

"Bea, I've been shot."

I sat up quickly, ignoring the searing pain in my lower half. We had pulled over beneath an oak tree in the middle of nowhere. The stench of manure drifted on the air. A pale-yellow sky cast a sickly hue over the landscape, or maybe that's just how it felt when I saw Jack for the first time in its light.

His skin was gray, and a thick gleam of sweat beaded across his forehead. Under his beard, his lips were pale and bloodless. Even his eyes—those beautiful, steel-hued orbs I'd found so bewitching—seemed devoid of color. Though we were parked, he still had one hand on the steering wheel; the other was pressed against the front of his left shoulder. As I watched, he pulled it away, revealing a red stain that stretched to his collar. He stared down at his wet palm, then back at me, parting his lips slightly.

The brightness of red against white pushed everything else

aside. I pulled him toward me, easing his body down onto the seat. He didn't argue. He didn't resist. And that scared me even more than the sight of his wound.

I unbuttoned his shirt with shaking fingers. He moaned as I pulled it off him completely. Blood soaked his undershirt. "Jack," I said with a calmness I did not feel, "I have to take this shirt off too."

He groaned as he raised himself enough for me to pull the shirt over his head. I balled the button-down into a makeshift pillow and tucked it beneath his head, a feeble attempt at comfort in an uncomfortable situation. Using his undershirt, I dabbed at the wounded area, searching for the point of entry. The skin was purple and splotchy, covered in both black, crusted blood and vibrant red waves. I wiped and wiped but never seemed to make any progress; it was if the entire area was one giant injury. Finally I saw a fresh swell of red rising from a spot just beneath his collarbone. Upon further inspection, I could see it: a hole, slightly larger than a cigarette, the jagged, ripped flesh visible for only a moment before another stream of blood trickled from its depths.

I squeezed my eyes shut. I knew nothing about gunshot wounds; the most I'd ever dealt with was a deep gash Eleanor had suffered on her leg after falling off a swing.

"Beatrice . . ."

My eyes fluttered open. One of Jack's hands slid limply into my own. His bare chest rose and fell rapidly beneath my other. When I finally met his gaze, I was surprised to find tears welling up in the corners of his eyes.

"I don't feel good," he whispered. "Am I . . . am I dying?"

I shook my head violently, throat too tight to speak, and tried to pull my thoughts away from the anxiety of the moment. What did I do to help Eleanor? I couldn't remember. It had been years ago, and a scrape from a rock was no comparison to a bullet. But still. My mind stretched even further. What would Alli do?

Alli. My heart lurched at her memory, at the uncertainty of her fate—a fate precipitated by the man now holding my hand. Perhaps he deserved what had happened to him.

And yet a part of me still cared. As foolish and stupid as it might have been, the memory of what we had shared—before—was strong. But it was more than simple nostalgia. I knew Alli, despite everything, would never just sit and let him die. Not even now.

She hadn't let me. She wouldn't let him. And that meant I couldn't either.

I twisted his undershirt into a long, thick rope and wrapped it around his shoulder. "This is going to hurt," I whispered. "But I have to stop the bleeding." I pulled the fabric into a tight knot, causing Jack to howl. He gripped my hand and let out a sob. I let him squeeze, refusing to flinch despite the pain, and bit the inside of my cheek to quell tears of my own. "I have to get you to a doctor," I finally managed. "You need—"

"No," he croaked, his voice sounding thick and dry. "No doctors."

"Jack, you need—"

"Please, Beatrice. I can't . . ."

But whatever Jack couldn't do was lost beneath a fresh outpouring of tears. His body shook as it alternated between pain and grief, fear and failure. Blood began to seep through my newly applied tourniquet.

"Okay," I said, pressing my hand against his chest. "Okay, okay. No doctors. But then where, Jack? Where am I supposed to go?" I glanced around. I had no idea where we were. Miles of prairie stretched out in every direction. Fields of dead grass and recently harvested wheat, broken only by the occasional tree or wayward cow.

We'd started the day in Wichita Falls, but we could be in Oklahoma, New Mexico, even Kansas by now. There was no way to tell.

His body quieted, his grip on my hand going slack. "No doctors," he repeated. Glassy eyes struggled to find mine before fluttering several times and then closing.

"Jack."

He didn't move.

"Jack!" The shrillness in my voice startled me in its ferocity; even from inside the car, it seemed to echo across the plain. But still he didn't move. "Jack!" I slapped at his body, trying to shake him without disturbing his wound. To my relief, his chest rose and fell, then rose and fell again. Steady. Rhythmic. *Alive.*

I took a shaky breath before moving myself into the driver's seat. My hip screamed as I tried to stretch my legs to the pedals and start the ignition. As the engine sputtered, coughed, and finally rolled over, I swallowed down my guilt. I hated Jack for betraying me, and yet now I was going to do the same.

I was going to take him to a doctor.

The pain in my leg was intense as I pressed on the gas and backed the car onto the deserted dirt road. But as I shifted it into drive, the engine gave another shudder and stopped completely. I noticed for the first time the gas gauge, its arrow pointed at a big red *0*.

I couldn't get him to a doctor. I couldn't get him *anywhere*.

Clasping the steering wheel with both hands, I jerked my arms back and forth in frustration and let out a shriek. Beside me, Jack didn't even stir.

We were stuck. The literal end of the road. And what an end. Even though I knew it was what we both deserved, it didn't stop the anger from coming, the indignation at a life full of pain and pleasure, intense love and even more intense regret, culminating in death or capture—whatever came first—in a perfectly mundane, ordinary, middle-of-nowhere field. The Dallas Desperado and his Salacious Sheba, the two brightest of criminal stars, extinguished in a field of cow dung.

I dropped my chin and let my hands fall from the steering wheel. Something between a groan and a wail passed over my lips as I raised my head again. And that's when I saw, out of the corner of my eye, a large black shape rising in the distance against the rapidly fading daylight.

A farmhouse.

CHAPTER THIRTY-EIGHT

NOW

"Jack Turner! We know you're in there! Come out with your hands up, or I can guarantee the next time you see the sun, it will be when you're pushing up daisies."

The bread from my small breakfast rolled in my stomach, mixing with the bitter coffee dregs. I was lucky I'd already replaced my mug on the table; otherwise it would have shattered on the floor beneath my numb fingers.

Lucky. The absurdity of that thought almost made me laugh out loud. Yes, Jack and I had been lucky, if that's what you wanted to call it. But all luck must end. And this, as they used to say in the theater, was the final act.

Rose remained standing at her place by the sink, peering out from behind the shabby curtains. The booming voice of the police officer outside hovered in the space between us, making the air both impossibly loud and unbearably quiet at the same time. Blood pounded in my ears, but still I could hear the rustle of Rose's dress as she shifted, the drip of water in the sink, the heaviness of breath that mirrored my own.

"Rose—" I started.

"What are you going to do, Beatrice?"

I started at the sound of my own name, spoken on the lips of a stranger. A stranger to whom I had lied, of whom I had taken advantage. "How long have you known?"

Rose turned around slowly, her eyes meeting mine. Swimming in their depths, I saw a myriad of emotions. And yet the one I most expected—anger—was the only one missing. "From the moment I laid eyes on you. I'm not stupid. I read the paper. Everyone from here to St. Louis knows the Dallas Desperado and his Salacious Sheba."

I curled my shoulders over my chest. That *name*. That stupid, ridiculous, disgusting *name*. I hated it. I hated the woman behind it, what she represented and what she had done. Why had I allowed myself to be called that? To be defined by that? My stage name, my famous name, the name on everyone's tongue. But hearing it now, with the man I loved dying on the couch in the other room; with Alli, the truest friend I'd ever known, captured or dead; with countless others wounded, physically and emotionally, in our wake . . . to hear it now, especially from someone who had shown me such unmerited kindness, brought me nothing but overwhelming shame.

"You have ten minutes, Turner! Or else we come in shooting!"

Their threat pulled the events of the past few days into focus. Alli. Emmett.

No more innocent blood. Not while I could still do something about it.

I sprang to my feet, the throbbing in my leg and hip rendered numb by panic. "You have to get out of here," I said. "Get your daughter and get out of the house." I grabbed a fold of her dress roughly, inappropriate given how little we truly knew one another, and used it to spin her toward the staircase. "Please. I mean it. You have to go."

"What are you going to do, Beatrice?"

Heat flushed under my collar. "Don't you understand? They're going to kill me! They could kill *you*, your daughter. They won't stop to—"

"What are you going to do, Beatrice?"

Every nerve in my body seized. "Stop it!" I screamed. My hands flew from her shoulders to my face, covering my cheeks and eyes as if I could truly hide from her words. "Stop saying my name! I'm not Beatrice Carraway! Not anymore!" Hot tears rolled down my cheeks, wetting the skin beneath my palms. "I'm the girl from the papers. That's who I am. That's all I can be now."

Silence filled the room after my outburst, broken only by my pathetic sobs. The truth was both freeing and excruciating. I was who I was. I had chosen my path, and I had chosen wrong. Bullets and bodies littered the journey Jack and I had forged. I was not the woman at the well, no matter what Alli had said. I was worse. I was the Salacious Sheba and Jack the Dallas Desperado. We'd hurt so many; we couldn't go back now. No, Jack and I were stuck, and we had to follow the course until the end. Until the very end.

But that didn't mean I had to take anyone else down with me.

My eyes burned as I pulled my hands away from my face and laid them once again on Rose's shoulders. "Please," I repeated, a thickness growing in my throat. "Please take Josephine and get out of here while you can."

Rose's chest rose and fell. Her lips pursed together in a grimace as she searched my face.

"Please," I whispered.

She stared at me for a few seconds—long, agonizing seconds in which the clock ticked down and the moment of reckoning raced forward—before giving me a small nod and moving out from beneath my grip.

The steps creaked under her weight. Goose bumps sprouted along my arms as I watched her go; it felt as if she took with her all the warmth and light in the room. Then suddenly she paused, one foot hovering over the next step, and turned to me.

"It's not true, you know."

I tilted my head.

"When I came down those stairs three days ago, I knew who you were. I'd read the papers, knew what they said. It should have been enough to cause me to go running for the police. But when I looked—really looked—I didn't see no Salacious Sheba. I saw only an injured man and broken woman, desperately in need of help."

My breath hitched. It felt as if a weight had slid over my chest. I turned my body away from hers, though it did nothing to quell the ache. "Why *did* you help us?" I whispered. "We didn't deserve it."

"None of us deserve it," she replied with a small shrug. "And yet . . . Jesus."

My mind flashed once again to Alli, to the way she had cared for me, even loved me, at my most unlovable. I'd never deserved an ounce of her kindness, nor of this woman's. Yet both of them had given it. Willingly. Selflessly.

Because of Jesus.

The Jesus who loved them . . . and gave them the strength and courage to love other people. Even monsters like me.

"You are more than what people call you. The names others

give us, those things they say about us . . . they don't define us. They're not who we are. The only one who can ever truly define us is the One who made us." Rose lifted her eyes to the ceiling, to the bowed, warped wood over our heads.

I knew this old house wasn't really what she meant. And for that reason, I couldn't bring myself to look at anything except my own feet, which were blurred by a fresh round of tears. All the things I'd ever been called in my life—not just Salacious Sheba, but *wicked, worthless, hopeless. Not good enough.* Jack's star. Eleanor's sister. Good or bad, the names and labels of others had always given me meaning. Made up my identity. I wanted so desperately to believe there was more to me than what others called me.

And yet . . .

"But . . ." Words choked my throat. I shook my head. I couldn't speak. I was afraid to hear the answer, yet it was the question I most ached to ask. "The things I've done . . ."

"Don't define you either," she finished. "We've all sinned, gone down the wrong path. But God is still right there, welcoming each one of us home with open arms. All we have to do . . . is turn around." She lifted her hand as if to touch me, then hesitated. Instead, she pressed it to her cheek and twisted one side of her mouth upward in a sad smile before turning and walking up the stairs.

I stared after her. The ghost of her words—of Alli's—hung in the air. How could it be that two different women, miles apart—strangers in life yet not in faith, both of whom had risked so much in their unwarranted kindness to me—could speak the same sentiment?

Could it be because the message wasn't really coming from them? Because this idea—illogical, unbelievable, and extraordinary—was more than just words?

Because it was truth?

My body felt empty, drained as if by a million invisible holes. My heart throbbed with shame and regret, pain and remorse . . . and inexplicable hope. The contrast of these emotions, swirling inside me simultaneously, made me dizzy.

I didn't want to go forward. I couldn't go back. But there was another choice. According to Rose, according to Alli, according to Him . . . I could turn.

"Five minutes left to live, Turner! It's your choice!"

The voice from outside rattled the windows, shaking me from my thoughts and causing the hair on the back of my neck to stand upright. Tearing myself from the stairs, I moved into the dim living room, where Jack remained motionless on the couch. I knelt beside him and took his hand in mine. He did not stir.

"Jack," I whispered. "Can you hear me?"

Beneath his lids, his eyes twitched but did not open.

I pressed his hand to my cheek, breathing in his scent. Gone was the musky fragrance of his cologne, the sharp, clean aroma of his freshly pressed suits. All that was left was tobacco and dust and his sweet-smelling skin.

I kissed his palm, letting my lips linger over his fingertips. "I love you," I murmured through tears. "If nothing else, I hope you know how much I love you. I regret a lot of things, but I will never regret how much I loved you." I swallowed heavily. "I only wish it had been enough."

He stirred beneath my touch. A small moan escaped from between his lips. The rise and fall of his chest was slow and imperceptible, the thud of his heart at the base of his throat so weak I could barely see it.

"I wish you'd found the love you needed. The one that was more than money, more than fame, more than me. The one you had all along but never truly saw. The one I had too . . . and the one I'm choosing now." I clutched at his arm, his hand, his chest, a sob rendering my next words a whisper: "I love you, Jack . . . but I think Someone else loves me more. Or at least, that's what I hope. And it's what I'm going to try to find out."

I kissed him one last time. He did not return it. He did not even rouse. But I hoped he felt it just the same. That he'd know, perhaps even somehow understand, what I meant. Then I stood and limped toward the front door. Taking a deep breath, I raised my hands and walked out into the fresh air, ready to greet whatever awaited me on the other side.

Ready to turn.

EPILOGUE

MAY 1933

"Carraway, you have a visitor."

I didn't look up from my desk. Eleanor had come a week ago, so I knew it wasn't her; she couldn't afford the time off work it took to travel all the way from West Dallas to Huntsville again so soon. And Eleanor was the only one who came to see me that I actually wanted to see.

"Carraway." A sharp clang as the guard tapped his baton on the cell door. "Did you hear me?"

"If it's my mother, I don't want to see her."

The last time my mother had come, right after the trial, she'd had a pile of photographs for me to sign. It was her newest boyfriend's idea, she'd said. He hoped to sell them at his shop and split the profits with her. People would pay good money for an autographed picture of the Salacious Sheba. When I'd refused, she'd screamed at me until the guards ushered her out, but it hadn't stopped her from writing letters, pleading with me to help her out. Letters I hadn't bothered to answer. It wouldn't surprise me if she'd shown up for another round of begging and belittlement.

"It ain't your mother."

"Oh? Which newspaper then? The *El Paso Herald*? The *Daily Panhandle*? I've already told them I've got nothing—"

"It ain't the press."

The scratching of my pencil paused. For the first time, I looked over my shoulder toward the cell door. It was open, the uniformed guard on the other side rocking back and forth on his heels as he waited. It was the blond one—Ernie, I reminded myself, the one with the gentle smile and the new wife at home he couldn't stop talking about. His normally heavily lidded eyes were wide-open, his lips parted slightly.

He's nervous, I realized. *And not because of me.* Despite my reputation on the outside, the guards all knew I was no threat; I'd never even raised my voice inside these walls. No, Ernie wasn't anxious about me.

My throat went dry in a way that had nothing to do with the spring air coming in from my high-set window. "Who is it?"

He tilted his head toward the door. "You better come see."

I stood on shaky legs and smoothed down my plain white dress, a silly but almost-unconscious gesture. Buttons up the front, a high V-neck, and cuffed sleeves—just like every other woman here. Long gone were the days of fashion, of silky material, dropped waists, and beaded belts, but I still found myself smoothing my dress every time I stood.

Old habits die hard.

My bad hip gave a sharp spasm; I waited for it to pass before grabbing my cane and following Ernie from my cell. We wove through several hallways before exiting the building into the bright sunshine. Ernie slowed his pace to fall into step with me.

"Warm again today," he said conversationally. "Triple digits by noon, I'm guessing."

"It's too early in the year for hundreds." I was trying to be polite, but my mind was not on the weather. The brick facade of Camp Goree's main building rose in front of us. In the distance, several inmates were engaged in a game of badminton; the wind carried the crunch of dried grass beneath their shoes as they raced for the birdie. Two guards were stationed on either side of the makeshift court. Farther in the distance, I could make out the shapes of the women on farm duty, pulling weeds from the fields. I grew thirsty watching them.

And then my cane was on concrete again and Ernie was helping me up the steps and into the main building. The interior gave relief from the sun but not much else; it was easily in the nineties inside, even with the windows open and the hum of half a dozen fans rotating around the room. I followed Ernie into a large open room that served as visitation quarters, holding my breath as we entered. Most of the tables were empty, save for one or two with an inmate and her guest, some children, some parents by the look of it.

Despite the stagnant, overbearing heat, a sudden coldness seized in my chest as my eyes landed on a woman sitting in the far-right corner of the room. The sunset-colored hair atop her head was much longer now than the last time I'd seen her. Her face was thinner, more drawn and somber. The terrified green eyes that had haunted my dreams, however, were once again vibrant.

"Alli," I breathed.

Although I knew she couldn't possibly have heard me, her gaze found me at that moment. Her lip gave a slight twitch as she stood . . . revealing a very large stomach protruding from beneath her sensible green-and-white smock-style dress.

I had been shocked to see her, but at this, I felt as if I would faint. It was only Ernie's strong grip that kept me upright. He half led, half dragged me toward the table and deposited me in a chair, taking the cane from my petrified grip and propping it up beside me.

"You alright, Carraway?"

It took a moment for Ernie's question to reach my brain; I was too busy trying to process the reality of the past few minutes. Alli was here. Alli was pregnant.

I licked my dry lips. "Yes," I said weakly. "I'm . . . I'm fine."

He nodded once. "Alright. I'll be right over there." He gave a small gesture to the front of the room. "You got fifteen minutes."

Alli eased into her seat as he walked away; she had to turn her chair sideways to allow for her large belly. I stared at her, taking in a presence I'd both longed for and dreaded these many months. There was something about being near her—the subtle movements of her body, the barely perceptible scent of her lilac perfume—that caused my heart to swell and break at the same time.

Across from me, she interlocked her fingers on the table, rotating her thumbs around one another. "You look well," she said softly. "Are they treating you okay?"

I nodded. "Yes. I . . . I have a bed and a bathroom and access to a doctor and medicine when the pain in my leg or hip gets too bad. I work right through there—" I gestured through the door, though I knew she didn't really know where I was meaning—"sewing uniforms for prisoners. It's not easy work, but it does pass the time. And it's better than being in the field or in the cannery."

"And the guards? The other prisoners?"

I gave a small shrug. "The guards aren't bad. There are a few, of course, that . . ." I let my words trail off, wanting to spare Alli the details of some of the seedier underworking of the camp. I didn't deserve her pity. "I try to stay away from them as much as I can," I said instead. "And the other prisoners are nice. Most are here because they were caught up in bad situations with the wrong kind of men. A few are violent, but they're kept away from everyone else. And drugs are an issue—mostly painkillers and hooch—but I stay away from that stuff."

She nodded but remained expressionless. I noticed her hands had come apart and were now clenched into two fists above her swollen belly. "I wanted to . . . to thank you. For whatever you told the police about me."

I swallowed, though there was very little spit inside my dry mouth. "The truth," I said. "I only told them the truth."

Alli had survived the ambush in Wichita Falls uninjured, only to be arrested and held in the county jail to await a trial in which she'd most certainly have been convicted for being a part of the infamous Turner Gang. When I'd surrendered, I'd been interrogated by a rough fellow named J. Edgar Hoover, the head of the United States Department of Justice's Bureau of Investigation, who was intent on using the termination of Jack's and my crime spree to advance his career. My statement, as well as Alli's impeccable record, convinced him I was telling the truth about her lack of involvement, and he agreed to let her go so long as I pleaded guilty, which I was only too willing to do.

Last I heard, his picture had now been in the paper almost more than my own.

"Even so," she said, "I appreciate it. Especially considering . . ." She gestured down to her stomach.

"It was the right thing to do," I said. "I mean, you weren't—"

"I've driven down here several times," she interrupted.

"You have?"

"The first time, I couldn't even bring myself to pull into the parking lot. I just drove right on by. The second, I parked but couldn't get out of the car. The third time, I actually made it to the building, only to be told the prisoners were locked down due to a smallpox outbreak. No one was allowed in or out."

I wrapped my arms around myself. That was only a few months ago; we'd been secured inside our cells, no activity or interaction with other inmates. Outside exercise was done individually. Meals were taken alone in our cells. It had been a dark period, especially for someone as new as me. But the break from interview requests had been a blessing. The fact I hadn't gotten sick even more so.

"I wanted . . . well, I wanted to check on you. No matter my own feelings about him, I know Jack's death must have been hard on you. And I know how it feels to lose the man you love."

I closed my eyes. I tried not to think about Jack's death, which had occurred in police custody before they'd even gotten him to the county jail. Not a single shot had been fired that day, but he'd died anyway. Instead, I tried to remember who he was before all of that, who *we* were. The present reminded me of the mistakes we had made, the bad choices we alone were responsible for. The love we shared was the one aspect of the past to which I could cling.

But Emmett . . . I thought about Emmett's death every day. I knew it was a shame I would—and should—bear for the rest of my life.

"Alli . . ." I fumbled for the right words, words I knew meant so little compared to the magnitude of her pain.

"I'm not here for an apology, Beatrice, although I do appreciate that you want to give one. But there's no need. There's nothing you can say that will bring him back." She ran her hands over her stomach, caressing the baby inside her as if she could already feel his or her soft skin. "I was pregnant at the time. Can you believe that? I didn't find out until later, of course, but I was pregnant. I wish Emmett had known, had gotten the chance to meet his child, but I feel grateful this baby was, in some small way, in his presence for a little bit. And that I still have this part of him."

I closed my eyes tightly, hoping to suppress tears, but one broke through anyway. When I finally allowed myself to open them, I saw Alli was crying too. The ache growing inside my chest flared into a throb. "I'm so sorry," I managed to whisper. "I'm so sorry for everything." I wanted to tell her it was Jack's fault—he had called them there; he had double-crossed them and insisted we flee—but I didn't. I knew it didn't make any difference. I was just as guilty, just as responsible. That day in Rose's house, I had made the decision to stop running, not just from the cops, but from myself. And that included no longer blaming others for my own bad decisions.

Jack's life was like a river current that had swept me downstream . . . but I was the one who had chosen to get into the water in the first place.

"I'm so sorry," I repeated through my sobs. "Alli, you didn't deserve any of this. I never meant—"

My words cut off as she grasped my hand. The shock of her skin on mine startled me into silence. Her touch was warm but firm, tinged with the memory of a thousand past embraces burned into my mind.

"I know, Beatrice. I know." Her voice was thick. Tears dragged mascara down her pale cheeks. "I'm . . . I'm just glad I didn't lose you too."

My body slumped over the table, my hand still holding hers. The weight of her words—both spoken and unspoken—was more than I could bear, and yet it felt as if they shattered the chains around a heart that had only barely been beating. Alli hadn't necessarily forgiven me; I don't know if I would have accepted it even if she had. My soul was still too broken, too guilt-ridden for that. But she was glad for my choice. The choice I had made to own up to my misdeeds, to turn from my crimes and face the consequences. The choice I had made not to go down in a hail of bullets with Jack. The choice I had made to *live*.

The excruciating choice. But finally, for once in my life, the right choice.

"Carraway," came Ernie's voice from somewhere outside my tear-filled haze. "Time's up."

Although every ounce of me cried out against it, I allowed the guard to pull me to my feet. My skin felt cold and tingly from the spot where I'd held Alli's hand. I leaned heavily on my cane as I tried to step away, keeping my eyes on my old friend. Alli remained in her chair, staring after me with tearstained cheeks and a small smile. I was halfway to the door when I heard her call out:

"Wait!"

I turned to see her waddling toward me, one hand cupping the bottom of her belly. By the time she reached me, she was breathing heavily, the baby and oppressive heat a double punch to her stamina. "Could I . . . could I visit you again sometime? Maybe?"

My heart soared with swelling gratitude. "Of course. I'll be here for a while. You know where to find me."

She let out a small chuckle. "Good. Okay. And . . . and I brought you this. I've already cleared it with the warden. It's gone through all the checks." From behind her back, she pulled out a small brown object.

My Bible.

It wasn't until that night, alone in my cell, that I found the small notation inside, tucked into the third chapter of Lamentations. Alli had underlined a few verses in bold black pen:

> I remember my affliction and my wandering,
>   the bitterness and the gall.
> I well remember them,
>   and my soul is downcast within me.
> Yet this I call to mind
>   and therefore I have hope:

> Because of the Lord's great love we are not consumed,
>   for his compassions never fail.
> They are new every morning;
>   great is your faithfulness.
> I say to myself, "The Lord is my portion;
>   therefore I will wait for him."

Despite it all, she hadn't given up on me. And neither had He. My soul still had a long way to go. But I had turned around. And now it was time to take that next step forward in the right direction. Gripping the Bible in sweaty hands, tears rolling down my dirty cheeks, I lowered myself to the ground and began to pray.

The Girl from the Papers was born several years ago while I was researching the Great Depression for my debut novel, *If It Rains*. The 1930s were the heyday of such celebrity criminals as John Dillinger, Pretty Boy Floyd, Baby Face Nelson, and—of course— Bonnie and Clyde. The last pair really caught my attention, and I ended up writing a short blog post about them on my website, where I often share stories and tidbits from the time periods about which I write. My editor at Tyndale happened to read that particular post and mentioned how she thought it would make a fascinating tale for a book, though she wasn't quite sure how I could turn it into a faith-based, redemptive book.

Challenge accepted.

After finishing work on my second novel, *Come Down Somewhere*, I immediately dove into the lives of Bonnie Parker and Clyde Barrow. What I discovered was equal parts riveting and heartbreaking. These two lovers, who would go on to become some of the most famous outlaws in American history, were raised in Christian homes and highly involved in their local churches. There was even a record of Clyde being baptized at the Eureka Baptist Church at age fourteen. And while it's easy to think the duo simply abandoned the faith of their childhood, those who traveled with the "Barrow Gang," as they and their associates were known, remarked on how both Bonnie and Clyde would pray frequently.

The seeds of faith were there. Not only that, they were also obviously strong enough to stay rooted well into their life of crime. And yet the two of them ended up hunted by law enforcement for multiple murders as well as a myriad of other crimes—a hunt that culminated in their own deaths in Sailes, Bienville Parish, Louisiana, in the early morning hours of May 23, 1934.

All I could think as I read about their lives was . . . what if? What if they had chosen to pursue faith over earthly glory? Peace over money? Humility over fame?

From these questions came the novel you now hold in your hands.

So while, yes, *The Girl from the Papers* is based on the lives of Bonnie and Clyde, it is also a work of fiction, born from my own musings about what a life redeemed from rather than pressed toward sin might look like. However, many incidents included in the story are real. For example, Bonnie and Clyde were both raised in rural poverty and moved to West Dallas in the mid-1920s. They also really did meet at a house party; it was, according to witnesses, love at first sight by both parties involved—even though Bonnie was technically already married (to a man imprisoned for murder).

Bonnie had screen aspirations and worked at a diner called Hargraves. Clyde was a petty thief and already had a criminal reputation by the time they met. In fact, he was arrested at her house less than a month after they began dating. But far from being horrified (like the fictional Beatrice), Bonnie stood by her man and actually helped Clyde escape, although he was later recaptured.

Many of the characters are also loosely based on real people within the world of Bonnie and Clyde. Jack's brother, Emmett, is based on Clyde's brother Buck, whom Clyde hero-worshiped as a child. Although he also dabbled in a life of crime, he tried to go straight after marrying a local preacher's daughter named Blanche Caldwell (the inspiration for Alli in the book). They joined Bonnie and Clyde in Joplin, Missouri, in April 1933, hoping to convince the pair to surrender to police before getting themselves killed. The talks were unsuccessful, however, and the foursome made plans to split up. Before they could do so, they were discovered by law enforcement. Because of the ensuing shoot-out, Buck and Blanche were forced to join Bonnie and Clyde in their life on the run for a few months before another shoot-out outside Platte City, Missouri, left Buck dead and Blanche with glass splinters in her left eye. She spent six years in prison for assault with intent to kill, and poor vision plagued her until her death in 1988.

If you're interested in reading about the lives of the real Bonnie and Clyde, I highly recommend Jeff Guinn's *Go Down Together* as well as Blanche Caldwell Barrow's autobiography, *My Life with Bonnie and Clyde*. Both books were invaluable in separating fact from fiction in the lives of these storied criminals.

Although my goal in writing this book was to highlight the what-if aspect of Bonnie and Clyde's lives, I also chose to veer into the realm of fiction in an effort to negate any perception of glorifying their life of crime, which history is wont to do. Their lives were a unique combination of the time period in which they lived and the choices they made. And as fascinating as it may have been, we cannot gloss over what their lives also were: short, violent, and wasted. Bonnie was only twenty-three years old when she died; Clyde, twenty-five. They are remembered only for what they took from this world, rather than what they gave.

And may we never forget that what they took wasn't just money and cars. At the time of their deaths, Bonnie Parker and Clyde Barrow were wanted in connection with the murders of

John N. Bucher of Hillsboro, Texas
Eugene Moore of Atoka, Oklahoma
Howard Hall of Sherman, Texas
Doyle Johnson of Temple, Texas
Malcolm Davis of Dallas, Texas
Harry McGinnis of Joplin, Missouri
Wes Harryman of Joplin, Missouri
Henry D. Humphrey of Alma, Arkansas
Major Crowson of Huntsville, Texas
E. B. Wheeler of Grapevine, Texas
H. D. Murphy of Grapevine, Texas
Cal Campbell of Commerce, Oklahoma

Because of the legends and myths surrounding all of the Barrow Gang crimes, the actual number of victims is unknown. There may have been others as well. Of these twelve known individuals, nine of them were lawmen.

Something about crime—particularly crime in the 1920s and 1930s—captures the imagination. It conjures images of Robin Hood or David versus Goliath, the grit of one world wrestling with the glamour of another. But at the heart of these stories comes the tragedy not only of their outcomes, but of their roots: the lie that any earthly possession or status can ever achieve more than the death of a humble carpenter on a cross thousands of years ago. Friends, I hope you know just how much Jesus loves you. It is a love you cannot earn, but also one you cannot outsin. If you find yourself walking along a path where the only view of Jesus is the one over your shoulder, it's not too late.

You need only turn around. I promise He will be right there waiting.

DISCUSSION QUESTIONS

1. Through her beauty pageants, Beatrice starts out as the center of attention in her family as well as a needed source of income. How does this shape her view of herself?

2. Beatrice encounters vastly different representations of Christianity in Charles Thomas and in Alli Turner. How does each influence her impression of faith? Who have been the defining spiritual influences—whether positive or negative—in your own life?

3. What draws Beatrice to Jack? Do you understand the appeal, both of Jack himself and of the life he offers Beatrice? Do you think their love for each other is genuine?

4. Though Beatrice doesn't want to follow in her mother's footsteps, she learns Emma Mae once had dreams very much like her own. In what other ways are the two women similar? How does Beatrice differ from her mother?

5. Both Beatrice and Jack comment on the lack of fun in the day-to-day drudgery of their lives. Do you believe fun is necessary to life? Why or why not?

6. Jack asks, "What kind of a God creates a world like this, then judges a man for doing the things he has to do to survive it?" How would you answer his question?

7. How do Beatrice and Jack justify their crimes? Is there any merit to their arguments about fairness and justice?

8. At different points in the story, characters view themselves as saviors for those they care about—Emma Mae Carraway with her marriage to Charles, Beatrice with Jack, Jack with the prisoners of Eastham. Why does each attempt ultimately fail?

9. Alli tells Beatrice, "Loving a person—truly loving them the way Jesus does—doesn't mean you ignore sin. God *is* love; therefore, any encouragement that steers you onto a path away from Him is unloving. So we love with truth, even if it's painful to hear." How does Alli attempt to love Beatrice in this way? Have you ever had to confront a friend with painful truth or had a friend point out such truth in your life? What was the result?

10. Beatrice goes through life with an underlying fear that she is not enough. How does that come out in her actions, her decisions? What names or labels have shaped your identity? Have you been able to break free of those that are untrue or harmful? If so, how?

ACKNOWLEDGMENTS

No man is an island, but being an author can sure make you feel like one at times. I am so thankful to the people in my life who make it a point to row out and check on me from time to time.

First and foremost, thank you to God, without whom none of this would be possible. He and He alone is responsible not only for my passion for writing, but for giving me the opportunity to use it as a way to glorify Him. Every door, every window, every crack in the wall—they've only been opened because of Him. Thank You, Jesus, for never giving up on me.

To my husband and two amazing kiddos: Thank you for loving me though all the crazy. You guys are my biggest cheerleaders and my most successful marketing campaign. (Thank you for telling everyone you meet, "My mom writes books!") None of this would mean anything without you by my side. I love you more than words can say.

To my agent, Adria Goetz: Thank you, once again, for being a fearless champion for this book. Yours is the feedback I covet the most because I know if you love it, then you will not rest until the manuscript finds its home. Others may call you a fairy godmother; I call you a warrior. And I am so grateful you are on my team.

To Jan, Sarah, Andrea, Andrea, Elizabeth, Isabella, Karen, Libby, and the entire team at Tyndale: Thank you for your tireless enthusiasm for this book. I am so thankful to be a part of a team that listens, understands, and always has my back. Thank you for the untold number of hours you put into making sure this book is the best it can possibly be and ensuring it finds its way into the hands of readers.

To my parents, sister, in-laws, and extended family: Thank you for your never-ending support. I both love and fear you all reading my books. Thank you for being so kind and gentle with your feedback.

To my TWC family: Thank you for the way you continue to fill my cup week in and week out. I could not pour out what has not been first poured in. Thank you for welcoming this sinner into your community.

To the myriad of author friends I've connected with over the past few years, specifically Susie Finkbeiner, Patricia Raybon, Katie Powner, Amanda Cox, Bethany Turner, Jaime Jo Wright, Stephanie Landsem, Michelle Shocklee, and Naomi Stephens: Thank you for being so generous with your time, feedback, and— most importantly—your friendship. Being a small part of this tribe of amazing female writers is one of the biggest honors of my life.

And finally, dear reader, to YOU: Thank you for reading. It has been such a joy to connect with so many of you, either virtually or in person. Whether you've been with me since my debut or this is your first dip in the water, please know how much I appreciate your readership. Your encouraging messages and unwavering enthusiasm are what keep me going when the writing gets tough. From the bottom of my heart, thank you. You are all, truly, such a blessing to me.

ABOUT THE AUTHOR

JENNIFER L. WRIGHT has been writing since middle school, eventually earning a master's degree in journalism at Indiana University. However, it took only a few short months of covering the local news for her to realize that writing fiction is much better for the soul and definitely way more fun. A born and bred Hoosier, she was plucked from the Heartland after being swept off her feet by an Air Force pilot and has spent the past decade traveling the world and, every few years, attempting to make old curtains fit in the windows of a new home.

She currently resides in New Mexico with her husband, two children, one grumpy old dachshund, and her newest obsession—a guinea pig named Peanut Butter Cup.

Keep an eye out
for the next historical
novel by
Jennifer L. Wright

COMING IN 2024 FROM
TYNDALE HOUSE PUBLISHERS

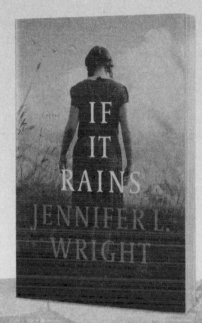
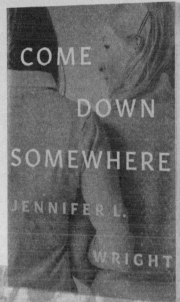

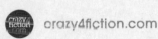
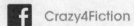
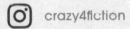
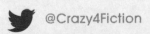

By purchasing this book from Tyndale, you have
helped us meet the spiritual and physical needs of
people all around the world.

Tyndale | Trusted. For Life.